GIFTS OF THE SPIRIT

Joanna stared, a smile

She had never seen Cha[...] bed, yes. She imagined a lot [...] features softened, lips slightly parted, eyelashes fanned out in black half-moons against his cheeks—no, she'd never even imagined.

Good thing, she told herself. If she had, she'd have had an even rougher time keeping her mind strictly on these favors they were supposedly helping each other out with.

Or *were* they still "favors"—just "business"—now? She wasn't sure after tonight. Tonight Chase hadn't come on business. At least, it didn't seem as if he had. Tonight he had been friendly, warm, willing to share.

Dared she hope?

TO MARRY AT CHRISTMAS
by Kasey Michaels

"You never cease to amaze me."

Elizabeth sighed happily. "Imagine driving all the way into New York just to have lunch. Anyone would think this was a special occasion."

But it is a special occasion, Nick thought nervously.

"You know, Nick," Elizabeth said, "you're spoiling me!"

"It's easy to spoil you," he assured her, checking his suit pocket for the tenth time just to see if the package was still there. He sat back abruptly, fumbling in his pockets. "Damn, I must have dropped it."

"Dropped what?" Elizabeth asked, already leaning forward to search the floor of the cab. "Oh, heavens, what's this?"

She sat up slowly, holding the small square box with both hands, eyeing it warily as if it were alive.

This was it; this was the moment he had been waiting for....

Dear Reader,

This is a special time of year, and we are delighted to bring you this distinctive collection—two full-length novels of Christmas cheer.

These heartwarming stories of love triumphing against the odds were carefully selected. We hope they will be a treasured addition to your holiday season.

Best wishes for a happy New Year!

The Editors

Christmas Celebration

ANNE McALLISTER
KASEY MICHAELS

Harlequin Books

TORONTO • NEW YORK • LONDON
AMSTERDAM • PARIS • SYDNEY • HAMBURG
STOCKHOLM • ATHENS • TOKYO • MILAN
MADRID • WARSAW • BUDAPEST • AUCKLAND

HARLEQUIN BOOKS

CHRISTMAS CELEBRATION
Copyright © 1993 Harlequin Enterprises B. V.
ISBN 0-373-15252-3

The publisher acknowledges the copyright holders of the individual works as follows:

GIFTS OF THE SPIRIT
Copyright © 1988 by Barbara Schenck

TO MARRY AT CHRISTMAS
Copyright © 1988 by Kasey Michaels

CONTENTS

GIFTS OF THE SPIRIT

ANNE McALLISTER

For James, Frances and Mark,
who shared the journey,
and for Joanne and Richard Yazzie
and for Tony Hillerman,
with gratitude for their patience and their help

Chapter One

"You're where?" Cassie Craig sounded as if she were sure she hadn't heard right. And at one o'clock in the morning, Chase Whitelaw thought, who could blame her?

"In jail," he repeated into the phone. "I need to talk to Brendan."

"Oh, dear." He heard her mutter something unintelligible, then stifle a yawn. The clatter and drone of police headquarters belied the time of night, and Chase, wide awake and fuming, drummed his fingers on the Formica-topped desk while he waited for Cassie to reach full alertness, still unable to believe what was happening to him.

"He's not here," she said at last.

"Not there? Where the hell is he?"

"He took the boys to Big Bear. They went camping."

"Damn!" Chase grimaced, seeing his last hope sinking below the horizon.

"C'mon, man. My turn now." The burly sailor in line behind Chase nudged him. He brushed the sailor off, then rubbed a hand across his face.

Cassie made a sympathetic noise. Then, "Chase?"

"Hmmm?"

"*Why* are you...in jail?"

"Don't ask."

Because he was a sucker for auburn hair and wide green eyes, that was why. Because he still hadn't learned his lesson. Because, damn it all, he'd looked for a woman who'd appealed to him instead of just grabbing the first one he saw.

If he hadn't, chances were he wouldn't be standing in the glare of the precinct headquarters right now trying to make bail; he'd have had his interview, got his story and been home asleep in bed where he had every right to be.

He raked a lean brown hand through jet-black straight hair and scowled into the unsympathetic stare of the uniformed woman behind the desk.

He knew *she* wouldn't believe that.

"Is it serious?" Cassie asked.

"I was working on a story." He ignored the snort of the officer at the desk.

"About what?"

Chase sighed. He didn't relish going into it all right now, but what the heck...

"Prostitution. You remember. Out by the pool that day you were telling Bren and me about the woman whose arm you set. The hooker? And we got to talking about it. Discussing women without choices and—"

"Hey, you don't have to give us no sociological claptrap, y'know," the sailor belched. "Just tell 'im to get the money an' get down here."

Chase stepped back hard on the sailor's toes.

"I remember," Cassie went on unawares, yawning again. "And Bren laughed and said you should write about it. And you agreed. And he said it would be just your luck to get picked up for solici—" Her voice faded and there was a long silence. Then, "Chase, you didn't...?"

He didn't say anything. He didn't have to.

A giggle. "You *did*!" There was another moment of silence while Cassie regrouped her thoughts. Then, "I'll come," she volunteered.

"No!"

He could just imagine that—Cassie Craig, eight months pregnant, driving thirty miles in the dead of a foggy summer night to bail him out of his own stupidity—even if she had been the inadvertent cause of it in the first place.

"What about Griff?"

"He's on the road. Took Lainie with him. I already thought of that. Susan's flying in from Miami on the red-eye. And Miles is still at work."

He ticked off their friends rapidly. He'd been through them all mentally a dozen times or more. He'd had damned little else to do as he'd been shuffled from one room to another, booked, fingerprinted, photographed except that—and curse the tall redhead with the come-hither eyes.

"I could call your grandfather," Cassie suggested.

"God forbid." Chase shut his eyes, grimacing at the very idea.

What Alexander DeWitt Chase IV would say if he were awakened in the middle of the night to bail his grandson out of jail for soliciting a prostitute—even in the interests of journalism—didn't bear thinking about.

"Your mother?"

"No way." Chase had spent thirty-five years knowing that his mother needed shielding from the harsher realities of life. "Never mind," he said heavily. "I'll think of something."

"Really, Chase... I don't like thinking about you down there."

"Don't worry. I'm fine. Maybe I can charm my way out," he added with more facetiousness than he felt.

"Like you charmed your way in?"

Chase groaned.

"Hey, buddy..." The sailor behind him poked him again. Harder. The woman at the desk gave him an arch stare and tapped her watch. Chase scowled at her. She looked pointedly at the line of men behind him still waiting for the phone. He glanced over his shoulder at the cross section of male humanity glowering and fidgeting behind him.

"I gotta go," he told Cassie.

"I'll come."

"No. Not now. If I haven't called you by nine in the morning, then come. All right?"

"Well, if you're sure..."

"I am."

"About time," the woman at the desk said frostily as he hung up.

Chase didn't reply. Whatever charm he might be able to muster he wasn't going to waste on her.

CHASE WHITELAW?

She had actually "hooked" *Chase Whitelaw*?

God must have a sense of humor after all.

Not that Jo had ever really doubted it. But sometimes, faced with the nitty-gritty of everyday life, she knew you had to look pretty hard to find much evidence of it.

Not so tonight.

Chase Whitelaw! Good grief!

She couldn't erase the grin on her face as she leaned back once more against the window of the all-night laundromat and waited for her next arrest.

Thank heavens he hadn't recognized her. She wondered with a grimace what he'd have said if he had.

He might not even have been surprised. His opinion of her was, without a doubt, pretty low. With reason, she was forced to admit.

The thought of those dark piercing judgmental eyes scrutinizing her sent a shiver right up her spine. She stiffened it and tossed her head back defiantly. She knew he thought that "finding herself" was a poor excuse for what she had done five years before. But she had only done what she'd had to do. And she certainly hadn't enjoyed doing it.

Anyway, Chase Whitelaw had no room for complaint. Things would have been far worse for both of them if she hadn't.

Besides, five years was a long time. It was old news now, not really worth remembering.

But telling herself so didn't make it easier to forget. And, as the night wore on, all the mental discipline and clear logical reasoning in the world couldn't seem to drive Chase Whitelaw out of her mind.

He was every bit as gorgeous as she remembered, and his presence still commanded attention. He was five feet eleven and a half inches of sheer masculine drive and intensity, a panther of a man with a shock of raven-black hair and a lean-muscled physique that evoked notions of carefully controlled power.

Chase Whitelaw was a force to be reckoned with. A man in charge of his destiny, a man who knew what he wanted and went after it—confident, direct, determined.

Terrifying when you got right down to it, Joanna remembered with a shiver.

Even tonight, thrown for a loop by her turning out not to be a hooker but a decoy, he still hadn't lost his cool. He'd been jolted for a moment, no doubt about that. But then he'd simply shut his mouth and retreated mentally, studying her narrowly, as if she were the guilty party, not himself.

Probably, Jo thought with irritation, he did have a perfectly legitimate, aboveboard reason for coming right up to her and asking, "How much you want, babe?"

But she'd still love to hear him telling it to a judge!

She giggled at the thought. It made wearing the ghastly tight blue satin dress, the black fishnet stockings, the half pound of eye makeup and the quart of hair spray more worthwhile than usual. Looking down at them now, though, she'd never have suspected they made her Chase Whitelaw's type—unless he'd changed far more than she'd imagined.

Probably he was doing a story. She'd heard plenty about his journalistic success. He was just beginning to make a name for himself five years ago. He was almost a household word now.

"Hard-hitting, gritty, but always objective," *Newsweek* had called him.

"A sock-it-to-'em journalist of the finest kind," *People* had labeled him in a personality profile.

"Gutsy. A man's man," her father had said.

It was all true. Joanna had read his stuff, had heard tales of his bravery and of the lengths to which he'd go to get a story.

She'd expected him to pull out his press card and tell Naylor, her plainclothes backup, exactly who he was. She was surprised when he hadn't. But beyond giving his name, he hadn't said a word.

That damned aristocratic shield had gone down over his eyes, and he had shut his mouth into a firm, stubborn line as Naylor led him away.

It was the same protective shield she remembered seeing five years ago. The same stubborn line.

But then they'd been standing at the front of a church where a priest had just asked her if she took this man to be her lawfully wedded husband.

And she had just said, "I can't."

CHARM HAD GOT HIM NOWHERE.

Chase hadn't really thought it would. Anyway, it was no big deal spending a night in jail. He'd spent nights in plenty more uncomfortable places.

But never because of a woman.

It wasn't because of a woman this time, either, he told himself sharply. It was because of a story. The last big story he was probably ever going to do, too, since his grandfather was retiring and he was going to be taking over the reins of the whole publishing conglomerate soon. He grimaced. What a heck of a way to go out.

But it wasn't the story that haunted him as he sat there in the crowded cell.

What tormented him was the memory of the woman with the gorgeous green eyes and dark auburn hair who'd landed him here.

What was it with him and redheads, for God's sake?

He ought to know better.

Well, he did now. And when he went after another interview for this—*if* he went after another interview—he was going to take the first woman he saw, not the one that made his hormones go into overdrive.

That had been his downfall. He'd passed a dozen women, maybe more, on his late-night stroll down that particular area of the Pacific Coast Highway, and any one of them could have answered his questions.

But no, he had to be choosy. He had to pass up the ones with vacant stares and shallow smiles. He had to put the question to the woman with the laughing eyes.

At the time he'd wondered what there was to laugh about. Now he knew.

A guard appeared at the cell door. "Hastings?" He scanned the room dispassionately.

A tall, slightly stooped, middle-aged man hauled himself away from the far wall.

"And—" the guard consulted the piece of paper in his hand "—Carrera?"

The short, barrel-chested man opposite Chase edged forward. The guard beckoned to them. Then came a rattle of keys, and the heavy metal door swung open. The two men walked out. The door clanked shut at once behind them. Chase sighed.

One by one as the night wore on, the remaining men left. Bailed out. Free.

All but Chase.

Every one of them, he would have bet, guiltier of the charges than he. And, he realized suddenly, he'd been so preoccupied by his idiocy in picking the red-haired woman that he hadn't even bothered to talk to them, find out their side of things.

So much for the intrepid reporter. He raked a hand through his hair.

"Hey," he said to the guard when he was leaving with Chase's last remaining cellmate. "Wait a sec."

The guard turned at the door, looking back at him, bored. "What?"

Chase got to his feet. "There's been a mistake."

The guard gave him a skeptical smile.

"I'm a free-lance reporter. I was doing a story when they picked me up and..." He was sure that sounded as lame to the officer as it sounded to him, and he wasn't surprised when all he got in reply was a loud bark of laughter. He felt the hot rush of blood to his cheeks.

"To get a little 'firsthand' experience?" The guard rolled his eyes.

"Well, I—"

"Spare me." The guard shook his head, still grinning. "It's been a long night and my feet hurt."

"Really. It wasn't—"

"One bit of advice, fella."

Chase looked at him hopefully.

"Tell it to the judge." And the door clanked shut against his back.

HE'D BE GONE BY NOW. Jo was certain.

They never kept them overnight. Just booked them and let them make their phone call. They were out on the streets within a couple of hours. Three at the most.

Pity. Somehow she couldn't help wishing she'd had a chance to see Chase again. Even just a peek through a cell grate. Especially a peek through a cell grate. She'd thought of him on and off for too many years not to want just one more glimpse—especially under such incredible circumstances.

But it wouldn't happen. Some gorgeous woman had no doubt been down at his first syllable to bail him out.

She knew from what her sisters said that he hadn't married since she'd jilted him. But she was equally certain that her behavior hadn't put him off women. There'd never been a noticeable lack of women in his life before their engagement. She doubted he'd become a recluse after. He was probably still looking for a suitable bride.

She might even know the woman he was dating. Another society belle, no doubt, she thought as she went into the women's room to change clothes.

She supposed one was almost as good as another when all he was looking for was the proper ornament to embellish his career and augment his grandfather's publishing empire.

Tabby Holmes, perhaps? Or Amelia Lattimer? Either of them would be satisfactory.

Though neither had her own impeccable credentials, Jo thought wryly. Neither of them was heir to a paper products empire that could streamline the efficiency of a publishing conglomerate. No, she would indeed have been the best choice.

What a coup it would have been for old Alexander Chase and Jeremiah Hancock-Smith to have cemented their informal arrangements by marrying off Alex's grandson and heir to the youngest Miss Hancock-Smith.

But the coup had failed because the youngest Miss Hancock-Smith turned out to have a mind of her own. The trouble was, she'd only discovered it at the last minute.

She had sent shock waves through California's high society when she'd said no that August afternoon five years before. But, as far as she knew, she'd scarcely affected the groom-to-be at all.

Of course, she doubted he'd been pleased by her defection. But that, she suspected, was because it made him look foolish rather than because of any particular attachment to her. In fact, according to her oldest sister, Whitney, he went right back to work the next day, and within a week he was in Washington, D.C., investigating some governmental agency's corruption as if it were the only thing that mattered in the world.

As far as Jo could see, the only thing that got put off was his providing the Chase family with its next heir. He hadn't done that yet, but perhaps he was being more careful whom he proposed to the second time around. He wouldn't want another disaster like her.

She had, in fact, been a disaster then. To her way of thinking, at least. Young and untried, she barely had an identity of her own.

The subsequent five years had been the making of her. When she got done with three years in Botswana in the Peace Corps—she'd liked it so much she'd reenlisted—and a year at Chico State doing a secondary teaching credential, she knew who she was and what she wanted in life. She was now in her second year teaching physical education and sociology in a less-than-prosperous southern California public high school. It wasn't the future her parents had planned for her, but it was the one that satisfied.

And if the Hancock-Smiths were less than thrilled, they took solace in the fact that nothing else she had done topped what she had done on her wedding day. These days they simply turned the other cheek and tried to pretend she was the same dutiful daughter she'd once been.

Joanna was happy to indulge them in their fantasy. It was easier, she'd decided, than trying to change them. And now that she was comfortable with herself, she could let them think whatever they wanted.

She kept out of their way as much as she could, and she kept the most horrible details of her middle-class life away from them.

The fact that she spent frequent weekends as a volunteer police decoy was one of them. She devoutly hoped, for her parents' sake, that it was something they never found out, more for what it would do to them than what they could do to her.

Well, Chase wouldn't tell them. One look into the floor-to-ceiling mirror on the far wall of the women's room reconfirmed Jo's opinion that there was no way he was going to equate the red-haired ingenue who'd left him at the altar with the gaudily painted tart who stared back at her out of the mirror.

She carefully removed the long golden hoops from her ears, and wriggled the tight skimpy dress over her head. Then she showered, washing the gallon of shellac out of her intricately piled dark auburn hair until it hung wet and shining clean halfway down her back.

· Dry at last, she dressed in the jeans and sweatshirt that were her more normal attire. She breathed deeply, snuggling against the roomy folds of the sweatshirt as she stuffed her feet into a pair of disreputable running shoes.

Then, picking up her purse, she swung open the door.

"I'm off now," she told Sharon behind the desk.

"See you next week?"

"I think so. I'll call." Jo was almost out the door when she turned back. Maybe it was childish of her, but she had to ask.

"Say, Sharon, one of those men I busted tonight..."

"What about 'im?" Sharon had distaste written all over her face.

"I was wondering about the, um, Native American."

Sharon's eyes widened. "You interested?"

Jo shook her head quickly. "I used to know him...when I was a kid."

"You knew him?" Sharon flipped through her log. "What's his name?"

"Whitelaw. Chase Whitelaw. He's a journalist."

"Well, I'll be damned. He *was* tellin' the truth, then."

Jo came back and leaned on the desk. "Why? What'd he say?"

"Didn't say nothin' at all for 'bout two, three hours. Then he tried to tell Kelly this cock-and-bull story as to how he's writin' some article about hookers." She gave a disbelieving shake of her head. "Kelly and me had a good laugh."

Jo grinned in spite of herself. She could just picture their reaction to Chase's story. Enough men told it every week. "You didn't believe him." It wasn't a question, but Sharon answered it anyway.

"'Course not. You reckon if we believed everything those guys tell us we'd ever prosecute anybody?"

"No. So...when did he leave?"

"Didn't."

"What?" Jo stared.

Sharon shrugged. "Couldn't make bail."

"You mean he's still here?"

"You can't make bail, ducky, you're still here."

Jo's mind whirled. Nobody had got him out? He had spent the entire night in jail?

"You want to see him?"

"I—"

Did she? Oh, heavens. Why did she feel as if God were snickering behind His shirt cuff and that the joke was suddenly on her?

See Chase Whitelaw again?

What would she say?

What would *he* say?

Her only communication with him since their almost wedding day had been the letter of explanation she'd tried to write. And he had certainly never written back an understanding response.

Still, she reminded herself, he'd spent the entire night in a jail cell. And she had put him there.

He'd put himself there, the other half of her argued.

Maybe you're just chicken.

Of course I'm not, she answered herself at once, chin lifting.

Well, then...?

Well, then... She sighed. *Why not?*

It might even be good for her. For both of them. She could prove to herself that she really was grown up, that she really had made the right choice and had no regrets. And she could prove it to him, too—just in case he had any lingering doubts.

Not that he would, of course.

He probably hated her guts.

"I'll see him. In fact," she added recklessly, "I'll go his bail."

It was Sharon's turn to stare. "Jo?"

But Jo hadn't got the Hancock-Smith jaw without the determination that went with it. "Sharon, I said I'll pay his bail."

HE SHOULD HAVE LET CASSIE come and get him. Jail was all right for an hour or two. It was instructive, interesting, intriguing for that long. But Chase learned his lessons quickly. It had to be six o'clock in the morning by now, and he wanted out.

He should have told them right away that he was doing a story. They might have believed him then. But telling them hours later, when the newness had worn off, well, that was the second stupidest thing he'd done tonight.

He sank back on the narrow bench again, slumping against the wall and staring at the tile floor between his feet, wondering why he couldn't get that damned woman out of his mind.

Aside from his infernal weakness for auburn hair, it was probably because she was so entirely different from Marlene, whom he usually dated.

Marlene was the cool, understated high-society type. In an earlier generation she would have spent her days giving teas and volunteering to speak on behalf of war bonds. As it was she ran a travel agency that specialized in European art jaunts and photographic big-game safaris for the super-rich with one hand, while she chaired the Fiesta Charity Tennis Tournament with the other.

She enjoyed Chase the way he enjoyed her, casually, undemandingly. That she expected him sooner or later to pop the question, he knew. But in the meantime, she had her life and he had his. Probably even afterward she'd have hers and he'd have his.

There was no intense passion, and certainly none of the provocative challenge and mocking laughter in Marlene that he'd glimpsed in the hooker's kohl-smudged eyes.

It was her expression that had nettled him. He'd wanted to challenge it—challenge her—the way she seemed to be challenging him. So he'd come on strong.

The joke, he thought sourly, had been on him.

The small window in the door opened suddenly and he heard a gruff voice right outside his cell door. "This one?"

His gaze jerked up. Had Cassie come after all?

"Whitelaw. Chase Whitelaw." The response was female, all right, but not Cassie. Slightly husky, it wasn't a voice he recognized at once, though it did seem vaguely familiar.

The owner of it was hidden behind the guard. Chase frowned, his curiosity piqued.

Who the hell . . . ?

Then the door opened, and he saw her.

The redhead lounged against the corridor wall, waiting.

Her come-hither look had vanished, and along with it the shiny blue dress. Instead she was now wearing blue jeans and a faded UCLA sweatshirt. Her lipstick was gone as well, as was most of the mascara. She just looked slightly smudged and hollow beneath the eyes now. And about fifteen years younger. And exactly like—oh, God—Joanna.

Chase swallowed hard.

He was hallucinating, of course. He did that sometimes under stress. In Lebanon once he'd thought he'd seen an elephant on the beach. And when he'd gone without sleep for seventy-two hours straight in Johannesburg last year, he'd carried on long conversations with his sister, who, he discovered later, had never left her home in suburban L.A.

But until now, even in his direst moments, he'd never conjured up Joanna.

He hadn't thought about her in years. Deliberately. Joanna Hancock-Smith was a part of his past he didn't dredge up easily. A part that just the thought of caused him to break out in a cold sweat. She was the only major part of his life that hadn't gone according to plan.

According to plan? That was a laugh. She'd practically tossed a hand grenade in his face.

So what made him think of her now?

The redhead, of course.

The coincidence of red hair and humiliation.

He gritted his teeth. What did *she* want, standing there like that?

Nothing, probably. She'd probably just come to lurk and smirk while he went on his way. He scowled at her.

"Let's go, fella," the guard said again, clicking his keys between his fingers impatiently.

Shrugging, unwilling to argue with a chance at freedom whatever the circumstances, Chase went.

He trailed silently after the guard into the outer office, where the woman on duty handed back his wallet, his car keys, his notepad and his pencil. He pocketed them all, then paused.

"How come you're letting me go?" he asked her. "You finally believe me?"

"You coulda been president for all I care, bud." The woman jerked her head toward the door. "She got you out. Paid your bail."

Surprised, Chase turned. The redhead met his gaze unblinkingly.

She neither simpered nor cooed. She didn't bat her eyelashes, either. But the challenge was still there. In spades. In fact she thrust her jaw out stubbornly, as if defying him to make something of it.

He remembered that jaw, remembered the last time he'd seen it lift like that.

God in heaven, it *was* Joanna.

He felt as if he'd been socked in the gut.

He looked again. Yes, it was Joanna, all right. The same Joanna. But also very different.

The Joanna he had been engaged to had been a demure twenty-one-year-old. A girl. Innocent. Ingenuous. Beautiful, but unawakened. And he had wanted desperately to be the one to awaken her.

This Joanna looked wide awake, and every inch a woman.

His eyes narrowed and his fingers dug into the countertop. He was suddenly flamingly angry.

"What in hell are you doing here?"

Joanna's eyes widened at his tone. "Working," she said with a cool self-possession that irritated him further.

"You *work* here?"

"I volunteer here," she corrected.

"As a hooker?"

"As a decoy," Joanna corrected again. Her voice contained a sharpness he didn't remember, either.

"It figures," he snapped finally. "You never were what you said you were."

He was gratified to see Joanna's face flame. "Look, I wrote you," she told him. "I said I was sorry."

"Sorry," he snorted.

"It would've been worse if I had married you!"

"I don't doubt that. Well, consider us even, then. Now you've sprung me from jail. I'll send you a check for the bail."

"It's not necessary."

"It is," he contradicted and brushed past her toward the door. He paused with one hand on the glass. "Glad to see you've 'found yourself,' Joanna. It's about time."

Chapter Two

The door swung shut behind him. Jo stared after him, stunned.

"I'll say you knew him," Sharon breathed, wiping her glasses on her sleeve. "Holy cow. You two fogged my lenses up."

Joanna grimaced.

"What was that about not marrying him?"

"We were engaged once," Joanna admitted. "I . . . broke it off." Which was putting it mildly.

"In a letter?" Sharon disapproved.

"Well, not quite. But the way it happened he never got to say his lines. Now he has." She sighed. "I hope he feels better."

She, quite frankly, felt worse.

The bitterness of Chase's reaction had shaken her.

The very fact that he'd *had* a reaction had shaken her. It made him human. Too human. The Chase Whitelaw she'd told herself she was walking out on had been a cardboard caricature at best.

Suddenly she couldn't just leave things there. "See you," she said to Sharon and flew out the door after him.

He was standing on the corner, hands in his pockets, staring down the street.

Joanna approached him cautiously, unsure of what to say. "What're you looking for?" she asked at last.

His back stiffened at the sound of her voice, but he deliberately didn't turn around. "A taxi. To get to my car. They didn't let me drive down here, as you might remember."

"You were caught solici—"

"I know what I was doing." He turned now and glowered at her. His tone was deadly.

Joanna fidgeted uncomfortably under his glare. "There aren't a lot of taxis around here at this time of morning," she offered.

"No kidding."

"I'll take you."

He stared as if she'd lost her mind.

"I'd be glad to," she heard herself saying.

"Thank you, no," he said with scathing politeness. "You've already done enough."

The double edge to his words made her burn. "Listen, Chase," she began, "I wasn't the one who got arrest—"

"Just drop it." He turned his back on her again, staring up the street.

She shifted from one foot to the other. He ignored her.

"Fine," she muttered finally. "Consider it dropped." She turned and headed for her car.

IT WAS HOT and it was smoggy, even though in theory at least L.A. didn't get heavy smog anymore. And Chase was breathing fire.

He had been up for God knew how many hours, and deck shoes without socks were not the sort of thing one wanted to walk five miles in. But his physical discomfort was nothing to the torment in his mind.

It had been bad enough when he'd simply thought he'd been done in by yet another redhead. Now that he knew that the redhead was Joanna, everything was ten times worse.

Was he going to go through his entire life with her making an idiot of him at every turn? She looked wonderful, damn her.

He jammed his hands in his pockets and trudged on. The makings of a first-class headache pounded behind his forehead. He was getting a blister on his left heel. He could feel the rawness increasing.

He focused on both. Cataloging his physical pains was a damned sight better than wallowing in the emotional turmoil of seeing Joanna again.

He'd thought he was completely over her.

He was wrong.

He was still angry. Madder than he ever remembered being in his life.

And she had the audacity to offer him a ride!

Did she think a ride and a couple of hundred dollars bail money was going to make up for what she'd done to him?

He didn't know what she thought.

Not now. Not ever.

If he had, he might've had some inkling five years before that the white-faced, thin-lipped girl who peered out at him from behind the bridal veil like a frightened rabbit was having more than an attack of prenuptial nerves. He might've guessed she was going to bolt.

He'd had no warning at all.

One moment he seemed within minutes of his heart's desire, and the next his world had come crashing down around his ears.

And he alone had been left to salvage respectability from the mess. He alone had faced the four hundred astonished guests, had comforted her parents and his mother, placated his grandfather, and then had got on with his life as best he could.

And now?

Now she had humiliated him again.

The police station was at least four miles from where he'd left his car. The blister was a dandy by the time he reached the corner where she'd nailed him.

He stalked right on past, not even pausing.

A young woman dressed in a hip-hugging dress of deep rose satin gave him a come-on smile. "Hey, sweetheart," she crooned. "How ya doin'?"

Another decoy? Chase wondered. Or the real thing?

He had no intention of finding out. He kept walking up the street toward where he'd left his car.

The streets were almost deserted. Sunday morning brought little traffic to this part of town. He walked another block, then stopped and frowned. He thought he'd only walked a block or two before he'd found her.

He knew he'd passed up several other women. Knew it only too well.

But all he saw on the street was a fat old Lincoln Continental, a rusty pickup, and a nondescript Ford.

He looked back down the way he'd come. Then he walked another block just in case he'd miscalculated.

He walked back down to where Joanna had picked him up, hurrying now, disbelieving.

"Hey, glad y're back," the pink lady cooed.

Chase ignored her, spun around and loped up the street again. The Lincoln. The pickup. The Ford.

"God Almighty," he breathed.

Someone had stolen his car.

THE POLICE WERE, suffice to say, surprised to see Chase back. And hardly more thrilled to see him than he was to be there.

But they were reasonably sympathetic this time—with the possible exception of the boot-faced woman behind the desk who seemed to think he'd got his just deserts.

Fortunately, though, she did the paperwork in haste, then dismissed him with a gruff "We'll let you know if we find it."

"You don't sound very hopeful," he muttered.

"We're not." She didn't even look up.

He glowered at her.

Cripes. A stolen Porsche and Joanna, too, and it was only 8:00 a.m. What next?

He was tempted to smash something, tempted to kick that smug woman right in her rear. Except, the way his luck was going, he would probably get arrested for assault.

Joanna, fortunately, was nowhere to be seen by the time he finished. There was that to be grateful for at least.

He asked to use the phone to call a taxi.

There weren't any available, the dispatcher said.

"What d'you mean, there aren't any?"

"Not down there. Not now. Nighttime they go down there. Now they're busy taking little old ladies to church."

"You don't have one lousy taxi?"

"Oh, maybe you wanta wait an hour or so..."

"An hour!"

"Hey, man, this ain't New York."

More's the pity, Chase thought. He slammed the phone down.

"Problems?"

His head whipped around. Joanna stood there, looking at him, her eyes warm, concerned almost.

He clenched his teeth. "What do you want?"

She shook her head. "Not a thing. I thought you might want something. A ride. I...heard about your car. I'm sorry."

Chase snorted. "Yeah. Right."

Joanna shrugged. "So don't believe me. Do you want a ride or not?"

He didn't, of course. Not with her. But then, how was he going to get home?

Los Angeles was not a city made for walking. He suspected his indecision amused her, and that made it worse.

"Look at it this way, Chase," she said with calm rationality, "what else can I do to you that I haven't already done?"

"All right," he snapped at last. "Give me a ride, then."

Joanna gave him a bright smile. "Since you so graciously asked."

Chase glared, feeling the hot blood course once more to his cheeks. He was grateful that his dark complexion made blushing virtually undetectable.

Joanna had started across the street. "Come on," she said over her shoulder.

He went, getting into her rust-pocked red Toyota and deliberately staring out the side window, willing himself not to pay any attention to her.

"Where to?"

"Manhattan Beach." He stared out the window, ignoring her.

She chatted on. "Really? Are you still in the same apartment, then?"

He scowled. "Yeah." He'd taken her there when they'd been engaged, though usually he'd gone up to Palo Alto to see her.

"Is Tucker still living there, too?" Griff Tucker, she meant. A major-league umpire who had been a college friend, he had shared Chase's apartment when he wasn't on the road.

"No," Chase said pointedly. "Griff's married. Has a kid."

Five years ago that hadn't seemed possible. Then it had seemed that Chase would soon be the old married man, and Griffin Tucker, the perennial bachelor.

For a moment Joanna was quiet, as though the news had surprised her. Then she said, "I see."

Chase doubted it. He doubted she saw anything beyond what she wanted to see. She had certainly never seen the pain that she had caused by her little flight from reality.

His fists clenched against the tops of his thighs. He stared resolutely straight ahead. Twenty minutes or less and he'd be home, able to put her out of his mind.

Joanna drove in silence for a while, then ventured, "It was too bad about your car."

"Yes." He kept his eyes trained out the window.

"Maybe they'll find it."

"They didn't seem to think so."

"No? Oh. What kind was it?"

"A Porsche. Silver."

She took her eyes from the road long enough to stare at him in astonishment. "You left a silver Porsche sitting in that neighborhood overnight?"

He glowered. "I had a choice?"

"Well..." Her voice faded for a moment, then she demanded, "Why'd you drive a Porsche down here anyway?"

"It's the only car I own."

"Well, if you're going to come down here you should've rented one."

"Next time I'll borrow yours," he snapped. "Fits right in."

"I've still got mine at least."

He didn't answer that. There was more silence.

Chase preferred the silence. He didn't like talking to her, stirring up memories, making new ones. He had all the memories of Joanna Hancock-Smith he needed, thank you very much.

They went up onto the freeway, whipping around Sunday drivers, heading west. Chase tried to make himself concentrate on the blister on his heel, on the license plates of the cars they passed, on anything except the scent of citrusy shampoo and spicy soap that periodically wafted his way. It recalled the way he used to feel about her—the way he never wanted to feel again.

They were almost to the off ramp before Joanna spoke again.

"I was surprised you were still there," she said. "I thought you'd be gone. Why didn't you call someone?"

"I did."

"And?"

"She couldn't come."

"She?" Jo flicked a glance his way. "Anyone I know?"

He looked at her. "Why should you?"

He was gratified to see her cheeks redden. "Well, I thought maybe she was...a...a friend of the family."

"She's *my* friend. Her name is Cassie Craig."

"Of the Harriman Craigs? The home furnishings Craigs?"

"The *baseball* Craigs," Chase said roughly. "She's Brendan Craig's wife."

Joanna turned her eyes back to the road. "Oh."

She drove along Aviation toward Manhattan Beach Blvd. Almost home, Chase thought, relieved.

"Was it for a story?" she asked him suddenly.

"What?"

"What you were...doing?"

"You mean, you don't think I was after your lovely bod?"

Her neck was closely approximating the color of her hair. "I didn't imagine you'd have to pay for sex," she snapped.

"Maybe I was wrong."

Chase's eyes narrowed. She'd developed a tart tongue over the past five years. He wouldn't have expected it. She'd been such a sweet, obliging little thing. Until she'd jilted him, at least.

"It was for a story," he conceded gruffly.

"Investigative stuff?" she prodded.

He nodded.

"Were you undercover last night?"

He looked at her then and gave a harsh laugh. "Not very successfully, it seems."

"You couldn't have asked?"

"For an interview?" He stared at her, incredulous. "Most people in your line of work aren't particularly forthcoming to the press."

"It's not 'my line of work,'" Jo reminded him sharply.

"Oh, right," he said, but his mocking tone denied his words.

"Well, after we arrested you, why didn't you say?" she demanded.

"I did."

"Not to me. Not in the first place."

"Would it have made a difference?"

She hesitated.

"I didn't think so," he said dryly. "Anyway, I thought I might get some good insights if I just went along with your cop."

"And did you?"

"No," he admitted. She waited, but he wasn't saying any more than that.

Jo changed lanes. "So what are you going to do now?"

"About what?"

"About your story?"

He shrugged.

"You *are* going to finish it, aren't you?" She gave him a searching look.

"Maybe."

"You must!"

Her urgent tone made his brows lift. He'd never seen her so worked up about anything before. "Why must I?" he asked her, his tone mocking.

"Because people need to know."

"About hookers?" He grinned, but she didn't return the smile.

"About the dangers of that sort of life," she said gravely. "About the pain. About the possibility of disaster. You could make a tremendous difference. People believe you."

Chase looked back at her, his dark brows lifting. Her vehemence surprised him. "And they don't believe you?" he asked her.

"I don't preach. I just stand on corners."

"Often?"

"A couple of weekends a month. Whenever they ask me."

He shook his head. "You're a fool, Joanna." He couldn't help himself.

She didn't reply, just stuck out that damnable chin of hers.

"It matters a lot to you?" he asked when it was apparent she wasn't going to be drawn into defending herself.

"Yes." Her knuckles were white against the steering wheel.

"Why?"

"Because you can do far more good with one well-researched magazine or newspaper story then I can do in five years of standing on street corners!"

"But why?" he probed.

"Why what?"

"Why does it matter so much?"

For a few moments he thought she wasn't going to tell him. He could actually see her body tensing, then finally she said, "I knew someone."

"A prostitute?"

"Yes."

He grinned. "Maybe I should interview her."

"You can't. She's dead."

Her bluntness robbed him of speech. He shifted uneasily in the passenger seat, looking down, then away, then finally back at her. "I'm ... sorry."

She looked at him, both wary and doubtful.

"I am." He'd seen death often enough. Most of the time he could steel himself against it, objectify it, write about it without letting it undermine his spirit. But other times ... other times there was no way to stop the hurt.

"Then write the story. Please." She looked at him, and, blinking, he met her gaze, and she held it so long he was afraid they might sail right off the road.

He sighed. "I'll see."

They drove the rest of the way in silence.

Joanna seemed to feel she'd got as much of a commitment from him as she was likely to get. And he was trying to regain the angry edge with which he had held her at a distance up till she had started talking about his work.

When they reached Manhattan Avenue, he took advantage of the red light to say, "I can walk from here."

"I'll take you all the way."

"It's crowded from here on. I—"

But he didn't get to finish his sentence because the light changed, and she shot down the hill and turned left on Ocean Drive.

"I'm surprised you remember," he said as she made the turn.

"I have a good memory."

There was a moment's silence. Then he said grimly, "So do I."

She pulled to a stop in front of his garage. "Look, Chase," she began.

But he didn't want to talk about it. It was over. Finished. And no amount of talking was going to change that.

He opened the door of the car. "Thanks for the ride."

"Chase, I—"

But before she could say anything else, around the corner of the building a tall, flaxen-haired beauty in tennis whites appeared.

Chase practically threw his arms around her. "Marlene!"

Marlene looked from him to the redheaded woman driving the car. The look she gave him said she wasn't sure if she had intended the "you lead your life, I'll lead mine" to go this far.

Chase slipped his arm around her and pulled her against him, glad that Joanna could see he hadn't been suffering from a lack of female companionship since she'd left him. "I'm glad you were here."

"Yes," Marlene said shortly. "Well, I was supposed to be here, wasn't I? You were the one who wanted to play tennis at eight-fifteen."

He winced, remembering. He hadn't even thought to call Marlene. She was a woman made for tennis dates and business dinners, not for jails in the middle of the night.

"I'm sorry. I got...tied up. Joanna here gave me a ride." He jerked his head in the direction of the car. He should introduce them. He wasn't going to.

"Joanna?"

"An old friend." He turned and gave Joanna a brief nod. "Thanks again," he said dismissively.

She looked at him, then at Marlene, then her mouth drew into a thin line.

"You're very welcome," she said and roared off in a cloud of dust.

Thank God.

Chase breathed again.

He almost sagged against Marlene. She turned under the sudden weight of his body and looked up at him. "Where have you been?"

"Working." He turned and headed for the front of the house.

"Working? All night? With *her*?"

"No, not with *her*. She just gave me a ride home. My car got stolen." He opened the front door and went in.

Marlene squealed. "Oh, Chase baby. Not your Porsche!"

"My Porsche."

"Oh, darling, you poor thing!" She hugged him. He let her.

He wrapped his arms around her, hugging her close, burying his face in her long straight hair, burrowing, trying to lose himself in the need for her. Desperate to eradicate the memory of shining red hair, citrus shampoo, and the faintest hint of spice.

Jo usually came home from her Saturday nights on the streets and fell into bed to sleep soundlessly until mid-afternoon. Today she couldn't manage to shut her eyes.

Every time she did Chase's lean dark face appeared on the underside of her eyelids. He smiled, he taunted, he made her squirm.

"It's nothing new," she reminded herself, flipping over in her bed and staring at the wall.

He'd made her squirm before.

But that had been different. She'd been no more than a child then, out of her depth, floundering.

"And you think you're not floundering now?" she asked.

She was. Badly.

The Chase Whitelaw she remembered jilting was not this Chase Whitelaw at all.

Oh, there were similarities. He could still be inscrutable, stern, hard, determined. But he could be more than that, too.

At least she thought he could.

The memory of his anger still astonished her. Her sisters had assured her he was as congenial as ever whenever he saw them, even right after their wedding had fallen through. Had he been bottling it up all this time? Had she really mattered to him, after all?

A daunting thought.

A scary thought.

A tempting thought.

Because today he had begun mattering to her.

She rolled over onto her back and stared at the ceiling, then at the clock—11:43—and then at the ceiling again.

She wondered who the woman was who'd been waiting for him. He'd called her Marlene. She'd looked familiar. Maybe she was someone Joanna had known. Or at least met.

Was he planning to marry her?

For the first time the thought of Chase with another woman was vaguely disconcerting. For five years she had rejoiced every time she heard he was dating someone steadily. It had eased her guilt. But the blond bomb he was so cozy with gave her no sense of relief at all.

She sighed and closed her eyes, telling herself to stop thinking about him. There was no point. She would do better to be thinking about lesson plans or what color to paint the kitchen. She tried.

It didn't work.

Usually she'd had three and a half hours of solid sleep by now.

A knock on the apartment door interrupted her reverie.

Jo scrambled out of bed.

Her sister, Lynsey, did a quick tap dance on the doorstep. *"C'est moi."*

Jo looked at her warily. "So it is."

Lynsey only ever appeared when her parents wanted Jo to do something they were afraid she would balk at. As Jo's favorite sister, Lynsey was generally deputized to see that they got their way.

Now she grinned at Jo's disheveled state. "Aren't you going to let me come in?"

Shrugging, Jo stepped out of the way as Lynsey pirouetted her way across the threshold.

"Don't tell me I got you up. I thought you were the gungho one in the family. Early to bed, early to rise, and all that."

"Even I can sleep late on a weekend." Jo didn't mention the reason she was still in bed. Lynsey knew no more than her parents did about Jo's weekends on the street.

"I suppose." Lynsey was about to flounce down onto the day bed when she stopped and looked at Jo carefully. "I'm not . . . interrupting anything, am I?" She cast a significant glance at the closed closet door.

"No, my dear, you're not," Jo said heavily. "Did you think I stowed my lover in the closet or something?"

Lynsey flounced to cover her embarrassment. "Well, a woman can hope, can't she?"

Jo gave her warning look. They'd had this conversation, or a variation of it, plenty of times before.

"You need a man in your life," Lynsey went on, just as she always did, as regular as a schoolroom clock.

"I don't," Jo countered just as she regularly did.

But just before the words fell from her lips, Chase Whitelaw loomed again in her mind.

Ruthlessly she shoved him away. "What do you want?"

Lynsey feigned hurt. "You mean I can't just come and visit without wanting something?"

"You could, but you never do," Jo pointed out, sitting cross-legged in the armchair and waiting until her sister got to the point.

Lynsey grimaced. "How observant of you."

She flipped her long dark hair away from her face and looked at her younger sister with serious dark eyes.

Jo considered her sister in turn. Lynsey was three years older and three decades more sophisticated. The family beauty, Lynsey could have been a tough act to follow if Jo had wanted to follow her. She hadn't, so they'd always dealt well with each other.

Even so, Lynsey wasn't above a bit of manipulation if she, or the family, thought it was in Jo's best interest.

Jo waited warily to see what was in her best interest now.

Lynsey studied her fingernails for a moment, then looked up at her sister and said offhandedly, "Dad wants to know if you'll play tennis with him."

It wasn't what Jo expected at all. Generally these little visits of Lynsey's were special missions dictated by her mother. And most led to invitations to charity balls, afternoon teas, or, at their most obvious, family dinners at which an eligible male was always present.

"Play tennis with him?" she repeated, looking for the trick. "When?"

"This week. Next week. The week after." Lynsey gave a negligent shrug. "He needs a partner."

"Why didn't *he* ask me?"

"He flew to Spokane this morning. So I volunteered." Lynsey gave her a bland smile.

Jo studied it suspiciously. "Play where?"

"Wherever." Another shrug. "You pick."

Jo's eyes narrowed. "Not the club?"

Her parents' country club had been the site of more than one attempt to introduce her to a suitable man. She avoided it now for that reason and because the rarefied atmosphere of wealth and privilege didn't appeal to her.

"If you want to, of course," Lynsey said offhandedly, buffing her fingernails on her linen pants.

"What if I want to play at the park down the street?"

Lynsey gave her a guileless smile. "I'm sure he wouldn't care. He just wants a good partner."

"Against whom?"

"I don't know. He's got the competition lined up." Lynsey straightened up. "Come on, Jo," she implored, "say yes. You know you love to play tennis."

Jo wavered. She did love playing tennis. Lynsey was right about that. And she had always enjoyed playing with her father in either singles or doubles. He was great competition and a good partner. They hadn't played together often since she'd come back to the L.A. area. The first time he'd asked her, she jumped at it, only to discover that her mother had lined up a beach-blond Fortune 500 executive to play in her father's place.

She wondered about this "competition" Lynsey said her father had lined up. They would know she wouldn't allow a substitute partner twice.

But opponents?

She suddenly recollected Marlene in her white outfit, scolding Chase for being late for their game.

Would her father want to play Chase?

Surely not. Not intentionally anyway. Not after what had happened.

But the thought, far from repelling, made her interest quicken.

"Is this a tournament we're talking about?"

"Well . . ."

"Is it?" Jo persisted.

Lynsey sighed. "Yes. Mixed doubles. Leading up to the Fiesta Charity Tourney."

It was the sort of thing Chase would play in. Maybe she would play Chase. Chase and Marlene. Jo chewed her lip thoughtfully.

"You know," Lynsey continued. "For the hospital. Lots of clubs are sending teams. Singles. Doubles. Mixed doubles. A round-robin elimination. Starts three weeks from today.

"That's why Daddy wants to start practicing with you," she went on, apparently deciding to make a full disclosure in the hope that, if Jo couldn't be tricked into going, she might still be nagged into it.

"He won the singles years ago, and he hasn't come close since," Lynsey went on. "He knows he can't take on that competition again, but he still thinks he can win in doubles if he has the right partner. You."

Jo stared out the window, thinking. It was an interesting possibility. Of course she didn't know if Chase was entering....

Lynsey drummed her fingers on the arm of the sofa, about to burst with impatience. "Jo..."

"Oh, all right."

Lynsey launched herself from the day bed and hugged Jo hard. "Great! Mom will be thrilled!"

Jo jerked back. "Mom?"

Lynsey's cheeks reddened. "Dad, I mean."

Jo eyed her sister narrowly. "I begin to have second thoughts."

Lynsey grabbed her wrists. "Come on, Jo! You promised. And you can handle Mom. You always do."

Jo grimaced. "It's a battle every step of the way."

"Yes, but you always win. Don't worry about it. He's nothing you can't deal with."

At last, the truth was out.

"He? Who is he?"

Lynsey shrugged, shaking her head. "I don't know. Someone she met in Santa Barbara when she went up to see Aunt Florence. Tall, blond and handsome, I understand."

"Why doesn't she introduce him to you?"

"She doesn't need to," Lynsey said bluntly. "I have no trouble finding my own men."

Which was certainly true. Lynsey had more men than the Rams had fans, and she never needed any help getting them. Or getting rid of them.

She flitted from one infatuation to another with the enthusiasm of a bee in a pansy patch.

"And where am I supposed to meet him?" Jo asked grimly.

"He's one of the opponents in your first match."

"Well, if it's mixed doubles, maybe his partner will be his wife."

Lynsey shook her head. "His mother."

"What?"

Lynsey giggled. "You heard."

Heaven help me, Jo thought. *My mother thinks I'm so hard up she's fixing me up with men who play tennis with their mothers.* "Swell," she muttered.

Her sister gave her another quick hug. "I can tell Daddy you'll do it, then?"

Jo sighed. "I suppose."

Lynsey grinned and ruffled Jo's hair.

"Come on, smile," she encouraged. "It won't be as bad as all that. The tournament will be fun, and you might meet the one man in the world who will interest you for a change."

"Maybe," Jo said softly.

But as she closed the door on her sister, she had the worrisome suspicion that she might already have.

Chapter Three

The notion was absurd, of course.

Chase Whitelaw was the last man on earth she should be interested in. He was certainly the last man on earth who'd ever be interested in her.

But whether it was right and proper or not, sensible and sane or not, the notion wouldn't go away. Over the next two weeks it cropped up time and time again.

When she was teaching her summer school sociology class, when she played tennis with her father, when she ran on the beach in the evening and found she was tempted to head for Manhattan, south of the pier, instead of Redondo where she normally ran—whenever and wherever Joanna happened to be, the memory of Chase Whitelaw would suddenly pop into her head.

It was aberrant, she told herself. Insane.

Perhaps Lynsey had a point after all. Maybe Joanna needed a man in her life more than she wanted to admit.

With that thought in mind, she made herself accept a date with her mother's great hope—the blond and tanned tennis-playing tax lawyer named Bob Danielson, whom she met, just as Lynsey had predicted, during the first match she and her father played.

Bob was urbane, witty and far less pompous than her mother's choices usually were. He was also a remarkably good kisser.

But the night she came home from their date, it wasn't the memory of his mouth on hers that kept her awake.

She couldn't get to sleep because her thoughts were still full of the lean, dark man she might have been married to now.

No, she told herself promptly. Most likely he'd be the man she was divorced from by now.

She couldn't imagine for a moment that, even if she had gone through with their marriage, it would have worked. He'd been a man of the world, and she'd still been a child. But she was a child no longer, and memories of Chase Whitelaw teased and taunted her day and night.

Was he still thinking about her?

Probably not.

Chances were he'd forgotten her the moment she'd driven away. He had the blonde to distract him.

The blonde, she had discovered, was Marlene Copley. Daughter of Preston Copley, tire magnate. Bitsy, her sister most caught up in the gossip mill, told her that. Bitsy said he'd been seeing Marlene for several months.

"It could be serious," Bitsy had said. "Maybe he'll marry her. Then perhaps you can get married, too."

It was her mother's notion that Joanna wouldn't marry until Chase had. Some outmoded sense of honor or some such nonsense—the idea that it would be more tactful to let him marry first. As if he cared.

"Maybe." Privately Joanna wondered how Chase's grandfather thought his publishing empire could be improved by linking his grandson up with a woman whose father was into tires.

But then she thought it was possible his grandfather had nothing to do with this liaison. Perhaps Chase liked Marlene for herself.

She spent a lot of time thinking about that. Far more than she should have. And as a result she wasn't getting much done on the stack of pop quizzes she'd given her summer school sociology class that morning.

It was a warm, sunny day in late June. The early-morning fog had burned off, leaving an idyllic southern California afternoon that had "beach" written all over it.

That was the real problem, she told herself. It was far too nice a day to be sitting in her classroom grading papers. She needed some tall, dark, handsome man to pop into the room and entice her away to play hooky.

Like Chase Whitelaw? she asked herself caustically.

But she couldn't help tilting back in her chair, idly rolling her pen between her palms and considering what she would do if he did.

When the door opened moments later, she practically tipped over in fear that the object of her fantasy might actually have appeared.

He hadn't, of course.

Standing just inside the door, a surly expression on his face, was Charlie Seeks Elk.

Dark, yes. Handsome, more or less. Not particularly tall. And certainly not destined to spirit her away. He was there because she'd told him that morning that if he wasn't in the door promptly at 1:05, she was coming after him.

Charlie was one of her students. She had him during the school year in P.E., in which he excelled. And she had him in summer school in sociology, in which he didn't. He was taking it because it was supposed to be easy. It was.

But not easy enough.

Joanna had offered him some extra help during the afternoons. Pep talks, actually, as well as tutoring. Because if he flunked this class, too, he wouldn't be able to run cross-country in the autumn.

And both he and Joanna wanted him to be able to do that. Desperately.

Charlie, because it was the one thing he did well.

Joanna, because she coached the team.

If Charlie couldn't run, she would be without one of the best distance runners in the whole school district. But, more importantly, if Charlie couldn't run, he would probably drop out of school.

All things considered, Charlie's passing was of terrific importance to both of them. But just how they were going to accomplish it, Joanna wasn't sure.

Clearly Charlie wasn't, either. He slouched into her classroom with none of the natural grace she saw in him when he ran. Leaning against the blackboard, his ebony hair flopping across his forehead, he watched her clear off her desk and thump several large weighty sociological tomes down on top of it.

He scowled. "Not gonna read these."

Jo gave him a baleful look. "Of course not. I expect you'll use them for weight lifting."

Charlie didn't smile.

Charlie rarely smiled. Only once, when he had been the surprise victor of the district championships last year, had Joanna seen even a flicker of joy on his face. If Charlie Seeks Elk ever felt happy, it was a well-kept secret.

"So, what'm I s'posed to do with 'em?" Charlie stuffed his hands in his jeans pockets and hunched his shoulders beneath the too-small T-shirt he wore.

"You could look through them. Read one. Whichever interests you most."

He looked at her as if she had suggested reading the Encyclopedia Britannica for fun. "What for?"

"You have to write a term paper to pass my class."

"So?"

"So these should give you some idea of what I'm looking for."

Charlie scowled again at the heap of books, then scowled even more fiercely at Jo. "You're lookin' for a *book*?"

"Not a book. But I am looking for something like one of the studies in the books. A paper on a subculture. Its values, its pecking order, the material things it holds important. Brief, but thoughtful."

Charlie wasn't mollified.

But when she simply sat there and made no move to open them for him or to say anything else, eventually he shoved himself away from the wall and came to glare down at them from beside the desk.

Finally he picked one up, grimaced as he weighed it in his hands, then flipped it open. "I can't hardly even read this. What's 'behavioral ram-if-i-ca-tions encountered in the second-generation pop-u-lace' for cripes sake?"

"In context I'm sure you could figure it out," Jo said briskly. "And the style, such as it is, is not the issue here, either. I want you to look at the titles."

Charlie shrugged and ran his finger down the page. "You mean like, 'Chronic Diseases of Displaced Trobriand Islanders?'"

"Not titles, then," she modified, cursing all the pedantic academics who persisted in polysyllabic obfuscation. "Subject matter."

Charlie shrugged again.

If Jo had a nickel for every time Charlie Seeks Elk shrugged, she would be a rich woman even without her trust fund.

"Look," she said finally, tamping down her exasperation, "maybe this wasn't a good way to start. But you need to think about it, Charlie. You need to see an overall view of what you are going to have to do. You're going to have to pick a subculture and write about it. And the reason I picked these was they all have something to do with family or small village studies. They are all handleable."

"Sez you," Charlie pointed out.

"Sez me."

Jo opened one of the books and proceeded to read the table of contents aloud to him, explaining the titles when they lapsed into obscure academic jargon, drawing parallels to local situations. Then she looked him square in the eye and said, "That's what I'm expecting of you."

"Huh!" Charlie got more skepticism into a snort than anyone she had ever met.

She looked at him levelly. "You can't do it?"

"I could." His lower lip jutted out and his dark eyes flashed angrily.

She waited. Charlie's scowl deepened.

"I have to write somethin' like this to pass?" he complained finally.

"Or you can get an A on my final."

"Fat chance."

"So I thought you'd prefer this."

"I oughta just drop out."

Jo shook her head. "Where's the future in that?"

Charlie's eyes were bleak. "Where's the future anyway?"

They'd had this discussion before. It was a perennial topic at her high school, which was largely populated by students who had no future worth contemplating at all.

They were the downwardly mobile, the marginally surviving, the down-and-out. Her cross-country team was made up of seven boys, only one of whom stood a fair chance of getting to college. If the rest even got through high school, it would be a miracle.

But it was a miracle that Joanna was going to try to make happen for all of them, especially Charlie Seeks Elk. But not at the expense of her subject matter.

If Charlie and his cohorts made it, it was going to be because they deserved to, because they had earned it. Joanna gave nothing away. Except her time and her support. She always gave unstintingly of that.

She looked at him expectantly now. He took the book out of her hands and glared at the list of titles she had just read him. Then he shut the book and handed it back. His dark face was closed, obstinate.

"Well?"

"Well, what?" he countered.

"Got any ideas?"

"No."

"Charlie!"

"What do I know about any Trobriand Islanders? I don't even know where they are."

"It doesn't have to be Trobriand Islanders."

He glanced at another of the titles. "Appalachian types, then."

"Write about what you do know."

Another skeptical snort. "The down-and-out in L.A. county, you mean?"

"Not everyone in L.A. county is down-and-out, Charlie."

"No, just everybody I know."

Joanna, considering this, thought it was for the most part unfortunately true. Charlie had limited horizons, limited opportunities, limited choices.

Charlie's sister, Lucy, hadn't thought she had any choice at all.

Lucy was the reason Joanna spent her weekends as a volunteer hooker.

She had been too late for Lucy. She didn't want to be too late for Charlie. She wanted Charlie to see other avenues, know other chances. She wanted Charlie to develop the tiniest bit of optimism.

But how?

"Positive role models," Charlie's guidance counselor, Mike Hoffman, repeated with monotonous regularity every time she brought it up to him.

"All the studies say that," he went on, shrugging. "But where're you gonna find 'em?"

And that was, Joanna admitted, a problem.

Charlie needed a positive male influence in his life.

He didn't need the bluff, beer-drinking, largely absent foster father in the family he was now living with. He didn't need Tony Hazel, the only other Indian boy in the high school older than he was, a boy who spent most of his time stealing hubcaps or worse. And he certainly didn't need the pimp who had got Lucy into trouble in the first place.

He wouldn't accept Mike.

"A WASP?" Charlie had merely snorted at the suggestion. "Don't need no white man. Gimme a break."

Charlie needed a successful Indian male to pattern himself after, Jo thought.

Charlie needed Chase.

"You're gonna catch flies you got your mouth open like that," Charlie said.

"What? Oh..." Jo shut her mouth, but her fingers gripped the desk till her knuckles turned white, and her brain kept right on whirling.

Charlie needed Chase. Of course he did! Why hadn't she thought of it before?

Because it was insane.

What on earth would Chase say if she turned up on his doorstep with a story about some orphan Indian boy who needed a positive role model in his life, and she was just wondering if Chase wouldn't like to take him on?

Well, the politest thing he would say would be "No. Thank you very much," just before he shut the door in her face.

The least polite she didn't even want to contemplate.

But she couldn't stop thinking about it.

Chase and Charlie.

No. It was absurd.

Still, knowing Chase would prove to Charlie that an Indian could survive in a white man's world.

Of course he could, she could hear Charlie saying, *if he had a million bucks and a granddaddy who owned a publishing empire that rivaled the Hearsts'.*

Anyway, Chase would say no.

But if he didn't...?

If he didn't, Charlie would have a role model.

And even if he did...?

Well, at least she would have seen him again.

Which just goes to show how disinterested your idea really is.

But even with her motive out in the open, bared to her own derisive gaze, it had some merit.

The question was, did she dare?

"I've got to run some errands, Charlie," she said, getting up and herding him toward the door, thrusting a couple of the least threatening books into his reluctant hands. "You just take a look at these. And I'll get back to you."

Charlie looked doubtful, but Joanna wasn't taking no for an answer.

"I'll see you tomorrow."

Charlie shrugged. "Might not be here tomorrow."

"Of course you will be. Where else would you be?" She gave him a steely stare.

Charlie shrugged.

Another nickel in the till.

"No matter what you've got to do, you've got to look these over, too, Charlie," she told him firmly. "I'm counting on you."

"Maybe," he conceded. "If I got time."

"Make time."

"You're a stubborn lady, Ms. Smith."

"Hancock-Smith. Two words. Like Seeks Elk. I don't massacre your name. Don't massacre mine."

A ghost of a grin flickered across Charlie's face. "Gotcha." And giving her a half-hearted thumbs-up sign, he hefted the books under his arm and left.

Joanna watched him go and wondered if she needed her head examined.

How, under the circumstances, could she even be considering the possibility of approaching Chase Whitelaw about Charlie?

It was a pretty audacious thing to do.

It was a damned audacious thing to do.

He would think she was chasing him.

Aren't you? she asked herself.

Not really, she answered.

She was curious. Nothing more.

Having pricked his reserve, having poked holes in the ice, she'd sensed a fire simmering beneath. During the brief time she'd spent in his company that Sunday morning, she'd sensed a man she'd never known during the whole seven months of her engagement to him.

She needed to know if those vibrations she'd felt were just in her imagination.

A good way to find out would be to see him again. Of course she could wait and see if she and her father ended up playing against him and Marlene.

But why wait? she asked herself.

Charlie was the perfect reason.

Besides, she needed to help Charlie. He, of all the boys on her team, was in the most desperate straits. Tran had a support group of Vietnamese that just wouldn't quit. Caleb and Douglas had Black Pride that they had come up with from somewhere. Manuel had eight brothers and sisters. And Kelly and Pat O'Reilly had each other.

But Charlie? What did Charlie have besides her?

Not much.

But if she introduced him to Chase . . . even ignoring her personal stake in the matter . . .

The possibility intrigued her. Tantalized her.

Would it help Charlie?

It might.

Would it help her?

God knew.

God also knew she didn't have a thing to lose.

HE WASN'T HOME.

Jo supposed she ought to have called first. But if she called, she reasoned, he could say no over the phone without even having to think about it, without having to see her hangdog expression, without her ever getting to see him again.

Charlie had hardly vanished from sight before she jumped in her car and headed resolutely for Manhattan Beach.

That wasn't to say she didn't have a misgiving or two on the way.

Actually she had several dozen. But none of them was sufficiently monumental to deter her.

She had once found the courage to say no at a point in her life when everyone else expected a yes. Whatever flak she got over this decision wouldn't begin to compare with that.

Half an hour later she was knocking on Chase White-law's door.

And getting no answer at all.

Damn. She knocked once more, loath to turn around and go home again. Loath to abandon all this courage without having anything—even a rejection—to show for it.

"Hi there."

Jo spun around to see a man peering at her out of the other front door that opened onto Chase's broad front porch. "Oh, hi."

"Looking for Chase?"

Embarrassed, Jo nodded. One more person to think she was chasing him besides Chase himself. "Er, well, sort of."

"He expecting you?"

"Well, no, not really, but..." She shrugged, backing to-ward the steps. "It was probably a bad idea. We were, er, are friends and I was...in the neighborhood—" a little lie wouldn't make any difference, she thought "—and I had something I wanted to ask him and...well, I'll try to call him sometime."

"No, wait." The man came out on the porch, an artist's brush in his hand, his unbuttoned shirt flapping in the breeze. He was about Chase's age, maybe a bit younger, with reddish brown hair and a rugged, smiling face. "He ought to be back soon. He's been out of town for a few days. Just got back this morning. From Boston, I think. He caught a few hours of sleep and just went uptown to get some groceries. Why don't you stick around?"

"He's not really expecting me," Joanna protested again.

The man shrugged equably. "I've never known Chase to turn away a pretty woman."

Somehow that wasn't as heartening as she expected he had intended it to be.

"Really, I—"

He stuck out his hand. "I'm Miles Cavanaugh. His neighbor."

Jo shook his hand. "Joanna Hancock-Smith." She supposed she could have added, "His ex-fiancée," but she couldn't quite bring herself to do it.

"You want to come in and sit down? Have a glass of iced tea? A beer?"

"I don't think—" But before Jo could protest again, Chase himself came around the corner of the duplex and stopped dead in his tracks.

He stared at her in disbelief.

"Er, Chase. Hello."

She managed a bright smile, which she hoped camouflaged the odd leap she felt at the mere sight of him. The vibrations, whatever they portended, were real enough. She knew that much now.

At least on her part they were. Chase looked as if the Loch Ness monster had suddenly appeared on his front porch.

For a moment they simply stared at each other, all the years of social etiquette that had been ground into each of them vanishing without a trace.

At last Chase nodded briefly. "Joanna." He sounded as if he were acknowledging the arrival of a natural disaster.

Miles looked from one to the other, amused.

"Well," he said briskly after an eternity of silence, "I'll leave you to it, then." And he disappeared back into his apartment.

Get on with it, Joanna told herself sharply. *Tell him what you've come for.*

But how? One look at the stony coldness with which Chase was regarding her and the notion that he and Charlie would be compatible fled.

He waited patiently, shifting the grocery sacks in his arms.

"Can I help you?" she volunteered quickly.

"No."

But before he could object, she snatched the key from his hand and stuck it in the lock. Then, shoving the door open, she said, "Go on in."

Chase paused and looked at her. "Thank you, I will." His voice was dry.

Jo's cheeks flamed. But she followed him into the apartment determinedly and shut the door behind her. If she left now she would look an even bigger idiot than if she plunged ahead.

Chase carried the groceries into the kitchen, but Joanna had stopped inside the door, looking around.

It was odd how little she remembered of his apartment from when she had been here five years ago.

In those days she had simply perched on the edge of the couch and watched Chase the whole time with the same fascination that a doe watches the wolf who's about to make a meal of it.

She had been totally preoccupied, at twenty-one, with her own feelings, emotions, experiences. She was so caught up in what was happening to her that she had paid scant attention to what his home might have told her about Chase.

Now she wanted to know.

It was a warm room, simply decorated in earth tones. A soft leather armchair and sofa, a couple of casual walnut and canvas director's chairs sat on a nubby sand-colored carpet that was overlaid with two exquisitely woven Navajo rugs.

Books and newspapers abounded. A small stereo unit and the stack of tapes against the far wall attested to an eclectic taste in music.

All in all, the room was lived-in and unpretentious. Jo liked it a lot.

"Thanks," he said gruffly, "for getting the charges dropped."

Jo smiled. "No problem. I explained about the story."

Chase nodded.

Neither of them spoke.

"So did they find my car?" Chase asked her, finally, when she didn't go on.

"Car?" she echoed stupidly.

"My Porsche. I thought maybe that was why you came." He was putting the groceries away and his dark head popped up and down behind the bar that separated the kitchen from the living room as he spoke.

Jo shook her head. "No. It's... it's not."

His head lifted. Dark eyes looked at her expectantly, as if to say, "Well, then what is?"

Jo took a deep breath. "I have a favor to ask."

"A favor?" She didn't realize so much negative emotion could be got into just two words when neither of them was "no."

"Not for me," she said quickly. "Or not mainly for me, anyway. For one of my students."

"Your students?" He frowned.

"I teach."

"You what?"

"I teach," she said firmly.

"School?" He sounded dumbfounded.

Joanna glared at him. "Did you think I was going to be a society deb all my life?"

"I didn't give it any thought at all," he said dampeningly as he stood up and pressed his palms against the bar.

Take that, she told herself. "No, I suppose you didn't. But, yes, I do teach school. Real live children."

"Where?"

She told him.

The brows lifted again. "What do you teach?"

"Right now sociology. Most of the year I teach physical education."

"Gym?" She didn't think his eyebrows could go up another millimeter, but they did.

Perhaps confounding his expectations was a plus. She nodded and gave him a quick hopeful smile.

He didn't smile back. "So, what's the favor?"

"Well, I have this student . . . Charlie Seeks Elk, and he needs—among a great many other other things—a positive role model. Someone who's made it, you know?" She looked at Chase for some sign of encouragement. She didn't see any.

She plunged on. "He's fifteen, hasn't got any family right now and he needs someone. Mostly a male someone."

Again she looked at Chase, still hoping. Nothing.

"An *Indian* male someone," she elaborated.

Still nothing.

Her throat was parched. She licked her lips. The further she got into this explanation, the less she wanted to finish it.

Chase's face was totally devoid of expression now. He looked as if he had been carved out of the side of a South Dakota mountain.

"Anyway, I, er, thought of . . . you."

There was an eternity of silence.

Chase stared at her, his features fixed, motionless. Then, "Me."

It wasn't quite a question.

If it had been, Joanna would have gone on with her fumbling explanation.

But there was nothing interrogative about it. It was more a tasting of the word. A testing. A sounding-out to see what it came out like.

It must have sounded odd even to him, because Chase frowned then, turning to look at her, and said almost incredulously, *"Me?"*

She gave him what she hoped was a terrifically encouraging smile. "Yes, you."

He didn't look encouraged. "Why me?"

"Well, why not?" she countered. "You're Indian, and you made it, and—"

"I don't know the first thing about being an Indian." Chase's voice was flat.

Joanna blinked. "You don't?"

He was one, wasn't he? How could he not?

"No."

"But—"

He looked at her suspiciously. "Is this a joke?"

"Of course it's not a joke!"

"Well, it sounds like one. No. It's absurd." He stalked across the room and stared out the window toward the ocean. "Forget it."

There didn't seem to be any room for argument in his mind.

"I see," she said quietly. She didn't.

A group of teenagers on roller skates hooted past, the noise from their jam box deafening even inside the apartment. Chase stood scowling out at the sea.

"It's not Charlie, is it?" Joanna said into the silence they left behind them. "It's us."

He jerked around, startled. "Us?"

"Or, more to the point, me."

"Of course not," he denied.

But she just nodded her head. "It is. I don't blame you, I guess. I suppose I'd feel the same way." She sighed and rubbed the back of her neck. "You still don't understand why I did it, do you?"

Chase didn't want to talk about any of this. The whole thing had a certain surreal quality about it, as if it were happening on another plane of reality altogether.

He had come around the corner with nothing more on his mind than getting a decent meal in his stomach and catching a couple of hours' sleep before dealing with his grandfather's latest coup, and there, less than ten feet away, was Joanna.

It was bad enough that she had popped up again two weeks ago; that had done enough to upset his equilibrium. He certainly didn't need her here now, asking favors, offering excuses for the past, infiltrating his life.

It was ancient history, better left undredged.

But it was going to be dredged, whether he wanted it or not, he could see that right now.

He sighed. "Obviously you weren't in love with me." He made his voice as emotionless as possible.

"It wasn't that."

"You were?" he mocked. "You sure as hell had a funny way of showing it."

"I don't mean that," Jo said. "Love didn't have anything to do with it."

"Now that I believe." He couldn't quite disguise the bitterness. He moved closer to the window and stood staring out of it, his hands tucked into the back pockets of his jeans.

He felt more than saw her come up to stand almost directly behind him. He moved to stand by the fireplace.

"It would've been wrong to marry you," Joanna went on. "It would never have worked. But I was too young, too stupid, to see that when you . . . when you proposed."

He looked skeptical. "And you had a blinding revelation as you were walking down the aisle?"

Jo sighed. "Not then. I—"

"Or maybe even later," he suggested sarcastically. "Like when you were supposed to say, 'I do.'"

She hung her head. "I didn't mean to hurt you."

He wasn't admitting she had. "You made a fool of me."

Her lips pressed together. She closed her eyes. "I'm sorry."

"Yeah. So you said."

She lifted her gaze then and looked straight at him. "I didn't mean to. It was wrong to let it go so far, but I didn't know how to stop it."

"You couldn't have talked to me?"

"Talked to you? When did I ever talk to you?"

He sighed and rubbed a hand around the back of his neck. She was right, of course. She *hadn't* talked to him. Nor he to her. Not really. Not much.

Not the way he knew that Miles and his wife, Susan, had talked when they were engaged.

"Why didn't you?" he asked. "Talk to me, I mean?"

"Because I was in awe of you. Because I was nobody special and you were somebody."

"Bull. You were Jeremiah Hancock-Smith's daughter, for God's sake!"

"Precisely. I was somebody's daughter, somebody's sister, somebody's granddaughter, and then, after you proposed, I was somebody's fiancée. I was never me! I didn't even know who *me* was!"

Chase shook his head, baffled. It didn't make sense.

She sighed. "You don't understand."

"You're right, I don't."

Joanna sighed. "You've never had a moment's doubt, I don't suppose?"

"About what?"

"About your identity. About who you are or what you're doing in your life?"

He considered that.

Who was he? He was Chase Emerson Whitelaw, son of Denise Chase Whitelaw and the late Emerson Whitelaw, grandson of Alexander DeWitt Chase, and, as such, heir to the Chase fortune and the Chase dream. No doubts there.

He couldn't ever remember not knowing that, not knowing what was expected of him, not expecting it of himself.

His grandfather had wanted him to start out as a reporter, to begin as he had done. And Chase had wanted that, too. He had succeeded admirably. He had learned the newspaper business from that angle, and he was now in the process of learning the business angle as well.

The time would soon come when he would take it over. His grandfather wanted him prepared. And so did he.

He had always been sure about it, and he had never wanted anything else. No doubts there, either.

The only questions he'd ever had in his life had been about his father—the man who had left an indelible stamp on his features and none on his life. But his questions had netted him few answers. His mother wouldn't talk. She went pale and teary-eyed at the mere mention of his name. His grandfather filled in the gaps as best he could. But he was quick to admit he didn't really know much about Emerson Whitelaw.

"A smart man. A good man. He would be proud of you," he often told Chase when the boy asked. And when

Chase had asked about his Indianness, his grandfather had simply shrugged it off. "It's not important," he'd said. "It makes no difference. You're a Chase, above all. What matters is what's happening now."

And, as plenty was always happening, Chase knew the old man was right.

"No," he said to Joanna, "I've never had any doubts."

She sighed. "Well, I have. I tried to explain that to you when I wrote."

Chase snorted. " 'I'm so sorry. I wish it hadn't happened this way. But I can't marry you when I don't know who I am. I need to find myself,' " he quoted in a sing-song falsetto.

Joanna's cheeks flushed. "I meant it. I didn't explain it well. If you haven't been there, you can't understand."

She brushed a hand through her hair. "Look, I'll say it again. I am sorry. Sorry for then, sorry for now. I should never have come today. It was a mistake."

Chase grunted irritably and dug at the carpet with his toe, wishing her sincerity didn't keep undermining his anger.

She moved to the door and opened it.

"He's managed this far without anyone. There's a cultural center for Native Americans in L.A. Maybe I can find someone there." She turned back on the threshold. "Thanks for doing the article on hookers, though. You did that much for him, anyway."

Chase frowned at the non sequitur. "Huh?"

"You remember the girl I told you about?"

The one who died, she meant. The one who had caused her to be a volunteer decoy.

"Yeah."

"She was his sister."

Chapter Four

You win a few. You lose a few.

But this was the first time in her life Joanna Hancock-Smith had ever suffered a knockout.

Well, she shouldn't have been surprised, she told herself as she drove home. She knew the possibility existed when she went.

Intellectually, at least. Emotionally, she realized now, she hadn't been prepared for his rejection at all.

Deep down, she admitted to herself, she had been hoping against hope that Chase would have had the same feelings she had.

Deep down she was hoping he would have let bygones be bygones and say, "Sure. Why not?"

Maybe, in the most outrageous fantasy of all, he would have even asked her out again. He would have decided that Joanna Hancock-Smith was worth getting to know all over again.

He didn't.

She sighed as she pulled into her parking place and got out of the car. She fetched the mail, riffling through it, as she climbed the stairs to her apartment.

She found three bills, two political circulars, an ad and— glory be!—a letter from Reg.

She laughed aloud. It must be mental telepathy. Reg Patton had got her through the trauma of Chase the first time. When she'd arrived in Botswana with her emotional life still in shambles, he'd taken one look at her and decided that she was as much in need of help as the students he was supposedly teaching math to.

For two years they had been known in ex-pat circles as "the bane of Botswana."

A couple of displaced Americans, and the only Anglo teachers in a village school fifty kilometers outside the capital of Gabarone, they had shared jokes and joys, sorrow and strife for twenty-one months.

If she had never been able to talk to Chase, she had never been able to keep silent around Reg. He'd been her sounding board, her counselor, her deepest, truest friend.

She wondered what he would think if he knew what she had done today.

She wondered what he'd think if, after all she'd said about how a marriage to Chase Whitelaw would never have worked, he found out that she had recently decided getting to know Chase Whitelaw again was a very tempting idea.

She knew exactly what he'd say about Chase's prompt rejection of the favor she'd asked.

"Spilt milk," he'd have told her just as he always did, sounding more like a mother than the thirty-year-old bearded beach bum/mathematics teacher he was. "It's over. You tried. You struck out. Mop it up, sweetheart, and get on with your life."

Jo laughed, too. A little sadly, a little ruefully. He was right, of course.

She sat down on the sofa, opened his letter and resolutely got on with her life.

"COPLEY CARAVANS and Safaris. Marlene speaking. May I help you?"

"Hi."

"Chase?"

"Of course."

"Well . . . I mean, you never call me at work."

"I just got back from Boston. How about dinner tonight? Then a little jazz? We could go down to The Lighthouse."

"Tonight?" Marlene sounded dismayed.

"I know it's short notice, but—" But he wanted—no, needed—to see her.

She sighed impatiently. "I'm giving a presentation tonight, Chase. We're doing a video of the Kenyan safari. Speakers. Music. A native meal. It's all arranged."

"Oh."

"You could come eat with us." She paused, reconsidering. "No, you couldn't. I've already given Edwin the number of place settings. Really, Chase, if you'd said something earlier..."

He hadn't known earlier. Until Joanna had shown up on his doorstep this afternoon, he hadn't felt this compelling need.

"Never mind," he said quietly.

"I should be done about ten-thirty. Eleven at the latest. We could catch the last set, perhaps," Marlene offered as consolation.

"Maybe. I shouldn't have called you at work. It was a bad idea."

"Well, as I said, I'll be free by eleven. Call if you want. And if you get the machine, leave a message. I'll get back to you as soon as I get home."

"Yeah."

There was a pause. "Are you all right, Chase? You don't sound like yourself. You sound tired."

"I am."

He was. It was the Boston trip, he told himself. Days of meetings. Nights of dining board members of the firm Alex had his eye on.

"Get some sleep," Marlene counseled. "And on the weekend we can— Oh, Mrs. Abercrombie is here. And I've promised her a quote on the Parthenon package. Well, you know what we can do," she said seductively. Then at once the businesslike tone was back. "You sleep, and I'll talk to you later, love."

The dial tone buzzed in his ear.

"BOY AM I GLAD to see you!" Susan Cavanaugh practically flung her arms around Chase as he dripped back up on the porch an hour later.

He hadn't slept. Couldn't. His mind kept coming up with images of Joanna. He tossed and turned, and she tossed and turned right with him. So he headed for the beach. An hour of volleyball and a brief swim had all but done him in. Now, perhaps, he could sleep.

But before he did, he managed to grin at his neighbor. "Miles leave you?" he asked hopefully.

"Something like that." Susan grimaced. "He was supposed to be home at three-thirty from the gallery. He and Leo are hanging a new show. Instead he's somewhere in the middle of La Cienega Boulevard behind a jackknifed produce truck and I've got an interview with Scott Flynn in twenty minutes."

Chase searched his brain. "The Olympic diver, Scott Flynn?"

"The impatient, doesn't-grant-interviews Olympic diver, Scott Flynn."

"Ah." He leaned against the banister. "I see it coming."

"What?"

"The request."

Susan smile sheepishly. "Obvious, aren't I?"

"Desperate, I'd say." Chase smiled at her. The same thing had happened before, but not terribly often. "How long will you be gone?"

"Two hours, max."

"And Miles?"

"Who knows?"

Chase sighed the sigh of the long-suffering. "It's napping, I hope?"

Susan raised her eyebrows. "It?"

Chase grinned.

"Is that your way of keeping your emotional distance?" Susan asked him. "You know you love him."

"I know I do." Patrick, he meant. Fourteen months old. Auburn hair. Full of the devil. And very close to Chase's favorite person.

Susan shook her head. "Sorry. Nap's over. Wide awake. Playful. Hungry."

"A bottle?"

"Spinach, peaches and Cheerios."

"Yuk."

"He likes it."

"What does he know?"

"What he likes," Susan said. "So, will you?"

"Of course."

Susan kissed his cheek. "Bless you." She took Chase by the hand and led him into her half of the duplex.

"I'm wet," Chase protested.

"So's he."

Patrick Cavanaugh was standing up, hanging on to the side of the futon, and the moment he saw Chase, he grinned from ear to ear and lurched away from the futon, heading directly for Chase's knees. He grabbed them with grubby fingers.

Chase groaned.

"By the way," Susan said, "who was the dishy redhead Miles was raving about earlier today?"

Chase shook his head. "No one."

Susan eyed him suspiciously, then smiled at his scowl. "I'll tell Miles he was hallucinating then."

"Do that," Chase said sourly.

He detached Patrick's death grip on his knees and hoisted the little boy into his arms to give him a damp hug.

"Did she hurt you?" Susan demanded, protective maternal fire flashing in her blue-gray eyes.

"For heaven's sake," Chase muttered, burying his face in Patrick's belly, blowing against the soft skin and making the baby giggle and tug at his hair.

"Did she? Chase!" Susan prodded when he ignored her.

"No. Of course not. She was an old...friend. Just dropped by to say hello. Don't you have an interview to do?"

Susan put her hands on her hips and frowned at him. "There's more to it than that."

Chase rolled his eyes. "Just go. Do the interview."

Susan stayed right where she was, obviously indecisive. Then, as he prayed it would, work beckoned.

"We'll see about this," she promised as she picked up her huge purse and notebook and kissed Patrick goodbye. She dropped a light kiss on Chase's cheek as well. "Don't think I'm going to give up easily."

He didn't. It would have been too much to hope for.

"What do I have to do to convince you to lay off?" he asked her.

She smiled. "Get married."

His head jerked up in surprise. Susan was the one who was always telling him to be patient, that the right person would come along.

"You turned me down," he reminded her. Three years ago he had offered for her. She had told him they didn't love each other enough. He thought then that love was a highly overrated emotion. Now that he'd seen it in the flesh, he wasn't sure.

If you had it—like Susan did with Miles—and it was reciprocal, well, then, he supposed there was something to be said for it.

But what if you loved and the other person—

He didn't even finish the thought.

"I'll see you when you get back." He shooed Susan out the door. "And we'll take your sloppy husband and your soppy kid and go out for a pizza."

So she thought he ought to get married, did she? he mused as he carried Patrick into his own apartment.

Funny. He'd been thinking the same thing all afternoon.

Maybe he should crash Marlene's safari night.

Yeah? he thought. And then what?

Marlene was not big on surprises. She liked everything planned out. If he showed up unexpectedly, that might end their relationship rather than intensify it.

He got a clean pair of shorts and a shirt out of his drawer, then headed for the shower.

"Bath," Patrick announced happily.

"For me, not you, old son," Chase said to him as he deposited Patrick on the floor, shut the door and turned on the shower.

Patrick hauled himself to his feet and butted Chase's knee with his head.

Chase reached down and tousled the soft mop of hair, feeling not for the first time an incredible envy of the parents of this marvelous child.

He might have had a child by now. Might have had more than one. If only...

And there it was again—the yearning, aching sense of loss, of "might have been."

Joanna had a lot to answer for.

He kicked off his trunks and stepped into the tub beneath the spray of the shower, letting the water drum down on his skull.

He felt a sudden breeze of cool air. He blinked the water out of his eyes and looked down. The shower curtain had been pulled aside and, shorts, T-shirt and all, Patrick was climbing right in after him.

"Cripes," Chase muttered. Then, "Oh, well, you needed changing anyway."

But though he tried, he couldn't stop thinking, as the warm water sluiced down over both of them, that Patrick wasn't the redhead he'd have chosen to share his shower with.

THE PHONE WAS RINGING when he shut off the water. Wrapping a bath towel around himself and a hand towel around Patrick, Chase dashed to answer it.

"So where the hell are you?" barked his grandfather. "Left a message on your answering machine not more'n an hour ago."

"What for?"

"Meeting. Davison Group. I told you they'd be in town today."

Had he? Chase didn't remember. He could grasp a million facts for an article, sort them, sift them, compare them and not lose a single one. Meetings didn't have the same impact on his consciousness.

"Maybe it's you getting senile, and not me," the old man went on.

"You don't have a senile brain cell in your whole body and you know it," Chase said.

"Good thing, too," his grandfather replied. "Saving your bacon, I am. Get down here."

"When's the meeting?"

"Right now. Half an hour ago, as a matter of fact. Don't you listen to that damned machine of yours?"

"Haven't had time."

"Make time. You have responsibilities now. The Davison Group among 'em. Harry Davison himself is in the other room sittin' on his thumbs."

Chase looked at the toddler in his arms. "But—"

"But what?"

"I can't," he started to say. But Alexander Chase didn't know the meaning of "can't."

"Hustle," he said and hung up without waiting for Chase's reply.

Dressing a wriggling fourteen-month-old was a trickier proposition than Chase had anticipated. And keeping track of the fourteen-month-old while he dressed himself wasn't exactly a piece of cake either.

Patrick had removed the cereal boxes from the kitchen cupboard and was gnawing on the top of one when Chase emerged from the bedroom knotting his tie.

He stared down at the little boy in consternation. "You're supposed to be hungry, aren't you?"

"Hung'y," Patrick agreed around the slightly damp cardboard in his mouth.

"C'mon." Chase scooped up him and the Cheerios in one arm and grabbed his sport coat with the other.

He made a flying pass through Susan and Miles's kitchen, writing them a note to tell them where he'd gone. Then he hunted up the bowl of pureed peaches in the refrigerator.

"What else did she say?" he asked Patrick, certain there had been a third item.

If Patrick knew, he didn't say, so Chase squinted again at the contents of the refrigerator.

"Oh, yeah. Spinach."

He scowled, rooting through the produce drawer. What he found looked like lettuce to him, but he tore off a leaf and ran it under the tap anyway, then stuffed it in a Baggie.

"We're off, chum. You can eat en route."

Settling Patrick in his car seat and piling the Cheerios box, the bowl of peaches, the green stuff and a spoon on top of him, Chase headed for the car.

It was a rental car. A four-door Ford Taurus with a dent in the front left fender and bright blue upholstery. Between it and the toddler in the car seat, Chase felt as if his identity had undergone a sudden shift.

Was this what it was like to be a family man?

Patrick was trying to pry the lid off the bowl of peaches. Chase took the peaches, the spoon and the Cheerios away from him.

The little boy objected vigorously.

"Sorry, chum." Chase handed him the leaf. "On the road all you can eat is this."

Patrick eyed the green leaf suspiciously.

"It's good," Chase told him.

"No," said Patrick.

Chase scowled at him. "Well, with dressing it would be," he compromised. "Sorry about that."

It took almost forty-five minutes to get to the newspaper offices, another five to get Patrick, the cereal, the peaches and what was left of the mangled green leaf out of the car and up the elevator to the seventh floor where his grandfather's office was.

"About time," Alexander Chase snapped when his secretary opened the door to the conference room to admit Chase.

His jaw dropped and his tone changed abruptly as he stared wonderingly from the baby to his grandson and said, "Chase?"

"Don't get your hopes up. I'm baby-sitting," Chase said.

He turned to the other men in the room, all of whom looked equally amazed at the baby he deposited on the floor. "Sorry I'm late. Please, let's begin."

It was a less than orthodox business meeting. But if Chase had learned anything at his grandfather's knee, it was to never show hesitancy or give any indication that you might be uncomfortable.

"Be forthright," Alexander Chase always exhorted. "Positive. Don't ever give them a chance to undermine your confidence."

So Chase didn't.

He proceeded with the negotiations as if it were an everyday occurrence to conduct them as he spooned pureed peaches into the mouth of a one-year-old child.

He pulled it off, too.

The Davison people moved from irritation to astonishment to rational business dealings at his lead. And before they left, the major points of the proposed merger of Davison Press with the DeWitt Chase Publishing Group were settled.

Old Harry Davison clapped Alexander on the shoulder as he left the room. "Wasn't sure about working with you, you wily old goat. But I like your grandson. A modern man, that one."

Alexander Chase was chuckling when the last of them exited the room.

He looked at Chase who paced the floor while Patrick, fed and comfortable, nodded sleepily against his shoulder.

"Not bad, my boy. Not bad at all."

Chase grimaced. "Not exactly the way I'd planned it."

Alex, still chuckling, shook his head. "Doesn't matter. Charmed 'em, you did. 'Specially Harry. Better'n coming on like gangbusters. Lulled 'em. Made 'em glad we were comin' in. They'll work better for us now. Good job."

He patted Chase on the shoulder, then patted the little boy, too. "This Cavanaughs' youngster?"

"Yep. Patrick."

"Doesn't look a bit like his mother."

"No."

Alex considered the two of them as Chase slowly paced the room. "Suits you," he said at last. "A baby."

"Mmm." Chase felt the same way, had been feeling that way all afternoon.

He liked the silky softness of Patrick's hair against his neck, liked the warm weight of the trusting little body nestled in his arms.

He felt again the ache he so often felt when he and Patrick were together.

"'Bout time you did something about it," his grandfather said for the several thousandth time. "Find a girl and—"

"I know how it's done, Gramps."

Alex snorted. "I wonder. Then do it, for pity's sake, boy. What'n hell you waitin' for?"

Chase shrugged.

"That Copley girl's a good'un," Alex offered.

"Mm-hm."

"Could do worse."

"Mmm."

"Already done worse," Alex said frankly.

Chase's head jerked around to stare at his grandfather.

The old man gave him a defiant look. "That Hancock-Smith girl."

"I know who you mean," Chase said.

"Bad choice."

"It had your blessing," Chase reminded him acidly.

"My mistake. Thought she'd suit you. You liked her, as I recall."

Loved her, Chase thought. That had been *his* mistake.

"Bounced back good, though, you did," his grandfather commended. "Damned sight better'n your mother did." He shook his head. "Don't do to get lovesick. Don't do at all."

"No," Chase said quietly, speaking from his own experience. It sure didn't.

"You aren't lovesick over the Copley gal, are you?"

Chase just looked at his grandfather.

Alex looked back, unblinking, refusing to admit he was overstepping the bounds. There were no bounds where Alexander Chase was concerned.

"I'm only sayin'," he went on in an aggrieved tone, "it'd be nice to dandle a great-grandchild on my knee 'fore I'm six feet under."

"You've got great-grandchildren," Chase reminded him. "Two of them. Maggie's."

His older sister had two daughters.

"Pah! Girls!"

Chase knew what Alex thought of girls. He'd heard if often enough. Mostly when his grandfather was telling off Maggie for her presumptuousness. Maggie had become a first-rate lawyer and she would happily have worked for Alex, but Alex wouldn't have her.

Women had their place, he'd often told Chase. In bed. Or in the kitchen. Not in the boardroom. So he ignored Maggie. And he would ignore her daughters, too, at least until they were old enough to marry off.

Then, Chase was sure, Alex would have suitors already picked.

"Look," he said quickly, not wanting to get into the discussion again. "I gotta go. Miles and Susan probably think I kidnapped their kid."

"Wish you had," his grandfather grumbled.

"I know, I know," Chase muttered. He hooked his coat with his spare hand.

"Hand me the Cheerios box," he said to his grandfather. Then, tucking it under his arm, he was out the door without looking back.

"YOU FED HIM *that*?" Susan looked at the soggy gummed leaf still clutched in a sleeping Patrick's fist.

"I meant spinach in a jar," she said as Chase deposited her sleeping son in Miles's arms and recounted the tale of Patrick's afternoon meeting with the board. "Anyway, that's lettuce."

Chase shrugged. "He didn't seem to mind. He had a great time."

Susan bent her head and kissed Patrick's forehead. He murmured and made a suckling sound with his lips. "I'll bet. I doubt if you did, though." She looked at Chase fondly. "I'm really sorry. I never meant for you to get stuck—"

"No problem. It worked out fine. He charmed them all. Especially my grandfather."

"I'm sure." Susan laughed.

Miles grinned. "Is he hankering after great-grand fatherhood, then?"

"He already is one."

"Maggie's, you mean?" Miles shook his head. "Not the same. He'd want yours. Carry on the line and all that. Look at my dad."

Miles and his father had barely spoken civilly for years. But within months after Patrick's birth, the elder Mr. Cavanaugh was making conciliatory noises. And while things were still sometimes strained between father and son, Miles and his dad had—thanks to Patrick—a better relationship now than they'd had in years.

"The line's already broken. I'm a Whitelaw, remember."

"In name only," Miles said. "You've been a Chase since the day you were born."

Susan agreed. "He's raised you, molded you, made you what you are."

"I guess." Chase sighed.

It had been a long day. A demanding day. Boston. The plane. Marlene. Patrick. The Davison Group. Joanna.

More than anything, Joanna.

He could have had it all now—everything his grandfather nagged about, everything he himself had dreamed about—if only...

He felt swamped with the loneliness he'd been holding off all day.

He looked at the sleeping child, nestled close in his father's arms, and all the "might have beens" he'd fought to keep at bay came crowding in on him.

He shut his eyes and swallowed hard.

Was surrogate unclehood as close to fatherhood as he was ever going to get?

He looked up and found Miles and Susan watching him, concern evident in their eyes.

He tried to smile.

"Ah, Chase," Susan said and gave him a hug. "It'll happen. Patience, remember? It just takes patience."

"Come on," Miles said, a shade more heartily than he needed to. "Susan said you were mumbling something about a pizza earlier. Let me put Patrick down and we'll go pick one up."

Chase went, glad to listen to Miles's laughing description of the jackknifed produce truck and the ensuing chaos, glad to be drawn into easy conversation with good friends, glad, for a time at least, to keep the sudden loneliness at bay.

But the loneliness came back later that night when he shut the door to his own apartment, stripped off his clothes and slid between the sheets of his wide, empty bed.

He thought again about Miles and Susan, about the way they looked at each other with secret smiles and laughing eyes, about the way they were no doubt loving each other this very minute.

He thought about Brendan and Cassie Craig whose daughter Katie, now two and a half, had occasioned his first sense of missing fatherhood and had prompted the proposal that Susan had rejected. They had each other, Katie, Keith and Steven, and now another one on the way.

He thought about Griff and Lainie Tucker, other friends, also married. Granted they'd had their problems, but at least now they had each other, as well as a ten-month-old son, Andrew, who was the light of their life.

He thought about Miles's brother, Austin, a free spirit if there ever was one. And yet Austin turned out to have been married longer than any of them.

Eight years ago he'd got Clea to the altar the first time. And though they'd made a second trip slightly less than a year ago, just to "confirm that they meant business this time," according to Clea, there was obviously no doubt in anyone's mind, least of all Austin's and Clea's.

Five weeks ago they'd had twins to prove it.

"'Double or nothing,' I told Clea," Austin had grinned when sharing the good news. "Why waste time?"

Chase smiled slightly, though his throat grew tight, remembering.

Good people, all of them. Brendan and Cassie. Susan and Miles. Griffin and Lainie. Austin and Clea. Lucky people who loved each other.

It had happened to them.

Susan said it would happen to him.

Yeah?

When?

He stared around the empty room, spread his arms out to stretch across the expanse of empty bed.

He had never felt so alone.

Except, he remembered, on his wedding night.

His jaw tightened. *Quit it,* he told himself sharply.

He was only feeling this way because he was tired.

Tomorrow would be better.

This was a phase.

It was stupid. It would pass.

He rolled over and punched his pillow, trying to get comfortable, to shake the mood, to convince himself that it was just a phase, that he'd be over it in the morning.

The phone rang.

He groped for it in the dark, knocked it over, picked it up. "H'lo."

"It's a boy!" said Brendan Craig.

It wasn't a phase.

It wouldn't pass.

And it wouldn't be over until he did something about it. Susan was wrong. Patience was getting him nowhere.

When Brendan hung up five minutes later, Chase didn't waste a minute.

He punched out a telephone number, waited, and when he got an answer, he took a deep breath and said, "Hi, Marlene."

Chapter Five

"He had a gun. I was sure of it." Carlos Castillo rested one hip on the edge of Chase's desk and leaned forward. "So I got out of there. Fast."

The young reporter breathed deeply and shook his head, marveling at his narrow escape.

Chase tilted back in his chair and peered up at him. "So how're you going to get the story, then?"

Castillo blinked. "Get the story? Well, I thought...I mean...hey, man, *he had a gun!*"

"So you said," Chase replied easily, folding his arms behind his head. "But what about the story?"

Castillo shrugged uncomfortably.

"Maybe I won't do it," he said after a moment. "Not worth getting shot over. It's only migrant workers."

"Whatever you think," Chase said equably.

"Besides," Castillo muttered, "everybody I talk to thinks I oughta be able to speak Spanish."

In his heart Chase knew what he'd do. And it wouldn't matter whether he could speak Spanish or not. He'd be back out there right now, digging in.

It was a peach of a story. The kind he'd give his eyeteeth to be working on. Migrant workers. Field conditions. Wealthy growers. Unions and union busting.

Rough stuff. Gutsy, demanding stuff. The very sort of thing that got his adrenaline flowing.

Instead of which he was up to his eyeballs in back-to-back meetings, legalese in triplicate and so much other administrative horse manure.

He itched to yank Castillo's sources out of his hands and get out into the field again. He couldn't, of course. Duty called.

Between duty and Marlene these days he didn't have time to be chasing around after migrant workers and wealthy growers—even ones with guns.

Especially ones with guns.

Marlene had made her opinion about his previous occupation very well known.

If he meant to have a future with her, gritty investigative reporting was not going to be a part of it.

And he was getting more and more determined to have a future with her. The birth of James Brendan Craig a week and a half ago had convinced him of that.

He was thirty-five years old. Ready to settle down. To have a family. All those things he would have had for five years if Joanna Hancock-Smith had not decided to pull her vanishing act.

But he wasn't going to think about Joanna. Thirty or forty times a day he told himself he wasn't ever going to think about Joanna again. She was the past. The future was Marlene.

Marlene had been surprised to hear from him the night of J.B.'s birth. Even though she'd told him to call, he knew she hadn't thought he would.

But she had humored him, had consented to taking in the last set at The Lighthouse, though she'd met him there rather than let him pick her up. And right after it was over, she'd given him a quick peck on the cheek and jumped back into her own car.

"What about 'after,'?" he'd reminded her.

But Marlene had simply shaken her head. "Sorry, sweetie, got a representative from an airline coming in tomorrow at eight."

And she had driven off, leaving him standing alone in the darkness, watching the taillights of her Alfa Romeo until she was out of sight.

Still, he reminded himself, she was seeing him more than she had been. He called her three or four times a week now, suggesting dinner, a movie, a walk on the beach. Chase realized it was a little bit calculated on his part. But he was past the age of serendipity.

He knew now that relationships didn't just happen. You had to work at them.

And he was determined to work at making one with Marlene.

"You think I should go back." Castillo looked at him accusingly.

"Hmm?" Chase tried to refocus on what the young man was saying.

"You would, wouldn't you?"

"Yeah, I would," Chase said absently, his attention caught by two men who had just come into the newsroom.

They stood just inside the main door surveying the chaos with obvious wariness. Amid the hustle and bustle of the frantic daily, they looked about as out of place as nuns in a brothel.

They wore dusty jeans and T-shirts, had thick straight almost blue-black hair and dark complexions, and, in Chase's mind, they had "story" written all over them. Their eyes raised, moving beyond the room to the glass-partitioned office where he and Castillo sat. They homed right in on him.

He had no idea who these two were, had never seen them before in his life. But he felt a faint stirring in his blood, a rush of adrenaline. The first he'd felt in ages. He might have promised his grandfather and Marlene he wouldn't go after any more stories. But he'd never said he would refuse one that came to him.

"Get lost," he said to Castillo.

Castillo did.

The men had reached the door of his office and waited. When Chase came to the door, the older of the two spoke. "Chase Whitelaw?"

Chase nodded.

The man held out his hand. "I am Joseph Begay. Born to the Red Forehead People. Born for Salt." He went on, giving his mother's name, his father's, his grandparents', an aunt and uncle or two. Then he nodded to the other man. "My brother."

"Curtis Begay," the other one said and gave Chase the same light handclasp and another list of relatives.

Chase smiled blankly. All those relatives undoubtedly had some significance, but he hadn't the faintest idea what it was. He waited for them to explain. They waited, too. For what, Chase had no idea.

The silence grew, punctuated only by the mutterings in the newsroom and the occasional whir of a printer.

Finally Joseph Begay frowned. "You are Diné?"

Chase frowned, too. "Diné?"

"Navajo."

"Oh." The light dawned. "Yeah. On my father's side, I am."

The men looked relieved.

"The son of..." the elder prompted.

He knew that much at least. "Emerson Whitelaw."

They waited expectantly again. "Clan?" Curtis prompted finally.

Chase began to understand quite clearly why Castillo got annoyed when people expected him to speak Spanish. He shrugged, feeling awkward. "I don't know about clans. I wasn't raised there. My father died before I was born."

The Begays looked at each other again, then briefly and worriedly at Chase.

He smiled hopefully. "Hey, I'm not your average Navajo."

"No." Joseph's disappointment was obvious. "But," he said after a moment, "you are the best hope we got."

Chase looked from one to the other, saw the weariness, the tension, the tired slump of shoulders and the road-worn clothes, and thought he understood. He'd seen it before in people who had come to him to get their story in print. The desperation. The grasping at straws. The hope that here, at last, they might find the man who would hear them out.

He shut the door and nodded at the chairs. "Sit down."

"We read your article," Joseph explained, his eyes examining the books lining Chase's shelves as he spoke.

Chase nodded. That was why people often came to see him. "Which one?"

"The one about the...prostitutes." Curtis cleared his throat uncomfortably.

"Good article," Joseph commended. "You know a lot of things. A lot of people."

Chase deliberately tried not to remember one person he'd met in connection with that article.

"Thank you." He waited patiently for what he knew would come next—would he please do an article on whatever was bothering them?

"Some of those girls you met," Joseph asked, studying the bookshelves, "they were runaways?"

Chase frowned slightly, the question unexpected. "Most of them," he agreed. "The younger ones, anyway."

Joseph eased out his wallet and opened it, then handed Chase a snapshot. "My niece, Jenny Tso."

Gently rounded Navajo features smiled at him out of the Polaroid picture. She was maybe sixteen, Chase figured. Looked even younger.

"She is missing," Joseph said.

"Runaway?" Chase was beginning to get the picture.

Curtis frowned. "Yes."

"We think she may have come to Los Angeles," added Joseph.

"And you want to know if I've seen her?"

They both looked hopeful. "Have you?"

Chase stared at the picture again.

He tried to remember the women he'd seen the night he'd run into Joanna. Some of them had been little more than girls. But he hadn't remembered any Indian girls.

After his encounter with Joanna, he'd found a real hooker, and through her introduction, he'd met several more. Most of them were young, and most of them minorities of one sort or another.

But none that looked like Jenny Tso.

He shook his head and handed the photo back. "No. Sorry." He stood up. "Wish I could help you. If there's anything else I can do..." he offered as a matter of course.

"There is," Joseph said abruptly.

Chase blinked. "Oh?"

"Find her."

"Find her?" Chase stared at them. "Find her? Me?"

The two Begays looked at Chase, their surprise at his astonishment as obvious as his at their suggestion.

"Yes. Please," Joseph Begay said simply.

"But—" Chase floundered. "Why me?"

"Because you wrote the story," Joseph explained. "Because you know the right people, where to go, who to ask."

"Because," Curtis offered the clincher with quiet confidence, "you, too, are Diné."

"THAT'S THE CRAZIEST THING I ever heard," Marlene said.

He could hear her muttering something under her breath as she talked to him. A list, probably. Every time he talked to her at work she was going over a list.

"They just walked into your office and said, 'Find this girl'?"

"Well, they didn't at first. I mean, I think they already hoped I'd know where she was. But when I didn't...yeah, they asked me to find her."

"As if you didn't have anything better to do!" Marlene was clearly astounded. "Why on earth did they expect you'd bother?"

"Because I knew where to start, they said. Knew the people to ask, that sort of thing. And," he hesitated, "because I'm Navajo."

"What?"

"I'm Navajo." Even as he repeated them, the words sounded strange on his lips.

"You're no more Navajo than I am," Marlene replied. The soft muttering continued.

"A little more," Chase corrected gently. But, in spirit, of course, she was right. Until they'd translated the word, *Diné*, he hadn't even known what it meant.

"Not really," Marlene disagreed. "You're all Chase."

Chase thought she was probably right about that. He had certainly felt "all Chase" today when confronted with what he thought of as "real Navajos."

He had felt woefully awkward faced with a set of expectations he didn't understand. All those relatives, those "born to" and "born for" clans. None of it made any sense to him.

And he'd continued feeling inadequate after they'd departed, pressing the photo of Jenny Tso into his hand as they did so, saying they were sure he would do the best he could.

How was he—Navajo in name only—supposed to find a runaway Navajo girl?

For the rest of the afternoon he had tried to struggle through a pile of merger reports that his grandfather had dumped on his desk with the admonition, "Get busy."

But time and again his eyes lifted from the columns of figures and speculation to rest on the Polaroid photo of the fresh-faced young girl.

Navajo or not, he wished he could help her. And he said so to Marlene now.

"Well, you can't go chasing all over creation looking for some runaway," Marlene said, "even if you want to. You have responsibilities."

You have responsibilities. It was getting to be a refrain, he thought. She and his grandfather could sing duets.

Chase sighed. "I know, but..."

He couldn't quite articulate what the photo of Jenny Tso meant to him. It had simply touched something deep inside him.

"Well, if you want to, and you don't have time, you must know someone who can," she said impatiently. "I mean, you know scads of people. Surely you must know one with the right sort of connections. Those Indians are probably right about that."

"Maybe."

"So call them. Delegate. That's what I do."

"Yeah."

"Speaking of which, I have to go to a meeting right now so I can delegate a bit more. I'll see you this evening."

"Uh-huh. Bye." But she was gone before he got the words out of his mouth.

Call someone, she'd said. Delegate.

Find someone who knows about Indians and hookers.

Surely you must know someone, she'd said.

He did.

He knew Joanna.

No. No way. He couldn't.

Why not? he asked himself, staring out the window of his office, not even seeing the parking lot below.

Because... He rocked back and forth on his soles, groping for a reason. Well, just because.

Great thinking, Whitelaw. Very convincing. He scowled at the setting sun, turned around, scowled at the merger reports, ran a hand around the back of his neck, rubbing at the tension knotted there.

There was no reason. Not really. Not if she didn't matter to him. And she didn't. No, she definitely did not.

So, ask her, the small inner voice prodded.

She'd be too busy. She was teaching. She had obligations just like he did.

She'd do it.

His scowl deepened. Yeah, probably she would. Anybody who volunteered to ''hook'' on street corners wouldn't mind looking for a lost girl at all.

But he wasn't going to ask her.

He was going to put her out of his mind, forget her, go get Marlene and take her to the Dodger game.

Then in the morning, Diné or not, he was going to finish the merger report and get on with his life.

IN THE MORNING, sleepless, irritable, frustrated, he went to see Joanna.

Absolutely *not* for himself.

For Jenny Tso. For Joseph and Curtis Begay. For the Diné. Whatever sense that made.

Not much, he had to concede. But after a sleepless night, spent tossing and turning, thinking about the man who'd fathered him, the man who'd never lived to see his son, he thought he owed his father's memory that much.

He didn't have time to do it himself. But if he could see that the Begays met someone who might be able to help them more than he did, then that would be enough.

Just because that person was Joanna was no reason to pretend she didn't exist.

If Jenny Tso was on the streets, it was for her that Joanna did what she did.

Surprisingly, he found her name and address in the phone book. Probably the only Hancock-Smith in the history of the world who was.

But he was glad to find her there, regardless.

It would save him time and no little embarrassment not to have to seek out one of her sisters or her father and ask where she lived.

He called in to the office and told them if anyone—meaning his grandfather—was asking for him, he'd be in later. Meetings, just like news, went on even on the weekend.

Then he got in his car and headed for Torrance where the phone book promised he would find Joanna Hancock-Smith.

He didn't. She wasn't home.

All the way over he'd been visualizing where she'd live. A posh condo, he'd decided. Rock gardens. Waterfalls.

He was wrong.

Her apartment wasn't posh. Far from it. It was not even, he was positive, a condo.

No one with any money would buy it.

Modest, spartan...cheap—those were the words that sprang to his lips.

One of maybe forty apartments in a two-story stucco building strung out along a busy thoroughfare, it was on the second floor overlooking a narrow strip of ground that had a few rocks, a couple of palm trees and some rather weather-beaten cacti.

And the only waterfall was the hose that somebody had left running when they'd been interrupted while washing the car.

Chase leaned against the railing outside her front door and considered his alternatives.

He could leave, of course. Forget the whole thing. Tell the Begays again when they showed up this afternoon that he couldn't help them, sorry. At least he knew he'd tried.

He could leave her a note telling her about the Begays, about Jenny, about what they wanted and let her handle it.

He could wait.

Before he had time to make a decision, he heard footsteps on the stairs.

Turning, he saw her standing there. She was wearing brief running shorts and a yellow tank top that clung to her. Her hair was tied back but a few tendrils stuck damply to her forehead and she was breathing hard from her morning run.

"Chase?" She sounded as astonished to see him as he was to be standing there.

He swallowed hard. If he'd thought the tight blue dress had made her look sexy that night on the street, it was nothing compared to what a pair of skimpy shorts and a thin cotton top did now. The mere sight of her made his heart somersault in his chest.

Irritated at his reaction, determined to keep this business and nothing but, he nodded curtly. "Joanna."

She edged around him to get to the door of her apartment, never taking her eyes off him.

When she had the door open, she looked at him warily. "D'you want to come in?"

"Thanks." He followed her in, looking around, curious in spite of himself, wanting to see if the inside reflected the outside of the apartment.

It was scarcely more lavish than the exterior. But it was warm, homey, comfortable just the same.

There were only three pieces of furniture in the living room—a low broad teak table, an armchair and a day bed loaded with brightly colored pillows. An African tapestry hung on the wall, and more big soft pillows lurked on institutional beige carpet.

Joanna fluffed up the pillows on the day bed and gestured to it. "Sit down. Would you like some orange juice? Some tea or coffee?" She sounded nervous.

It made him feel better. Still standing, he shook his head and got right to the point. "I need to talk to you about Indians."

Jo blinked. "Indians?"

He paced across the living room, then back, aware of Jo's eyes following him.

"A couple of men came to see me yesterday. Navajos. They're looking for a runaway girl. They think she might've come to L.A." He looked at her.

Curled in the armchair, Jo nodded.

"They wanted me to find her."

"You?" she asked politely, obviously recalling his denial of any Indian ties.

Chase snorted. "That's what I said. But they said I was their best hope, because of the hooker article. Because I'd know people. And because I'm—" he paused at the word

"—Diné. It means Navajo," he explained. "'The People' actually." This morning, before he'd come over, he'd looked it up.

"I know."

"You do?" He stared at her.

Jo shrugged. "College anthro."

Chase stuck his hands into the back pockets of his jeans. "Yeah, well, I'm sure you know a lot more than I do," he said gruffly. "That's why I'm here."

"You want to know if I've seen her?"

"Sort of." Chase fished out Jenny's picture and handed it to Joanna.

She studied it carefully, then shook her head. "No."

He sighed. "It was really too much to hope."

"I suppose," she said. "I'm sorry."

"Yeah." He took the photo back and slipped it into his wallet. "Thanks."

"You're welcome."

He paused, trying to figure out how to phrase the next part. "I...uh, don't suppose you've got any other ideas. Places to look, I mean." He shrugged awkwardly, looking at his feet. "So maybe I can make some suggestions, you know. When they come back."

He lifted his eyes and found Joanna looking at him, her eyes warm and compelling, a slight smile on her face.

Flushing, unnerved, he looked away at once. "But it doesn't really matter."

"Of course it matters. Why would you have come if it didn't matter?"

Again he shrugged. His collar felt tight, his palms damp.

"When are you meeting them again?"

"Later this morning."

"I'll come with you."

Chase swallowed, not having counted on that. "You will?"

Joanna paused. "If you want me to," she amended.

Did he?

Curtis and Joseph Begay would. There was no question that Joanna could do far more for them than he could. But he personally?

"Just business," he said abruptly, stalking to the far end of the room before he turned to face her.

"What?"

"If you do, that's all this is—business."

Her eyes widened slightly.

"I don't want to get involved again. I won't," he said stubbornly.

"Fine." The Hancock-Smith chin lifted. "Consider yourself uninvolved."

Chase felt his cheeks burn. He knew he was being defensive, but he couldn't help it. There was something about her that still touched some primitive chord deep inside him and set it to vibrating. "Sorry," he muttered. "I just want it understood."

"I understand," Joanna said, her voice heavy. "Now, do you want me to meet them or not?"

"Yeah ... if you would."

"Let's go."

JOANNA EXPECTED to make her own miracles. The Peace Corps had taught her that.

But if someone else wanted to make one for her—like planting Chase Whitelaw on her doorstep—she wasn't one to question it.

She had almost resigned herself to never seeing him again. Had almost—but not quite—convinced herself that her world and his would never overlap. And there he was, in the flesh, and asking a favor, too.

She would have done anything legal he asked of her, and quite possibly, several things that weren't. But to be asked to help with something so near and dear to her was absolute joy.

She liked the Begays at once. They liked her. They seemed much more comfortable talking to her than they did talking to Chase. And he seemed much more comfortable letting them. He busied himself at his desk, shuffling papers and muttering, while she and Joseph and Curtis talked. But all the while they talked, Jo was terribly aware of him sitting there.

Jo forced herself to concentrate on what Joseph and Curtis were telling her, tried to put herself in Jenny's place.

It wasn't hard. Jenny had been unhappy at home. There were lots of brothers and sisters, not much room. Jenny was the one with ideas, aspirations, plans. Never one to settle for the status quo, she was always the odd one out. Joanna knew just how she felt. For all that they were light-years apart in the societies in which they had grown up, the feeling of restlessness, of having to find oneself, was something they shared. Joanna had fled an imminent wedding. Jenny had simply met the challenge of one of her sisters. "If you don't like it here, why don't you just go somewhere else?"

One day, out of the blue, Jenny went.

At first no one had missed her. Used to her disappearing for hours at a time, for days occasionally when things got bad and she went to stay with a grandmother, no one noticed anything unusual until several days had passed and Jenny was nowhere to be found.

Then the searching began. Locally at first, then Joseph and Curtis began checking with more distant relatives. With a cousin in Cortez, with an uncle in Phoenix, an aunt in Teec Nos Pos.

But no one had seen Jenny.

And then someone remembered that she was the only one who ever got a letter from the other odd man out in the family, her sailor brother, Wilson.

Of course no one knew if she'd got a letter recently, because Jenny was the one who usually picked up the mail.

But it was a thought, a straw to grasp at, and just about the only one they had.

Wilson had enlisted in Long Beach several years ago. Maybe he was in port. Maybe he had written. Maybe Jenny was in L.A.

A lot of maybes, a long shot at best. But they loved Jenny. They had to come. They had to check.

"She's so young," Joseph said. "So naive."

And Curtis simply shut his eyes at the thought of what might already have befallen her.

Joanna wanted to shut her eyes, too. But shutting one's eyes never made the problems go away.

So she arranged to check out Long Beach to see if the Navy would help her find Wilson Tso, and she agreed to take Joseph and Curtis with her.

"We want to come," Curtis said. "It's better than sitting in a motel room waiting, doing nothing."

Joanna, understanding, agreed. "I'll pick you up at your motel in the morning," she told them, then waved aside their thanks. "Thank me when we find her." She purposely did not say "if."

They left and Chase looked up from where he'd been sitting. "I'm sorry."

She looked at him, startled. "Sorry?"

He grimaced. "I think I saddled you with quite a job."

"I'm glad to do it."

He stretched. She watched the muscles in his chest flex under the blue oxford cloth shirt he wore. She swallowed and turned away.

"You think you can find her?" he asked.

"I intend to try."

He hesitated. "Thanks."

"You're welcome."

There was a moment's silence; he rubbed a hand around the back of his neck, kneading the muscles. Then he dropped his arm and glanced at his watch. "You've missed lunch. And almost supper, too. Want something to eat?"

It was a truce offering.

She knew it. It meant he was almost apologizing for having announced that today was "just business." She looked at him long and hard. He gave her a faintly sheepish look in return.

She grinned. "All right. Let's."

He took her to a seafood place in Redondo. It wasn't fancy. Not the sort of place he'd ever taken her when they had dated. Those had been calculated to impress; this was like going home. She enjoyed it immensely.

She thought he did, too, when he forgot to keep his distance and relaxed enough to tell her about some of the places he'd been, some of the things he'd done. She marveled that she'd ever thought him reserved and stuffy. But then, five years ago, he hadn't talked to her with the ease he did tonight.

Perhaps it was because she was more at ease, too. She wasn't in awe of him anymore. She felt like an equal now, not a child allowed to stay up and talk to an adult dignitary. She found herself telling him about her years in Botswana, about the differences between putting herself through grad school and the pampered undergraduate existence she'd led at Stanford. She even talked about her cross-country team and laughed when he told her about his escapades on the track team in college.

They ate scallops and shrimp and coleslaw and they drank two pots of coffee, and awareness quickened between them as the evening wore on.

It was almost ten when he took her home. Jo debated inviting him in, wondering if she dared. But as they walked up the steps, he seemed to shift gears, becoming suddenly more formal, as if he wanted to reestablish the business footing they'd forgotten for several hours.

"I appreciate your coming along," he said when they reached her door. "You did far more than I could do. If there's ever anything I can do for you . . ."

"There is," Jo said promptly, unable to help herself.

He blinked. "What?"

"Charlie."

Chapter Six

How could she have forgotten Charlie?

"Hey, come on. I don't know the first thing about being an Indian role model."

"But you are one," Jo said, "whether you want to be or not. It comes with the genes. I'm not asking you to teach him how to make a tepee, for heaven's sake. I just want you to spend some time with him. Shoot pool. Play video games. Talk. Listen. Nothing very difficult."

Chase wasn't sure about that. "Teenage boys are a foreign species."

"You were one yourself."

"At a prep school in Rhode Island."

Jo shrugged. "Then you can tell him how the other half lived."

"I don't think—"

"You owe me," she reminded him.

He knew that. She'd been super all day, had been everything he could have hoped.

But it didn't keep him from stalling. What did he know about teenage Indians? he asked himself. Less even than he knew about teenage white kids. And there was the time factor. All his administrative responsibilities were every bit as demanding as his grandfather always claimed they were. And what about Marlene? He could just imagine her enthusiasm.

But, most of all, there was Joanna herself.

Seeing her so that he could put her in touch with the Begays was one thing. But the more he saw of her, the more he found that he wanted to see. And if he got involved with her student . . .

"Business, you said," she reminded him mercilessly when he started to hedge. "Just business. Think of it as a deal, Chase. Tit for tat. The Begays for Charlie." Her eyes implored him.

Chase shut his, then opened them. Still she looked hopefully at him. He sighed. "Once."

She beamed. "Great. Next Saturday?"

"Saturday?" That seemed precipitous to him. "Do we have to decide now?"

"I want to have something concrete to tell him."

"You mean you want to tie me down to specifics," Chase countered.

Jo grinned. "That, too."

He raked fingers through his hair. "All right. Saturday. An hour or two. That's enough."

"How about the afternoon?"

"A whole afternoon?"

"He doesn't have a contagious disease, you know. Besides, how well can you be a role model in an hour?"

"Quality time?" Chase offered hopefully.

Jo rolled her eyes. "Only parents can use that excuse."

"Okay, okay. The whole afternoon, then." He could just imagine telling Marlene he'd be tied up half the day—and why.

Joanna beamed at him. "Thanks, Chase," she said and kissed his cheek. "You won't regret it."

Cheek tingling, hormones humming, he already did.

JOANNA KEPT HITTING dead ends with the Begays.

Wilson Tso, she discovered, had been discharged six months ago. If he was still in the L.A. area, she didn't know. And if Jenny Tso had taken to the streets, they weren't any streets Joanna and the Begay brothers walked down, though they certainly walked down enough of them.

It was discouraging. Frustrating. Joanna would have liked to have someone to talk to about it. Someone to bounce ideas off. Someone like Reg, she told herself.

She meant someone like Chase.

She hadn't seen him all week, though she thought about him constantly. His distance surprised her because she half expected him to at least try wriggling out of his commitment to see Charlie. But by Thursday night she had heard nothing and was just congratulating herself on having convinced him, when the phone rang.

"I can't on Saturday," Chase said without preamble. "I've got a tennis tournament." He named a big charity event. The same one she and her father would have been playing in if he hadn't pulled a hamstring last weekend.

"No problem," she said promptly. "Charlie will love it."

"But—"

"I'd sympathize," she said in a tone that said she didn't at all, "but I've got both your Begays all day. Want to trade?"

The silence on the other end of the line told her that Chase didn't.

"The kid's gonna be bored out of his skin," he said finally.

"I doubt it. He'll probably find it endlessly fascinating. Like watching *Dynasty*. He'll think his TV set has come to life."

Chase laughed at that.

"I mean it."

But she would have said it even if she hadn't because over the past couple of weeks she'd seen less and less work out of Charlie. He needed something to galvanize him. She was pinning all her hopes on Chase.

But on Saturday morning she wondered if she'd hoped for too much. It was now nine fifty-seven and the moment of truth was at hand.

It was the only thing that was. Neither Chase nor Charlie was anywhere to be seen.

Joanna glanced at her watch and wondered if they'd both
stand her up. Neither had been exactly thrilled. Charlie,
when she'd told him, no more than Chase.

"What do I want to see him for?" he asked.

"Because I think you might like him," she said. "Be
there," she'd added in a tone that brooked no argument.

So she hoped he was. She couldn't wait around long to
find out. She had promised to pick up the Begays at their
motel in Inglewood at eleven for another afternoon of
searching. If she left here by ten fifteen, she might make it.
Barely.

"So I'm here," Charlie said, materializing suddenly right
behind her.

He stood with his hands shoved into the pockets of his
pants, his black hair falling over his forehead, a scowl on his
face.

For all his negativism, though, he'd managed to come up
with something other than the two T-shirts and the faded
jeans he seemed to live in at school. He wore a faded blue
polo shirt and a pair of canvas pants. A hopeful sign.

Joanna smiled, feeling a momentary wave of relief, then
the beginnings of the rebuilding of apprehension.

Where was Chase?

She scanned the street traffic hopefully.

"So who is this guy?" Charlie demanded, propping his
hip against the light standard. "Not your boyfriend, is he?"

"No. Just a friend. I've known him for years. He's Indian. I thought perhaps you two would..." Her voice fal-
tered.

"Have something in common?" Charlie finished dryly
for her. "Old Hoffman's been at you, has he?"

Poor Mike, blamed for everything. "Mr. Hoffman
thinks—"

"Thinks he can save me from myself." Charlie didn't appear to share the opinion. "This guy rich? Like you?"

Joanna had never mentioned her upbringing or her trust
fund. She'd never mentioned prep school or Stanford. She

dressed conservatively and informally. She wore no jewelry. Yet still Charlie knew.

"He's . . . got money," she admitted.

Charlie pursed his lips. "Don't know why you want me to talk to him, then. I ain't never gonna have any."

"You might," Jo snapped at him. "If you work hard."

Charlie snorted. "Does he? That how he got it?"

"His family has money," Jo admitted frankly. "But he works as well. Works hard."

Charlie looked doubtful. "Doing what?"

"He's a journalist. He writes in-depth investigative articles."

"Like those ol' Watergate dudes?"

"Sort of like that."

"I don't like to write." Charlie folded his arms across his chest and dared her to dispute that.

"I don't expect you to learn to write from him."

"What do you expect?"

"I—" Joanna was fast beginning to have no expectations at all.

But before she had to answer, a nondescript Ford Taurus turned into the lot with Chase at the wheel.

"Ah, here he is now."

Charlie stared, reserving judgment.

Chase seemed to be reserving it, too. At least Jo could find nothing discernible on his face as he shut off the engine and climbed slowly out of the car.

His gaze shifted from her to Charlie, and she saw Charlie stiffen and stare back. The two of them reminded her of a couple of alley cats, weighing strengths and weaknesses, sizing each other up before a fight. Swell.

"Chase, this is the student I wanted you to meet, Charlie Seeks Elk," she said quickly. "Charlie—" she fixed Charlie with a determined smile, willing him to respond "—this is my friend, Chase Whitelaw."

All those years having social graces drummed into him did Chase some good at least. He stuck out his hand. "Pleased to meet you."

Charlie considered the hand, then grudgingly clasped it with his own. "You, too."

Then abruptly their hands dropped and they both looked at her, duty done, now obviously expecting she would pick up the conversation.

Bravely she plunged in. "Chase is going to be playing in a tennis tournament today," she told Charlie cheerfully. "He thought you might like to come along."

Chase gave her a hard look.

"Tennis?" Charlie sounded as if she were speaking Greek.

"Two rackets. A ball. You know," Chase said grimly.

"And a lot of money," Charlie said. "Rich man's sport."

Chase gave him a narrow look. "Think of it as a journey into another culture then," he said flatly.

Jo gritted her teeth. "I'm sure you'll enjoy it, Charlie," she said. Then she turned to Chase. "I'm sure he will."

She meant, he'd better, and Chase knew it.

"I have to go," she added. "The Begays are waiting."

Chase got the point. "Right. C'mon," he said to Charlie. "Match is at twelve."

Charlie frowned, then looked at his car. He turned to Joanna. "I thought you said he was loaded."

Color flooded Jo's face. "I never—"

She saw the first sign of a grin tug at the corner of Chase's mouth. He lifted a sardonic eyebrow in Charlie's direction. "You don't like my car?" he asked silkily.

Charlie shrugged, stuffing his hands in his pockets. "'S'all right, I guess. I just figured, bein' rich, you'd have somethin' better."

"Yeah, well, you're right."

"Yeah?" Charlie looked skeptical.

"I had a Porsche."

Jo thought she saw a split second's flicker of interest in Charlie's eyes.

"So where is it?" he asked doubtfully, jaw jutting.

"It got stolen."

Interest definitely flared. "Yeah? Where?"

"It doesn't matter where," Joanna said hastily.

"Just off Pacific Coast Highway," Chase told him, unperturbed.

Joanna hoped Chase didn't go into detail about the circumstances. But Charlie wasn't interested in the circumstances. He only cared about the car.

He moved toward the Ford and got in. "D'you know who took it?"

Chase slid behind the wheel. "If I did, I'd get it back."

"How'd they get it? Hot-wire it? It's not hard, hot-wiring," Charlie assured him, speaking with more authority than Joanna had ever heard from him. She wanted to die.

"Charlie..." she began.

But Charlie didn't hear her. "My friend Reno showed me," he went on enthusiastically. "He says all you gotta do is..." He began to explain in great detail.

Chase looked at Joanna and lifted his eyebrows.

She shrugged helplessly. "Have a good time."

"Right," Chase said, but she couldn't tell if he was being sarcastic or not.

"I bet you'll learn a lot," she said to Charlie.

Chase grinned then. "I bet we both will."

"WHO'S YOUR FRIEND?" Austin Cavanaugh, Chase's doubles partner, jerked his head in the direction of the boy leaning against the white-shingled clubhouse wall.

Chase glanced across the court, then wiped the sweat from his forehead and took a long swallow of water from the flask Austin offered him. "Name's Charlie."

"Not a relative, is he?"

"No."

"Didn't think so." Austin grinned. "No little alligator on his shirt."

Chase flicked his mop-up towel at the younger man, then shot another glance at Charlie.

The boy hadn't moved during the entire doubles match. He was still propped against the clubhouse wall, studying everything and everyone unblinkingly. Exactly as Joanna had predicted—as if *Dynasty* had come alive before his eyes.

At least, Chase thought, he was still there. He'd been half afraid Charlie might be out in the parking lot hot-wiring BMWs or Jags.

The kid certainly knew enough about it. All the way to the country club, he had regaled Chase with tales of Reno's exploits, and had ended by saying, "He's teaching me everything he knows."

Swell, Chase thought.

So far, however, so good.

"So who is he?" Austin asked.

"He's a—" Chase groped for a word to answer, not finding any suitable "—project, I guess you might say. A trade-off."

"Huh?"

But the referee was beckoning them now to start the second match. "Tell you later."

"Right." Austin grinned. "One thing at a time. Let's go stomp 'em."

It took a while because they did a reasonably good job of it. At tournament's end, Chase and Austin were handed grimy slips of paper that, proffered at the correct time during the awards banquet Sunday night, would net them each a first-place doubles trophy.

Chase was ready for nothing more than a long cool drink and twelve hours in the sack.

He had totally forgotten about Charlie.

Charlie, however, was right where he'd left him seven hours before, still leaning patiently against the wall, observing with expressionless taciturnity the spectacle of wealthy Angeleno society that paraded before him.

The only change that Chase noted was that now he had a napkin and a stub of a pencil in his hand, and he was scribbling something.

Not prospective license numbers to give to Reno, Chase hoped.

"We'll go as soon as I shower."

Charlie gave a short shrug.

Austin, following Chase into the locker room, gave him a backward glance. "Talkative, isn't he? Where'd you pick him up?"

"He's the student of a . . . friend of mine."

"Woman friend?"

"What difference does that make?"

Austin grinned as he stripped off his sweaty shirt. "Just can't see you knocking yourself out otherwise. What sort of project is he?"

Chase grimaced. "I'm his 'positive role model.'"

Austin laughed. "Yeah, right."

Chase shed his shirt, shorts, socks and shoes, then grabbed a towel and headed for the shower. "I suppose you'd be a better one?"

Austin followed him, taking the shower stall next to his, flicking on the water. "I'm a respectable married man, at least."

"Respectable?"

Austin grinned. "Well, married anyway."

Chase laughed, then ducked his head under the spray, letting the hot water pour down over his body, drinking in the moisture, the relaxation, the feeling of success, of a job well done. It was the best he'd felt in weeks.

The way he usually felt after he'd wrapped up a story. The way he rarely felt now that stories were out and meetings were in.

He wanted to savor it, revel in it. But Charlie was waiting.

He sighed and shut the water off again.

Charlie had moved by the time Chase came out. In fact he was nowhere to be seen.

Chase checked the court area, the deck and, with bated breath, the parking lot.

No Charlie anywhere.

About to give up, at last Chase found him behind the clubhouse sifting through the trash. "What the hell are you doing?"

Charlie looked over his shoulder. "Research."

"What?"

"Research." The boy straightened up. "Sociological research. For my term paper."

Chase looked at him blankly.

"My 'journey into another culture,' isn't that what you said?"

Chase remembered some sort of semi-sarcastic remark along those lines. "So?"

"So that's what I'm doin'. Pick a subculture, Ms. Hancock-Smith told us. We gotta write ten to twelve pages about its structure, values. That rot. She showed me what she meant in a book. All about Trobriand Islanders."

"Trobriand Islanders?" Chase wasn't following.

"That was the culture in the book," Charlie explained patiently. "They interviewed 'em, lived with 'em, dug through their junk piles. Sounded good to me." Charlie grinned.

Chase was amazed at the transformation.

"I found my subculture." The boy waved his hand to encompass the lavish clubhouse and its environs. "The country club elite. It's amazing," he confided, "what you can find in their trash."

"Hi. This is Marlene. I'm off on safari right now. But if you'll leave your name and number, I'll get back to you as soon as I bag my lion."

It was the fifth time he'd heard that. And the fifth time he'd hung up after opening his mouth without saying anything.

What should he say?

This is Chase. I've gotta tell you, this kid I took to the tennis tournament today is unreal. He's got a new lease on life now since he's discovered the archeology of the rich and famous.

It wasn't answering machine material.

But Chase had to tell someone. It was too marvelous not to share. He'd been bubbling over with it ever since he'd dropped Charlie off at the gas station where he worked and had met the infamous Reno. By day, at least, Reno was a garage mechanic. By night...well, Chase figured he'd draw a veil over that.

What mattered was the transformation in Charlie.

The sullen, grim-faced boy of the morning was gone. He was enthusiastic, talkative. He rattled on to Chase all the way home.

"Ms. Hancock-Smith says travel is broadening," he told Chase. "I think she must be right."

Chase grinned, remembering. It didn't have to be travel measured in miles, either. Up or down the social ladder could make an equally big difference.

He had come home as enthusiastic as Charlie and had gone straight to the phone to share the news with Marlene.

That was the first time he'd heard the answering machine message. He supposed it wasn't surprising. Marlene had headed the committee that had set up the tennis tournament. She had been running herself ragged for days. And no doubt she still had odds and ends to sort out.

But Chase wondered, if she was so fond of delegating, why she hadn't delegated a bit more of it, when he called her a second time, a third, a fourth and finally a fifth still without finding her at home.

He went over to see if Miles and Susan were around. Their apartment was dark. He came back into his own apartment and tried Marlene one last time.

"Hi. This is Marlene. I'm off on safari right now. But if you'll leave—"

"Right," said Chase. He left.

WHEN THE DOORBELL RANG, Joanna didn't want to answer it. It was after ten. No one came by after ten except her sister, Lynsey, and her friend, Reg. She knew it wouldn't be Reg because the letter she'd got said he was coming to town later in the month. And Lynsey she didn't want to see.

Lynsey would come for only two purposes: either she would want to know why Joanna had recently turned down three dates in a row with Bob Donaldson whom she had earlier agreed was a nice guy, or she and Lydia would already have come up with a new man and she would be attempting to talk Joanna into something when her defenses were weakest.

The doorbell rang again, more insistently this time. That was the trouble with a one-room apartment. It was hard to pretend you weren't home when all the lights were on.

Sighing, she shoved away the stacks of bibliography cards she was going over for her class and went to answer the door.

"Don't start. Just don't—*Chase*?" Her voice wobbled, her jaw dropped.

But even after she'd blinked, he was still there.

He grimaced. "I know it's late, but—"

"Come in," she said. "Come in."

She had been wondering all day how things had gone with him and Charlie, but she had expected to have to wait and try to pry the information out of Charlie on Monday. She motioned Chase toward the chair, trying to determine from his demeanor just how disastrous the encounter had been.

He didn't look angry at least. In fact he had an air of suppressed excitement about him. But what it meant she didn't know and was afraid to guess.

"Can I get you some coffee? Tea?"

He shook his head and handed her the brown paper sack he was carrying. She took it, peering inside to see a six-pack of beer. She winced, then lifted her eyes and met his.

"To drown your sorrows? Was it that bad?"

He shook his head, grinning. "To celebrate."

"Celebrate?"

"Charlie has found a subculture."

Joanna looked at him, baffled.

"For his term paper," Chase told her. "He said you told them to pick one."

"I did." She gestured to the stacks of bibliography cards all over the table, none written up by Charlie Seeks Elk. "And he hasn't."

"He has now."

"He has?"

"Mmm." Chase was laughing. "He's picked the rich and famous of L.A."

"What!"

"You were absolutely right. He was fascinated. I thought he'd be bored out of his mind. He wasn't. He didn't blink all day. Just stood there taking notes like mad." He took the beers from her and took out two and opened them, then handed her the rest, which she dutifully put in the refrigerator, her mind whirling all the while.

Charlie taking notes? Charlie fascinated?

"He has whole conversations transcribed." Chase shook his head in amazement at the dialogues Charlie had captured and reproduced for him on the ride home. He flopped down on the floor, lying back and tucking one of the jumbo pillows under his head. He took a long draft of the beer. "You wouldn't believe. And then he went through the trash."

"He did *what*?" Joanna spluttered into her beer.

"Went through the trash. They did it on the Trobriand Islands, he said."

"Yes, they did," Joanna agreed. "But— He went through the Country Club trash?" She winced, then shrugged, laughing. "Oh, Lord, what have I wrought?"

Chase stretched out against one of her oversize brightly colored, down-stuffed pillows and folded his arms behind his head, smiling at her. "Good question."

She smiled back. "Thank you," she said, "for taking him."

"I enjoyed it." He was surprised to find that he meant it. "It was fun. We might do it again."

"Go through the trash?"

"And other things." He took another swallow of the beer. "How about you? What happened with the Begays?"

Joanna sighed. "Not much." She told him about further fruitless searching. About going to the cultural center, about meeting a few families of relocated Navajos, about none of them having seen or heard of Jenny Tso.

"You had better luck than I did," she told him.

"I'm sorry."

"I'm not. I just wish I'd had some luck, too." She sighed and stretched. "Maybe I will tomorrow."

Chase frowned. "You going again tomorrow?"

"Until I run out of places to go."

"Determined, aren't you?"

"Yes."

They looked at each other, Chase on the floor, Joanna on the day bed, each of them slightly sleepy, each of them slightly amazed to find themselves here together, talking, not sparring for once, each of them feeling things they weren't quite sure how to handle.

"Ready for another beer?" Joanna asked at last.

"Thanks."

He was high, and he knew it. Not on drink. Not on drugs. But on the sheer physical exhaustion that came from a day-long ordeal on the tennis court followed by the serendipitous success of his encounter with Charlie Seeks Elk and the pleasure of having someone to share it with. Having Joanna to share it with.

She handed him the beer and he raised it in a toast. "To Charlie," he said solemnly.

"And to his term paper," Jo added. "At least he's found an interest."

"Two interests," Chase corrected.

Jo's eyebrows lifted in query.

"Don't forget Reno and the stolen cars."

"Don't remind me. All that nonsense about hot-wiring." She shuddered.

"It wasn't nonsense. He knows it backward and forward."

"Academically, I hope," Jo said fervently.

Chase nodded his head slowly and shut his eyes, lying back against the pillow, sinking in. "So far," he murmured.

He liked lying here talking to her, too mellow and too pleased and too tired to move. She was easy to be with, making no demands, no suggestions. She didn't rattle on about ice sculptures or the perks included in Parthenon packages like Marlene would have. She just sat across the table from him, sipped her beer and let him be.

There was something soft and instrumental playing in the background. He didn't recognize the artist, but he remembered the song. "The Nearness of You."

He could hear the words singing themselves inside his head, spinning round and round, weaving a spell in his consciousness, lulling him, drugging him. He let himself drift.

"I'm so glad it went well," she was saying. "How was the tournament part? For you, I mean."

He smiled again. The beer was shutting down the circuits in his brain one by one. He figured about half of them were gone by now. "Terrific," he assured her muzzily. "We won."

"Really?" She sounded thrilled, far more so than Marlene had.

He got both eyes open in order to see her smiling at him. "Yeah, we did. Men's doubles. Me 'n' Austin Cavanaugh."

Jo beamed. "Congratulations."

She was extraordinarily beautiful when she smiled. He wanted her to smile some more.

He wanted to edge across the space that separated them and lay his head in her lap and let her smile down on him, but he felt absolutely boneless. He lifted the beer bottle and poured the rest of it down his throat. He shut his eyes and listened to the music.

"Can I get you another?" Jo asked him.

"'Nother?"

"Beer. There're three left."

He ought to say no.

God knew he didn't need any more beer in his system helping it on its way to oblivion. But if he said no, then he ought also to say goodbye.

Good manners, proper upbringing and all that.

But he didn't want to say goodbye.

Not now.

Not yet.

He wanted just to lie here, to listen to the music, to watch the fan swirling gently overhead, to bask in the afterglow of his day's triumphs, to rest against this heavenly down-filled pillow and let Joanna Hancock-Smith smile at him.

"Jus' one more," he said.

Joanna smiled. "Coming right up."

He returned the smile and lay back watching her jeans-clad hips sway slightly as she went to the kitchen.

Then he shut his eyes, the memory of those hips inked indelibly on his brain. They were lovely. Almost as lovely as her smile. When she got back he would think about her smile again, he decided. Until then, he thought, sighing softly, he would concentrate on her hips.

WHEN SHE GOT BACK he was fast asleep.

Joanna stopped and stared, a beer bottle in her hand, a smile on her face, an ache in her heart.

She had never seen Chase asleep. Had never even imagined it.

In bed, yes. She'd imagined a lot about that. Especially lately.

But simply sleeping, features softened, lips slightly parted, eyelashes fanned out in black half-moons against his cheeks—no, she'd never even imagined.

Good thing, too, she told herself. If she had she'd have had an even rougher time keeping her mind strictly on these favors they were supposedly helping each other out with.

Or were they still "favors"—just "business"—now? She wasn't sure after tonight. Tonight Chase hadn't come on business. At least it didn't seem as if he had. Tonight he had been friendly, warm, willing to share.

Dared she hope?

She didn't know how long she stood there above him, just watching him breathe. It might have been a minute. It might've been a quarter of an hour.

But however long it was, Chase never stirred. He slept on soundly. Once his lips twitched into a smile, and Jo felt her heart twist.

What was he dreaming about? *Who* was he dreaming about?

Fifty bucks said it probably wasn't her. But it didn't stop her wishing just the same.

Sighing, she carried the beer back to the kitchen and poured it down the sink.

Then she turned off the kitchen light, went into the bathroom, washed her face, brushed her teeth, slipped into the oversize T-shirt she wore to sleep in and went back to the living room.

She'd known the minute she saw him lying there that she wasn't going to wake him. If he woke up by himself, well, that was simply part of the natural course of events. But if he didn't . . . that was part of the natural course of events, too.

Joanna was a firm believer in letting nature take its course.

She fluffed up the feather mattress on the day bed, then slid the summer-weight comforter and light cotton blanket out from the trundle bed beneath it. The blanket she tossed on the bed for her own use. The comforter she carried over and, bending down, she tucked it gently around Chase's sleeping form.

He smiled again—this time, she decided, for her—and rolled over onto his side, pulling his knees up slightly. An ebony fringe of hair fell across his forehead, and before she could stop herself, Joanna brushed it back.

His forehead was cool, the skin smooth and soft against her fingers. And when she touched him, he smiled again.

"Oh, God," she muttered and got hastily to her feet, retreating to the safety of the day bed, flicking off the light and rolling over to face the wall, her own face hot, her whole body tingling with her need of him.

How on earth was she going to get any sleep tonight?

Chapter Seven

Chase could sleep anywhere. Anytime. But never for long.

It went with his job—the forty winks on the staircase of a row house in Belfast, the half-hour zonk on the plane between L.A. and San Francisco or the five-hour night on the transatlantic run, the catnaps in his car while waiting for contacts who only sometimes showed up.

And he woke just as promptly, alert and aware. Always prepared, always knowing just where he was.

Which was why the sunlight streaming in the window hitting him in the face was such a shock.

So were the smell of coffee and the sound of heavy traffic right outside the window.

What the hell? His eyes jerked open and he sat up, looking around.

He saw a small living room, a day bed, a teak table, an African weaving and a digital clock that read 10:42.

He groaned, disbelieving.

He had spent ten hours sleeping on Joanna Hancock-Smith's floor? He couldn't have. And then he thought, yes, given the circumstances, maybe he could.

It was beginning to come back to him now—the tennis, Charlie, the elation, the beer.

He looked around for some sign of Joanna herself, but didn't see any. The day bed was plumped up just as it had been, the gay profusion of pillows scattered across it. He guessed she'd slept there, but he wasn't sure.

He got to his feet. His head felt slightly thick, as if the beer had solidified and established residence between his ears. He gave it an experimental shake and winced. A bad idea.

He found a clean towel and a wash cloth on the table. With it, there was also a note. He picked it up.

You do sleep the sleep of the just, don't you? After yesterday you deserve it. I've taken the Begays to talk to a cop I know. Help yourself to a shower. There's fresh o.j. in the fridge, French toast keeping warm in the oven and lots of coffee. Thanks again for helping Charlie.

It was signed simply, "Jo."

Chase took a shower, drank the orange juice and coffee, ate the French toast, washed the dishes, put them away. He took his time, stretching things out, in no real hurry to go. He liked being here, liked the cool morning breeze that blew the curtains in the kitchen window, liked the controlled clutter of school papers and mail that half took over the kitchen table. Mostly he liked the feeling he got when he looked around. It was a comfortable feeling. The only place he'd ever had it was in his own home.

The feeling surprised him, unnerved him. Joanna unnerved him. He knew this was supposed to be business. But it was beginning not to feel like business at all.

It was nearly noon before he left. He wrote her a note, too. It said, "No thanks necessary. Tell Charlie we'll do it again. The French toast was great. Thanks for the use of your floor." He was almost out the door when he went back and added, "We're building a sand castle for a contest in Manhattan today. If Charlie wants to come, I'll introduce him to an eccentric millionaire."

He didn't write, "If you want to bring him." But he didn't know any other way Charlie would be able to get there, either.

THE CASTLE WAS ALREADY underway when he arrived at the beach.

He spied Austin first, his golden hair a beacon in the noonday sun. But it wouldn't have been hard to find him in any case. His castle was by far the most elaborate on the beach. The sand itself had already been piled and compressed into two sets of wooden forms. Austin stood atop the third form, sculpting a rather delicate-looking tower while Miles and Susan were squaring off a portion of the other set.

Clea, Austin's wife, was busy trying to prevent Patrick from teaching their six-week-old cousins, Brent and Sara, how to eat sand.

"Oh, wonderful! Reinforcements!" Clea beamed when he dropped his towel down next to her beach umbrella. "Look who's here."

Susan looked up. "About time. Did you sleep in?"

"He probably slept out," Austin said, grinning down at him.

Chase flushed. "I was tired," he said. "I'm not as young as you are," he reminded Austin severely.

"Oh, right. Sorry," Austin replied, wholly unrepentant.

"Patrick!" Clea protested, shooing her sandy nephew away from his cousin. "Miles, corral your son."

"Can't," Miles said cheerfully. "Your husband will have my head. I have to finish this." He gestured at the row of parapets he'd just begun to work on.

Chase reached out and snagged Patrick away from the twin he was currently trying to feed and hoisted him up onto his shoulders. Patrick's fists tugged at his hair and small sandy feet bounced off his chest.

"Bless you," Clea said.

"Where's Marlene?" Susan asked.

Chase shrugged. He'd tried to call her when he got home. She was on safari again according to her machine. He didn't know if she was coming down today or not. He'd invited her last week, but she'd ticked off seventy-five other things she had to do.

"You've been spending a lot of time with her lately," Susan went on.

"Mmm." Chase agreed.

"Things getting serious?" Susan asked hopefully.

"Susan!" Miles admonished his wife.

Susan brushed him off. "Well, are they?"

Miles, knowing his wife well, looked at Chase and gave him a "what can you do?" shrug.

Chase smiled wryly at her. "When I find out, you'll be the third to know."

"So how'd things go with your project?" Austin asked him.

Chase grinned. "You'll never guess." He proceeded to describe Charlie's proposed project.

Austin laughed. "Sounds like my kind of boy. I'd like to meet that kid."

"Yeah, well, I thought he might like to meet you, too, sometime."

"Like now," Austin said, squinting up the beach.

"Huh?"

Austin gestured with his spatula. "Isn't that him?"

Chase spun around, making Patrick giggle on his shoulders. Sure enough, Charlie—and Joanna—were walking across the beach.

"I begin to understand the reason for the project now," Austin said to him, ogling Jo. "What a dish."

"It's the redhead," Miles said appreciatively.

Susan looked at Chase narrowly. Her gaze said quite clearly, "What about Marlene?"

Chase ignored her. He grinned at Joanna. He couldn't help it. It was as if the day had suddenly come into focus, as if something he hadn't even known he'd been waiting for had finally come to pass.

He hadn't realized how much he'd counted on seeing her again until this minute.

It didn't hurt, of course, that he was seeing her in a swim suit. Even five years ago, Joanna'd had a tall slim, leggy figure that made her gentle curves enticing. But there was more to her now. More substance. More woman. He felt a stirring in his loins.

Get a grip on yourself, Whitelaw, he instructed himself sternly. *Adolescence is over.*

"Hi," he said, walking up to meet her and Charlie. "You got the note."

"Yes. Couldn't pass it up." She gave him a broad smile.

"Hey, uh, thanks for... last night." He shrugged awkwardly, not knowing exactly what to say.

"No problem. My floor is your floor, as they say." She grinned again, then looked up at Patrick. "Who's this?" she asked Chase.

He told her, then introduced her to Patrick's mother, to Austin and Clea and their twins. "You've met Miles already."

Joanna nodded, returning Miles's grin. Then she introduced Charlie all around. The boy looked a little nervous.

Chase clapped a hand on his shoulder. "Not exactly research material, most of 'em," he told Charlie. "Except him." He nodded at Austin. "You're rich and famous, aren't you?"

Austin grinned. "Who, me?"

Clea laughed. "Infamous, I'd say."

Chase saw Austin's gaze flicker for just a moment over his children before settling warmly on his wife. A long look passed between them.

"Infamous maybe," Austin said to Charlie, "but very definitely rich."

And Chase understood that it wasn't a matter of money either. It was the sort of wealth he coveted—the wealth of love and caring—the only kind that mattered. His fingers tightened around Patrick's ankles and he felt a curious thickening in his throat.

He stole a quick look at Joanna.

Austin beckoned to the boy. "Come on and give me a hand. I'm trying to carve a tower. You can help me and I'll tell you how I made my first million."

Charlie looked wary, obviously trying to judge whether Austin was joking.

"He means it," Chase assured him.

Charlie considered that, considered Austin. "You made a million making sand castles?" he asked skeptically.

Austin shook his head. "Clerestory windows, believe it or not. That's how I made my first million. Made my second on hot tubs. Then redwood furniture and decking."

Charlie's eyes grew wide, then narrowed. He looked once more at Chase.

Chase nodded. "It's true."

Charlie smiled faintly. "Okay," he said and took the spatula Austin offered. "Show me how."

Chase looked at Joanna and she looked at him. They both smiled.

"If you want to sit down, Joanna," Clea offered, shifting over one of the twins, "there's plenty of room on the blanket."

Joanna, still looking at Chase, shook her head. "Not yet, thanks." She smiled briefly at Clea, then turned back to Chase. Her eyes looked like smoldering green fire, enticing, beckoning.

He wanted her. The feeling, of course, wasn't new. But the intensity of it was. It rattled him.

"I could use a swim," he said, almost desperately.

Patrick bounced enthusiastically on his shoulders. "Swim!"

Miles came over. "Want me to take him?"

Chase shook his head, his fingers still wrapped around Patrick's ankles. "No."

He needed Patrick. He couldn't have said why precisely. He just knew there was something solid and tangible about the little boy's presence that kept his emotions in line, his hopes in perspective, his feet on the ground.

Until Joanna reached out and tickled Patrick's toes, at least.

Patrick giggled and kicked. Chase felt the feathery brush of her knuckles and his discomfort grew. He edged away.

Joanna grinned up at Patrick, oblivious. "Do you like horsey rides?"

Patrick grinned back and banged Chase on the head with his fist. "Horsey, go," he said.

"He wants you to give him a ride," Joanna said.

"I know." He wanted to give *her* a ride. His face flamed.

"You sure you don't want Miles to take him, Chase?" Susan watched him with avid curiosity, obviously prepared to make sure Patrick wasn't *de trop*.

Chase turned away. "He's fine. C'mon, sport," he said quickly. "Let's go take a dip."

He headed toward the water at a brisk clip.

"I'll go with you," Joanna said.

He wasn't sure what kind of idea that was, but it turned out to be a fantastic one. It was an enchanted afternoon. Warm and clear with a light westerly breeze, the sort of weather that southern California is famous for. But it wasn't the weather that enchanted Chase, it was the company.

Joanna matched him stride for stride down the beach, plowed right into the surf alongside him, then dived under an incoming wave, surfacing to laugh and then lift Patrick down off his shoulders so he could do the same.

The three of them jumped the breakers together and then moved out beyond them so that the soft swells lifted them gently, then dropped them again to the sandy ocean floor.

Joanna still held Patrick, his small body snug against her chest, his arms around her neck. He beamed at her, then tugged her long auburn braid. "Go up," he said. "Go down."

"We will," she promised. "Watch for the next wave." She showed him with her hand the way the waves coming in would lift them. "See?" she said seriously. "We can't do it alone. The waves do it for us."

Patrick's hair was just the color of Joanna's, and Chase, watching the two of them, was smitten with another overwhelming urge toward fatherhood. He swallowed hard and looked away.

Just then Patrick said, "Uh-oh," and Joanna added, "Chase..." with some urgency, and he looked up to see a swell growing mightily on the horizon.

He swallowed, looking apprehensively at Patrick. "Wave of the day?"

"You could say that," Joanna replied even as it grew, beginning to show signs of cresting just beyond them. "In or out?" she asked him, while Patrick's eyes grew wider and wider.

The wave peaked and broke, a crashing wall of water surging almost upon them.

"Under," Chase said and, without thinking, wrapped his arms around them both and ducked down.

The water pounded over them, Patrick wriggled between them, Joanna's long smooth legs tangled with his own, and then he straightened, shoving them all upward and they broke the surface, clinging together, water streaming down their faces, hearts thundering in unison.

Patrick rubbed his eyes with his fists, his lower lip jutted out as he debated the wisdom of tears. "Big'un," he said.

"I'll say," Joanna agreed. "Knocked us right off our feet, didn't it?"

Was that what it was? Chase wondered.

He didn't think so. Not for him at least. What knocked him off his feet was Joanna.

"Had enough?" Jo asked Patrick.

He looked toward the shoreline. "'Nuf," he said. "Go Mommy."

They made their way toward shore, dripping, swinging Patrick by his hands between them.

"Big'un," Patrick told his mother and father, pointing at the ocean.

"You don't say." Miles took his son and tossed him up into the air.

Susan didn't say anything; she just looked speculatively from Chase to Joanna, and then she smiled to herself, noticeably pleased.

Chase reached down and tossed Joanna a towel, then grabbed his own. She dried off, then spread her towel and lay down on her stomach. He dropped on his back right next to her, remembering how her body had felt against his with the wave surging around them. He closed his eyes and groaned.

Patrick toddled over and plopped down in front of Joanna, handing her a pretzel. It was sandy and less than appetizing, but Joanna took it with a grin and broke it in half, giving a piece back to him to eat while she ate the other herself.

At least, Chase thought thankfully, it broke the mood. It was a mood that needed breaking. This was Joanna Hancock-Smith, for heaven's sake. But somehow he couldn't shy away.

"Good?" he teased, watching her nibble the sandy pretzel.

Joanna laughed. "The best." Her smile began to restore the mood rather fast.

Patrick, pleased with her response, went back and raided the pretzel bag again, returning with a handful, which he proceeded to feed to Chase and Joanna alternately. Then he climbed on Chase's chest and bounced up and down.

Thank God, Chase thought. Distraction was what he needed right now.

"Hey, you lazy bums," Austin hollered at them. "We've got to get this done in less than two hours. Lend a hand, will you?"

"Me?" Joanna asked. "Really?"

She looked delighted at Austin's nod and jumped up, leaving Chase watching, Patrick still using his chest for a trampoline. He felt the faintest bit relieved.

"You, too," Austin beckoned to him.

"Me?"

"You can show her what to do."

Warily Chase got to his feet, handing Patrick to Susan.

"Here." Austin gestured to a wall that needed finishing. "See the way I started? Do that all along here. You do the upper level and Jo can do the lower one. Show her, Chase."

Taking a deep breath, Chase showed her. It wasn't easy. He had to take her hand and guide it at first. He had to move so his body practically covered hers. And even when she got the hang of it, he was too aware of her smooth skin, her damp hair, the way her sandy leg on occasion brushed against his.

"You need a steady hand for this," Austin said.

Joanna lifted her arm to brush a stray lock of hair away from her eyes. Chase saw the lift of her breasts in the scant blue bra that covered them.

"A steady hand?" he repeated hoarsely. "Yeah, sure."

"Look who's here," Susan said suddenly.

Chase looked up, the spatula slipping from his hand. Marlene was picking her way across the sand, the full skirt of her white silk dress lifting in the breeze, displaying a tantalizing glimpse of long tanned legs. The legs ended, incongruously enough, in a pair of spike heel shoes and on her head she wore a wide-brimmed summer straw hat, anchored by one desperate hand. It wasn't exactly "beach," but it was pure "Marlene." He glanced quickly, nervously at Joanna. She seemed to be mesmerized by the sight.

Marlene was oblivious of the effect she was having. "You really must get a portable phone," she said to him. "I've been trying to reach you for hours."

Chase opened his mouth to mention her own rather lengthy "safari," but she went right on. "Hello, Miles, Susan. Nice to see you."

She nodded to the rest of them, even Joanna, then turned back to him, continuing briskly. "It's almost four, you know. And we have to sit at the head table tonight, so you'll have to be there by six-thirty."

He grimaced, having forgotten the awards banquet.

"But you don't need to pick me up," Marlene said. "I'm on my way there right now. I just stopped to drop off your tux. I picked it up from the cleaners. And, oh yes, I sent myself some flowers, and I billed them to you. All right?"

Chase almost got the word "Fine" out of his mouth before she cut him off. "Come up with me now and take the tux. I don't want to leave it hanging on the porch. Who knows what might become of it?"

"Cripes, yes, Chase," Austin said gravely, "Don't get your tux stolen."

Chase managed a weak grin. "Right."

"I don't have a lot of time," Marlene reminded him when he didn't move.

"Yeah." He handed Miles the spatula, looked at Joanna for a split second, wanting to say something, not sure what. But Joanna looked suddenly remote.

Finally he shrugged awkwardly. "See you later." Irritated at having to leave—albeit irrationally, he told himself—he followed Marlene back up the beach.

JOANNA TOLD HERSELF she should have known. Hadn't Bitsy said it might be serious? Hadn't Bitsy said that Chase might very well marry Marlene Copley?

Yes, of course she had. But Joanna had been too dumb to listen. She had only heard what she wanted to hear. And because she had suddenly discovered an interest in Chase after all these years, she had imagined he would rediscover an interest in her.

So much for self-delusion.

Oh, no doubt he was no longer furious with her. He couldn't be and have drunk beer with her and fallen asleep on her living room floor. He couldn't be and have decided to seek her help with the Begays. He couldn't be and have left her a note that she interpreted as practically "inviting" her down to the beach today.

But "not being furious with" wasn't the same as "hankering after," either. He was treating her the way he would treat a friend or—God help her—a kid sister.

Joanna winced.

She watched Chase and Marlene disappear into his apartment and sighed. *Why are you surprised?* she asked herself. Marlene was exactly the woman he had always been looking for—pretty, social, organized, someone who would fit in well with the publishing pooh-bahs, who would be able to hold her own in any situation. A woman who could arrange a banquet for several hundred, remember what needed fetching from the cleaners and order herself flowers at the same time.

A social paragon, in other words.

Not a pariah. Certainly not a woman like herself.

Jo tried to force her concentration back on the castle, but she couldn't. She felt as if she was there under false pretenses. Or, rather, false expectations.

And she had to leave, had to be miles away when—if—Chase came back. Because if he came back now, she wouldn't know what to say or how to act.

But before she could move, Miles said, "Here come Griff and Lainie," and Jo looked up dismayed to see a couple carrying a toddler making their way toward the castle.

Oh, God. Of all the people in the world, the last person she needed to see right now was Griff Tucker. Griff, who had been best man at her disastrous almost wedding. Griff, who would quite rightly wonder, probably aloud, just what the devil she was doing here. She looked around frantically for a means of escape.

Susan moved toward the tall blond man and his brown-haired wife, saying, "About time you got here. Miles and Austin are having to do all the work."

"It took Andrew a while to wake up," Lainie said.

"And when he's asleep you want to enjoy the peace and quiet," his father added with a slow smile. "He never shuts up."

Susan laughed. "Not his father's son?"

Griff's smile broadened. "Not in that way at least." Then his eyes found Joanna's and quite suddenly he stopped in his tracks.

"Oh," Susan said quickly. "I almost forgot. This is Joanna, a friend of Chase's. I'm sorry," she said to Jo, "I don't even know your last name."

"Hancock-Smith," Griff supplied smoothly, and Susan turned to stare at him.

Jo held her breath, waiting for Griff's censure, waiting for him to say what so many people had already said. But he didn't say a word. After a moment he held out his hand to her and the beginnings of a new smile found his mouth.

"Nice to see you, Joanna. You're looking good."

She breathed again. "You, too, Griff." She took his hand.

Susan looked at the two of them curiously. Joanna heard unspoken questions filling the air.

But before Susan could ask any, Austin intervened. "Doesn't matter how long it took you, Tucker, you're here," he said briskly. "Come on. We've got work to do if we're going to finish by the deadline. You, too, Susan," Austin prodded his sister-in-law.

Griff handed Andrew to Lainie and went to help Miles and Austin. "Where're the Craigs?" Joanna heard him say.

"Brendan's coming down with the boys and Katie later. Cassie's staying home with J.B."

Joanna remembered Cassie Craig. She was the one Chase wouldn't let drive across town to bail him out. She remembered Brendan, too, now that she thought about it. She'd even met him once long ago, when she had been engaged to Chase, and Brendan had dropped over to see Griff.

Another reason to leave at once. Sooner or later someone less circumspect than Griffin Tucker was going to come along and make things even more awkward. She had no business here, Jo realized. The dream was over.

"Charlie! We've got to go."

The boy looked around the side of the castle, frowning at her. "Now?"

Joanna tapped her watch. "Now. I have to go to my parents'."

He sighed. "Yeah. Can I wash off first?" He nodded toward the ocean.

She glanced quickly up at Chase's. He wasn't anywhere to be seen. Surprise. As if he would leave the lovely Marlene to rush right back down to the beach. "I guess," she said. "If you're quick."

Charlie handed Austin the sculpting knife and sprinted toward the water. "Too bad," Austin said to Joanna.

She started. "What?"

"Your boy. He's got some talent. He doesn't knock things down like some I could mention." Austin cast a disparaging glance at Griff who seemed to be all thumbs as he squared off one of the battlements. "Wish you didn't have to take him."

"I really do have to go." Joanna shrugged awkwardly, wishing he wasn't so nice, wishing she didn't want to stay.

"Don't you want to wait for Chase?" Susan asked.

"No." She gave a quick shake of her head and started up the beach. Charlie dripped along after her.

As she passed his apartment she gave it a quick glance. "I think," she said in a low voice, "that I'd have to wait a very long time."

"WHERE'S JOANNA?"

Susan looked up from drying off Patrick after another quick dip. "What?"

"I said," Chase repeated, shifting from one foot to the other. "Where's Joanna. Where'd she go?"

Susan shrugged. "She left."

"Left?"

"Left." Susan began drying Patrick's hair with another towel.

"But—" Damn. He'd only been gone thirty minutes. Forty-five at most. Marlene had twenty things he had to remember to pick up on his way to the awards banquet, and she'd insisted he sit down and make a list of them before she would leave. And she wouldn't leave even then until she was sure that the tux still fit him—and that meant taking a quick shower and trying it on for her.

When at last she was satisfied, had planted a light kiss on his jaw, and had flown off again to make the next stop on her itinerary, he had scrambled back into his trunks and had headed back to the beach. Too late.

He'd told himself he wasn't going to come back. Had told himself that distance was what he needed right now. But he hadn't convinced himself in the least. Chase scowled. "When'd she leave?"

Susan shook her head. "Fifteen minutes ago, maybe."

He squinted hopefully up toward The Strand, but of course she wasn't there. If she'd left fifteen minutes ago, she'd be long gone by now.

He stalked over to where the others were working on the finishing touches of the castle. "D'you know where Joanna went?"

Miles looked up from the wall he was carving. "Thought she said something about her parents' place. Didn't she?" He looked at Austin for confirmation.

Austin nodded.

"Her parents?"

"You know," Griff drawled, "the Hancock-Smiths." He arched a brow. "Remember them?"

Chase stopped and stared, aware suddenly of Griff's presence, remembering what Griff knew. "Did she say anything to you?" he demanded.

Griff shook his head. "Nope."

"Did *you* say—"

Once more Griff shook his head. "Me?"

No. Of course Griff wouldn't. Not his style. He, of all people, would never say a word.

Chase grimaced, raking a hand through damp black hair. "Right. Well, I gotta go. See you guys later." He pivoted and started back up the beach.

He was halfway home when a voice behind him said, "Joanna's looking good."

He turned, saw Griff following him, and slowed his pace. "Yeah."

Griff caught up with him. "Grown up."

"I noticed," Chase said dryly.

"Quite a woman."

Chase didn't reply.

"Going to try again?"

For a minute Chase didn't answer. Then he said, "I tried once."

"So?"

"You got a short memory?"

Griff smiled slightly. "Maybe the timing wasn't right."

"You can say that again." There was a bitter twist to Chase's voice.

"Maybe now it is," Griff said quietly.

Chase stopped and looked at his friend. He saw worry as well as kindness and compassion in Griff's eyes. Behind him he heard the slap of a volleyball, the cawing of a gull, the muted rush of waves against the shore.

Was the time right?

"Maybe," he said finally. "But the real killer, Griff, is how can you know for sure?"

Chapter Eight

Being Griff, of course, he didn't give Chase any answers. It was enough that he was there just as, three years earlier, Chase had tried to be there for Griff and Lainie during their troubles.

Was it the same? Chase wondered.

Was Joanna to him what Lainie was to Griff?

Once he'd thought so and had been proved wrong. And now?

Now he didn't know.

He was beginning to realize, however, that what existed between Marlene and him couldn't come close to the feelings that existed between Miles and Susan, Griff and Lainie, Austin and Clea. No matter how much he might've wished they were.

Marlene managed to give him an absent smile and put a proprietary hand on his arm when he arrived at her side just before they went into the awards dinner. But she didn't pause in her conversation with the CEO of a big valley manufacturing firm, and she certainly didn't lace her fingers through his the way he noted Clea's were at that moment laced through Austin's.

Chase felt similarly detached. He went through the dinner mechanically, blessing his mother for all those years of pounded-in etiquette. He could make small talk while comatose, and very nearly did.

While he ate filet mignon and twice-baked potatoes, he wondered where Joanna was and what she was doing. While he listened to the president of the Fiesta Charity Tennis Tournament introduce the woman who had made it all possible, he wondered if she had really gone to her parents and taken Charlie. Or was it, he wondered as Marlene walked to the podium, just an excuse?

"... lovely tonight, doesn't she?" his mother said in his ear over the generous applause.

Chase blinked, trying to swim back to the reality at hand. "Sorry?"

"I said, doesn't Marlene look lovely tonight?" Denise repeated. "Of course, she always does."

"Yes," Chase agreed, watching as Marlene took the microphone and began her speech. She did look lovely. Lovely and poised and confident. And remote.

He watched her move quickly through the program, handing out awards, praising players and supporters alike, treating everyone with equal aplomb—even himself when he and Austin went forward to accept the men's doubles trophies—and in his mind he could see her twenty years from now doing the same thing. Only she'd probably be doing it better. She thrived on it.

Did he? No, not really.

What he thrived on was his writing. And that was turning into a thing of the past now, too. Well, that couldn't be helped, but he and Marlene ...

He had to talk to her, see where things stood. Tonight.

His grandfather leaned across the table and clinked his champagne glass against Chase's. "To the next generation of tennis players."

Chase brought his glass to his lips, but didn't drink.

"What's the matter?" Alex demanded. "Won't be long now. I can see the way the Copley girl looks at you."

"Mmm," Chase said noncommittally.

"We just want to get you settled, dear," Denise put in before Alex could say the same thing in earthier terms.

"I can settle myself," Chase said shortly.

Alex snorted at that. "Doin' a damn poor job of it, I'd say."

The only way to handle Alexander Chase when he was in top autocratic form was to run right out and do what he said or change the subject so completely that he forgot what command he'd just issued.

Since Chase had no intention of marrying anyone that evening, he changed the subject, grabbing the first thing that came to mind that he was sure would provide a smoke screen.

"Funny thing happened the other day," he told them, "I was sitting in my office and a couple of Navajos walked in the door."

The change in both Alex and Denise was instantaneous. Alex's white brows drew down and his jaw thrust out. Denise's hard-won tan bleached pale.

"Navajos, you say?" Alex barked, making the people around them jump. "What'd they want?"

Well, at least he'd forgotten Marlene. "They were looking for a runaway. A girl."

"A runaway? Why'd they come to you?"

"Because I wrote a story about hookers. Runaways sometimes end up there."

"Not because they thought you were Navajo?" his grandfather demanded.

"I am Navajo," Chase said quietly.

Alexander thrust his jaw upward and fixed his grandson with a steel-plated stare across the table. "You are my grandson. You are a Chase. And don't you forget it."

He took his daughter firmly by the arm. "Gettin' damned hot in here. Too much racket for an old man. Goin' home. Get your wrap, Denise," he said brusquely. "I'll meet you at the door."

Chase's mother gave him a wan smile. "Yes, Dad." She touched Chase's arm briefly, held his eyes for a mere instant, then melted into the crowd.

Chase watched her go, feeling the familiar guilt descend, wishing he could take back the words, wishing he'd thought of another way to distract the old man. Wishing he could think of another way to distract the old man now.

Alex had turned and was glaring at him. "I trust you told these Indians to shove off."

"No, I didn't."

"Why not?"

"They needed help. I introduced them to a ... friend." Chase wasn't saying which friend. No doubt his grandfather would have plenty to say about that, too.

"Not you?" It was a question and a statement both.

"What good would I be?" Chase asked, tasting bitterness, not champagne.

"You wouldn't be," Alex said flatly. "And I'm glad you realize it." He looked at his grandson squarely. "You can't be both, Chase. It's impossible."

Alex drained his champagne glass, then started to move away. Arthritis was slowing him down, Chase noticed. He looked older tonight. Vulnerable. More like the eighty-two he was than the fifty he often seemed. No longer entirely the indomitable old codger who ruled the west-coast publishing world and would rule it into eternity.

It was time for him to retire, while he could still enjoy life, still travel, still have a chance to put his feet up and enjoy his dotage—something he'd never had time to do while single-handedly building an empire and standing in as surrogate father to his daughter's children.

Chase felt a sudden rush of affection for the old man. Irascible, opinionated and stubborn though he was, he was still the only father Chase had ever known. He'd done what he could and always for the best.

All things considered, he'd done a damned good job.

"There're others, you know, if you don't want Marlene." His grandfather changed topics completely as he often did, letting Chase know that for all his efforts at sidetracking, he hadn't succeeded at all.

He smiled. "I know."

Alex grunted. "You got someone in mind?"

Chase hesitated. "Maybe."

The old man's eyes narrowed. "Don't wait too long."

Chase shook his head. "I won't."

"Fair enough." His grandfather squeezed his arm. "You'll have breakfast with me Wednesday?"

Chase nodded. "If you want."

Alex laid an arm across his grandson's shoulders. "I want."

Everyone, it seemed to Chase, knew what he wanted. Except himself.

He stood around watching people leave the banquet arm in arm and felt in as much of a quandary as ever. It would help, he thought, if Marlene would throw herself into his arms and act as if she couldn't live without him. Or at least walk past and kiss his cheek.

Instead she sent him off to see if he could find the head groundskeeper who had the only set of keys to some cupboards she desperately needed entrance to. And when he got back from that, she left him cooling his heels in the kitchen while she went over a list with the caterer about which serving dishes belonged to him and which to the country club. He stuffed his hands into the pockets of his black tux trousers and fumed.

"You don't have to wait," Marlene told him in passing.

"I want to talk."

She shrugged equably. "Fine. Let's talk. Come on. You can talk while I get the chairs counted. Can you believe Marjorie Harris left without doing it. You can't trust—"

"About love," he said doggedly, following her.

"Mmm?" Marlene was tapping her teeth with a long polished fingernail. "Love?" she echoed vaguely.

"What I'm looking for in a relationship..."

"Oh. 37, 38, 39..."

"Caring, love... that sort of thing," he went on, determined.

"51, 52, 53, 54..."

"Damn it, Marlene!" He grabbed her arm and hauled her into the anteroom next to the main hall. "Quit counting the blasted chairs and listen to me!"

Marlene stared at him as if he'd lost his mind. "I don't need this," she told him sharply. "I don't need it at all."

It was Chase's turn to stare. "What do you mean?"

"All this caring you're talking about. This 'love' business. Romance—" she made it sound faintly dirty "—who needs it? What good is it?"

"Good?" Chase echoed.

"We're friends, Chase," she said simply. "We have a good time together. We could do well together our whole lives. We've had the same experiences, know the same things, the same people. The rest—the romance part—" she shrugged "—it's highly overrated, if you ask me."

He remembered saying much the same thing to Susan once. He didn't believe it anymore. The "love business," as far as he was concerned, was the most important—and the riskiest—part there was.

"You don't agree?" Marlene asked him.

"No." He shook his head adamantly. "I don't."

She reached up and gave his cheek a pat. "Then it isn't *me* you need." And she turned on her heel and went right back to the dining room to count chairs. "Is it?" she asked over her shoulder.

He smiled ruefully after her. "No, it's not."

It was, God help him, Joanna.

EIGHT MORE OUTLINES and she could call it a night. Thank heavens.

Joanna sighed and stretched, then curled again into the corner of the day bed where she sat surrounded by evidence of her students' work. On the stereo John Williams played Bach on his guitar, a choice made in an effort to soothe.

But Joanna wasn't soothed. She should be grateful, she supposed, that she was dealing with outlines. Bare structure was about all she could manage tonight. Her concentration had been on the wane all evening.

Her mind was still on the beach. On what a colossal fool she'd been.

She'd read far too much into Chase's exultant arrival on her doorstep last night. He'd been high on his tennis triumph and on having dented Charlie's impervious indifference. That was all.

He'd shared it with her because she'd brought him Charlie. No more, no less.

She shouldn't have presumed on him and showed up at the beach this afternoon, despite what she had interpreted as a veiled invitation. His friends had made her welcome, of course—even Griff. Chase himself had seemed glad to see her. But it was Marlene he really wanted, Marlene he'd followed up to the apartment. Marlene who was his girlfriend.

Joanna might have made it to "friend" status, but certainly nothing more than that.

Let that be a lesson to you, she told herself and, indeed, she tried to, determinedly bending her head over the outlines once more.

By midnight she was about five pages further and getting slower by the minute. Ready to give up anyway, she was grateful to hear a knock on the door. It was a hesitant knock, tentative. Reluctant almost.

A far cry, she couldn't help thinking, from the confident rapping Chase Whitelaw had given that same door the evening before.

She sighed and got up from the day bed, wondering who would be calling now.

It was Chase.

Joanna stared, dumbfounded, disbelieving.

He wore a white dress shirt and a black tux. The cummerbund was trailing out of his coat pocket, and the tie dangled from the collar of his shirt. His hands were tucked into the pockets of his slacks, and his black hair drifted across his forehead. He wore a serious, hesitant look on his face.

There was no exultant smile in evidence tonight, no joy, no enthusiasm. He looked as worried as she felt.

"Hi," he said softly.

Joanna's fingers tightened on the doorknob. "Hello." She opened the door cautiously.

What was he doing here? What did he want? Was he going to tell her to please stay out of his life? Mortification flooded her. *You don't have to,* she wanted to tell him. *I will, I promise. I already know.*

One corner of his mouth quirked up in a ghost of a smile. "I didn't know where else to go."

Where else to go? Joanna was confused. What did he mean? Wordlessly, still amazed, Joanna opened the door wider and stepped back to let him in.

He bent his head slightly as he walked past her, and when he saw the piles of papers stacked on the coffee table and heaped on the day bed, he grimaced. "Oh, cripes, I'm sorry. I don't want to interrupt your work."

Joanna shook her head, scooping the ones on the day bed aside so he could sit down. "It doesn't matter. I was getting ready to quit anyway. Please." She swept her hand toward the day bed, offering him a seat.

He sat, but he didn't lean back and relax the way he had last night. Instead he perched right on the edge, leaned his forearms on his knees and knotted his fingers together, staring at them as if they were an intricate oriental puzzle he was obliged to solve.

"Coffee?" Joanna offered tentatively.

He shook his head.

"Tea? Gatorade?"

He smiled slightly. "No. Nothing, thanks. I...I came to—" He stopped, groping for words, not finding them. "I...needed to," he said at last, looking at the floor between his feet, then almost desperately, up at Joanna.

Joanna waited, uncertain how to respond.

"When I came back this afternoon, you were gone."

"Yes, well, I'd butted in," Joanna explained quickly. "You shouldn't have had to put up with me. I—"

"No!"

His ferocity surprised her. "No?"

"I was glad you came."

"Well, I know you said in your note that you'd introduce Charlie to your friend, but that was no reason for me to—"

"I hoped you would."

She gulped. "You did?"

"Uh-huh." He looked up at her a moment, then his gaze dropped.

"But I thought...when Marlene came..." Her voice trailed off. "I thought..."

"No."

"No?"

He met her gaze, his dark eyes burning. "No. It's not on. Not Marlene and I. It...wouldn't work. It never would."

Joanna felt a flame of hope.

"She said so herself," Chase went on.

The flame in Joanna's heart died. Marlene had dumped him.

"But she didn't have to," he continued. "I'd already begun to figure it out this afternoon. She wasn't what I wanted." He still looked at the floor.

Joanna waited, and when he didn't go on, finally she dared to ask, "What did you want?"

He looked up at her then, and she saw a faint flush along his cheekbones. "You."

The word rang like a gong in her ears.

"But—"

"'But' is right," he said roughly. "There are a thousand of them, and I'm having trouble dealing with them all."

So was she. What she was hearing was so far from what she'd been thinking that her mind boggled. He still wanted her?

Glory hallelujah!

But Chase didn't seem to think it was glorious at all. He looked pained.

"Listen, Joanna," he said, "when I first saw you again, I wanted to run in the other direction again as fast as I could."

"And now?" she asked. "Do you still?"

He cracked his knuckles. "I don't know. I don't know what I want anymore. I don't know if it will work."

It was a triumph of hope that Joanna found something to be optimistic about in his confusion.

"We never talked like this before, you know," she told him.

He frowned. "Like what?"

"Like people who are trying to understand each other. Like people who care about what the other person thinks."

"I always cared about what you thought," he told her.

Maybe he had. Probably she just hadn't noticed. She'd been far too much in awe of him in those days to imagine that he spared her very many thoughts at all.

"I didn't realize," she said softly.

Chase sighed and leaned back, folding one arm behind his head. "Well, it's true."

Their eyes met again, more gently this time. There was a warmth in his that made Joanna's toes curl. She smiled. He smiled. John Williams's guitar wove smiles all around the room.

"Come here," Chase whispered and held out his hand to her.

Mesmerized, obedient, Joanna rose and came to him, taking his hand, feeling it clasp hers strongly as it drew her down onto the day bed next to him.

They touched. Her knee and his thigh. His arm and her shoulder. Her hair and his cheek. Their fingers twined.

Joanna's heart tripped as lightly as Williams's fingers across the frets of his guitar, and she breathed first shallowly, then deeply, drawing in the essence of Chase. A hint of sea breeze mixed with pine.

He turned her head slightly so that she was looking at him. Their eyes were scant inches apart, their noses almost touching. Closer now—except for their embrace under the wave today—than they'd been in years.

Joanna remembered that closeness. She remembered the tension in him, a leashed urgency, a demand denied. She hadn't understood it then. She comprehended it perfectly now.

She felt it herself, growing within her, throbbing, aching, needing. Needing Chase.

He moved closer, tilted his head, and his eyes closed as, finally, his lips touched hers.

Their caress was feather light. A hint. A question. Perhaps a promise.

And then she saw him smile.

"To new beginnings," he said.

THIS TIME, Joanna was determined, it would be different. Everything in the past had been laid out for them, cut and dried, by her parents, by his grandfather, by the society in which they lived. It wouldn't happen again.

Chase had to learn to trust her again. She had to teach him to trust her again, had to prove to him that this time she knew her own mind, knew who she was and who he was.

She had to make sure he knew that if he asked again and she said yes again, this time there would be no going back.

And so she began cautiously, offering to fix him supper the next night.

"You cook?" he asked.

"After a fashion," Joanna said. "For you I'll make the effort."

He said yes.

The dinner consisted of meat loaf, baked potatoes, fresh broccoli, and homemade ice cream for dessert. Chase was impressed, also worn out from having to crank the freezer.

"You never cooked for me before," he remarked as they washed up afterward.

"Didn't know how," Joanna reminded him. "It wasn't one of the social graces."

"I liked you anyway." He dropped a light kiss on her forehead.

"I hope you like me better now," she said frankly.

He smiled. "I think I might."

He came back the next night, too, sitting cross-legged on the floor and going over her outlines with her, adding insightful comments, making her smile when he told her that correcting the outlines was far more interesting than attending meetings the way he'd done all day.

"I like writing better," he said, stretching his arms up over his head to ease cramped muscles and to tantalize Joanna with a view of his chest.

"So write," she said.

He shook his head. "Can't. I've got to be the CEO now."

"You want to?"

"It's expected. So pass me another outline. I'll make do with that."

Wednesday after school he played hooky from his meetings and picked up her and Charlie and took them on a drive through Beverly Hills.

"Old home week," he teased Joanna.

She shrank down and wailed, "I wish I'd worn a disguise."

Happily they saw no one they knew.

It was, Joanna thought, a week to remember. One in which things kept getting better and better. For herself and for Chase, for Charlie. Possibly even for the Begays, for on Friday Gloria, the policewoman to whom she had shown Jenny's picture, called. She'd seen a girl in the neighborhood where she'd been working who answered the description of Jenny Tso.

GLORIA WASN'T SURE, of course. The girl she saw was maybe Jenny, maybe not.

None of the other people Joanna asked—and she asked a lot that afternoon as she and Chase carted the Begays around the neighborhood—was sure, either.

"So many girls," one sailor told her. "So little time."

Chase put his hand on Joanna's arm, restraining her. He was beginning to recognize the uplifted chin. It meant that Joanna Hancock-Smith was taking on the world.

She had certainly taken on him. And he, slowly and carefully, was taking her on again, too.

She seemed to understand his need to move slowly, to rebuild. She made it easy for him, offering companionship, an easy smile, a gentle laugh, a touch of her hand. And she always left him burning for more.

This Joanna was the one he'd dreamed about. A joy to be with. Serious at times, silly at others. Open, yet mysterious. And the more he knew, the more he wanted to know. She was getting into his blood.

He had always wanted her—and he'd always known it—but he was beginning to understand that the way he'd wanted her five years ago was a mere shadow of the way he wanted her now.

Then he had wanted her body and he'd wanted her social acumen. She'd been lovely and she'd have looked good in his bed and on his arm.

She still would, of course. But he spent less time thinking about it now.

Now he thought about her stubborn chin, her generous smile. He thought about the way she encouraged Charlie, the way she listened intently and without interrupting when Joseph Begay talked, the way she persisted, looking for Jenny Tso in the face of very formidable odds.

"You can give it up, you know," he told her as they sat on her tiny deck Friday afternoon and watched the sun go down. He knew how much time she was spending, because every moment she was not with him or teaching, she was busy looking with no further leads.

Even the Begays were conceding defeat. They had no more money for motel rooms and no more vacation time from their jobs. In the morning they were driving home. It seemed to Chase that Joanna had every right to call it quits, too.

But Joanna shook her head. "You aren't giving up on Charlie," she said.

He wasn't, but Charlie was turning out to be considerably more rewarding.

Twice when he hadn't joined Joanna and the Begays following false leads about Jenny Tso, Chase had picked Charlie up after school and had taken him to the Craigs' or picked up Keith, the oldest Craig boy, and had taken him to Charlie's.

There he had the two of them point out the differences between their life-styles. Then together they had discussed the differences in the values they perceived.

It was an education for Charlie and Keith, but it was just as much an education for Chase. He had spent his childhood taking all that for granted and his adulthood scrutinizing everyone else's background but his own. He found he was learning a lot.

"I like Charlie," he told Joanna quite honestly, stretching out on the chaise longue and smiling at her.

"The feeling appears to be mutual." She smiled back, lifting her glass of beer and toasting him with it. "And there's an additional benefit, too."

"What's that?"

"He doesn't sleep through class anymore. In fact, he even contributes."

"He's growing by leaps and bounds." Chase grinned. "The next thing you know he'll be developing social responsibility."

Joanna lifted her hands with all fingers crossed. "Do you suppose we've wrought a miracle?"

Chase grinned. "Could be."

The phone rang. She got to her feet. "You want another beer while I'm up?"

He shook his head. "I'm mellow enough tonight." He had plans for this evening, and they didn't include any impairment of his faculties, however slight. He smiled at Joanna, a warm and tender smile, heartened when he got a similar smile back.

She went to answer the phone, and Chase let himself drift off into a fantasy in which they made up for five years abstinence in one night.

It was going to be warm and delicious and wonderful. And he was just getting to the good part when Joanna came back out onto the deck, a frown on her face.

He lifted his eyebrows. "What's up?"

"It's Charlie. He wants to talk to you." She sank down into the chair and shook her head. "I think perhaps our miraculous hopes were a bit precipitous."

Chase got to his feet. "What hopes?"

"The social responsibility hopes."

He looked at her, baffled.

"He wants you to help him steal a car."

Chapter Nine

Not just any car. A silver Porsche.

"It's yours! I know it is! C'mon, man, time's wastin'!"

"Hey, Charlie, slow down." Chase leaned one hip on Joanna's kitchen counter and tried to make sense out of what Charlie Seeks Elk was telling him. It wasn't easy.

He almost didn't believe it was Charlie on the other end of the line. Still seldom given to bursts of loquaciousness, Charlie wouldn't shut up now.

"I been seeing it around. A 911 SC Targa," he said. "Some dude's been drivin' it around here on and off. Hot-doggin', y'know? Showin' off for his girlfriend. Thought it might be yours, but I didn't wanta say till I was sure. Just got me a good look. Filled it up myself right here not half an hour ago. Unleaded premium."

"There's more than one silver 911 in L.A.," Chase argued.

"Yeah, well, this guy isn't the silver Porsche type, y'know what I mean?"

Chase wasn't sure.

"Not rich enough," Charlie told him. "Don't move right. Swaggers, doesn't glide. Hasn't got the polish for it. What you said when me and Keith were talkin'—" Chase could almost hear him concentrating "—about *savoir faire*?"

Chase grinned. So sociology had its practical uses after all.

"Still might not be mine," he said.

"Black leather upholstery? Scratch on the left front fender? Pink fingernail polish on the passenger door handle?"

It was the fingernail polish that did it.

"Damn, it is mine." Chase was standing up straight now.

Marlene had provided the polish the night before the Porsche had been stolen, getting into it to go to the theater while her nails were still drying. She'd complained about what it had done to her nail polish. Chase had bitten his tongue about what it had done to his car.

"Where is it?"

Charlie told him the cross streets. "I'm in a phone booth by the shoe repair."

"Did you call the cops?"

"You think the cops are gonna run right over to look at a maybe stolen car on *my* say-so?" Charlie was scornful. "Friday night in L.A., man, they got better things to do. You want your car, you better come."

"I'll be right there."

Chase went back out to the deck. "I gotta go," he said to Jo.

"You couldn't get him settled down over the phone?"

"I didn't try to settle him down."

She stood up. "Why? What's happened? Where are you going?" She came after him as he strode back through the apartment toward the front door.

"To help him."

"Help him?"

"Steal my car."

"Your Porsche? He found your Porsche?"

"He says so." Chase was prepared for an argument. He could imagine the one he'd have got from his grandfather, from his mother, from Marlene.

"Fantastic," Joanna said. "I'm coming, too."

IT TOOK MORE THAN half an hour to get there. Friday evening traffic on Pacific Coast Highway was thick in spots, but it was faster, Chase figured, than going clear over to the freeway, then having to come back west again. Still, he feared the dude and the Porsche would be gone by the time they found Charlie.

They weren't.

Charlie was leaning against the phone booth outside the shoe repair, looking as nonchalant and bored as ever, when Chase pulled into the parking lot.

"Is he gone?" Chase demanded.

"'Course not." Charlie slid into the back seat and gave Joanna a nod. "It's right over there." He dipped his head in the direction of a liquor store halfway down the block.

Chase looked. Sure enough, there was a silver Porsche— *his* silver Porsche—sitting benignly in the parking lot.

He stared at the Porsche, then turned his head slowly and stared at Charlie. "It's still there? How come he stayed so long?"

There was the faintest glimmer of amusement in the teenager's dark eyes.

He lifted his hand and showed Chase several inches of black wire with a cap at each end. He smiled.

Chase grinned. "So where is he?"

"Lookin' for a mechanic, I reckon." Charlie shoved a lock of black hair off his forehead with a greasy hand. "Or maybe he's bright enough to know what he's missin'. Then he's prob'ly gone to get it."

"How long's he been gone?"

"Half 'n hour. Left his girlfriend an' some dumb fat guy in the store."

"How long will it take you to put that back on?"

Charlie shrugged. "Couple a minutes."

"Let's go."

"What about the police?" Joanna asked.

"What about 'em?"

"Why don't we just call them now?"

But Chase didn't want to be bothered any more than Charlie did. The car was half a block away. Who knew how long it would take the cops to get there? To ascertain it was his? To impound it? To fill out forms and take statements?

Who cared?

"Forget the cops," he said to Joanna and drove the Ford up into the parking lot alongside the Porsche. Then he turned to Charlie. "C'mon, doc, let's see you do your stuff."

Charlie was out and had the hood up in a flash, bending over to reattach the wire. Chase got out to watch him.

Suddenly Joanna said, "Is that the girlfriend?" and he looked up to see a blowsy blonde, carrying a paper sack with what was probably a fifth of something potent in it, emerging from the liquor store. She stopped stock-still and stared at them and at the Porsche in consternation, then moved briskly in their direction.

At Joanna's question Charlie glanced up from beneath the hood. He grimaced. "Yeah, that's her. That's the fat guy, too."

A mammoth of a man, carrying an open bag of cheese curls, waddled out of the store after her.

Chase sucked in his breath. Suddenly the cops didn't sound like a waste of time after all.

But Charlie was under the hood again. "Don't worry. I'm almost done."

"Yeah, but—"

"What are you doing?" the blonde asked them.

Charlie pulled his head out and gave her a wide grin. "This your car, ma'am?"

She nodded, suspicious, shifting the paper sack. The fat man took another handful of cheese curls and stuffed them in his mouth. On closer inspection, Chase noted with considerable concern, he didn't appear to be quite so much fat as muscle.

"Your friend," Charlie said easily, "that tall dude...the one with the black beard..."

"Maurice," the blonde supplied.

Charlie nodded. "Yeah, Maurice. He was at the gas station where I work. Said you had some trouble. Sent us to fix it up for him." He jerked his head to include Chase.

"Two of you?" the blonde asked.

Charlie shrugged. "I'm new. He's my boss." He jerked his head again in Chase's direction. "Come along to see I did it right."

"Are you almost finished?" Chase asked him on cue.

Charlie nodded. "Why don'tcha get in? See if you can start 'er up."

Chase gave the blonde and the fat man what he hoped was the sort of smile a man used to not quite competent help would give. Then he slid behind the wheel.

It felt like coming home, but he couldn't revel in it yet. He slipped his key into the ignition.

"Ready?" he asked Charlie out the window.

Charlie slammed down the hood. Chase winced. "Ready," Charlie said.

"Get in here then, if you ever want a chance to sit in a Porsche." He gave the blonde an apologetic look and asked tentatively, "You don't think Maurice will mind, do you? The kid's never been in a Porsche."

She pursed her lips, half acquiescence, half pout. "I guess not . . . if you hurry."

"We'll hurry," Chase promised as Charlie slid into the passenger side and shut the door. He turned to Joanna and gave her a speaking look. "Home," he mouthed.

She lifted her brows, but she started the Ford.

"Here comes Maurice now," said the blonde.

Chase didn't bother to look. He had no desire at all to see the man who had put another fifteen hundred miles on his car.

He flicked the ignition, gunned the engine, thanked God Maurice had parked heading toward the street rather than toward the store wall, and shot across the sidewalk and off the curb into the street.

He was five blocks away before he ever looked back.

"Whooooeee!" Charlie's grin split his face. "Hot damn! We did it!"

"I'll say we did!" The thrill of accomplishment sang through him. Chase grinned and wiped damp palms on his chinos and glanced into the rearview mirror to give the thumbs-up sign to Joanna.

She wasn't there.

His head whipped around. What the heck . . . ?

"Whatcha pullin' over for?" Charlie demanded.

"I don't see Joanna."

Charlie frowned, then turned around and craned his neck. "Me, neither."

Chase shut his eyes briefly. Where was she? As far back as he could see through all the traffic, there was no Ford Taurus anywhere in sight.

"You gonna go back?" Charlie wanted to know.

Chase wavered. Should he? What good would it do? Surely she wouldn't still be sitting there in the parking lot next to Maurice and cohorts.

He shook his head. "No. I told her we'd meet her at home. She probably just took another street."

"Yeah," Charlie agreed, then he paused a beat and said, "You don't s'pose they grabbed her, do you?"

"Of course not!"

"Yeah, I mean, what could they do? Keep her hostage or somethin'?" Charlie grinned hopefully.

Chase laughed. "That's stupid." And, of course, it was. He hoped.

They got to Joanna's promptly and stood leaning against the fenders of the Porsche to wait in triumph for her arrival.

She didn't come.

"What'd you tell her?" Charlie asked when they'd been waiting half an hour.

"Home," Chase said. "I told her to come home."

"Maybe she thought you meant your place."

So Chase went to the pay phone down the street and called Miles, but Miles said Joanna wasn't there.

"If she comes, tell her to stay there," Chase instructed. "I'll call you later."

"Everything all right?" Miles asked.

"I think so," Chase said. He had his Porsche back, for heaven's sake. Everything ought to be wonderful.

It would be if Joanna would only show up.

Suddenly the car didn't matter much. He tucked his fists into the pockets of his pants and went back to lean on the car next to Charlie.

The boy's shoulders were hunched against the evening breeze, and Chase was pricked by another concern.

"You cold? You want to get in the car? You want me to take you home?"

Charlie shook his head. "I'll wait. You think she's okay?"

"Sure," Chase said. But he wasn't. Not anymore.

They waited together another hour, more. Until at last a pair of headlights turned into the parking area behind the apartments, and both of them straightened up.

"At last," Chase breathed.

"Oh, no," Charlie muttered when the car came closer.

It wasn't Joanna at all.

It was the police.

The patrol car stopped next to them and a burly policeman got out. "You Whitelaw?" he asked Chase.

Chase nodded numbly.

"You can come with me, both of you."

He couldn't believe what was happening. He didn't even *know* what was happening. "Come with you?" he echoed. "Where? What's going on?"

"You have to make a statement. Tell us what happened. To corroborate Miss Hancock-Smith."

"Miss Hancock-Smith? You have Joanna? Where is she? What are you doing with her?"

A million awful possibilities cascaded through Chase's mind. "She's not in jail, is she?"

The policeman laughed. "In jail?" He shook his head. "Hardly. She made a citizen's arrest."

"A CITIZEN'S ARREST?" Chase was looming over Joanna as she lay on the day bed four hours later. "A *citizen's* arrest?"

"Well, it wasn't really," she protested. "I had a policeman with me."

"One you went and found."

"Of course. You didn't want them to get away with it, did you?"

"I got my car. That was the main thing. At least it was until I couldn't find you."

Joanna cocked an eyebrow, grinning. "Worried, were you?"

"Hell, yes. Charlie thought they'd taken you hostage."

Joanna laughed. "But you knew better."

"I didn't know what to think. I sure didn't expect you to go running off to find the nearest policeman and spend half the evening tracking down Maurice and company."

He still found himself tempted to strangle her. He couldn't believe that while he and Charlie had been racing for home, she'd been rounding up first the police and then the criminals.

"But aren't you glad I did?" She smiled at him, warmth lighting her eyes as she reached for his hand.

He shrugged, shaking his head, grinning, giving in. He sank down onto the day bed beside her, bracing himself over her so that he looked down into her laughing eyes. "I'm just glad you're all right."

"I'm fine," she assured him softly. "Are you?"

He sighed, still shaky. "I guess." The panic of the evening was still catching up to him.

He touched her cheek. "Don't do it again," he asked.

She smiled. "Not even for your Porsche?"

"Not for anything. Promise?" Touching her with his hand wasn't enough. He bent his head. Their gazes were less than a foot apart now.

Joanna nodded her head slowly, her auburn hair moved, fanning out against the pillow.

"Promise." Her voice was soft and low, enticing him. Her eyes widened, her lips parted. He could see the tip of her tongue, the edges of straight white teeth.

Then, he was too close to see anything more than her eyes, warm and beckoning, wanting him the way he wanted her. Totally. Desperately.

And finally there was no more distance between them at all.

There was warmth and yielding. Joanna's lips were soft and welcoming beneath his own. He eased himself down onto the bed so that he lay next to her, his hands learning her shape the way his mouth learned her lips.

For so long he had held back, reined in every libidinal urge that had threatened to surface, that now, once begun, he had no control at all.

All he could think was that he wanted her, needed her. That for years he hadn't been able to have her, and now she was his.

And not, he thought exultantly, passively his, either, for Joanna's hands sought him as well. They tugged his shirt up, they stroked across the smooth expanse of his chest, they fumbled with buttons and zippers as desperately as his own hands did.

In the back of his mind he knew that five years ago he would not have made love with her the first time this way. He would have preserved his restraint. He would have been gentle, tentative, cautious almost.

Not now.

Now the adrenaline was pumping, the need was surging, the desire demanding. He wanted Joanna—wanted to be part of her, wanted her to be part of him.

It was what Joanna wanted, too.

Whatever fantasies she'd had, whatever girlish thoughts had floated around her immature brain, none of them held a candle to the reality of how she wanted Chase tonight.

When she'd agreed to marry him five years ago, she might have been a different person. For that matter, so might he. Both of them then had seemed insubstantial, two-dimensional, puppetlike almost. She, a marionette guided by her parents, and he, simply the man they had selected for her. In his own way, though he'd been an adult, she knew he'd been as influenced by his own grandfather as she had been by Jeremiah and Lydia Hancock-Smith.

There was no outside influence between them tonight.

Tonight they met on their own terms, accepted each other on their own terms. Loved on their own terms.

And it was right.

Five years ago Joanna would have accepted Chase's loving, but she wouldn't have returned it. Not with equal fervor and equal desire. Not the way she returned it now.

Now she was a woman—a woman who knew who she was, what her strengths and weaknesses were, what she wanted out of life—and whom.

First, last and always she wanted Chase.

Her father would laugh and say, "I told you so." Her mother would shake her head and cluck and tsk. No doubt half of high-society Los Angeles would do the same.

But Joanna didn't care.

What mattered was knowing it for herself, making up her own mind at last, loving Chase because she wanted to.

And she did, she knew now, truly love this man.

And so, deliberately and intently, she set about showing him how much.

They moved together with a desperation that each of them understood, and they touched each other with a reverence that each of them held.

It was a time of sharing, of discovery, of giving and taking. And when the storm of climax hit them it brought with it a sense of completion that sent tears of joy streaming down Joanna's face.

Chase raised his head, his chest heaving, his body still shuddering in the aftermath, and he touched her face.

"Are you...all right?"

Joanna half gulped, half laughed. "F-fine." The tears were running into her ears. She felt like an idiot. She hugged him tight.

"Are you sure?" He didn't look or sound convinced. His voice trembled slightly, apprehension clouded his features.

"I'm sure." Embarrassed by her tears, she wiped a hand across her eyes.

"I hurt you." He sounded stricken.

She shook her head violently. "No."

"I did. I didn't know you... you hadn't... done it before."

He didn't sound as if he was blaming her. He sounded astonished, awed, worried and, underneath it all, she thought he sounded pleased.

She shook her head again, less vigorously this ti~ "No," she said quietly, "I hadn't."

He touched her face again, one finger stroking down h~ cheek following the trail of a tear. "I never imagined you'd still be a virgin."

He said it with a kind of wonder, and she thought she understood why.

He had no way of knowing that she hadn't thrown eve-rything over when she threw him over, had no way of guessing that she had not found anyone else to give her lov to over the past five years.

"Why, Jo?"

"Because it was a very important part of me. And b~ I gave myself away to anyone else, I needed to know wh~ was."

He shook his head slightly as if he still didn't under-stand. "But surely you learned before—" there was a ghost of a grin on his face "—half an hour ago."

"Yes," she told him. "I knew. But even after I figured it out, I still had to want to share who I was with someone else. Until you came along again," she told him softly, laying her hand along his cheek, "I never did."

He bent his head and touched his lips to hers. "Oh, Jo," he murmured. And then he rolled onto his side, curved his arm beneath her head and began to love her all over again.

This time he was gentle.

Probably the way he should have been the first time, he thought wryly.

The first time.

Her first time.

He wondered at it. Marveled at it. He had felt the resistance—the physical barrier he hadn't expected—and had been astonished by it at the same time he had known he could not stop.

If only, he thought. If only...

But the only if that mattered, thank God, was still there in her eyes afterward. In them—he breathed a sigh of relief—he still saw love. At least it looked like love to him.

It was new and fragile, like a day-old infant or the earliest bloom on the earliest rose.

It scared him almost. He wasn't sure he trusted it or quite knew how to handle it.

And yet he couldn't deny it, either.

They loved and then they slept, and, close to morning, he awoke to love her once again. Joanna wrapped herself around him, gave to him and accepted from him, then nestled down in the crook of his arm and tumbled off to sleep once more.

MORNING CAME, and with it the thud of the *Times* against the door, the revving of the motorcycle of the neighbor next door, the "Tonio, for heaven's sake, hurry up," that Jo heard from Mrs. Rivas every morning.

But when she turned in Chase's arms and opened her eyes to find him smiling at her, all that faded away. And what she felt was far closer to the sacred than the mundane.

"All right?" His voice was soft.

"Mmmm." She smiled back at him.

"No regrets?"

"Hmm-mmm." She shook her head. "You?"

He swallowed. "No." His gaze was serious, as though he was still working things out, and she wanted to reach out and touch the furrow between his dark brows, smoothing it, soothing him.

But then he reached for her, slid his arms around her, and drew her into his embrace, and she stopped worrying and instead thought how perfect things were, how absolutely right, and how they ought to go on like this forever.

And then, of course, the telephone rang.

They looked at each other. Chase sighed. Joanna grimaced. Then she hauled herself up and snagged the receiver, curling back down into his arms before she said, "Hello?"

"I think I found her," a female voice said.

Joanna stiffened. Chase frowned at her. She touched his lips, reassuring.

"Gloria?"

"Yeah," the policewoman said. "Your girl. Last night I think I saw her."

Joanna sat up. "Where?"

Gloria told her the neighborhood. "I don't usually work there," she went on, "so I don't know too many of the regulars. But besides the ones who were obvious pros, I saw some new girls I've never seen before."

"Hooking?"

Chase sat up, too, scowling, obviously getting the drift of the conversation from Joanna's responses.

"Lurking mostly," Gloria said. "Your girl, she doesn't fit in too well."

"I can imagine," Joanna said dryly.

If Jenny Tso were even remotely a well-brought-up Navajo girl, she wouldn't be making eyes at men on the street, let alone offering what most of the girls there offered.

"Where is she now? Did you talk to her?"

"Couldn't," Gloria said. "I wasn't there on a lost child detail. I did try to get close to her, find out if someone knew her. But there were men all over, and it's first things first, you know."

Joanna knew. But it didn't stop her regretting that Gloria hadn't made contact.

"Did you find out who she was with?"

"I'm checking. I know a couple of the regular girls. They'll let me know. I'll call you. Just called you now so's you could pass on the news to the uncles."

But it was too late for that. Bright and early this morning Joseph and Curtis had gone on their way.

It was perhaps a blessing that they had missed the news anyway, Joanna thought. After all, it wasn't certain—just a hope—nothing more. Yet.

If, or hopefully when, it became something more concrete, then Joanna would let them know.

"I think I'll drive down and nose around. I'll put on the answering machine so you can leave a message when you hear. And Gloria, thanks."

"Jenny Tso," Chase guessed when Jo had hung up.

"Jenny Tso."

"A brief appearance?"

"Seems like."

"So we have a place to start at least."

"Yes, we do."

"Then let's."

AFTERWARD JOANNA THOUGHT it was probably for the best that Gloria's phone call had broken things up. It would have been marvelous, without a doubt, to make love with Chase again, to luxuriate in his caresses, to caress him in turn. But eventually there would have come a moment when they would have had to face separating, pulling back, retreating into themselves again. And it would have been awkward and fraught with potential for misunderstanding.

This way it was natural. Jenny Tso was, they hoped, alive and well and somewhere in south L.A., and, knowing that, they couldn't stay in bed all day, even though they wanted to. They had to find her.

Chase seemed to realize it as much as Joanna did. He went off to grab a shower as matter-of-factly as if he had been doing it in her bathroom all his life.

And afterward when he came out toweling his hair dry, he said, "You go ahead and shower now. I'll fix breakfast," just as if he were used to doing that, too.

They ate quickly, not lingering as they had the first time, though they smiled frequently and often touched. But they were content to wait because hopes were now realities, wishes were now facts.

Jo washed the dishes while Chase made up the day bed, and within half an hour they were heading down the steps to the car.

The area in which Gloria had thought she'd spotted Jenny was in the same general direction as they had gone last night to retrieve the Porsche. Joanna had been there early in her search with no luck at all. She hoped they'd be luckier today.

It was a hazy morning. The early-morning fog still lingered inland, softening edges, painting everything subtle shades of gray, and the ocean dampness clung, making Joanna shiver.

"Want to go back for a jacket?" Chase asked her. They were already in the car.

Joanna shook her head, crossing her arms across her chest. "It's all right."

He smiled. "I'll lend you an arm then." He raised his right one and slipped it around her shoulders, drawing her close. "I'm beginning to like this car. It has certain advantages over a Porsche."

"Don't tell Charlie. He'd be crushed."

"I doubt it. Charlie knows there's more to life than cars."

Joanna considered that. "Girls?" Were girls ready for Charlie? she wondered.

"Mmm."

"Maybe we'll have to introduce him to Jenny Tso."

"We have to find her first."

But, even having narrowed down where she was, it wouldn't be easy, and they both knew it.

Joanna had never volunteered in this neighborhood, but she might as well have. It possessed the same wide dirty sidewalks, the same peeling stucco buildings, the same pawn shops, cheap jewelry shops, discount record stores, and run-down laundromats. The same sad-eyed, long-faced people abounded.

Chase parked the car and got out. "You want to start asking down one side while I do the other?"

"I don't want to ask."

He paused on the curb. "How're we going to find her if we don't ask?"

"If we ask, she'll hear about it before we even get close. She'll think we're pursuing her. She'll panic and run, and then we'll never find her."

"So what do you want to do?"

"Leave a message."

"A message?"

"So she can come to us."

"Where?"

"The laundromat for a start. Usually they have bulletin boards. Then we'll look around and see where else. Okay?"

One corner of his mouth lifted. "I bow to your superior wisdom. You're the hooker."

Joanna socked his shoulder lightly, then she grew serious. "Let's hope Gloria's right and Jenny's not into hooking yet."

Chase nodded. "Let's."

The bulletin board in the laundromat was exactly as she'd expected. Joanna borrowed a pen from Chase and wrote on one of the cards: "Jenny Tso: call me. I'll help you," and put her first name and phone number.

If Jenny was in the neighborhood, it was a good bet she'd see it there. She'd be far more likely to show up in the laundromat than the record stores or jewelry shops.

Jo did venture into the pawn shops with Chase on her heels. Here he took over, examining the pawn beneath the glass-topped counters. Whenever he found turquoise jewelry, which wasn't often, he asked to see it, wondering aloud how long it had been there.

"You Navajo?" the pawnbroker in the third shop asked while Chase was examining a wide silver bracelet set with polished oval turquoise stones.

"Yes."

"You know the real stuff, then?" The man jerked his head toward the piece in Chase's hands. "Girl told me it was, but I dunno. Ya don't see much a that stuff hereabouts."

"Who told you?" Chase asked casually, his eyes on the bracelet.

"Girl that pawned it. Indian."

Chase undid the clasp and put it around Joanna's wrist. "What do you think?"

"I think it's lovely," Joanna said. She also thought the girl was Jenny Tso, and she knew Chase did, too.

"You want it?" The man smiled a snakelike smile. "Hundred fifty dollars."

Chase undid the clasp. "Too much." He handed it back.

"It's fake?" The dealer sounded offended. "Mighta known. No wonder she didn't come back." He snorted. "Kids."

Chase cocked an eyebrow. "You take pawn from kids?"

"Not a kid," the man said hastily. "Just young, y'know. Hard to tell with them Indians." Then he realized who he was talking to and backtracked there, too. "Nice complexion. Smooth. Not a wrinkle on her. Maybe she was twenty. I dunno."

"Maybe younger, though?" Joanna ventured.

"Coulda been. I doubt it. What d'you care?"

Chase didn't answer. "You remember her well."

"Oughta. She wanted a hell of a lot for it. Told me she'd be back in two weeks."

"And she didn't come?"

The man shook his head. "Been a month. So I'm sellin'."

"I'll give you fifty," Chase said.

"I paid more'n that," the man squawked.

Chase shrugged.

"She didn't wanna pawn it," the man said. "Acted like it was real valuable." His eyes narrowed and he squinted at the bracelet in his hand again, then looked up and considered Chase. "It must be, no matter what you say."

Chase shrugged again. "I didn't say anything except I'd give you fifty."

"Hundred," the man said.

"Sixty."

"Hey, man, I tol' you, I give her more'n that."

Chase just looked at him.

"I gotta get what I give her outa it."

Chase didn't say a word.

"Seventy-five."

Chase turned and started to walk toward the door. Taking his lead, Joanna followed him, crossing her fingers inside her pocket.

"Ah hell, take it for sixty-five."

Chase wheeled around and pulled out his wallet. He counted out the money and handed it to the dealer, then took the bracelet. "Hold out your arm," he said to Joanna.

She did. He slipped the bracelet around it again, more carefully this time, and fastened the clasp. Then he scribbled a phone number on the back of a card. "Here," he said, passing it to the dealer. "Give this to the girl if she shows up and wants it back."

The man looked at him suspiciously. "You gonna sell it to her?"

"If I do," Chase promised him, "you'll get a cut."

"How much do you think he paid her?" Joanna asked him as they left the shop.

"Maybe thirty, forty at best."

Joanna was horrified. "That little?"

"He's not a charity."

"He's a weasel."

"I've known nicer weasels," Chase said.

Joanna shivered involuntarily. "You think it was Jenny, don't you?"

"Yep. Don't you?"

"I think so. I *hope* so," Joanna said fervently. She considered the dingy neighborhood, the blowing papers, the unwashed windows and the peeling paint. "If she was down to pawning this a month ago, I wonder what she's living on now."

"Don't ask," Chase said, taking her hand in his.

"Do you think she'll call?"

"Who knows?" Chase said. "But it's one more base covered."

"Now what?" Joanna asked him.

"Now we go home and wait."

Chapter Ten

The trouble, Chase realized shortly thereafter, was that Joanna had listed her number on the laundromat card and he had put his on the one he gave the pawnbroker.

So they went home and waited, all right, but they waited apart.

"It's just as well," Joanna consoled him with a hug. "I've got to finish grading my papers. And while I'd really rather be with you, you know I wouldn't get anything done if I did."

"You'd get something done," Chase told her with a grin.

Joanna smiled. "Yes, but it wouldn't be grading papers."

Which was true enough. Still he wasn't thrilled to go home alone and wait for the phone to ring. Partly because he was missing Joanna, and partly because the phone didn't ring. If he was going to be self-sacrificing, he wanted results to show for it.

He wondered if Joanna was grading Charlie's term paper.

"He turned one in," she'd said, awe in her voice.

"Of course he did." Chase was indignant.

Jo smiled. "You've done wonders with him."

"He's done it himself actually," Chase admitted. "All it was was finding out what he was interested in."

"Fame and riches!"

Chase grinned. "It's a start."

Indeed it had been. Charlie's research could have gone on indefinitely. And he and Keith Craig had become fast friends. Keith's life-style might not have been exactly that of riches and fame, but it was distinct enough from Charlie's to give both boys new insights. Keith was teaching Charlie, and Charlie was teaching Keith, too.

"Not about stealing cars," Charlie had assured Chase. "I'm teaching him about my life and he's teaching me about his."

The mutual information pact might go on forever, but there were time limits to the term paper, so Chase made him get going on that.

He read it when Charlie had finished the rough draft. He corrected the spelling, made a couple of organizational suggestions, then read Charlie's finished product. He was impressed.

He hoped Joanna would be, too.

Chase sighed and stretched out on the sofa. It would justify her faith in asking him, too.

A tapping on his window made him look up. Miles, Patrick snug in one arm, the other looped over Susan's shoulders, grinned down at him. "Want to go for a swim?"

Chase glanced at the phone. Jenny hadn't called, but he couldn't sit here forever just waiting. "Let me turn on the answering machine. I'll catch up with you."

Miles was no more than a dark speck out as far as the pier by the time Chase joined Susan and Patrick on the sand. "Aren't you swimming?" he asked Susan.

"Not with my buddy." She nodded at Patrick who was filtering sand onto his knees with great concentration. "He sinks."

"I'll watch him. You go ahead."

"Not much of a swim for you."

Chase shrugged equably. "I don't mind. Patrick's as much fun as a swim any day, aren't you, fella?"

Patrick grinned up at him. "Fun," he agreed.

"So says the man who can go home childless at night," Susan replied dryly. But she got up and brushed herself off, then gave him a quick peck on the cheek. "Thanks, Chase."

He sat down on the sand next to Patrick and watched her go, watched her dive cleanly beneath an incoming wave as she swam out to join Miles, and he remembered how once he had wanted her to be his wife.

She had been right to say no, right to tell him that there was more to love than what they felt for each other. He had shut out those feelings since the first time he'd loved Joanna. He hadn't wanted to admit that anything ran that deep. It hurt too much when things went awry.

But now, now he was about ready to admit it again. There was no way to deny the feelings that existed between him and Joanna. Especially not after last night.

Last night. The memory of it, the sweetness of it, made him groan, made him ache with wanting again. His fists curled in the sand and he felt a quickening in his loins. She was so sweet, so innocent, so—

A determined redheaded tornado butted him in the chest and knocked him flat.

"All done sand," Patrick said and clambered onto Chase's chest. "Horsey now." He clapped sandy hands over Chase's face, sending a fall of sand into his mouth.

"Wretch," Chase muttered.

"Wetch," Patrick agreed happily. "Horsey?" He gave Chase a hopeful look.

Chase groaned. How could you say no to a face like that? All the assertiveness training in the world wasn't proof against a sixteen-month-old's smile. He swung the little boy up onto his shoulders and headed down the sand toward the sea as he gave Patrick a ride.

"Sucker," Miles chided, meeting him on the way in and holding out his arms.

Chase grinned. "I guess." He handed the little boy to his father, then turned and accompanied Miles back up the beach.

"Aren't you going to swim?" Miles asked.

"Nah."

"Thought that's what you came down for?"

"Came down so my phone would ring."

"Huh?"

"Doesn't when I'm there," Chase explained.

"Joanna?"

"No."

Miles looked surprised. "I thought she was it, I really did."

"I think she is it," Chase said quietly as they sat back down and Miles bent his head and swiftly began to dig a large hole. "This is something else."

Miles nodded his head. "I'm glad."

"Glad about what?" Susan came up beside them and dropped down onto a towel. Patrick immediately pounced on her, but Miles fielded him deftly and plopped him into the hole he'd been digging.

"Sit there," he said in his sternest father voice.

Patrick's eyes opened wide, but he did as he was told. Then Miles began to cover his feet and legs with sand, packing it down around him, making the little boy grin. "I'm glad Chase has decided that Joanna's it," he said to his wife.

Susan beamed. "Have you asked her?"

He shook his head quickly. "No."

"Why not?" Susan gave him an impatient look.

Trust Susan to be blunt.

"Because I . . . because . . ." He groped for an explanation. He didn't know if they knew about his history with Joanna or not. He imagined not. Griff knew, but Griff rarely said anything to anyone. "Because I don't want to rush her this time," he said vaguely, helping Miles pour sand onto Patrick.

"This time?"

"We go back a long way."

Susan's eyes narrowed. "She's not the one you were—"

Chase met her eyes. "The one I was engaged to? Yes."

"The one who jilted you?"

Patrick's forehead furrowed and his lips puckered at his mother's tone of voice.

Chase gave a wry shrug.

"You're kidding," Miles breathed. Then he looked at Chase's face and said, "You're not."

"She had her reasons," Chase defended her. "She was a kid," he said, trying to tell them Joanna's side the way she had told it to him. "A senior in college. She didn't know who she was. Apart from being her parents' daughter, I mean. She didn't have an identity of her own."

"She agreed to marry you," Susan reminded him.

"She got a lot of encouragement. Pretty substantial encouragement."

"Pressure?"

"You could say that." He shrugged again and shook his head. "I don't completely understand how she feels," he admitted. "I mean, I *always* knew who I was and what I wanted, but I guess some people don't."

"I didn't," Miles said.

"Didn't what?" Chase asked.

"Know what I wanted. Actually that's not quite true. I knew precisely what I wanted. I wanted to be a priest." He grinned. "Turned out I was wrong, but it took someone forcing me out of the seminary to get me to see it." He looked down at his son who was now encased up to his chest in sand and was patting it happily. "I'd like to spare him the same trauma."

"Huh." Susan gave him a playful shove. "You think marrying me was a trauma, do you?"

"No," Miles said seriously. "But what I went through to get there wasn't easy. I'd like Patrick to have it easier."

"It doesn't have to be a trauma," Chase told him. "I've never had one."

"Then you're blessed," Miles said.

JOANNA WISHED he was there. After last night it seemed the cruelest irony that they should spend this night apart. Now, of all times, when they had finally—at last—got together, to be separated seemed to be tempting fate.

It wasn't that she didn't love him. She did. And it wasn't that she didn't think he had cared for her at the time they'd made love. She thought he did.

But in the clear light of a mid-August evening, as she sat alone in her apartment and tried to concentrate on the term papers in front of her, she could think of a lot of misgivings and second thoughts that might well be plaguing Chase.

It would have helped a lot if Jenny Tso had called, but the phone was determinedly silent.

At last, right before bedtime, it rang and Jo leaped for it hopefully. Jenny, she prayed. Or if not Jenny, then, please God, Chase.

It was her mother proffering an invitation to a lawn party the following Saturday evening.

"You can bring a guest if you want to, dear," Lydia said smoothly. "Or I can invite someone for you if you prefer."

"I'm afraid I can't come at all, Mother."

"A date?" Lydia asked hopefully.

"Mmm." Jo figured she might be able to stretch a prior commitment to stand on street corners as a decoy into a date, but she preferred to sound noncommittal and let her mother make the necessary inference.

"With Bob?"

"Not with Bob."

"But with someone," Lydia concluded, as Jo hoped she would. "Thank heavens. I was afraid after what happened you'd sworn off men indefinitely."

Lydia never overtly mentioned "what happened." Most of the time she pretended that it hadn't. Joanna wondered what Lydia would think when she found out who the "someone" was.

"Well, I'm sorry you won't be able to make it, love," Lydia said. "But I'll enjoy myself more knowing you'll be enjoying yourself, too."

"Thank you, Mother," Jo said and hung up with a sigh of relief.

It wasn't as easy to convince Lynsey half an hour later.

"Who is he?" she demanded when Jo answered the phone.

"Who is who?" Jo countered though she knew perfectly well. She hadn't a doubt in the world that Lydia had called Lynsey without even having put the receiver down.

"Your man."

"Mother spreading gossip?" Jo asked.

"Mother hopes she's spreading the gospel truth. Is she?"

"More or less," Jo admitted.

"More?" Lynsey asked. "Or less?"

Jo sighed. "More. I hope."

"Then I repeat, who is he?"

"I'm not going to tell you."

"Jo! Why not? Have I ever stolen your men?"

"No, of course not. It's just...I...don't want to jinx things."

There was a pause. "Oh," Lynsey said in a small voice. "I see what you mean. After...last time."

"Yes." Thankfully it didn't occur to Lynsey that the man was the same man as last time.

"When are you going to be sure?" Lynsey demanded, all hesitation fleeing once more.

"I'll let you know," Jo promised.

"Deal," her sister said and rang off.

She had scarcely done so than the phone rang again. Jenny? Joanna wondered hopefully as she answered.

It was Chase. Her heart kicked over at the simple sound of his voice.

"Did she call you?" Jo asked him.

"Nope. You?"

"Nope."

There was a pause, then Chase said, "We can't stay home forever on the off chance that she rings, can we?"

"Not really," Joanna agreed, smiling.

"We've got lives of our own to live, right?"

"Right."

"I'll be right over," he said.

The next few days were as close to heaven as Joanna reckoned to get on earth. She finished teaching her summer school class, finished grading all the term papers, had the satisfaction of making a well-deserved B on Charlie Seeks Elk's report card, and managed to work Saturday night on the street under Chase's watchful eye, so that in strictest honesty she could tell her mother she *had* been out with a man that night.

Best of all, though, she knew that every minute of every hour her relationship with Chase was, just like the old Beatles song, "getting better every day."

CHASE AGREED WITH HER. In fact, things were going so well he was loath to push at all, to suggest more, to in any way rock the boat. Another month or two of steady courting and then he would be ready to make it official again. Marlene called him once just to see if he had changed his mind. He said he hadn't, and he concentrated all his efforts on spending time with Joanna.

He even found something nice to think about the administrative side of publishing. The meetings were easier to control than the research had been. And while administration wasn't as fulfilling as writing, it did leave him far more psychic energy to expend on Joanna.

In fact, he even went into it with more zeal than he had previously. He did a better job, too. His happiness rubbed off on everything he touched.

Alexander Chase was quick to notice.

"You're getting the hang of it now," he said after the next board meeting. He leaned back in his chair and smiled at his grandson. "Everything else going good, too?"

Chase, still shuffling through the meeting's papers, looked up.

"The girl you're interested in," Alex spelled out.

Chase grinned. "Yep."

"Do I know her?"

Chase bent his head and concentrated on filing the papers in his briefcase, then reached for his sport coat. He

didn't like not being straight with his grandfather. But jus
for the moment, he hoped that silence would deter the old
man.

Predictably, it didn't.

"Who is she?"

"I'll tell you when I'm ready," Chase said quietly.

"Ashamed of her?" Alex blustered, standing up behind
the heavy walnut table and thrusting out his chin, like a
bulldog asking for a fight.

Chase didn't take him up on it. "Of course not. It's just
that I prefer to handle things my own way this time."

Alex opened his mouth, then shut it again. He cleared his
throat and loosened his necktie. "I see," he muttered. He
scowled, then took one last stab. "But if you're afraid
something like last time will happen again, don't even think
it, my boy. That Hancock-Smith girl had rocks in her head."

"She might've been right," Chase said mildly.

Alex snorted in clear disbelief. "Nonsense."

Chase shrugged into his sport coat. "Well, it doesn't
matter anyway. This time is not last time. This time I'm doing it my way."

"You and Frank Sinatra," Alex grumbled.

Chase smiled and patted his grandfather on the arm. "Me
and Frank Sinatra."

JOANNA AND FRANK SINATRA were singing "High Hopes"
together that evening when the doorbell rang. Joanna let
Frank hit the high note because he did it better than she did,
even though she had hopes as high as Everest these days. She
still hadn't heard from Jenny Tso and neither had Chase,
but everything else in her life was fantastic.

"Lookin' good," said the tall, freckle-faced man standing there grinning at her.

"Reg!" Joanna wrapped him in the same enthusiastic
bear hug that he gave her. "I thought you were going to call
from the corner store first."

He shrugged, still smiling. "Why call when you can make
an entrance? Do you mind?"

"Of course not." She tugged him inside, motioning for him to toss his duffel bag in the corner. "I'm just so glad to see you. You look fantastic."

Ten pounds heavier than he'd been in the Peace Corps, Reg had lost his gangliness. He simply looked muscular and well built now. He still had his perennial sunburn, but his thatch of red-blond hair, even more vivid than her own, had definitely benefited from the attention of a more competent barber than she'd ever been.

He reached out and tipped up her chin, studying her carefully. "So do you," he said. "A damned sight better than I remember from the last time I was here."

Jo smiled, remembering the last time. Life had been busy and full, but not much else. There hadn't been the spark that ignited her now. There hadn't been Chase.

"Things looking up?" Reg asked.

"Mmm."

"Met a man?"

"Mmm."

His grin broadened at the mischief in her eyes. "Serious, is it?"

"I hope," Jo told him fervently. Chase hadn't sprung the big question yet, but she didn't blame him. She knew he was taking his time. They both were. But she thought she knew by now which direction things were heading in.

"Tell me."

"Come have a beer." Jo led him into the kitchen, got them both beers and then took him out on the deck. When he had settled into the chaise longue, she perched on the chair opposite him. And when he leaned back and took a long draft of the beer, she leaned forward and said, "It's Chase."

His swallow seemed suspended for an eternity. Then his eyes widened, he gulped and said, "Chase? The one who—"

"Mmm."

Reg gave a low whistle. "Well, I'll be damned. How'd that happen?"

She told him, first about their encounter on the street corner, then about the jail, about Charlie and Jenny Tso and everything else that had happened between them. He was amazed.

They talked all through the beer, all through a frozen pizza and another beer, and they were still talking when her sister, Lynsey, waltzed in.

"Mother wants to know if—" she began, then stopped dead at the sight of a strange man lounging out on the deck.

"If what I told her about having a man was true?" Jo finished, even though she knew that Lynsey wouldn't have been that blunt.

Lynsey nodded. "Is that him?" she hissed at Jo, never taking her eyes off Reg, who unfolded himself from the chaise and ambled toward them.

Joanna introduced them. She did not say, "This is Reg Patton, the man in question," but neither did she say, "This is Reg Patton, an old friend and that's all."

She simply told Lynsey they'd been in the Peace Corps together. The obvious familiarity and rapport between them spoke loudly enough. Lynsey drew her own conclusions.

Reg didn't contradict anything Joanna said, and he didn't volunteer anything that would correct Lynsey's erroneous impression. He simply let Joanna take the lead and followed along, all amiability, until at last Lynsey departed.

"He's gorgeous," she said to Joanna through clenched teeth as she left. "Trust you to nab the only decent looking man left in the western half of the United States."

Surprised, Joanna said, "I'm sure there are one or two others."

"Not that I've met," Lynsey said. "And I've met plenty." She sighed. "Well, congratulations, kiddo. I wish you well, and I hope you bring him up to scratch."

Watching her leave, Joanna felt a tad guilty for allowing Lynsey's self-deception. She felt even guiltier a few moments later when she turned away from the open door and went back out on the deck and Reg said, "Why didn't you tell me you had such a gorgeous sister? Is she single?"

"Um, yes."

Reg smiled. "Good."

"She thinks you're mine," Joanna confessed.

"There will be time enough to correct that," Reg promised easily. "You just get your romance on target now. We'll worry about mine after."

Joanna put her arms around him and hugged him, laughing. "You saint," she said and gave him a kiss.

"Bad timing, kiddo," he said in her ear.

Joanna blinked. "Huh?"

She followed Reg's gaze and glanced over her shoulder. Chase was framed in the doorway, looking as if he'd been shot.

Reg stepped around her and held out his hand in greeting. "Hello. I'm Reg Patton, an old friend of Jo's from Botswana. You must be Chase."

Joanna had seen pit bulldogs with more benevolent expressions than Chase's. It seemed an eternity until his hand moved to take Reg's. But finally it did, and then she could breathe again.

Chase wasn't finding it so easy.

The sight of Joanna in another man's arms shocked him. He had driven over here whistling to himself, thinking how well everything was going, how smoothly, how this "step by step" business was exactly right, how "nice and easy" was the way to go.

Instantly he changed his mind.

Joanna reached for his hand and he gripped hers tightly, pulling her against him. If it looked like he was staking out his territory, he was. He didn't know what Joanna might have told Reg Patton about her love life. But he intended Patton not get any wrong ideas. Joanna was his.

At Joanna's suggestion the three of them went out on the deck. Then she brought him and Patton beers and fetched an iced tea for herself. There was only the deck chair and the chaise to sit on. He took one, Patton the other, and before Jo could make a move Chase hauled her into his lap.

Only there, with her body warm and firm against his, could he listen with equanimity to what Patton was saying about why he'd come to southern California at all.

To be fair, as the evening wore on, Patton didn't seem like much of a threat. He treated Joanna as cavalierly as Chase treated his own sister. They reminisced about Botswana, but a part of what they reminisced about was how badly Joanna had felt at the way she had handled the breaking of her engagement. Chase got a very good idea of how dependent she'd been just then on Patton. He supposed he ought to be grateful that she'd had someone so solid and sensible to talk to.

Instead he felt a primitive desire to punch out Reg Patton's lights.

Maybe he wouldn't have if Joanna were committed to him again. But she wasn't. Not yet.

He had to do something about that. Taking it slow wasn't enough. He glowered at Patton and Joanna who talked on, oblivious.

It was well past eleven when Chase began to get the awful feeling that Patton had no intention of leaving that night.

They had moved into the living room from the deck about ten-thirty when the evening began to cool. But instead of walking to the door and saying how much he'd enjoyed the visit, Patton dropped down onto the day bed, crossed his feet at the ankles and went on reminiscing about Saturday mornings at the President's Hotel and about a native woman named Boitumelo who had shared Joanna's half of the duplex and everything else Joanna owned.

Joanna curled up against a plump cushion on the floor and grinned sleepily up at him. Chase, cross-legged next to Joanna, glowered and glanced at his watch.

Finally Joanna caught him at it and reached behind him to massage the taut muscles of his neck. "Sleepy?"

"It is getting late," Chase said pointedly.

"Don't feel you have to sit here and listen politely on my account," Reg told him. "You want to go home and go to sleep, go right ahead."

Chase's jaw tightened. What he wanted was for *Reg* to go home and go to sleep or, failing that, to go to his hotel and go to sleep. Anything, just so long as he left Chase alone with Joanna.

"I'll give you a ride," Chase offered.

Reg's eyes widened slightly and he looked at Joanna, then cleared his throat.

Joanna grimaced, her hand still against his neck. "I...invited him to stay here, Chase."

Chase stared at her. Reg Patton was staying here? With Joanna? While he got in his car and drove home?

Like hell.

"Then come home with me."

Joanna's green eyes were wide and wondering as she stared at him.

He caught her hand. "Please."

It wasn't etiquette, God knew. It would have stood Miss Saunders of Dancing and Decorum infamy on her ear. But Chase didn't care. He was beyond propriety now. Beyond etiquette. Beyond anything except wanting Joanna to be his and his alone.

Then faintly she said, "All right," and he could breathe.

She showed Reg where the clean towels were. She provided sheets, a pillowcase, a lightweight comforter, instant coffee, a loaf of bread, and a jar of marmalade. Then she gave him a sisterly hug and, toothbrush, hairbrush and clean underwear in hand, she left with Chase.

"I can't believe I did that," she said as Chase tucked her into the Porsche and went around to slide in beside her.

"Believe it," was all Chase said, but there was as much pent-up emotion in his voice as she ever remembered hearing, and, hearing it, she did believe.

There was no way she could have said no.

The journey back to his apartment was accomplished in virtual silence. Tension hung between them, taut and vibrating, singing with an intensity that Joanna had felt growing since he'd walked in the door earlier that evening.

Perhaps it had been because of Reg's presence. Perhaps Chase had been jealous, though heaven knew there was nothing to be jealous of. But whatever the reason, gone was the Chase she'd grown accustomed to—the warm, easygoing, smiling man who had replaced the stern-faced, remote man she'd known five years before.

This Chase was neither. Or rather he was both—and more.

He pulled into his garage, took her hand and practically hauled her into the apartment after him. Once there, and with the door shut between the two of them and the rest of the world, he drew her into his arms and his mouth sought hers.

There was a need in him she'd never seen before, a desperation that, until now, she'd never met. But finding it, she found it matched by her own.

She kissed him back, reveling in the taste of him and the hard warmth of his mouth against hers. And when he began undressing her, right there in the living room, she didn't demur.

Her hands moved, too, tackling the buttons of his shirt, the snap of his jeans, the elastic of his briefs. He groaned, kicking their clothes away and easing her back on the sofa. He slid between her thighs and sighed as Joanna welcomed him. Then he propped himself up on his forearms and looked down into her face. His was taut with passion, his eyes in the moonlight glittering ebony, his nostrils flared.

"I love you," he muttered and then he began to move.

Joanna moved with him, as demanding and intense as he was, matching him, urging him, loving him, until the sensations overtook them both and, shuddering, together they spun out of control.

For a long while then there was no sound beyond breathing, faster, than gradually slowing, and the steady rhythmic pounding of the waves against the shore. Joanna felt as if she were suspended, waiting. But waiting for she knew not what.

And then Chase spoke. His voice was the barest whisper, a breath, no more, barely audible above the sound of the surf. "Will you...marry me?" he asked. "This time?"

Joanna looked at him. His face was shadowed and unreadable, moonlight only etching the emotion and the hesitation on it that she heard in his voice. And she realized, perhaps for the first time, the depth of the pain he had suffered at her earlier rejection. She knew what it cost him to ask again.

"Oh, yes." She reached out and brushed a lock of hair away from his forehead, then touched his cheek and let her fingers trace the strong line of his jaw.

His eyes met hers. "You mean it? You know who you are now?"

"I know exactly who I am. I am Joanna Victoria Hancock-Smith, daughter, sister, gym teacher, activist, volunteer hooker, friend." She smiled. "And, most of all, I am the woman who loves Chase Whitelaw very much."

Chapter Eleven

It wasn't going to be the production it had been last time. Both Chase and Joanna agreed on that.

It was going to be a small wedding, a private wedding, a personal wedding. Not a media event. Not a society do. Not a merger of the family fortunes.

Fortune was incidental. A future—their future together—was what was important. *All* that was important. It had all gone wrong once. This time it was going to go right.

Chase told Miles and Susan. Joanna told Reg. Word didn't go beyond that.

"Are we chicken, do you suppose?" Joanna asked Chase one evening the following week when they sat on the porch railing of his place and looked out across the ocean.

"No, just experienced."

Jo smiled. "I suppose you're right. Have you got things sorted out yet with that Father Morrisey you mentioned?"

Jack Morrisey had married Miles and Susan and had officiated at the church ceremony between Austin and Clea. Their marriages seemed to be thriving, and while Chase was not especially superstitious, he did like what he'd seen of the man.

"He's on retreat." Chase made a face. "Should be back a week from Sunday, the church secretary said. Do you mind waiting?" He grinned and shook his head self-deprecatingly. "Stupid question. *I* mind waiting. It's just that this time I want it right."

Joanna reached out for his hand. "Me, too. I'll wait as long as you want."

The wait wasn't as hard as Chase thought.

For one thing, Joanna didn't start back to school with preliminary workshop week until the following Monday, so she spent most of her waking hours and a great many of her sleeping ones with him.

For another, Reg had finished his business and had gone back where he'd come from. Once he'd claimed his bride, Chase found he could tolerate Reg Patton quite well. But he was just as pleased not to have to share Joanna with him now.

The third reason life was better and waiting not so hard was because his grandfather seemed pleased with the progress he was making in taking over the administrative side of their publishing interests. A pleased Alexander Chase was a happier, less irascible Alexander Chase. And that made life pleasanter for everyone.

For another—and the biggest surprise of all—Jenny Tso showed up.

The phone was ringing one afternoon just as Chase got out of the shower.

"Jenny called," Jo said without preamble.

It had been almost three weeks since they'd put the messages up. Three weeks with no response whatsoever. At first they had lurked by the phones or hurried back to listen to answering machine messages. But after a week or two with no word, they had begun to lose hope.

They hadn't spoken about it, as if doing so might ensure that she would never call. But Chase had felt it, and he knew Jo had. Every time he watched her pick up the phone to hear someone else's voice, her face fell.

Now her excitement was evident. "Just a few minutes ago."

"Where is she?"

"She said she was calling from a McDonald's right off Pacific Coast Highway." Jo told him the cross street. It wasn't far from the laundromat. So chances were she'd always been in that neighborhood. He suspected that meant she'd had the number for quite a while.

"What'd she say? What made her call now?"

"I don't know."

Chase paused. "Is she all right?"

"I don't know that either."

"Can we go get her?"

"I said I'd come down and meet her there. Just to talk."

"I'll drive you."

"I think maybe I'd better go alone. So as not to scare her off."

"I'm scary?" Chase asked.

"Not to me," Jo assured him. "But to her, maybe. Strange men and all that."

"You sure?"

"Yes. Besides, I thought you had a board meeting today."

"I can cancel."

"Go to your meeting," Jo told him. "Call me when you get back."

Chase hesitated.

"Really," Jo told him. "Jenny was my job anyway. Charlie was yours."

"All right," Chase agreed reluctantly. "But I'm coming over as soon as I get done."

IT WAS ODD seeing someone in three dimensions that you'd only seen in two dimensions for weeks. It was odd meeting someone in person you'd only met through hearsay. It was even more odd expecting to be greeted by a smile and have Jenny Tso virtually ignore you.

She was sitting at the table in Joanna's minuscule kitchen, chopping tomatoes while Joanna fried hamburger for tacos when he arrived. He noticed at once that the turquoise bracelet he'd bought from the pawnbroker was on her wrist.

She had been saying something, but when Chase appeared in the doorway, she stopped abruptly.

He stayed right where he was and smiled at her. "Hello."

Joanna looked over her shoulder, saw him and smiled. "Ah, there you are. Jenny, this is my friend I told you about, Chase Whitelaw. He's Navajo, too. At least his father was."

"Navajo," Jenny repeated under her breath. It sounded almost like a question. She looked at him surreptitiously.

Chase felt the same discomfort he had when first confronted by her uncles. He shoved it away. She was only a teenaged kid, for heaven's sake. He offered her his hand.

She managed a polite but faint, "Hello," took his hand briefly and let go almost at once.

"Your uncles came to me to see if I could help them find you," he told her, hoping that would establish some rapport.

It didn't seem to.

"Oh." Jenny's eyes settled back on the tomatoes.

Not all cultures were obsessed with a need to watch the other person while he talked, Chase thought. But all cultures held conversations, for crying out loud. He wished she'd hold up her end.

She chopped tomatoes.

"I'm glad you're here, Jenny," he said gamely.

"Thank you," she said to the table.

Chase looked at Joanna for help. She shook her head and shrugged. Her whole manner seemed to say, we were doing all right till you walked in.

"Really glad you got here. You can chop the onions," she said aloud in a clear attempt to make him feel welcome. "How was your meeting with your grandfather?"

Chase shrugged, picking up the onion and sitting down opposite Jenny at the table, concentrating his visual attention on the onion, though he was aware of every move the girl made, just as he knew she was aware of his.

"Boring. This one perhaps a bit more boring than most." He wasn't going to say he couldn't even remember what it was about, that his mind had been on Joanna and Jenny the whole time. "I write for a newspaper," he explained to Jenny. "Maybe Joanna told you. That's how your uncles found me."

Eyes on the table, she said, "Yes."

Chase sighed. "Speaking of the uncles, have you tried getting ahold of Joseph or Curtis?"

"I thought I'd let you," Jo replied.

Unspoken he heard her telling him that she thought the proper protocol would be for him to be the one to do it.

"What do you think, Jenny?" he asked her.

Jenny darted a quick glance Chase's way. "Are you a cousin?" she asked him.

"A cousin? Not that I know of."

She frowned. "Then why did they—" She started to say something, then thought better of it, waited a moment, then finally blurted, "What clan were you born to?"

The same question he'd got from Joseph and Curtis. Chase shut his eyes.

"I don't know."

Jenny did look at him then, all good manners forgotten. She simply stared in wide-eyed astonishment. "You don't know?"

He shrugged awkwardly, wishing he knew something. If his mother hadn't wanted to talk, he should at least have looked something up. "What do you mean, 'born to'?" he asked her.

"You really don't know?"

"I wouldn't ask if I did," he said roughly.

She nodded, convinced. "Your mother's clan."

"My mother's white."

"Oh, that's too bad."

Chase hadn't thought about it that way before. He blinked, nonplussed.

"What about your father's clan?" Jenny asked.

"My father died before I was born. I was raised by my mother and my grandfather. My mother's father."

"Oh," she said. "I see." There was a pause while he could almost see her assimilating this astonishing knowledge. "All right," she said at last.

But Chase understood as the evening wore on that it was clearly far from all right in the world of Jenny Tso.

She scarcely looked at him again. It was as if he weren't even there. Or as if she wished he weren't. Clearly she didn't know what to do with this Navajo who didn't even know what clan he was. And he didn't know what to do with her, either. Nor did he know what difference it made what clan his father had belonged to. In thirty-five years, it had made none at all, but it seemed to make an enormous difference tonight.

Jenny looked enormously relieved when, soon after dinner, Chase said he thought it was time for him to go.

She couldn't have been more relieved than he was, Chase thought as he gave Joanna a surreptitious kiss as he went out the door.

He didn't drive straight home.

He drove up into Palos Verdes, turning off onto a private lane that led to the house where he'd grown up. His grandfather had sold it several years back when the twists and turns had become too much for him. And Chase had been half tempted to buy it himself. It held a lot of him, a lot of his past. And when he'd been engaged to Joanna the first time, he'd thought it might hold his future. But when Joanna left, so did his interest in the future. And when the house went on the market, he had been in Lebanon and had missed the entire sale.

Since then he'd rarely given it a thought. But tonight he couldn't keep from driving up there. He didn't know who had bought it, didn't care. He wouldn't see them. He simply wanted to find the lookout bluff on which he'd sat as a child and sit there again.

He didn't ask himself why. At least not until he'd left his car pulled over onto the shoulder of the lane and had hiked through the waning twilight up across the wooded hillside to the cliff that overlooked the sea. There, sitting silently, arms wrapped around his knees, he finally wondered why he'd come.

The answer surprised him. It had to do with a dozen old memories, mostly buried, of other times when he'd felt awkward, uncomfortable, fatherless, alone. Once it had been because a boy he knew had taunted him about not having a father. Another time he'd come from a boyhood game of cowboys and Indians when he couldn't be a cowboy.

"You're the Indian," one of the boys had said. "You gotta be. Can't be a cowboy. Not a redskin like you."

Couldn't he be? he'd asked his grandfather.

Alexander had been furious. "You can be any damned thing you want," he'd stormed. "You're a Chase! My grandson! Don't you ever forget it. And don't let anyone else forget it, either."

Chase hadn't. The next time it came up, he'd pounded a neighbor kid into the dirt.

He'd pounded a few kids into the dirt before he was grown. Fewer and fewer, of course, as time went on. His lack of a father didn't matter so much since he had a grandfather like Alex. He learned to accept fate. And for the most part, once they got to know him, people forgot there was a Navajo side of Chase Whitelaw. Chase forgot it himself.

Or he had until the Begays. And Jenny.

What did it matter what clan he was, anyway? Why did she care?

Why did he?

He knew who he was, after all. It was scarcely a question. There were no kids to pound into the dust now. Still, he didn't like the awkwardness, didn't like feeling ill at ease, didn't like not knowing what by rights he ought to know.

He got to his feet and drew a deep breath. He had to know. He had to ask.

THE EVENING hadn't been a rousing success.

Jo slid a clean pillowcase on the trundle bed pillow and

then set about fluffing up the feather mattress and covering it with a fresh set of sheets. She could hear the shower running in the bathroom, and even though there had been tension, she still felt a tremendous satisfaction.

She knew where Jenny Tso was.

That was, for the moment, enough. All evening Jo had been telling herself to take it slow, but it hadn't been easy because if ever a girl needed some mothering and a shoulder to lean on, it was the thin, sad-faced girl whom she had found sitting outside McDonald's that afternoon.

Jo had wondered if she'd recognize Jenny. School pictures were not always reasonable facsimiles of the people who were in them.

But she would have known Jenny anywhere because Jenny looked just the same way Lucy had. Her slumped shoulders wore the same line of defeat, her eyes the same weariness. It was all Jo could do to get casually out of her Toyota and walk nonchalantly across the parking lot instead of bolting out and streaking across to grab the girl in her arms. But to do so, she knew, would be disastrous.

So she had forced herself to be casual. Concerned, but not overbearing. She'd introduced herself, had said she hadn't had lunch yet, and wondered if Jenny would like to share a hamburger with her while they talked.

Jenny hadn't been sure. But when Jo had shrugged and said, "Suit yourself," she had decided she might after all, which was a good thing, because when Jo came back with the food, Jenny had proved herself plenty hungry.

Over hamburgers and Cokes Jo had explained who she was and how she came to be leaving a message for Jenny. She'd hoped that doing so would encourage Jenny to talk to her. Very gradually, Jenny did.

It turned out that her uncles' long shot wasn't so far off after all. She had been staying with her brother. But when she heard the rest of the story, Jo couldn't blame the Begays for not considering him a possibility.

The brother, Wilson, was no longer in the Navy as Joseph had thought. He was a merchant seaman now, but he had been between tours, and Jenny, having kept up a rather sporadic correspondence with him, had known it.

She'd found him living with a white girl not far from where his ship was berthed in San Pedro.

Wilson had succeeded in the world off the reservation, she had told herself. He had been just as desperately unhappy at home as she had been. He would help her make it, too. She'd been sure of it.

Wilson, to his credit, had tried. He had been dismayed to find Jenny on the doorstep of his girlfriend's house. But he was Diné and she was family; he didn't consider turning her away.

He did, however, try to persuade her to go home. She wouldn't hear of it.

"To do what?" she had told Joanna angrily, recounting the conversation. "To sit and stare at the rear ends of sheep all day? I want more out of life than that. There is more to me than that! I know it!"

Jo had nodded sympathetically, understanding. At the age of twenty-one and facing a far more palatable, but just as predictable, future, she, too, had panicked and run away.

But she had been older, better educated and, in the structure of the Peace Corps, had had a far greater chance of proving herself than Jenny'd had.

Jenny got minimal verbal support from Wilson eventually and bare tolerance from his girlfriend, Deb. But when Wilson's ship departed for six months in the Far East two weeks ago, even that evaporated.

"Deb threw me out two days after he left," Jenny said.

She spent the next two weeks trying to keep her head above water. But she couldn't live on the sort of jobs she'd been offered. And a future on the streets was even less appealing than one staring at the rear ends of sheep.

At the end of her rope, money and hope all but gone, the street the only other alternative, Jenny had made a choice.

There was no way she wanted a life on the street. She'd take a life in the family hogan before that.

So she fished out the phone number she'd found at the laundromat the last time she'd washed her clothes. For two days she had stared at it, then she called.

This afternoon it had brought her Joanna.

The shower had stopped running. Jo finished making up the bed for Jenny, then made up her own and slipped into an oversize T-shirt. She considered calling Chase.

He had left far earlier than he normally did, his exit as awkward as his presence had been. All the progress she'd made with Jenny had seemed to evaporate the moment Chase walked in the door.

Any hopes Jo might've had that his being Navajo would give him more of a common ground with Jenny had vanished almost equally as fast. Jenny had been far warier of him than she had of Joanna. The whole evening had been tense.

She could tell that the girl's attitude bothered Chase, seemed, indeed, almost to hurt him. Knowing how inadequate he felt about his lack of knowledge concerning his Navajo background, Jo felt bad for him. But she didn't know how to remedy it.

She wanted to call him and commiserate, but before she could do so, the door to the bathroom opened and Jenny emerged.

"I've made this up for you," Jo told her briskly, nodding at the trundle bed. "I'm sorry I don't have a guest room."

Jenny gave her a shy smile. "I spent my life in a hogan with eight brothers and sisters," she said. "I've been used to plenty of other people. And I'll have to get used to it again."

It was the first reference Jenny had made to actually going home. Jo breathed a sigh of relief.

"Yes, I suppose you will," she replied matter-of-factly. "Would you like Chase to call Joseph in the morning?"

Jenny looked surprised. "He left a phone number?"

"Yes. It isn't his?"

Jenny shook her head. "Couldn't be. No phone out there. It's probably at the trading post. That's about fifteen miles. They would send a message." She paused, considering. "I'd rather write a letter." Her gaze flickered to Jo momentarily. "If you don't mind."

"I don't mind." Jo could understand Jenny preferring the privacy of the mails. "You're welcome to stay here as long as you want."

Jenny smiled. "Thank you." She slid between the sheets of the bed Jo had pointed out to her. "You're very kind. Thank you. Good night."

"Good night." Jo shut off the light and slipped silently into her own bed. It felt empty without Chase there to share it. *She* felt empty without Chase.

She wished she'd had the chance to call him tonight. In the morning she would call him, she decided. First thing. Bright and early. He probably wouldn't sleep any better than she did.

IN THE MORNING first thing, bright and early, the phone rang, but Chase was already gone.

He was on his way to see his mother.

If his grandfather knew why, he would be furious. For thirty-five years he had assiduously protected Denise from questions about her late husband, even questions from her own children.

Until now Chase had always accepted that. Granted, there was much he didn't know about his father and his father's people, but he probably didn't need to know it, either, not to get by in the life he was living. But now, not for himself, but for Jenny, he needed the answers to just a few questions.

He didn't even know if his mother even knew those answers. But perhaps if he caught her early and in the right mood, he might find the way to ask.

He found her, as he'd hoped he would, out working in her gardens. She was kneeling beside a row of yellow roses, digging out weeds, and when she saw him walking toward her across the dew-dampened grass, she straightened up, brushed her dark hair back off her face and smiled.

"Well, fancy seeing you here so early. Have a breakfast meeting with Grandad?"

Chase shook his head. "No. Thought maybe I could persuade you to have breakfast with me for a change."

"Me?" Denise looked surprised.

"Why not? We used to do it before I got so involved in all this administrative rot. Remember? Whenever I'd get back from doing a story overseas we'd go out."

"I remember," his mother said. "But don't malign the 'administrative rot' too much. Your grandfather deserves to retire after all these years."

"I know." Chase held out a hand and pulled her to her feet. "He's worked far longer than anybody should. He should've handed over the reins to someone else years ago."

Denise shook her head. "He wouldn't hand them over to anyone else. No one but you."

Chase knew that, appreciated it, but couldn't help saying, "Margaret would've—"

His mother shook her head. "He's far too old-fashioned, and you know it. Women don't run things in Alexander Chase's world."

Chase smiled wryly. "And the world always does Alexander Chase's bidding."

Denise nodded slowly. "Yes, the world always does."

She always did, Chase knew that. Never a strong woman, Denise Whitelaw had been no match for her determined father. Sometimes Chase felt sorry for his mother. Now, for example; when she got a faraway look in her eyes, and he wondered what sad thought had brought it this time. But then she seemed to shove it determinedly away, for she smiled at him again and said brightly, "I'd love to go to breakfast with you, darling. Just let me get washed up."

She washed up in the potting shed next to her greenhouse, and when she would've gone inside to change into something more suitable than her gardening corduroys and madras blouse, Chase overruled her.

"You look fine," he assured her. "And if you go back inside and Grandad is up, we'll have to invite him along."

"And you don't want to?"

Chase shook his head and gave her a conspiratorial smile. "Not today. I see him all the time. I don't always get to see you."

Denise smiled and took his arm. "Then let's be off."

He took her to a beachside coffee shop in Santa Monica, and over blueberry pancakes and coffee, he talked aimlessly about everything under the sun. Denise listened, smiled at him, talked a bit, too, more than she usually did when Alexander was there to dominate the conversation. Chase thought, not for the first time, that he really should get his mother out alone more often. It would be good for her.

He felt vaguely guilty for having an underhanded reason for having asked her out this time. And he was startled moments later when she said, "Why don't you stop beating around the bush and get down to what you really want to say?"

The coffee cup in his hand tipped and slopped over into the saucer. "Huh?"

Denise steepled her hands and peered at him over the top of them, her dark eyes smiling at him. "I keep noticing that while we've talked about everything else this morning, we've never once mentioned women."

Chase, in the act of trying once more for a swallow of coffee, decided that now was not the time and set the cup very firmly back down in the saucer. "Women?" he parroted, trying to fathom this particular woman's brain.

"Grandad says you've found one."

"Well, I..."

"And that you won't tell him who it is."

"I don't want..."

His mother leaned forward and reached out, taking one of his hands in both of hers, holding it tightly. "I know, dear," she said. "I understand. You don't want anything to happen like last time. I don't blame you. But it's better that it happened then rather than after, Chase. Believe me." She pressed his hand.

He swallowed, confused at her urgency. "I . . . I do believe you." He shook his head in bewilderment.

His mother stared back, equally bewildered at his reaction. "I thought that's why you asked me out," she said at last. "To tell me. It's not?"

He raked a hand through his hair. "Not really." He debated how to tell her what he really wanted, then decided the only way was simply to plunge in.

He told her briefly and simply about Jenny Tso.

She listened without interrupting. He saw the faraway sadness come back into her eyes, but he didn't let it stop him this time. He chronicled the search, the messages, the response they'd got yesterday at last, and finally Jenny's reaction to him last night.

"I'm not sure why," he concluded, "but I think it has something to do with this clan business. Like I'm supposed to know what clan I am," he said awkwardly. "And I don't. So I was wondering . . . do you?"

For a long time his mother didn't answer. The waitress came and refilled their coffee cups and took away the empty plates, a fire engine on its way to somewhere careened down the street right outside the window, the baby at the next table sent a glass of milk cascading to the floor, and all the while Denise Whitelaw stared just past Chase's right ear. But what she was seeing he didn't know.

Finally, when he had all but given up and was wondering how to extricate them from this situation he'd created, she spoke. It was as if she had faced some inner demon and done battle, but when he heard her voice, Chase wasn't sure who'd won.

Her voice was soft, mechanical almost. "You don't have a 'born to' clan, of course, because I am white. But you were born for Bitter Water. That's your father's clan."

"And what was *his* father's clan?" Chase asked. "Do you know that?"

"Mexican clan," she said softly. Then she pressed her lips together and her eyes dropped. Her fingers clenched white on the coffee mug in her hand.

Chase nodded slowly. A thousand other questions leaped into his head, begging to be answered. But he had seen the struggle that had got him just this much. He didn't know what occasioned that struggle, what made his mother so much more vulnerable than other widows he had known. But he appreciated the effort she had made for him. He reached out and took her other hand. It was cold against his palm.

He smiled gently. "Thanks, Mom."

IT MADE all the difference in the world to Jenny Tso.

She talked to him now. Even laughed occasionally and batted her eyelashes now and then, much to Joanna's chagrin.

"Now she knows you're not related clanwise, she's going to flirt with you," Jo complained as they sat on the beach and watched Jenny and Charlie cavorting in the water, but she was smiling as she spoke.

"You think she's got a crush on me?" Chase grinned and adjusted the baseball cap that was shading his eyes from the afternoon sun. He had grown to like Jenny, had enjoyed getting to know her over the week she'd spent at Joanna's place.

"She'd better not," Jo replied, tugging the cap down over his eyes, "or I'll pitch her right back out on her fanny before she gets a reply from Joseph."

The reply, they figured, should be coming any day now. Jenny had written at the end of last week. Chase wished it would hurry up as much as Joanna did. As much as he enjoyed Jenny, he didn't like going home every evening alone.

He missed being able to reach out and find Joanna beside him. And now that she was back in school, he couldn't see her during the day, either.

"Jack's due back next Wednesday," he said optimistically, which would solve one problem if not the other.

But on Tuesday, they got a call from Joseph Begay, so they got to deal with Jenny first.

Joseph was relieved, he was pleased, he was worried about how he was going to get Jenny home.

"We'll bring her," Chase said. "We'd be happy to."

He hadn't thought about it before. But as the words came, he thought, why not? Just once he would like to see the land his father had come from.

But, *"You'll* have to take her," Joanna told him when he'd hung up. "I'm teaching, remember?"

"But—"

But she had no choice. The school year had only got underway the week before. Jo was finally beginning to know her classes and just getting the cross-country team working well. Personal-leave days were available, yes. But not for the amount of time it would take to drive Jenny home.

"We could put her on a plane," Chase said the following afternoon when they were walking on the Redondo pier.

Jo shook her head. "No. They'd have to go miles to pick her up. Besides," she added, putting a hand on his arm, "you'd like to go, wouldn't you?"

He shrugged, feeling awkward and rather juvenile. It really didn't matter, he thought. It was just idle curiosity, after all.

"It's a way of finding out a bit without hurting your mother," Jo reminded him.

"I guess."

Jo smiled, squeezed his hand and kissed his cheek. "So go. I know you don't want to hurt your mother by asking her any more questions. But there's no reason you can't go there and ask a few on your own."

Chase rubbed a hand around the back of his neck, kneading the muscles, still unsure. It seemed almost disloyal to go asking questions behind their backs. They'd never done anything behind his. "I don't know."

"Maybe you need to," Jo said. "Like I needed to go to Botswana."

Chase shook his head. "No, I don't."

Jo shrugged. "Whatever you say."

His gaze followed Jenny. She and Charlie were walking half a pier's length ahead of them, their heads together, laughing about something. Jenny had bowled Charlie over. When she turned on the charm, no one was immune. He was glad she hadn't ended up on the streets. And after all this, he did want to see her safe home.

"I guess I will." He turned and looked at Jo. "But I still wish you could come."

"So do I." Jo smiled at him again for a moment, then made a face. "I could be your chaperon."

Chase laughed, his gaze seeking out Jenny again. She had turned and was waving at them to hurry now. "You reckon my virtue might be in danger?"

"It better not be," Jo said darkly. "I'm planning to have a little chat with Jenny before you go."

Chapter Twelve

It looked more like Mars than America. Huge gray humps that looked like monstrous half-buried elephants, miles of unbroken, uncultivated desert, red rock mesas jutting up out of the plateau—all of them gave Chase the sense of having been dropped into an alien world.

He had spent time in El Salvador, in Addis Ababa, in Nepal and Guatemala. But none of them had seemed as alien as this. Somehow all those back issues of *Arizona Highways* he'd read as a child hadn't even begun to prepare him.

Only the twang of country-western guitar on the radio seemed at all familiar. And that, too, lost its familiarity the moment the song ended and the rapid-fire nasal tones of the Navajo announcer filled the air with words Chase couldn't understand.

He spoke Spanish fluently. He spoke passable French, a smattering of German, a little Greek, enough Russian to get by. But he knew he would perish if he had to make himself understood in his father's native tongue.

It made him nervous, and he found himself continually rubbing the back of his neck to ease the taut muscles that seemed to tighten as he drove. He wanted to go home to Joanna. He couldn't imagine why he'd come.

On the contrary, the farther they had driven northeast of Flagstaff, the more relaxed Jenny had become. At first worried about the reception she would get from her family, now she was just eager to come home. Whenever Chase glanced at her, she was smiling slightly at the passing landscape.

The heat, which to him felt like a blast furnace whenever they cut off the engine and opened the doors, seemed not even to faze Jenny. And the wariness he'd seen in her when they'd first met and which had lasted to some degree even during most of the time she'd been with Joanna, seemed slowly to seep out of her here. She was relaxed, at home.

It wasn't until midafternoon on the second day as they drove east toward Window Rock, the closest town to her home, that he saw Jenny begin to sit up straight again.

"Not far now?" he asked her.

"Hmm?" She glanced at him, distracted, then smiled briefly. "Not too far. Go south on Route 12."

She leaned forward in the seat as he took a right at the turn-off. To the northwest clouds were gathering. Occasional lightning flickered, and Chase glanced back over his shoulder, wondering if the flash floods he'd read about were likely to become a reality anytime soon.

Jenny didn't even seem to notice. Her eyes were busy scanning the narrow asphalt road, the rugged red rock country with its covering of piñon and juniper trees, the scattered hogans as if she were checking to make sure nothing had changed.

Chase was sitting straighter, too, more apprehensive than ever. The countryside made him feel alien enough, but in mere moments he would have to confront a lot of people who would make him feel even more like an outsider looking in, more aware of everything he didn't know.

He'd spent the last few days at the library poring over books about the Navajo, and they had given him a smattering of knowledge—enough so that he thought he might not stick both feet in his mouth. But mostly they just increased his feelings of inadequacy by highlighting all the things he didn't know.

"Turn left there." Jenny pointed ahead to a place where a worn dirt track led off toward the red rock bluffs.

Chase slowed, signaled, turned. The moment the truck hit the heavily rutted road, he renewed his thanks that he hadn't driven the Porsche.

Jenny had been disappointed when he'd said, "I'm borrowing a truck."

"Everyone drives a truck," she'd complained.

"Good." He would stand out enough as it was without driving an unsuitable car.

He was originally grateful when Austin and Clea offered the use of their six-year-old Subaru pickup, and even more so when Austin volunteered to drive it down from San Francisco. But he was most grateful right now as they bounced along the rutted track toward the bluffs where just round the bend he could see two hogans not far apart, a couple of other smaller shedlike buildings, a lean-to, a corral and two pickups just about as seedy as the one he was driving. It was no place for a Porsche.

No one was outside when they arrived, and when he cut off the engine, still no one appeared.

He glanced over at Jenny, expecting her to go hurtling out. But nothing moved except her eyes, which traversed the scene for long slow minutes. Finally a woman—Jenny's mother, Chase guessed—came to stand in the doorway of the hogan. Only then did Jenny draw a deep breath and open the door of the truck.

The woman came forward from the doorway, followed a few moments later by a much older woman wearing the old-fashioned long full skirt and a purple blouse, her hair in the traditional bun. Two other girls slightly younger than Jenny seemed to hover in the doorway, and a couple of young boys peeked out past them at the new arrivals.

Two men who had been behind one of the sheds appeared and began walking toward the truck as well.

One of the men was Joseph Begay, and when Chase saw him, he began to get out.

If Chase had been expecting Jenny to get an exuberant welcome, he was wrong. The younger woman said a few words to Jenny, smiled, touched her hand. So did the older woman and the man who wasn't Joseph Begay. Joseph nodded to her, but walked past and came directly toward Chase.

"Thank you," he said, giving Chase the now familiar lightly pressed handshake.

"You're quite welcome." Chase smiled. "I'm glad she turned up."

"Yes." Joseph nodded. "It is a blessing. Come. I'll introduce you."

Chase met Jenny's parents, Frank and Milly Tso, her mother's mother, Lizzie Littleben, her sisters, Alice and Caroline, her younger brothers, Tom, Jim and Joe, an aunt, Maria, and two cousins, Juanita and Catherine. There were two more brothers, they told him—Anson and Ben. But Ben was herding the sheep and Anson had a job at the gas station in Window Rock. There was another sister, too, Sylvia, but she was married to a Many Goats Clan man and lived in Teec Nos Pos.

Chase smiled, he shook hands, he felt himself sinking fast. So many faces, so many names, so many clans, so many smiles.

"He doesn't have a clan," Joseph explained to them. "His mother is *belagana*."

A white woman. Chase understood that much.

"Ah." There were nods. Chase thought he heard a sigh of sympathy. He remembered Jenny's similar reaction. Then it had seemed odd. Here, in the context of an extended family like hers, it made much more sense.

"But," Jenny reported quickly, "he was born for the Bitter Water People."

"I have a sister who married a Bitter Water man," Mrs. Littleben said. "Who is your father?"

One of the things Chase had learned was that Navajos did not speak the names of the dead if they could help it. So he said simply, "He died in the Korean War. A few months before I was born."

Mrs. Littleben nodded. "Yes, some did."

"Chase might still have family around though," Jenny said quickly. She had been talking about finding him some ever since they'd started their trip, as if it was something she could do for him in exchange for all he'd done for her. Chase hadn't encouraged her, but now, faced with murmurs of concern, he didn't object.

"Yes," Mrs. Littleben agreed. She looked out across the land, thinking. Everyone waited in silence. "I could ask my sister who's married to the Bitter Water man. My cousin, John Chee from over by Chinle. He is Bitter Water, too. He might know." She went on mumbling names and relationships, aided by Jenny's aunt and two cousins, while Chase's mind reeled.

"You'll stay for supper," Jenny's mother said when Mrs. Littleben and the aunt had drifted off into a discussion in Navajo.

He hesitated, then thought, why not? When would he ever have another chance?

"You should look for your family," Jenny's mother said to him while they were eating the meal of green chili and mutton stew, peaches, fry bread and coffee.

Chase shrugged. "Maybe."

"I had a Mr. Whitelaw at school last year," Jenny's brother Jim said. "You think he's a cousin?"

Chase shrugged again. But the thought was intriguing. Might he have a cousin here? If so, it would be the only cousin he had. His mother had been an only child. He had a sister, two nieces, a grandfather. Nowhere close to the number of relatives of Jenny Tso. He looked around the crowded hogan and felt a prick of envy.

"You like fry bread?" Jenny's mother asked, offering him some.

"I've never had any."

Tom and Jim and Joe looked at each other, amazed. The idea of a Navajo who had never tasted fry bread was the funniest thing they'd ever heard, though they did their best to stifle their giggles when their mother frowned at them.

Chase didn't mind. He winked at them when Milly looked away, and that made the giggles worsen.

"You were a big hit," Jenny told him after supper as she walked him back out to his truck. They stood beside it taking advantage of the evening breeze that had taken the edge off the baking heat of the day. It still hadn't rained, and, glancing at the clouds, Chase was beginning to suspect it wouldn't.

Reading his thoughts, Jenny said, "It won't rain. You can't expect it. Not here." She gave a weary sigh.

Chase looked down at her, wondering what she was thinking, how she was feeling. She rarely talked about it.

But she had to be a different person from the girl who had left. She had been gone over two months. She had seen more, done more in that time than she probably had in the rest of her sixteen years. And now even though she was back where she started, he knew that everything else might be the same, but Jenny, undoubtedly, was different.

"You going to be all right?" he asked her.

She leaned against the bumper of the truck and nodded. "I'll survive." She pushed her hair back out of her eyes.

"It's funny, you know," she went on after a moment. "I couldn't wait to leave. But I didn't leave—not really. I took it with me, all this." She waved a hand, encompassing the land, the hogan, her family.

Chase could see how she would have. You couldn't forget it once you'd seen it. It was too stark, too elemental, too beautiful. And to have lived in it all your life...

"But sometimes you have to go away to know who you really are. Joanna told me that. She said she did. I think I did, too. I'm not going to just sit here though," Jenny went on with determination. "I'm not going to let life pass me by. Joanna said I might make a teacher. There's a community college at Tsaile. I could go there."

Joanna, it appeared, had said a good many things. Chase smiled at Jenny.

"Good idea." A far better one—a far safer one—than the streets of L.A. "I'm glad things are going to be okay."

She looked out across the red earth. "They will be." Then she turned to him. "Thanks. Thanks a lot."

"Any time."

She paused. "I wish I could do something for you."

"Go to school. Be a teacher. Do that for me."

"Yeah, I will. But I mean something just for you. Find you a cousin or something."

"A cousin would be nice," Chase said, more because of her earnestness than anything else. "You look around and find me one. If you do, write me, okay?"

"Really?"

"Sure."

"I'm going to write Charlie."

He wasn't surprised. Jenny's flirting with him had tapered off as her flirting with Charlie had been on the rise. The two of them had found quite a lot to talk about over the last few days. He opened the door to the truck.

"Are you going home in the morning?" Jenny asked him.

"Yeah."

"Couldn't you stay just one more day? I could probably find you a cousin by then."

"In one day?" Chase grinned.

Jenny shrugged. "I could try."

A cousin in a day? Joanna would say, do it. It was the sort of thing that would appeal to her.

Chase slanted a glance at Jenny. "You really think so?"

"Sure. My grandma knows everyone. Probably more than one cousin. A whole family, maybe," she said expansively.

"Don't strain yourself," Chase teased.

Jenny made a face at him. "You'll stay? I could take you around. Show you the area."

Chase pressed his lips together. Why not? His grandfather was undoubtedly right—a person couldn't be both. But a little bit of roots never hurt anyone. And there'd been a time when he'd wanted to know. Maybe he'd want to again, to answer the questions of his own children. "Fair enough."

"See you in the morning, then?"

"I'll come by. It won't be early."

"Don't worry. I won't tell my grandma," Jenny said. "She thinks any self-respecting Navajo should be up at dawn."

THE SELF-RESPECTING Navajos probably were, but Chase slept until past ten.

He'd gone back to the Window Rock Motel and had taken a swim in the pool. Then, somewhat rejuvenated, he'd hiked past the tribal headquarters, taken a look at the hole in the sandstone cliff that gave Window Rock its name, then walked up the highway across the state line to the donut shop, bought himself a cup of coffee and two donuts and walked back to his motel again.

By that time it was dark enough so there wasn't much to see, so he bought a copy of the *Gallup Independent* and carried it back to his room to read before he called Joanna.

He had put off calling her all day, savoring the anticipation, making himself wait until he had read the paper, taken a shower and, finally, slid between the cool white sheets in the motel room bed.

Then, and only then, had he let himself dial.

She picked it up on the first ring. "I was hoping it was you."

"Who else would it be?"

"You'd be surprised," she said dryly. "My mother, wanting to know why I'm rejecting all her attempts at matchmaking. My sister, wanting to know how my romance is going with Reg, all the time hoping it isn't so she can pick up the pieces, or—" he could hear her grimace "—more likely one of the boys. I've had three call me tonight with shin splints or turned ankles or some such."

"The joys of the cross-country coach." Chase laughed softly.

"Mmm. The cross-country coach wants to know when you're crossing country toward home."

"Wednesday," Chase promised. "I decided to stay around tomorrow. Jenny wanted me to. Said she was going to find me a cousin."

Joanna laughed. "How is she?"

"Adjusting. She quotes you every other sentence."

"She's a good kid."

"Yeah."

"She still flirting with you?"

"Uh-uh. She knows I'm yours."

"Are you?" Her voice was soft, seductive, teasing him. It curled his toes and made him wish he were driving home that minute.

"You'd better believe it. We're going to track down Jack Morrisey the minute I get there."

"You and me and a couple of witnesses."

"And my cousin." Chase grinned.

Joanna laughed. "And your cousin."

CHASE PICKED UP JENNY just before noon. She was standing alone by the lean-to when he pulled into the track in front of the house. He grinned at her. "What? No cousin?"

She scrambled into the truck. "I'm working on it."

He raised his eyebrows.

"The grapevine." Jenny gave him a confident smile. "Come on. I'll take you around."

She took him through the arts and crafts guild that was practically next to his motel, pointing out the best rugs, the best jewelry, the best pottery.

He saw the name Whitelaw on one of the cards displayed by a rug. "My cousin?" he teased.

Jenny shrugged. "Who knows?"

They bought cans of Coke from a vending machine and foil-wrapped burritos made of canned corned beef, chilies and potatoes wrapped in tortillas from a little girl in the parking lot. And then, as they got in the car munching on them, she directed him onto the highway west.

"We came this way," he reminded her.

"We're going to Ganado," she said. "To the trading post. Part of your education. Pretend it's a field trip."

"Right," Chase said. He drove west as she directed him.

They visited the trading post, talked to the Navajo woman weaving there.

They walked around the old buildings, down to where the reeds grew. Jenny told him the Navajo name for the place, which had to do with the reeds growing there, introduced him to one of the rangers who really was a cousin, then they headed back for Window Rock.

He took her to the Fedmart so she could buy groceries for her mother, then filled the truck with gasoline so he'd be ready to leave in the morning.

Afterward he drove Jenny back home.

"Have supper with us," she said when they were bouncing back along the rutted track toward the hogan.

"Thanks, but I'd better be getting on." He pulled up near the corral to let her out.

"You sure?"

"Gotta get moving sometime."

"I guess." She sighed. "I'll miss you. Will you come see me? You and Joanna?"

"Yeah," he promised. "We will. You come see us, too." He winked and touched the tip of her nose. "And if you find him, bring my cousin."

HE WAS GLAD HE'D STAYED. He'd at least got a taste of life as the Whitelaws might be living it. But he was just as glad Jenny hadn't come up with the promised cousin. There would be little point in establishing contact. Their lives were far too different. And if he did, he knew he would feel guilty.

His grandfather didn't even know he'd made the trip. What would he say if Chase came home talking about long-lost cousins? And he could hardly lie and pretend he hadn't met them. He and his grandfather had always had a relationship based on truth. Chase didn't want to jeopardize that.

So it was better to leave that stone unturned. Better not to hurt either his mother or the old man.

He ate a light supper in the motel dining room, then wandered once more through the shops in the shopping center just down the road. He stopped and bought a newspaper, then picked up a couple of postcards. He wouldn't mail them to Joanna, but he could take them home. He could show them one day to his children.

It was past eight when he tucked the newspaper under his arm and walked back to his room. He went in and flipped on the television. Nothing looked good, not even Schwarzenegger killing off someone on HBO. He flipped it off again and sat down to read the newspaper.

There was a light knock on the door.

Chase frowned, then shrugged and got up to answer it.

A man was standing there. He wore a pair of clean but faded blue jeans and a summer-weight long-sleeved plaid shirt. He was probably in his mid-fifties, his thick shock of hair still jet black, but his face definitely lined. He was, like almost everyone else staying at the motel, a Navajo.

Chase lifted one brow inquiringly. "Can I help you?"

"You are Chase Whitelaw?" The man spoke his name slowly, as if he were testing it on his tongue.

Chase nodded. Was he going to meet a cousin after all, no matter what?

"Yes, I'm Chase Whitelaw," he said.

"Your mother is Denise Chase?"

Chase frowned, looking at the man closely. How had he known that? "Yes, she is," he said cautiously.

The man nodded, smiled slightly. Then he held out his hand to Chase. "So," he said. "My name is Emerson Whitelaw. I am your father."

Chapter Thirteen

Chase didn't call.

Probably he'd got involved talking to the cousin Jenny had promised him. Or maybe he'd changed his mind and got an early start home instead. Perhaps, Joanna thought hopefully as she took a swipe at the bookcase with her dust cloth, he left last night instead of waiting until today.

If he had, and if he'd driven all night, he'd be home this evening. That notion made her pirouette happily through the last of her cursory Saturday morning dusting and vacuuming. It encouraged her so much that, humming, she went to clean the toilet.

He would be exhausted, of course, completely bushed. Quite unable to do anything but sleep. Joanna didn't care.

She just wanted him home again. In her arms. To stay.

Jack Morrisey had called this morning. Of course he'd marry them, he'd told her. It would give him great pleasure.

"First Miles and Susan, then Austin and Clea. Now you two." He had laughed. "Miles and Susan are getting to be extraordinary matchmakers."

Indeed they were. And they were a wonderful advertisement for marriage.

They'd dropped by with Patrick the night before, knowing that she'd be missing Chase, and had invited her out for a pizza. She hadn't wanted to leave in case Chase called, so

Miles went out and brought a pizza back. The four of them consumed it while she waited for Chase's call.

It hadn't come, of course, and she had been chagrined.

But then, both Susan and Miles comforted her, a watched phone never rang.

Probably they were right, Joanna thought.

But it wasn't ringing this morning either. And she hadn't been staring at it at all. In the afternoon she didn't have time to stare at it. She had a cross-country meet to coach, a set of lesson plans to prepare, and some papers to grade for her sociology class.

The Falcons were running at their home field, which meant it was her job to make sure everything was ready for the meet. That required getting there an hour or so ahead of time. She did, needing something to occupy her mind.

Charlie, equally at a loose end, was already there. He was leaning against the chain link fence, wearing his red and white school shorts and shirt, his dark hair blowing in the wind.

His eyes followed her all the way across the parking lot, and when she came through the gate, he almost smiled. He'd been doing more of that lately.

Joanna smiled back. There was a determination in Charlie now. A sense of purpose. He stood straighter, talked with more assurance. Got to the point at once. As he did now.

"Did he call?"

Joanna didn't have to ask who "he" was. "Night before last."

"How is she?"

Joanna didn't ask who "she" was, either. "Chase says she's fine. Readjusting."

"Oh." Charlie chewed his lower lip, contemplating that. Then he tilted his head to one side and looked at Jo. "You believe that?"

Joanna nodded. "Yes, I do."

Charlie looked glum. "Swell."

She touched his arm. "It isn't as bad as you think. She'll write."

Charlie shrugged. A classic Charlie Seeks Elk shrug. Not everything had changed. But he said, "Maybe," as if there was at least room for the possibility. And Joanna thought she saw a hint of hope in his eyes as he pushed away from the fence.

"I'll get the stopwatches," he said.

The stopwatches proved two hours later that Charlie was getting better and better. The whole team, in fact, was improving by literal leaps and bounds. They came in second in the meet, their best finish all year. Joanna was hoarse from all her cheering.

She took them out for pizza to celebrate, deliberately pushing aside the notion that Chase might already be home waiting for her. Let *him* wait for a change, she thought determinedly.

But when she drove home, she did so with a smile on her face and anticipation in her heart.

In her mind's eye she could see Chase sitting in the living room waiting for her when she opened the door. He would be tired and hungry, but smiling, reaching for her, ready to take her in his arms.

She mounted the steps, eyes closed, savoring the image.

When she got to the top Lynsey was sitting on the porch. "I was in the neighborhood and I thought I'd drop by."

Jo's face fell. "So I see. You haven't...seen anyone else?"

Lynsey lifted her brows. "As in who?"

Jo shrugged. "Just...anyone." She opened the door, looking around the room hopefully, aware even as she did so that it was as empty as when she'd left.

Lynsey followed her in. "The only person I saw was that fat lady across the way. The one who yells at her kid."

Jo nodded. "Mrs. Rivas."

She motioned Lynsey to have a seat, but she couldn't sit down herself. She filled a pitcher and began to water her plants.

Lynsey watched, scowling. "You're going to drown them. This one—" she nodded at a Swedish ivy "—is already soaked. When'd you water it last?"

Jo shrugged irritably. "This morning."

Lynsey gave an indignant yelp. "Then put that pitcher away. What's the matter with you?" She looked at her sister curiously. "Did you and Reg have a fight?"

"Reg?"

Lynsey rolled her eyes. "Your boyfriend. Surely you remember him?"

"Oh, right. No. No fight." Joanna reluctantly put the pitcher away, then came back into the living room, running her fingers over the phone as she passed it.

Lynsey made a moue of dissatisfaction. "Rats. I'd hoped you'd dumped him by now."

"I . . ."

"Just kidding, sweetie." Lynsey tugged Joanna's braid. "You look tired. Is everything okay?"

"Fine. Just fine," Jo said. She sat down, then popped back up again, walking to the window to stare down into the parking lot.

"Expecting him?"

"Who?"

"Reg," Lynsey said with exasperation.

"No. I just . . . can't get settled down. We got second in a big meet today," she offered as explanation.

"Congratulations. That's not what's got you keyed up, though." Lynsey knew her too well. "Want to talk about it?"

Jo shook her head. Since she hadn't mentioned Chase to Lynsey yet, she could hardly start talking about him now.

Lynsey regarded her with a mixture of sympathy and exasperation. "Whatever." She shook out her mane of long dark hair and said brightly, "I'm off to the folks' for dinner. You wouldn't like to come along, I don't suppose."

Jo shook her head. "No. I . . . I've got work to do." She gestured at the pile of sociology papers on the table. But her eyes strayed again toward the phone.

Lynsey's gaze followed. "Right."

"Thanks." Jo walked her sister to the door. "See you."

"I hope it rings," Lynsey said as she went down the steps.

But it hadn't by midnight when Joanna finally fell into a deep, uneasy sleep.

AT FIRST SHE THOUGHT she dreamed it. The ringing was loud and insistent, and in her sleep Joanna answered it, only to find the ringing continued.

She sat up, disoriented, blinking.

Once more the phone shrilled, and this time she leaped for it. "H'lo?"

"Jo?"

"Chase! Are you home? Why didn't you just come here? I thought you might get here last night."

"I'm . . . not home."

She sank down onto the day bed again, brushing her hair out of her face, frowning. He sounded odd, and now that she was paying attention, she could hear the crackle of the long-distance line and the sound of faint voices and clattering dishes in the background. "What's wrong? Where are you?"

"In Arizona."

"Still?" He sounded reluctant, she thought. As if the words were choking him.

"Mmm."

She waited. For a long moment he didn't say anything else, and she tried to cast about for a reason for him to have stayed. Car trouble? A sudden change of heart on Jenny's part?

Then he cleared his throat. "It wasn't a cousin."

"What?"

"The relative Jenny found for me." She heard a hollowness in his voice, a flatness she'd never heard before.

"Chase—"

"It was my father."

"Your—"

"Father. Dad. Papa. You know, the man who was married to my mother." There was a hard bitter edge to his voice, now.

"The one who died—"

"The one who *didn't* die in the Korean War." Every word dropped as if it had a fifty-pound weight attached.

Joanna shut her eyes. "Oh, Chase. Oh, my God, Chase."

His reaction exactly, Chase thought. Even now, thirty-six hours later, he was having trouble fathoming it.

He'd stopped doubting it, though. It all made too damned much awful sense for him to doubt it anymore.

But he had been frankly disbelieving when Emerson Whitelaw had made the announcement at his motel room door.

"My...father?" Chase's eyes had widened. He knew that in Navajo culture even more so than in white, it was impolite to stare. But etiquette wasn't his top priority just then. "You're my...father?"

The older man had nodded, taking Chase's hand in a light clasp, his eyes meeting Chase's own, then dropping to look at their linked hands.

"No." Chase had shaken his head, starting to smile, to brush him off. "I think you're mistaken. My father died in—"

"Korea? No." Emerson shook his head. "I didn't."

Chase swallowed. There was something calm and matter-of-fact about the man's demeanor that he found even more disconcerting than he would have found high-pressure insistence. "But—"

The man looked past Chase into the room. "May we talk?"

Chase wet his lips. "Yeah. Sure. I guess. I—" He broke off, stepping back, allowing the man called Emerson Whitelaw to enter the room and take a seat in the chair by the door.

"You want a Coke?" Chase asked, nodding to the six-pack that sat on the dresser by the television. Polite to the end, he thought grimly. His mother would've been proud.

"Thank you. I would like that."

Chase popped the tabs on two, handed one to the older man, then stood staring down at him. He felt almost as if, were he to take his eyes off Emerson for even a second, the man would simply evaporate. His *father*?

Emerson took a long slow swallow of the Coke and closed his eyes for a moment, as if gathering his thoughts. Then without looking at Chase, he began to speak.

"I was in the Army when I met your mother. Stationed near Los Angeles. I was young, foolish. A country boy enamored of a big-city world. Enamored," he said, his voice dropping and his eyes focusing on the painting across the room, "of a big-city girl."

Chase took a swallow of the Coke and sat on the edge of the bed, his eyes still on the man who pressed his lips together, then spoke again.

"I was different from her usual boyfriends, too. Intriguing." One corner of Emerson's mouth lifted. "A chance for a bit of rebellion, I think."

Chase frowned. Rebellion? His mother? Quiet, unassuming Denise Chase Whitelaw? "I don't think—"

But Emerson shook his head. "You don't think she was a rebel?" He gave a slight laugh. "Well, you are right, of course. But in those days," he sighed, "neither of us knew that."

Outside a truck backfired. Farther down the highway, a semi shifted gears.

"We were in love. We were enchanted. Opposites attracted," Emerson went on slowly. "We got married just before I shipped out. Her father, to say the least, did not approve."

Chase shook his head. He couldn't remember his grandfather ever having spoke ill of his father. But then, he recalled, his grandfather had scarcely spoken of his father at all.

"It was not easy for Denise to be married. To be married to me. She was at home. I was thousands of miles away. She was young. Impressionable. Worried." He paused. "Pregnant."

Chase looked at the man closely. He seemed almost in pain. Chase knew it would be polite to look away. He couldn't do it.

"But I was home by the time Margaret was born," Emerson went on. "I was there for that, if nothing else." His gaze shifted away from the painting, found Chase for a brief moment, then moved on. "How is your sister?"

"She's . . . fine." Chase swallowed against a lump in his throat. "She's married, has two daughters. She's a lawyer."

"Ah." Emerson bowed his head.

This wasn't happening, Chase told himself. It was a dream. He'd repressed all his questions about his father too long. And now, coming here, they had all surfaced in his mind, clamoring, plaguing, haunting him. He shook his head, trying to break the hold of the dream.

But the reality was Emerson taking a brief swallow of his Coke, studying his knuckles, sighing softly. And no matter what Chase tried to tell himself, the reality didn't go away.

"When I came back, at first I thought we would manage living with your grandparents. Navajos do it. But for us, no. There was no living with your grandfather. He was not happy with me. We were not happy there. We found an apartment. We moved." Emerson's eyes grew dreamy and faraway. Then he shook his head sadly.

"But that was not the answer, either. Your grandfather was a strong man, a determined man. I was not in his plans. Your mother needed her parents, their support, their love. Her parents did not need me." He paused, then added even more quietly, "And I, to be honest, found out I could not be a city boy, either."

Chase sat, numb, unspeaking, waiting for the end.

"I said to her, 'You can have parents—my parents. Come with me back to my land,' I said. 'You love me. You can do that.'" He shook his head ruefully. "And she said, 'You love me. We can stay here. You can work for my father.' But her father did not want that. *I* did not want that. Never in a million years."

Emerson stared unseeing across the room. "He came to me, the old man did. He wanted to know if it was true, that I had asked her to come with me to the reservation. He said, 'I cannot believe even you are such a fool.'" Emerson shook his head at the memory. "But for a brief time, I was. Not long. It wouldn't work. Even I could see." He bent his head, contemplating the toes of scuffed work boots.

"She could not come. She was not made for that kind of life. No more than I was made for hers. 'Get a divorce,' her father said. 'Don't be a fool, man,' he said. 'She will die out there.'"

She would have, even Chase could see that. But was this man saying that his grandfather had engineered the whole thing?

Emerson gave a fatalistic shrug. "It was true, what he said. Your mother and me—it wasn't going to work. So he fixed things, got us the divorce. He took me to the train station himself."

Chase stared. "And you left? Just like that?"

Another shrug. "And I left."

"But what about—" He couldn't keep the anguish out of his voice.

"What about you? What about Margaret?" Emerson anticipated the question. "I started to say something about when I would see Margaret. Your grandfather said, 'Don't. Navajos stay with the mother's clan,' he reminded me. 'Maternal uncles are more important than fathers.' This is true.

"'What would she do if a Navajo father popped up every now and then?' he asked me. 'Break it off clean,' he said. 'Go away and leave them both alone. If she ever wants to see you, let her get in touch with you.' He can be very persuasive, your grandfather." Emerson's tone was bitter as he set the Coke can down on the table with a soft clank. "I went. I never even knew she was pregnant with you."

For an eternity silence weighed in the room. Outside a family with children walked by, chattering, a horn honked, the faint bass of honky-tonk radio drifted in on the evening breeze. Within, a whirlwind had been let loose.

Chase shut his eyes. "God."

In his mind he examined it all, probed the words, the meanings, tested them for holes, for flaws.

He found none.

It was ghastly. Horrible. Frightening. But most of all, it was true. He knew it was true.

"They said you were dead," he rasped. His voice felt raw. His throat ached.

Emerson looked straight ahead. "I'm not surprised."

Chase lurched to his feet, slamming the Coke can on the dresser. "Dammit, *why*?"

The whole room throbbed in the ensuing silence.

Then Emerson said quietly, "I imagine it was because he wanted you."

Of course, Chase thought numbly. What else? Alexander had an empire to govern, and with Chase he had an heir at last to inherit it.

His grandfather had done that? Had lied? Deliberately? Manipulatively? Had withheld his father from him all these years?

The man whom he revered most in all the world?

The man whom he'd always sought to emulate?

"No," he muttered. Then louder, "No!"

He fell back on the bed and ground his fists against his eyes, then stared up at the ceiling and saw nothing but the tatters of his belief in what he'd always held dearest in his life.

"I'm sorry," Emerson said.

"Sorry?" Chase croaked.

Emerson spread his hands in a gesture of self-disgust. "Perhaps I should not have told you."

"And let me live a lie?" Chase said bitterly.

"I do not know."

"Yeah." Chase gave a broken half laugh. "Neither do I." His fist slammed down on the mattress.

"When I heard...when I was in town for water and old Mary Gorman said your name...I wondered. I wondered. Could it be? Was it possible? After all this time did I have a son? Was he seeking me? What did it mean? What should I do?"

What should I do?

Emerson had wrestled with his demons, had made his decision. He had chosen to seek out the man called Chase Whitelaw. To see if the name meant what he suspected it might. And one look had told him. Chase was his son.

But for Chase the decision was still to be made.

What should he do?

With four words Emerson Whitelaw had turned his world upside down.

Emerson stood up quietly. "I am staying in the room four doors down. I will be there if you need to talk." He went out as silently as he had come in, shutting the door behind him.

He might never have been there, Chase thought, an almost hysterical laugh breaking through. But he had been.

And the world was a different place.

He was a different man.

But who? Who would he have been if he had known his father? If his grandfather hadn't lied? If he had been given both halves of his heritage? If he'd been a Whitelaw in more than just name? If he had grown up knowing that he was Diné too?

And who would he become now that he knew?

He shrugged into a jacket, let himself out of the room and began to walk. Mindlessly. Determinedly. Neither seeing nor caring where he went. How far he walked, he couldn't have said. He followed the highway, followed the waning sun until it disappeared beyond a distant mesa and he stood in the darkness of a high desert night and looked around him, lost.

Stars winked overhead. More stars than he had ever seen. Without the glow of city lights to dim them, they gleamed like isolated specks of sunlight against ebony velvet. He shook his head. Even the sky was different, strange.

The night was cold. Once the sun disappeared the altitude took over, dropping the temperature suddenly. Chase didn't notice. It wasn't the weather that made him cold. But he was, in fact, frozen. Clear through.

A pair of headlights moved closer. He heard the rumble as a semi rushed past, heading back from where he'd come. And then, once more there was silence. Silence outside, at least.

Inside his head was filled with the sound of a lifetime of lies.

His mother, weeping, declining to talk about his father, the memory of his "death" causing too much pain. His grandfather, putting an arm around Chase's young shoulders, telling him how proud his father would have been of him. There were more memories, hundreds more, all of them based on deceit. They crowded his mind, crushed his soul.

He didn't know when he became aware of the headlights coming up from behind. He didn't care. He tucked his hands in his pockets, hunched his shoulders and walked on.

The pickup came abreast of him, then moved ahead and cruised to a stop. The passenger door swung open.

"Get in," Emerson said.

For a long moment Chase didn't move. And then, slowly, he obeyed. Got in the truck, shut the door, stared straight ahead.

Emerson swung the truck in a narrow U-turn right in the middle of the deserted highway, then headed back toward Window Rock.

Neither of them spoke. They covered the distance in fifteen minutes, maybe less. Emerson parked in the lot outside his own room, but he walked Chase back down to his room, took the key from Chase's nerveless fingers and opened the door.

"Sleep now," he said and touched Chase's shoulder. "In the morning we will talk."

In the morning they did. At length. Over blueberry pancakes and hot coffee. A menu that struck Chase as su-

premely ironic having just shared it with his mother the week
before.

Emerson told him about his second wife, Nora, his children, his job. Chase's mind reeled at the thought of seven
half brothers and sisters he'd never dreamed existed. He
listened with fascination as Emerson talked about where he
lived now, about where he'd grown up.

Then, haltingly, emotionlessly, Chase talked to him.

They spent the day talking, driving, meeting Nora and the
two daughters who were married and lived close at hand, the
sons-in-law, the grandchildren.

"Your grandmother would like to meet you," Emerson
said to him late that night.

"My grandmother?"

Emerson nodded. "My mother. She lives in Canyon de
Chelly. Would you... like to meet her?"

Chase said yes. But first he had to call Joanna.

Joanna.

It was the first time in a day and a half he had thought of
her. Joanna. The most important person in his life, and he
hadn't remembered her once.

But he didn't say that to her now as he told her what had
happened. He just shook his head and tried to make sense
on the telephone. "I'm not coming. I'm... going to stay for
a while."

"Stay where?"

"With my grandmother."

"Your grandmother?"

"I need to. To sort things out."

There was silence on the other end of the line. He wondered what she thought.

Probably that he'd lost his mind. It wasn't far from what
he was thinking himself.

But a quick glance out the window and he could see
Emerson filling the truck with gas while he waited for Chase
to make this call. His father. The truth.

He couldn't do anything else.

"When... will you be back?" he heard Joanna say.

"I don't know."

There was another silence. Then Joanna said, "Where does your grandmother live? What's her name?"

"Canyon de Chelly. Her name is Maria. Maria Whitelaw."

"Oh," Jo said softly, then, "Is he really your father, Chase? Are you sure?"

"I'm sure." He'd spent time enough trying to turn the clock back, trying to pretend it was a nightmare. It wasn't.

"What about your grandfather? Your mother?"

"What about them?" he asked roughly.

"What'd they say?"

"Nothing yet. I haven't talked to them. They're next. What can they say?" he asked bitterly. "I trusted them and they made my whole life a lie."

He hung up without another word.

There was a bitterness and implacability in him that Joanna had never heard before.

His whole life a lie? Well, yes, given his grandfather's determination, she could see what he meant.

Joanna wondered what old man Chase would have to say to that.

SHE DIDN'T HAVE to wonder long. Scarcely forty-eight hours later while she was in the midst of folding her laundry, there came a hammering on her front door.

She didn't answer it at once. It wouldn't be Chase. And she wasn't in any hurry to see anyone else.

The hammering came again, stronger this time.

"Hold your horses," she muttered. Whoever it was, she intended to send them away with a flea in their ear.

Alexander Chase stood there, red-faced and bristling, on her doorstep. "About time," he snapped and pushed past her into the living room.

She hadn't seen Chase's grandfather since the day of their almost wedding. He hadn't improved with age.

Her fingers tightened on the doorknob. "Please come in," she said though he already had.

He spun around, steely gray eyes nailing her. "You've got nerve!"

"Excuse me?"

"Don't play dumb with me, missy. You know damned well what I'm talking about, you—" He left off, sputtering, apparently unable to come up with any words adequate to describe his opinion of her.

Jo felt a determined calm settling over her. She shut the door carefully, then stood her ground regarding the old man in silence. He was barely as tall as she was, but his sheer rage made him seem to fill the room.

"You heard from Chase," she said quietly.

"Damned right I heard from Chase!" He snorted. "Might've known it was on account of you! Do you know what you've done?"

"What *I've* done?"

"What *you've* done, girl! Wasn't enough you had to walk out on him five years ago, make him feel a fool. Make him *look* a fool! Oh, no, now you come back to mess his life up again! Raking up the past! Poking your nose into things that don't concern you! Damn you!"

The calm Joanna felt was ruffling considerably. "I don't see—"

"It's your fault! All of it!"

"*My* fault?" Joanna stared. "You've told him all his life his father was dead, and it's *my* fault?"

"Told him that for his own good. He was never cut out to be some dirt-poor Navajo sheepherder! Didn't want him thinking he was. He's *my grandson*!"

"And his father's son."

Alexander bristled. "His father didn't need him. I did. And now, thanks to you, he's gone, girl. Gone!"

"Well, I don't think—"

"And he isn't comin' back! Wouldn't work for me if I was the last publisher on earth!"

Jo's eyes widened. "He said that?"

"Damned right he did." Alexander continued to glare. His fists clenched and unclenched.

"I don't think—"

"No, you don't! If he'd had an ounce of sense he'd've never got involved with you again. I should've guessed," he spat. "Him lookin' all starry-eyed over some new girl. Stupid fool!"

"I don't see how I—"

Alexander slammed his hand down on the end table, scattering the magazines to the floor. Ignoring them, he stalked up to her, tilted his chin and stared her right in the eyes. "I don't care what you see and what you don't. You started this. You found that Indian girl and got him to go there. You encouraged him. You get him back!"

Joanna didn't remind him that Chase had come to her for help in looking for the girl in the first place. She knew the old man was in no mood to hear it. He brushed past her, flung open the door and slammed it behind him. Joanna heard his footsteps echoing as he pounded down the stairs.

The phone rang.

Still dazed, she went to answer it.

"Joanna?" It was Susan.

"Mmm?"

"Chase's grandfather was here this morning," Susan said hesitantly, "looking for his girlfriend. Miles . . . mentioned you. Afterward we thought the old man looked a little out of sorts. So I thought I should warn you. He might be dropping by."

Out of sorts? Joanna thought. Oh, just a little.

"He dropped," she said.

"Oh, dear." Susan gulped. "What'd he want?"

"Blood."

JOANNA THOUGHT that Chase's grandfather was overreacting. Of course Chase had been mad, he'd had every right to be. But after Chase had a week or so to get acquainted with the Whitelaw family, she was sure he'd be back.

Things might not be the way they'd always been between him and his grandfather. There would be a rift that would have to heal. But she didn't doubt that it would.

Not at first anyway.

But when one week without him turned into two and then three, she began to wonder.

There had been no more phone calls, and even though she thought he would write, there'd been no letters.

Periodically Charlie asked if she'd heard from him, and she always shook her head and put the best complexion on his silence that she could. But at night, staring at the four walls of her apartment, she began to have doubts.

Feeling a bit like a fool, she had asked Miles and Susan, but they hadn't heard from him either.

"Not a word," Susan said. "Do you reckon he's okay?"

And Jo said blithely, "I don't see how he could be getting into any trouble out there." But still she worried.

"He's a big boy," Miles reminded her. "Don't worry. He'll be back in no time. It's like the phone, you know. If you expect it to ring, it doesn't happen."

"I guess," Joanna said. "Anyway, he's got Austin and Clea's pickup. He can't keep it forever, can he?"

"He didn't. He gave it back a couple of weeks ago," Miles said.

"Then he's there? In San Francisco?"

"Nope. Austin said he drove it up, turned right around and flew back."

And when Joanna found that out, she knew the waiting was over. She was going to find Chase.

THE HEAT THAT HIT HER in the face the moment she stepped out of the airplane in Phoenix reminded her of Botswana. But the bloodred mesas, sagebrush, piñon and juniper that she encountered on her drive north toward Canyon de Chelly did not.

Just as well, Joanna thought. Nostalgia was not the issue at the moment. The issue was Chase.

If he had taken Austin's truck back without even mentioning it to her, if he had flown directly back to Arizona, then there was more going on in his mind than she'd thought.

She requested her personal leave days, tacked them onto a weekend, packed her bag and flew to Phoenix early Thursday morning. There she rented a four-wheel-drive Jeep, unsure what kind of land she would be driving over before she was through. Then she began the long trip north.

She reached Chinle late on a cloudless October afternoon and went into a gas station cum quick-stop grocery store to buy a bottle of pop and, since this looked like the nearest town to Canyon de Chelly, to see if she couldn't find out where Chase's grandmother lived.

The girl behind the counter knew. "Old lady Whitelaw?" she said. "Sure."

Ninety minutes later, bumping along the bottom of Chinle Wash, Joanna spied the hogans that the girl had directed her to.

She slowed almost to a crawl, gathering her wits, suddenly nervous, hoping she was doing the right thing, wondering what else could she have done. It had been three weeks. Three weeks of silence from the man for whom twenty-four hours a day in her company had scarcely been enough.

She cut the engine, drew a deep breath and waited. For what, she didn't know. A sign from on high perhaps? A throng of welcoming Navajos? Courage?

Probably the last.

He had never invited her. He had never encouraged her at all. But he loved her, she reminded herself. And she loved him.

Her eyes swept over the sheer red rock walls of the canyon, over the cottonwoods and willows that clung to the stream banks, over the hogans and lean-tos that seemed so remote from her everyday world.

It seemed unlikely that she would even find Chase—urbane, cosmopolitan Chase Whitelaw—here.

And then she saw him.

His hair was longer and shaggier. He wore a pair of dusty faded blue jeans and a red T-shirt. In his hand he carried a battered-looking Stetson.

Stetson? Chase?

He was just coming around a bend in the wash, walking with a young boy, listening to him intently, oblivious of her. He looked, she thought heavily, as if he belonged.

Slowly Joanna got out of the Jeep and shut the door. The sound echoed off the sheer straight red walls of the canyon, and Chase looked up.

For a moment he didn't move, just stood there, his face blank, his hands at his sides as he stared at her. Then he spoke to the boy who promptly ran off toward the hogans.

And Chase came walking toward her.

Joanna stood still, waiting, wishing, wanting. Hoping and praying that he would sweep her up into his arms and hold her, making the nightmare go away.

He stopped three feet in front of her. His expression was unreadable. The man she thought she knew wasn't even there.

"Hi." She spoke softly. The canyon seemed to demand it. She gave him a hopeful smile, wanted to reach out and touch him, but felt oddly afraid to.

Chase smiled back, but it was an apprehensive smile, not the confident one she knew so well. "Joanna." His voice cracked. "Are you...what are you...?"

She shrugged and tried lightness. "I wondered what had become of you."

He rubbed a hand against the back of his neck, kneading the muscles, then shrugged wordlessly.

"Well, when you didn't come back and didn't come back..." Her voice trailed off. She wanted him to take her hand, to put his arms around her. She wanted to feel his lips against her own. But when she stepped forward, he stepped back, and she looked at him with real alarm.

"Hey, listen," he said quickly. "Since you're here I want you to meet my grandmother." There was pride in his voice, and before she could say a word, he was walking toward the hogans.

Worriedly Joanna followed him.

There were two hogans built of logs and daubed mud, squat and sturdy beneath the towering canyon walls. Beyond them Joanna saw what had been a brush sleeping shelter for the nights that were too hot to spend indoors. Nights were cool now, though. So she supposed he would spend them in the hogan.

He led her past neatly planted rows of corn and squash, a few peach trees, then past the corral where three horses stood.

Stopping at the door of the hogan, he peered inside. *"Shinááléh?"*

The sound of Chase speaking Navajo—any Navajo—was the biggest jolt yet.

"Come on in," he said when he'd got a response. His grandmother was standing by the stove, a small woman wearing a traditional voluminous long skirt and dark velveteen blouse, stirring tonight's mutton stew. "I'd like you to meet my friend, Joanna," he said to her, then to Joanna, he said, "My grandmother."

Joanna smiled and nodded. "I'm happy to meet you."

His grandmother said something in Navajo that Joanna didn't understand, then she nodded, smiled and added, "Happy, too," in English.

Joanna had no trouble understanding that.

"You stay for supper," Chase's grandmother invited. "Stay tonight."

Joanna looked at Chase. He nodded. "Thank you," she said. "I'd like that."

"Come on," he said. "I'll show you around."

She followed him outside again, wondering when they'd talk. But Chase didn't seem inclined to talk. He led her toward the other hogan, which he said was his father's sister's. She met his aunt, a smiling woman with the unlikely name of Guinevere, and his cousins, including the boy who had been with him, whose name was Andy. She got introduced to the horses, the sheep, the mangy brown dog who came nosing up to them as they stood by the corral fence.

There was perhaps two feet between them, but they might have been standing on opposite sides of the ocean. Chase stared off into the corral and talked rapidly about this sheep and that horse, this cousin and that uncle. He never talked about the two of them. He never talked about coming home at all.

Jo let him talk—all the rest of the afternoon, all evening. She listened. But she listened less to his words than to the tone of his voice, less to what he said than what he didn't say.

And in the morning, after having spent a fretful night on a sheepskin-covered mattress in Guinevere's hogan, she met him by the pickup, getting ready to go into town for water, and decided she had waited long enough.

"What now?" she said to him.

He set the last of the large silver milk cans they used for hauling water in the bed of the pickup and turned his head. "What do you mean, what now?"

She was tired and grouchy. She was worried. She had listened to him all evening and had noted that he'd scarcely even asked about her—her job, her life, Miles, Susan, Patrick, Charlie. It was as if nothing existed beyond the walls of Canyon de Chelly.

"When are you coming home?"

"Home?" He sounded as if the word were as foreign as Diné had been two months before.

"Manhattan Beach?" Jo said irritably. "Your half of the duplex on The Strand? Surely you remember that much?"

"Of course, I remember."

"Well, then . . ." She glared at him impatiently.

He shook his head slowly. "I'm not."

Joanna stared. "What?"

"I'm not," Chase repeated, his tone patient, as if she were a slightly stupid child. "I'm not going back to that. It was a lie. All of it."

"A lie?" She couldn't believe what she was hearing.

"What my grandfather said—"

"What your grandfather said, yes! That was a lie. A self-serving falsehood told by a manipulative man. But the rest of it—"

"The rest of it was based on his lie. Who I was, what I did, what I was going to do. It was my life, but he ran it. I never had a say in it at all. I don't even know who in the hell I really am!"

"But—"

"But nothing. I'm not going back. I'm through."

"What about your writing?"

"I'm not writing."

"But—"

"I have other things to do."

"Chase—"

"No."

"I didn't believe him when he said—"

"Believe who?"

"Your grandfather."

"He talked to you?"

"Yes, he came by and—"

"Is that why you came, then?" he demanded angrily. "Is he using you to get at me now?"

"Of course not! I came because I wanted to. Because I don't know what's going on with you."

"I'm living my own life for a change!"

"By holing up in the middle of nowhere?"

He stared at her. "My God, Joanna, I would've thought you, of all people, would have understood."

She looked at him blankly.

"You did it yourself, for God's sake. You went to Botswana," he reminded her. "Left me standing at the altar. Remember?"

She remembered. She closed her eyes, then opened them again frantically. Surely he didn't mean . . .

"What about us?" she asked faintly.

He shook his head. "You were right about that, too. I understand that now. You can't get married when you don't know who you are."

Chapter Fourteen

Poetic justice.

That's what it was. And Joanna thought that at some far future date she might be able to appreciate the irony of it.

But now, though it was already a month since she had left Chase to find himself in Canyon de Chelly, she was still too close to it for that.

Now she simply hurt. Agonized. And despaired.

Why not? she asked herself.

After all, what were the chances that when—*if*—Chase "found himself" he would also find that he was still in love with her?

It might've happened once, as it had this past summer when she'd discovered her love for him. But the odds had been against them even that time. She wouldn't bet on it happening again.

She tried to tell herself that she would get over it, that life would go on much as it had always gone on. She would still have her family, her job, her friends.

But intellectual acknowledgment and gut feeling were sometimes—as they were now—poles apart.

She felt rotten.

Charlie's first-place finish in the regional cross-country meet cheered her a bit. But she felt, as she knew he did, that there was someone missing in the cheering section when he crossed the finish line.

"Wish he'd been here," he said to her afterward when the rest of the boys had gone home and she and Charlie were standing outside the locker room.

"Yes."

They rarely spoke about Chase. It was almost as if he'd died and to mention his name would cause untold pain. But now it was hard not to.

Charlie slung a towel around his neck and accompanied her to her car. "You dunno he's not comin' back," he reminded her. He meant to sound hopeful.

Joanna shrugged. "Maybe. But you remember Lonna?"

"Lonna Jones?" Charlie rolled his eyes. He had dated her last year. Lonna couldn't get the time of day from him this year. He had places to go, things to do. He'd changed.

"Would you go back to Lonna now?"

Charlie just looked at her. "No way."

"My point precisely."

Charlie didn't say any more about Chase.

Susan and Miles weren't so pessimistic. They tried to buoy her spirits, encourage her hopes.

"I know Chase," Susan told her firmly. "He'll be back. Just you wait."

But as October turned into November and November turned into December and no one heard from him, even Susan seemed to have her doubts.

"I don't understand him," she muttered.

"I do," said Miles, and the words didn't sound as hopeful as Joanna might've wished.

She told herself that by Christmas she would be on the mend. She would find a new interest or two in life. She would collect donations for the Salvation Army, knit antimacassars for the chairs in rest homes, take up tatting. And if all else failed, the French Foreign Legion was a tempting thought.

"Buck up," Reg told her on his next swing through L.A. "Third time's a charm."

For some, maybe, Joanna thought. But not for her.

She told Lynsey the truth, introduced her to Reg as a possible date, and took as much satisfaction as she could in the fact that her sister's love life seemed to be improving even as her own went down the drain.

"Can't I do something for you?" Lynsey asked her as they Christmas shopped. "Introduce you to my dentist or something?"

Joanna laughed. "For a root canal, maybe. Not for anything else."

"I hate to see you like this." Lynsey cocked her head and considered Joanna's pale complexion and the dark hollows under her eyes.

"I'll be fine," Joanna assured her. "All it takes is time."

And heaven knew, she had plenty of that.

IT WAS IMPOSSIBLE to cram thirty-five years into a few weeks or months. But Chase tried.

He had lost so much, had missed so much. A father. A grandmother. Stepmother. Half brothers and sisters. Uncles, aunts and, of course, the ubiquitous cousins. And more than just family, there was a Navajo way of life, a Navajo reality, a different way of seeing the world.

He wanted it all. Desperately. He needed it. So he could come to terms with himself.

"You want to stay?" His father had sounded surprised when Chase brought it up.

Chase nodded. "If you don't mind."

"You are my son. You are always welcome," Emerson said. "You can stay with my mother. She will teach you."

Everyone taught him. His grandmother, his father, his half brothers and sisters. Even the youngest children. He learned to herd sheep, to haul water and not to waste a drop. He learned which plants sheep could eat and which they should stay away from, which trees made the best firewood and which gave the best shade. He learned about Changing Woman and Monster Slayer, about the *Yei* and Coyote and the Blue Flint Boys.

And finally he learned the bounds of his anger, too.

It wasn't enough to live fortified by anger. He needed more. He needed purpose, promise, love.

"Hozro," his father said the afternoon they drove up into the Lukachukai Mountains to cut wood for the winter.

"Huh?"

"Hozro." Emerson groped for a translation. "Beauty, they sometimes say. Harmony. Balance. What you need in your life to make it worth living."

What did Chase need?

He wished he knew.

He couldn't put his finger on the exact moment when things began to come together, when past began to mesh with present and he felt, at last, ready to deal with the future.

It could have been that day up in the Lukachukai Mountains with his father when he first started thinking about *hozro*, about beauty, about fulfillment in life. It could have begun the morning he sat on the rim of the canyon at dawn and for the first time opened a notebook and began once more to write.

But the fifth night of The Night Chant, sung in early December for his ancient uncle Jefferson Sam, brought things into focus at last.

That was when Chase, along with a number of others, had been initiated into the mysteries of the *Yei*. Most of them were young and doing it for the first time. But age didn't matter. What mattered was the understanding gained.

There, for one long moment, as he looked through the mask of the *Yei*, he saw, as did all the initiates, that the fearsome beings were only mortal men. For Chase himself the significance was even greater. For the first time he looked beyond the masks of the people in his own past. He understood then that his grandfather, too, was a mortal man who could be wrong, who could make mistakes. So could his mother, and his father. So could Chase himself.

No one was perfect. No one had all the answers. The world was far too complicated a place. And as he put the mask aside and covered his head with the blanket again, he understood at last that it was less a betrayal than mortal men and women trying to do their best with the reality at hand.

And, realizing, he finally began to forgive.

He allowed his grandfather fallibility, he permitted his mother weakness and his father fear. He allowed himself need and uncertainty and, finally, hope. He put the past behind him, accepted the present and looked toward the future. He understood at last the gifts of the spirit—of love, of understanding, of generosity, of determination—that he'd been given through all of them.

It was, he knew, time to grow up.

It was time to go home.

AND SO HE WENT.

Not to be head of the DeWitt Chase Publishing Group.

He wouldn't do that. Executive administration, he had determined, wasn't one of the gifts he'd been endowed with.

But Margaret had. And he would do considerable leaning on his grandfather until, he hoped, Margaret got her fair share.

He was going to be the writer he knew now that he was. His grandfather had been correct about that much. He hadn't been free of words and images, even when he'd been sitting out in the middle of nowhere, his only companions a herd of sheep. Inside him there was a need to seek, to understand and finally to express. And so he would.

Perhaps for his grandfather's periodicals, perhaps not. But wherever, he would bring a greater sensitivity, a deeper compassion, a fuller understanding of other people—their joys and their sorrows, their hopes and their limitations—because now he had come to terms with his own.

His grandfather had been right about something else, too. It wasn't possible to be both Navajo and white. Not fully. No one could have two entire identities, save perhaps a schizophrenic. But for people born of two cultures, it was equally impossible to deny one totally and embrace the other.

It was part of the beauty, part of the harmony of being who he was to discover the balance between the two in his own nature and, then, to find his appropriate place in the world.

It made him understand finally what Joanna had tried to tell him about why she had fled their wedding all those years ago.

And it made him hope to God that when he walked up her steps and knocked on her door in less than ten minutes, she would be equally understanding of him.

It seemed like a good time. Christmas Eve was the sort of goodwill time that might predispose her to at least listen to what he had to say. Though he knew he shouldn't blame her if she did not.

He hadn't said, "Wait for me."

He hadn't said, "I'll be back."

He hadn't held out hope.

He had known better than to do that, of course, just as she hadn't made any promises when she'd jilted him.

But he hoped. Oh, God, he hoped.

For all that he had immersed himself in a Navajo way of life—for all that he had arisen to greet the dawn with his grandmother, had gathered piñon nuts and herded sheep with his nieces, nephews and cousins, for all that he had attended a Night Chant, a Ghostway, and a Blessing Way and learned the efficacy of each, for all that he had learned about himself—the most important thing he learned was that no matter who he grew to be, he would always love Joanna.

And he hoped to God she still loved him.

He was tired and grubby and he'd been up since before daybreak. He had stayed in Arizona until this morning so he could share in the celebration of the wedding of his youngest half sister. Then it had snowed, and though he and his father had got up at two in the morning so Emerson could drive him to Flagstaff to catch a plane, nothing was flying in or out for hours.

Finally late in the afternoon, they had opened the airport and he had managed to get a flight. He had rented a car at L.A. International and had driven straight to Joanna's house. He hadn't even bothered to go home first.

It was cutting things close, he knew. But even if Joanna planned to go to her parents' later on, he thought she would be home in the early evening.

He was wrong.

There was no light on in her apartment when he mounted the steps. Her car wasn't in the lot.

She could have gone grocery shopping, or maybe out for an evening run. Chances were she would be back in a few minutes. He hoped so, anyway. He sat down on the steps to wait.

She didn't come. But about forty minutes later, Mrs. Rivas, her neighbor, did, her arms full of groceries.

"Hi." Chase smiled gamely up at her.

"You waitin' for Joanna?"

Chase nodded.

"You'll have a long wait, I bet." She gave him a knowing look.

Chase sat up straighter. "Why?"

"I wouldn't be home soon if I went out with him."

His eyes narrowed. "Out with whom?"

Mrs. Rivas gave an eloquent shrug. "Don't know. Blond fella." She smiled as if she were savoring the words. "A real hunk."

Blond fella? A real hunk?

Chase felt sick. So much for Joanna waiting. He got to his feet. Reg? he wondered. Was it Reg?

Reg was sort of blond, though Chase would have called it reddish. And he wasn't sure "hunk" was the proper word for him. Still, some women might describe him that way. And was he supposed to hope it was Reg or not?

He jammed his fists into the pockets of his jeans. "Thanks," he muttered, heading down the stairs.

"You're welcome," Mrs. Rivas called after him. "Merry Christmas."

Merry Christmas? Chase gave her a baleful look over his shoulder.

Yeah, sure.

T'WAS THE SEASON to be jolly.

Joanna knew that. Susan had even said so right before they'd left, and Miles had added a sympathetic "Ho, ho, ho" before giving her a quick hug of thanks for spending Christmas Eve babysitting while they went to Brendan and Cassie's for a get-together and then on to Midnight Mass.

She had been invited along as well.

"We'd be delighted if you'd come," Cassie had told her on the phone last weekend, and Susan and Miles had seconded it, as had Griff and Lainie and Austin and Clea.

But Joanna couldn't go. She couldn't put on a happy face for an entire evening, not even Christmas Eve—especially not Christmas Eve—and she knew it. God knew how often lately she had tried. So she'd declined.

She'd told Susan and Miles, "I appreciate the invitation more than you know. But I can't. You go and leave Patrick with me."

It hadn't been hard to convince them. Nor had it been too difficult to convince Griff and Lainie to leave Andrew with her as well.

"He'll be company for Patrick," she told them. "Really," she added when they hesitated. "I wouldn't offer if I didn't mean it."

She told the same thing to Austin and Clea.

"You can't be serious," Clea said. "Four kiddies?"

But Joanna was entirely serious.

The more the merrier, as far as she was concerned. She loved kids, loved Christmas, and maybe the combination of the two would provide enough distraction that for once she would be able to get Chase out of her head.

She needed to. Desperately. She hadn't heard a word from him in almost three months. And she wasn't going to, she knew that now.

"Bring 'em all on," she said recklessly.

So they did.

Austin and Clea and the twins, down from San Francisco to spend the holidays, had arrived earlier that afternoon. And when Joanna called to say that the water pump had gone out on her car on her way home from her stint as the Salvation Army bellringer, and it was in the shop for the holidays, Austin had said he'd come and pick her up.

He had arrived just as Sally Rivas was going out, and she had beamed to see Joanna, after several months of moping around, once more in the company of a handsome man.

"About time," she'd approved. "You have a good time, now."

And Joanna, not wanting Mrs. Rivas to think things hadn't really improved at all, had pasted her brightest smile on her face and had said gaily, "Oh, I will. I will."

If she did, it would be because Patrick and Andrew and the twins succeeded in distracting her. So far nothing else had.

Miles and Susan's apartment looked like a day-care center. Besides the gaily lit Christmas tree in the corner and the blazing fire in the fireplace, the room was filled with toys, high chairs, portacribs and disposable diaper boxes. Lainie was busy making out a list of phonetic transcriptions of Andrew's vocabulary so that Joanna could understand him. Clea was nursing Brent, while Miles bounced Sara on his knee, and Patrick and Andrew were using Griff's chest as a wrestling mat as they tussled with each other in the middle of the floor.

"You're a braver soul than I am," Susan said, coming out of the bedroom, still brushing her long dark hair.

"I'm going to enjoy it," Joanna assured her.

Miles looked doubtful. He handed Sara to her father and wrote Brendan and Cassie's phone number in huge letters on the bulletin board by the phone. "Call if you need anything," he said. "Promise?"

"I promise."

Six adults hovered by the door, looking at her with varying degrees of concern and sympathy.

Joanna smiled and shook her head. She reached for Sara, taking her out of Austin's arms, then took Brent from his mother. "Go on," she said. "Stop worrying. Nothing's going to happen. Nothing at all."

Nothing except that ten minutes after they left, Andrew suddenly noticed that his mother and father were gone.

His lower lip jutted out, his eyes filled with tears and he headed straight for the front door emitting a long wail.

"Oh, Andrew." Joanna plopped the semidozing Brent into the nearest portacrib and hurried to the little boy's side, still holding Sara in her arms. "It's all right."

But Andrew didn't think it was all right at all. He wailed even louder and threw himself against the door.

Sara, a sympathetic sort, got the idea. Her small angelic face screwed up and she began to sob, too.

The noise roused Brent, who lifted his head, frowning hazily. Then he hauled himself to his hands and knees, took one look at Joanna over the top of the crib bumper and began to howl.

Joanna looked warily at Patrick.

He gave her a blithe grin. "Babies crying," he said.

"Tell me about it," Joanna muttered and flew to the refrigerator for the bottles that Clea had said would tide the twins over in the event of an emergency.

Joanna wasn't sure this qualified as an emergency. But an ounce of milk was worth a pound of crying, the way she figured it. And it sounded like it was going to be a very long night.

She gathered Andrew into her arms along with Sara and trundled them over to the futon, plopped them both down, then reached for Brent, who kept on wailing. Settling herself onto the futon, she lifted Sara into one arm and Brent into the other, wedging bottles firmly between their lips, then told Patrick, "Get me a book. We'll read to Andrew, okay?"

The first book Patrick toddled over with was something about "perspectives on nudes." Miles's, undoubtedly.

"Not that one," Joanna said, relieving him of the book and stuffing it up out of his reach. "*Peter Rabbit*, okay? Or *Winnie the Pooh*."

Patrick looked momentarily perplexed. Then he toddled back over to the bookcase and brought her another offering. This time it was a book on tennis greats. Probably Susan's.

"Never mind. I'll get one myself." She edged her way up off the futon, hoping that Sara and Brent could hang on to their own bottles long enough for her to nab a suitable book and come back. She grabbed an assortment, then plopped down again, scooping the babies up and seating Andrew, still sniffling loudly, and Patrick, ever curious, on either side of her.

"Now then..."

She read them *Goodnight Moon*. She read them *Where the Wild Things Are*. She read them the entire volume of *When We Were Very Young*. Patrick listened. Sara and Brent drifted off to sleep. Andrew sobbed on.

Joanna felt like sobbing with him.

IT SOUNDED AS IF they were killing him. Or as if they'd abandoned him. It sounded awful, heartrending, and wholly unlike Patrick.

And it had been going on for ages.

Chase heard it the minute he got home. He ignored it, opting instead for the solitude and privacy of his own apartment, a shower and a glass of whiskey, neat.

He wasn't fit company for anyone right now, least of all Susan and Miles. Miles might respect his privacy, allow him his silence, tolerate his reticence. But not Susan.

Susan could get an interview out of the Sphinx, and in the shape he was in at the moment, his deepest secrets wouldn't be safe from her skillful prying questions. She would do it with the best of motives, of course. Even he knew that. But just the same, he couldn't handle it right now.

So he showered, long and hot, blotting out the noise of the crying next door, feeling lousy enough himself. But when he shut off the water, he could still hear it.

What were they doing to the kid? And on Christmas Eve yet?

He shrugged into the dark red terry cloth bathrobe that still hung on the hook of the bathroom door right where he had left it three and a half months before, just as if he were the same man who had left it there.

But he wasn't. Time went on.

And so did people.

It was only what he should have expected, he reminded himself grimly, sloshing a bit more whiskey into the glass and sinking down onto the sofa to contemplate his bare toes and the gaping void that loomed now in his life. There was no balance—no beauty—without Joanna.

The wailing continued.

"Cripes," he muttered, knocking back the whiskey. Maybe the kid was sick.

The thought of Patrick sick worried him. The thought of Patrick next door beckoned him.

Next to Joanna, he had missed Patrick most. His half sister, Teresa, who lived near Rock Point, had a son Patrick's age. His name was Jimmy, and sometimes, playing with Jimmy, Chase had been overcome with such a longing of homesickness that he physically ached.

It was an ache not unlike the one he was feeling now.

Maybe if Susan and Miles couldn't get Patrick calmed down, he could. After all, he'd done it before.

But that meant facing Susan. He debated. The sobbing, which had slacked off for a moment, increased again. Chase thumped the whiskey glass down on the counter and strode out the door.

He crossed the porch, banged unceremoniously on Miles and Susan's door, then jerked it open and said, "What in God's name are you doing to that—*Joanna?*"

Halfway through the chapter on Pancho Gonzales while Andrew screamed and Patrick listened, Joanna stopped dead and stared.

It was the first time in almost three months she hadn't been thinking of Chase, and, unbelievably, there he was. She thought she might be dreaming.

"Chase?"

"Chase!" Patrick scrambled down off the futon and threw himself at the man who stood in the doorway. And then Joanna knew it was true.

Unconsciously Chase fielded him, lifting him into his arms, hugging him close.

Joanna? Here? His mind reeled. It didn't make sense.

Where was the "blond fella"? The hunk? Her date?

He looked around cautiously. There didn't seem to be any blond guy in the room besides Andrew Tucker, still sobbing his head off and gnawing on his fist, and he didn't qualify as a hunk.

Joanna didn't know what to do, what to say. She might have rehearsed things a thousand times in her mind, but she'd never even envisioned circumstances like these. Besides, what could she say over Andrew's screams?

"What's the matter with him?" Chase asked.

"Misses his mommy and daddy. And I think he's teething."

Chase grimaced. "Give him here."

Joanna looked doubtful.

Chase dumped Patrick down on the futon next to her and reached for Andrew. "Doesn't look like you're making any headway, does it?"

"No..." That was obvious enough.

"Then give him here." Without waiting for her consent, he scooped Andrew into his arms and strode off toward his own apartment.

Joanna stared after him amazed.

Andrew looked back at her over Chase's shoulder, his last sob caught mid-gulp, his eyes widening.

Patrick waved cheerfully to him. "Bye-bye."

Joanna looked at Patrick. Patrick beamed at her.

There didn't seem to be any sound coming from Chase's apartment at all.

Jo didn't know how long she sat there, stunned by the turn of events. She only knew the blessedness of silence and the amazement of the knowledge that Chase was just a few yards away.

Why had he come back now? What did it mean? Was he simply passing through on his way back to Arizona or had he—dare she hope?—come to stay?

Patrick thrust the tennis book at her. "Read."

"Read?"

"Read Pancho," said Patrick.

Mind reeling, Joanna read.

They had finished Pancho Gonzales and had started on Pancho Segura when Chase returned. Andrew was sound asleep in his arms.

"Where should I put him?"

Joanna stood up and peered down into the now angelic face, then looked with real awe at Chase. She pointed toward the bedroom. "In there as long as he isn't going to wake up again."

She had put Sara and Brent in their respective portacribs and had already wheeled them in there. If Andrew was asleep for the duration, fine, but she didn't want the infant chorus starting up all over again.

"He won't," Chase promised. He disappeared into the bedroom with the sleeping child.

A minute later he was back without him, his eyes wide. "My God, this place is wall-to-wall babies!"

"Babies," said Patrick happily.

As long as they were sleeping, it didn't matter to Joanna. "How'd you do that?" she asked Chase, mystified. "Get him to sleep, I mean?"

"Old Indian trick," Chase told her.

"What is?" she asked warily.

"Rubbing oil of cloves on their gums." He shrugged, then smiled. "But I didn't have any oil of cloves."

"So what'd you use?"

He grinned. "Whiskey, of course."

Joanna shook her head, smiling back at him. Unable to keep from smiling, no matter what he'd come to say.

It was that smile that undid all his best intentions. That smile that snapped his control, undermined his explanations, and had him reaching for her.

"Oh, God, Jo!"

And Joanna, no proof against his need, reached for him.

It felt like coming home, like reaching a haven in the midst of a storm, and Joanna gave herself over to the sensation wholly, savoring the feel of his arms hard around her, his face buried in the softness of her hair, the thrum of his heart against her breasts.

And then she stepped back and looked into his eyes. "Does this," she asked, "mean it's on again?"

Chase grinned. His eyes were suspiciously damp, his hair tousled. "God, I hope so," he said.

"You mean it?"

"Every word."

"You found out who you were?"

"Yeah, I did. But more than that, I found out that whoever I am, I don't want to spend the rest of my life without you."

"Oh, Chase!" It was a miracle. She buried her face into his shoulder, wrapped her arms around him, needing the warm, solid feel of him against her for now, forever.

And Chase needed her, couldn't get enough of her. How had he lasted so long without her? Why hadn't he known earlier?

"Because beauty can't be forced," Emerson had told him. "Because it simply has to grow."

And then he was kissing her again.

Joanna wasn't sure how long that kiss lasted. She was only sure that it was the most wonderful one she had ever experienced, and that it might have gone on forever if small hands had not tugged insistently at her jeans and the hem of

Chase's bathrobe. She looked down into an upturned hopeful face.

"Me, too," Patrick said.

Chase scooped him up, laughing, hugging him between them. "You, too," he said, kissing Patrick's nose, then he eased the little boy onto one arm and drew Joanna down on the futon so that the three of them nestled together. Patrick bounced on his chest.

"You're very good with children," Joanna said.

"I should hope."

"Want some?" she asked.

"You bet."

"Soon?"

"Mmm." He nibbled her earlobe.

She laughed. "Like in nine months?"

"Sooner, I thought."

She pulled back. "What?"

He was still smiling but there was a seriousness in his eyes. "I was thinking on the way home that, if you'd have me...er, maybe we could give some thought to having Charlie as well."

Joanna's eyes grew round. "Adopt Charlie?"

Chase shrugged awkwardly. "It was just an idea. If you don't think—"

"I think it's a terrific idea."

"Yeah? Well, Charlie probably won't. At best he'll probably shrug."

Jo touched his cheek tenderly. "Charlie might surprise you."

"Life is full of surprises," Chase agreed dryly, and Joanna knew he thought they'd had their share.

She smiled. "Gifts. Life is full of gifts."

Her eyes drifted to the soft glow of the colored lights on the Christmas tree, to the gaily wrapped presents beneath it, to the bright-eyed little boy who had clambered down and was sitting on the floor watching them, to the man with whom she was going to spend the rest of her life.

"And you are my greatest gift," she told him.

"Ah, Jo." And Chase enfolded her in his arms as his lips met hers once more.

In the middle of the room the small boy looked up thoughtfully, his gaze moving from the Christmas tree to the two adults who were wrapped in each other's embrace, oblivious for the moment to any world beyond it. He smiled.

"Always kissing," Patrick said.

TO MARRY AT CHRISTMAS

KASEY MICHAELS

To Anne, the beautiful bride,
and Eric, her handsome groom,
from the ecstatic Mother of the Bride.
All love, health and happiness to you,
my darlings, now and forever.

Chapter One

Elizabeth Chatham moved the small cardboard Sale sign precisely one and one half inches to the left, then stood back to admire her handiwork. "There," she said, tilting her head to one side and narrowing her eyes to inspect the display of food processors. "That's perfect, Judy, a real work of art. Just let Mr. Lancaster try to find something wrong with it this time!"

"I didn't say he didn't like it, Ms. Chatham," the chubby redhead put in, pushing herself away from the counter that she had been leaning against just as the bell sounded over the loudspeaker, alerting the employees that it was ten o'clock and Lancaster's Department Store was open for business. "I just said he looked at it sort of funny when he walked by it Saturday while you were on your lunch break."

Elizabeth wrinkled up her small nose in distaste. "And, according to you, that funny look is known as the kiss of death around here. Right, Judy? I've only been here a week, but I've heard enough stories about our esteemed boss to figure out he's a perfectionist. No matter who's responsible, he holds the head buyers guilty as charged for everything and anything that goes wrong within a department.

And to think I believed life would be easier here than at my last job."

Judy Holland, who was still in awe knowing her new supervisor had worked at the famous Bloomingdale's department store—in New York City, no less—looked admiringly at Elizabeth's fashionable mauve cable-knit sweater and soft wool plaid skirt and gushed, "Bloomie's! How could you ever bear to leave all that to come back to dinky Bethlehem, Pennsylvania? I'd die to work there!"

"It wasn't all that glamorous, Judy," Elizabeth told the young salesclerk while walking around the counter to check the display from another angle. "Housewares are housewares and bosses, unfortunately, are bosses. Besides, I happen to think that Bethlehem is beautiful. All our lovely old Moravian homes and everything, you know."

As Judy went off to help a woman who was intent on dismantling the blow-dryer display—in an effort to uncover a "pink one to match my bathroom, you understand"—Elizabeth walked through the large third-floor department, giving it one last inspection before heading for her office and the mountain of correspondence waiting for her there. Although she was stationed in the main store, she was housewares buyer for all thirty-six Lancaster department stores that were spread up and down the East Coast, and that meant a lot of paperwork.

She was happy in Bethlehem, she thought comfortably, smiling to herself as she hung a wire whisk back on its hook. Life was less hectic here, with not nearly as much hustle and bustle as in Manhattan, and she definitely didn't miss rush hour on the subway. Her family's huge three-story Victorian home was only a mile from Lancaster's, on quiet, tree-lined Spring Street, and she enjoyed the walk to and from work under the lovely old Hill to Hill Bridge.

Elizabeth was a small-town girl at heart, having grown up the eldest of four children in a loving, middle-class family. Besides, it wasn't as if she had left the love of her life behind her in New York. During her three years at Bloomingdale's she had rarely dated, and she knew firsthand that a person could live a long time in New York City and—although she had made many friends—still feel very much alone.

Pulling a wry face at these thoughts, she knew her grandmother's pointed comments the night before—it was her contention that Elizabeth must be the only unmarried, unsettled twenty-six-year-old female left in civilization—had a lot to do with her current introspection; she stopped in front of a display of cookware and shook her head.

"I'll never understand it," she groused, once again a demanding buyer, picking up the hammered metal roasting pan with some effort and turning back the way she had come. "This thing weighs a ton!"

Rushing a bit in her eagerness to get back to her office and dash off a nasty note to the jobber who had shipped the pan, Elizabeth rounded the corner of the next counter sharply— and ran smack into a tall, immovable object.

"What the—" Nicholas Lancaster had known there was a new head buyer in the housewares division of Lancaster's Downtown but, as Chief Operating Officer, he had never felt any pressing need to immediately introduce himself to every new employee.

His usual method was much more subtle, even sneaky: strolling into the department unannounced within a few days of the latest hiring to observe his newest employee firsthand before making his identity known. This morning had seemed like a good time to observe Ms. Elizabeth Chatham. Although the staff eventually recognized their boss, the initial element of surprise had served him well over the years, and he prided himself on keeping his employees hopping.

But this morning the tables were turned, and it was Nick who was suddenly hopping because his newest employee had come barreling around the towering aisle-display of toasters, which he was inspecting, and violently crashed into him, the roasting pan she was carrying dropping squarely on his foot.

"Oooh!" Elizabeth exclaimed, her breath partially knocked out of her by the force of the impact, while Nick cursed silently, knowing there had to be better ways to meet his new employees. By reading her name tag, he realized at once that the woman was the new buyer, a random conclusion that flitted swiftly through his mind, just a second before the jarring pain in his foot completely registered in his brain.

After the shock of the initial impact was over they both stared blankly at each other for a moment, mumbled startled apologies, then bent down to retrieve the pan, only to bump heads and apologize again, bend down again, and bump heads a second time.

Nick and Elizabeth both ended up sitting rump down in the carpeted aisle, she still furiously apologizing and offering to send for the store nurse, and he, suddenly, inexplicably breathless, holding his injured foot and surreptitiously waving away the three apprehensive salesclerks who were hastening to assist their boss.

"Oh, I'm *so* sorry, sir!" Elizabeth repeated earnestly, one hand to her mouth, knowing deep in her heart that the man she had barreled into could be none other than her boss. Who else could it be, what with her legendary poor timing? Lordy, how she hated Mondays! And why was he staring at her like that?

"Yes, I believe you've already covered that," Nick replied absently, flexing his injured foot and deciding that two things in this department had to go—the high display, and the heavy pan. Then he stole another look at Elizabeth and blinked hard. *She's gorgeous!*

"I know I must sound like a broken record, but then what else can I say? Are you sure you're really all right?" Elizabeth continued breathlessly as she knelt forward to quickly unlace his shoe and massage his stockinged foot, her chestnut head bent over her task and hopefully hiding her flushed cheeks.

Nick leaned back on his hands, doubting what he was seeing, what he was feeling. He felt as if someone had punched him in the stomach, as if he should be gasping to regain his breath, and his heart was pounding at twice its normal rate. He felt like Christmas and the Fourth of July and his birthday had somehow all come at once, without warning, and he had just been given every gift he'd ever wanted. "You—you don't have to do that, you know," he felt honor bound to say, secretly hoping she'd never stop.

It was silly—something she'd only read about in novels—but when her hand made contact with his foot, a tingle moved through Elizabeth's fingers and up her arm. A few seconds later, their gazes met, and held, and the tingle spread throughout her body, warming her blood and turning her bones to water.

"It must hurt terribly, I'm sure. Isn't that just the stupidest pan you ever saw? I was taking it to the stockroom just so something like this wouldn't happen. Arnold Schwarzenegger would have trouble with that thing. I mean, really! Can you imagine a housewife trying to lift that pan with a fifteen-pound turkey in it?" *That's it, Elizabeth,* she congratulated herself. *Keep talking, just keep talking. Maybe then he won't notice that you're eyeing him as if you're a starving fool and he's a juicy porterhouse steak. Lordy, but he's gorgeous! So dark, so handsome!*

"I can't imagine," Nick murmured, still feeling somewhat bemused. *Her hair wasn't red—sort of burnished brown, maybe? It looks warm. Perhaps if I touched it—*

"I'm sending all of them straight back to the supplier, of course. I can't help but wonder what the previous buyer could have been thinking of when he ordered the things, can you?" *Why is he staring at me like that? Chatham, for pity's sake—enough, already—close your mouth!*

"Maybe, with all this carrying on about physical fitness and incidental exercise, he was hoping to add his bit to the effort?" *Oh, that's good, Lancaster. Ha, ha. Good grief, what a stupid, stuffed-shirt thing to say!*

Elizabeth tilted her head to one side as she considered what he had said, wondering why she thought each word to be a pearl of the greatest wisdom. "Do you really think so? And here I was, imagining the designer as a woman hater, doing his darndest to kill us all off come Thanksgiving. I guess I won't enclose a nasty note after all. There," she ended, giving his foot a final rub, hating to break this small physical contact. "I don't think anything's broken, and my offer still stands to send for the store nurse. I really am sorry about this."

Nick watched as Elizabeth deftly replaced his shoe and then neatly tied it, giving the finished bow a quick pat as if to put her personal seal of approval on the job. He was desolate with disappointment now that her touch had been withdrawn, but tried not to let it show. "Is that it? My mother used to kiss my boo-boos to make them all better," he teased provocatively as he helped the new buyer to her feet. *That's even worse than your last jewel, Lancaster. Now you sound like a cheap pickup artist trying out the same old tired line. What's the matter with you?*

"She did, did she? How nice for you." Pushing a hand through her hair in order to rearrange it behind her ears, Elizabeth looked up at him and smiled, unknowingly sending another stunning blow straight to Nick's midsection as she decided his eyes somehow managed to be both blue and green at the same time.

Nick returned her smile, unsurprised to find himself wondering if all their children would have such beautiful, clear skin. "Yes, she did. And then she put a bandage on it, whether it needed it or not."

"You were a very lucky child," Elizabeth told him as he bent down to pick up the roasting pan and place it on a nearby countertop, barely suppressing her desire to lean down herself and run her fingers through his thick, dark hair. "I was always told to stop sniffling, blow my nose and run out to play like a good girl."

Nick felt a sudden, mad urge to take Elizabeth in his arms and kiss her from head to toe to make up for any time she had cried and been denied comfort.

"I'm sorry," he heard himself say inanely, holding on to the countertop because he felt in danger of falling into the velvet soft depths of her wide brown eyes. Her lips would taste like sugary cotton candy, he was sure of it, and he had to hold himself back before he took her in his arms right in the middle of the sales floor. He shook his head slowly, wondering when it was that he had lost his mind. *I've heard about love at first sight, but this is ridiculous!*

"There now," Elizabeth said, pushing the roasting pan away from the edge of the countertop, deciding it might be safest if she pretended she didn't know who he was. "If you think you can trust me not to assault you with a pastry brush or something, perhaps you can tell me how I may help you. I'm Elizabeth Chatham, by the way, and although I'm fairly new here, I believe I can be of assistance. What will it be? A four-slice toaster? A microwave? Or how about a gourmet frying pan?"

"How about lunch, Ms. Chatham? You see, I'm not a customer. I'm Nicholas Lancaster, and your boss," Nick replied, forgetting that it was only a few minutes past ten, and the store had just opened.

Elizabeth tilted her head to one side, the single dimple in her left cheek making a startling appearance as she looked up into his face, and with her answer made Nicholas Lancaster the happiest man on the face of the earth. "Thank goodness!" she said frankly, feeling her heart skip yet another beat. "I thought you'd never ask."

"Liz, pass the potatoes, wouldya? Liz? *Liz!* Hey, *Lizzie,* I want the spuds!"

Elizabeth shook her head, as if waking from a dream, and looked across the dinner table at her brother. "I'm sorry. Did you say something, Johnny?"

"Oh, brother!" Fourteen-year-old Paul rolled his eyes and nudged John with his elbow. "Liz looks like Meggie when she's mooning over some creep. You know—stupid."

"You always look stupid, *Paulie,*" Megan, who had just turned seventeen and was totally disenchanted with younger men—especially younger brothers—shot back, her voice spanning two octaves.

"All right, children. That will be quite enough, thank you." The three youngest Chatham children were immediately reduced to glaring at one another in silence. Gloria Chatham, resuming her seat at the foot of the table after bringing in a fresh loaf of bread from the kitchen, shook her head and complained to her husband, "Jack, can't you keep these children from open warfare for two minutes?"

Smiling at his wife, Jack Chatham then turned and winked at his mother, who sat to his right at the other end of the long table, before answering. "Nope. One minute is about thirty seconds over my limit. Besides, I can bellow all day long and they just keep right on talking. You're doing a great job, hon. You just tell them to stop and they stop. I don't know how you do it, and I'm not going to go upsetting the applecart now by trying to take your job away from you. Right, Mom?"

"Don't look at me, son. For myself, I'd like to send them all to reform school, nasty little beggars."

Megan giggled, then leaned over to give her grandmother a kiss on the cheek. "Oh, Gammy, you're such a monster. Last week you wanted us all to sign up with the Foreign Legion. You even rented *Beau Geste* for the VCR."

"Yes, well," the woman muttered, shifting in her seat, "I figured it was worth a shot. You can't blame an old lady for trying."

"Gammy, you're adorable! Old lady, indeed. You'll never be old; not if you live to be a thousand." Elizabeth leaned back in her chair and lovingly cast her gaze around the table. "You may all think I should be locked up for saying this but, gosh, am I glad to be home. Unbelievable as it seems, I really missed this madhouse when I was living in New York."

Rose Chatham, her petite blond beauty only slightly faded with age, blushed at her oldest granddaughter's backhanded compliment, then declared, "You're pretty adorable yourself, sweetheart. Now pass John the potatoes before he climbs across the table on all fours to get them himself. My stars, child, you were a million miles away a minute ago. You meet your Mr. Right today or something?"

Seeing her oldest daughter's obvious embarrassment at her mother-in-law's blunt question, Gloria broke in hurriedly. "Elizabeth, is that a new sweater? I particularly like the color; it looks lovely on you."

"This old thing? Why, no, I—"

"Of course it looks lovely," Rose interrupted, "it matches her flaming cheeks. You don't really think you can hide anything from your old Gammy now do you, child? Come on, what's his name? Did you meet him at work or did he try to pick you up on your walk home? I told you that you should take my car. I hardly ever use it anymore, and the bus stops at the corner if I really want to go anywhere all that badly. I ride half fare, you know, now that I'm an official old lady. Is he handsome, or are you just feeling desperate after our little talk last night? Well, don't just sit there, child—talk to me!"

"I think Elizabeth's waiting for you to take a breath, Mom, so that she can get a word in edgewise," Jack suggested, earning himself a speaking look from his parent. "Uh—right. I'll stay out of it. John, save some of those potatoes in case somebody else wants a second helping. I know the coach told you to bulk up, but you don't have to do it all in one sitting."

Shoveling one last heaping spoonful onto his plate, John passed the bowl over to his father. "Coach says I need more upper-body strength for basketball. I have to build up my muscles. Here you go, Dad. Hey, can't you see Liz going to work in Gammy's car? What a riot!"

Megan leaned over to whisper to Elizabeth. "If you ask me, Johnny's got plenty of upper-body muscle already—and it's all right between his overgrown ears."

Paul, not hearing his sister's remark, quickly contradicted his brother, saying, "I don't know if that would be so bad. One look at that old heap of Gammy's and her boss would give her a raise right on the spot, just so she wouldn't leave that wreck in his parking lot anymore."

"If you've all quite finished?" Rose interjected dryly before clearing her throat and commanding: "Megan, I think your mother needs some help with the dishes. Boys, take a hike before I change my mind about driving you over to Eddie's this Saturday. Jack, go read your paper in the living room. Elizabeth Anne—*sit!*"

Elizabeth, who had risen along with her mother and was already beginning to clear away the dinner dishes, her own nearly untouched plate included, sighed in defeat and sank back into her chair. Gloria Chatham might maintain control through her own basic good nature and femininity, but Rose Chatham had no time for the niceties. Age, she always said, had its privileges, a theory Elizabeth had been hearing from the woman as long as she could remember, and she knew she had only two choices open to her when Gammy gave an order.

She could sit down and answer the woman's questions, or she could run away. The only problem was that she couldn't hide forever. Sooner or later her grandmother would find her and proceed to hurl embarrassing questions at her until she had ferreted out every last secret. With Gammy, nothing was sacred, and she had the tenacity of a bulldog when it came to getting her own way.

The fact that her oldest granddaughter had been living on her own for the past three years in Manhattan hadn't changed Rose's assumption that she was entitled to know about every facet of the young woman's life, and to have some say in whatever Elizabeth did. Elizabeth thought fleetingly of that saying "you can't go home again," and smiled. You could go home again, she decided, but only if you left your newfound independence on the doorstep.

She decided to give in early—at least this time—and save her energy for Gammy's reaction to what she had to say. "Yes, Gammy," Elizabeth agreed as the rest of her family escaped as quickly as they could. Holding her hands up in front of her as if trying to ward off blows, she whimpered, "Anything you say, copper. I'll talk, honest. Only please, no thumbscrews."

"Elizabeth, behave yourself," her mother warned quietly as she returned to the dining room to gather the last of the dinner dishes onto a tray. "Gammy's only being curious."

"Gammy's only being nosy, Mother," Elizabeth corrected, handing her mother a glass. "But I don't mind. She's old now, you know, and has to live vicariously through us."

"*Elizabeth!*" Gloria exclaimed, shocked, while Rose laughed out loud.

"Oh, Elizabeth," Rose complimented happily, "much as I love those three ruffians, you'll always be my favorite. You're just as sassy as I ever was. Gloria, close your mouth and go away. Your daughter and I have some catching up to do—don't we, dear? You went straight to work at Lancaster's the moment you moved back home, and I hardly ever see you. I knew more about you when you were kicking up your heels in New York. At least then I had your letters."

Elizabeth reached her hands across the lace tablecloth and squeezed her grandmother's heavily ringed fingers in her own. "I didn't mean to ignore you since I'm home, Gammy, but you know how it is in retailing. The hours are awful and, besides, I have a whole department to learn, a whole new system of doing things."

Gloria looked at her daughter and Rose without jealousy. She knew the two shared a special bond, and had since Rose had been widowed and moved in with her and Jack when Elizabeth was just about ten and Megan was a baby. Both of them had felt like displaced persons, Rose missing the husband she had lived with since she had been a girl of sixteen, and Elizabeth confused by the presence of a baby in the house. The two had been naturally drawn to each other.

When John and Paul had followed Megan into the world within three years, Gloria had been more than happy to have Rose's help with her oldest child. If she had missed out on some girlish confidences during Elizabeth's teenage years, Rose's renewed interest in life had made that loss easier to bear.

Gloria Chatham was a sensitive, loving woman, and her greatest happiness came in seeing those around her happy. Now, able to detect a slight glimmering of tears in Rose's eyes, she quietly withdrew into the kitchen, leaving the two good friends alone.

"So, child," Rose said after a few moments, "what's his name?"

Elizabeth withdrew her hands and laid them in her lap. Concentrating her gaze on her tightly clasped fingers she whispered, "Nicholas—Nicholas Lancaster."

"Nicholas Lancaster," Rose repeated quietly, her own hands sliding slowly from the tabletop and onto her lap. "Henry Lancaster's boy? How about that. Whoever would have thought it."

"You know Mr. Lancaster, Gammy? I understand he retired from Lancaster's a couple of years ago, although he still comes into the main store fairly often. Gee, I didn't think about it before, but the two of you must be about the same age. Did you go to school together? Is Mr. Lancaster one of the million boys who chased you until Grandpa caught you? Was he the one with the rumble seat? I'm all ears. Tell me *everything*!"

"Down, girl, down." Rose shook her head, banishing some private thought, and countered, "Don't think you can change the subject and start me off on one of my stories, young lady. So, this young man of yours is also your boss. You're my granddaughter through and through, starting right at the top. I've always said it's just as easy to love a rich man as it is to love a poor man, not that I would have traded your Grandpa for ten millionaires."

Elizabeth flushed hotly, her brown eyes flashing. "He's not my 'young man,' Gammy, and his being rich has nothing to do with it. Besides, we only had lunch together—a business lunch. Really, in a minute you'll be calling Father Chuck to have the banns posted."

"Is he handsome? As I recall, Henry Lancaster was quite a looker."

Elizabeth began tapping her heels agitatedly against the parquet floor beneath the table. "His face wouldn't exactly make little children run from him, screaming."

Rose grinned—wickedly, to Elizabeth's mind. "A regular Adonis, is he? And he's crazy about you, of course. Oh, to be young again!"

Suddenly it wasn't the same. Elizabeth had always confided in her grandmother, told her all about her dates, every detail of her conversations with her many boyfriends. But this was different. This was private; her feelings were too new, too intense to be shared, even with Rose. Jumping to her feet, Elizabeth declared airily, "You've been watching too many soap operas, Gammy. We met, we had lunch together in the store cafeteria, we're having dinner together tomorrow night. That's the beginning, the middle and the end of it. Honestly, Gammy, Nicholas Lancaster is just another date."

Rose stood up, carefully refolding her napkin and placing it back on the table. "We had roast beef, mashed potatoes and gravy for dinner tonight, Elizabeth," she intoned importantly, as if she were a prosecutor about to reveal an important piece of evidence. "Your all-time favorite. I made the gravy nice and dark, especially for you."

"My goodness," Elizabeth said warily, "now that's a news flash. So what?"

"Sooo," her grandmother replied, dragging out the word on purpose, "you only ate three teeny bites of meat and two forkfuls of potatoes. You didn't even touch the corn, but as you never were a good sport about your yellow vegetables, I won't count that against you. Besides, the meat and potatoes are evidence enough. You, my precious child, are in love."

"*In love!*" Elizabeth shouted, then quickly lowered her voice because, in the Chatham household, even the walls seemed to have ears. "In love?" she repeated much more softly. "Don't be ridiculous. So I didn't have much of an appetite tonight. Big deal. I don't think we'll have to alert the media. Maybe I just wasn't hungry. It happens, you know, impossible as that is for you to believe. Now please excuse me, I'm going to help Megan and Mother finish up in the kitchen."

"What's today's date, Elizabeth?" Rose asked as her granddaughter turned to escape from the room.

"September twelfth. Why?"

Rose walked around the table to reach up and kiss her granddaughter on the cheek. "Good. That gives us just about enough time. Christmas weddings are so romantic, don't you think?"

Elizabeth opened her mouth to speak, then closed it again, knowing there was no arguing with her grandmother once the woman got something into her head. Sometimes—almost all the time—it was easier, and less aggravating, to say nothing. Leaning down to return the woman's kiss, Elizabeth only whispered, "Bah, humbug, darling," before heading for the safety of the kitchen.

Rose watched her granddaughter's retreating back until the kitchen door swung closed behind her. "Hank Lancaster," she mused aloud. "Let's just hope the son's got as much gumption as the father."

Chapter Two

Nick was fairly certain the strip steak had been prepared just the way he liked it, but he couldn't have sworn to it, any more than he could remember if that had been orange or raspberry sherbet he and Elizabeth had shared for dessert.

As they walked across the nearly deserted parking lot to the car, Nick smiled in the darkness, the warm glow that had filled him from the moment he had met Elizabeth at the employee's entrance having multiplied a dozen times over as the evening progressed.

"The prime rib was really delicious, Mr. Lancaster," Elizabeth told him as they stopped on the passenger side of the car and he unlocked the door for her. "I don't believe I've ever tasted better, even in New York. How was your steak?"

Nick opened the car door before answering, his forearm resting lightly against the roof as he faced her, effectively blocking her way. "Beats me," he admitted honestly, frowning down at her. "They could have put boiled shoe leather in front of me, for all the attention I was paying to what I ate. Elizabeth, we've been talking almost nonstop all evening, about anything and everything, right? So, tell me; why don't you call me by my first name?"

"Why don't I...well, um, I...after all, you're my...that is to say, we've really only just met, and—" She stopped talking and hung her head before adding, "Feel free to stop me at any time, okay?"

Nick lifted her chin with one finger, freeing her face from the sleek curtain of hair that had fallen forward to hide her perfect features. "The workday ended for us at six o'clock. Your boss didn't ask you out to dinner, Elizabeth, I did. Allow me to introduce myself. The name is Lancaster. Nicholas Charles Lancaster, actually, but my friends call me Nick. Hello, Elizabeth."

Tilting her head to one side, Elizabeth smiled up at him, her brown eyes twinkling with amusement. Her voice suddenly lower, huskier, breathier, she said, "Well, hello there yourself—Nick."

He had always been rather indifferent to his name, thinking it ordinary and not all that spectacular, but when he heard his name on Elizabeth's lips, suddenly it sounded important, even majestic. Swallowing hard, Nick pushed himself away from the car and slid his arms lightly around Elizabeth's back. "Promise me you won't scream, please. I've been longing to do this from the first moment we met."

"I—I prom—" Elizabeth said on a sigh, her eyelids fluttering closed as his mouth descended slowly, searching for hers, only to pop open wide as his warm lips claimed hers, setting off an instantaneous explosion deep inside her body. She was overwhelmed with sensation, and a sudden physical weakness enveloped her, causing her eyelids to close once more and her knees to wobble. Raising her trembling hands to his shoulders, she clung to him as her world narrowed to exclude all but the two of them.

She fit into his arms perfectly, her lips molded to precisely the right shape beneath his, her softness complementing his lean, muscular frame. She was his other half. She made him whole. She was the reason he had been born; his reason to go on living. He loved her—had loved this woman from the moment he first saw her.

And if he told her all this now she'd probably call a cop and have him locked up. Nick withdrew his lips a fraction, his embrace slackening as he prepared to back away and put some sanity-inducing space between them. He was being Noble Nick, he told himself, he was being civilized.

But then he made one small mistake. With their faces only inches apart, he opened his eyes and looked straight into hers. She was looking at him with her heart laid bare, with all her secrets revealed and his for the taking. He realized that she had felt it, too, this wild, unbelievably sweet communion.

"Again, Elizabeth," he whispered hoarsely, not even aware he had spoken, and once more they kissed each other, held each other, alone together in the dark, the rest of the world forgotten.

"You have the latest sales figures for the Baltimore branch yet, Nick?" Henry Lancaster sat at one end of the long conference table, his back to his son. When there was no answer to his question he swiveled in his seat to see Nick standing in front of the floor-to-ceiling window, staring out over the city. "Nicholas, wake up. You're woolgathering again. It has to be a woman. What's her name?"

His father's words rudely interrupting his pleasant daydream, Nick reluctantly moved away from the window and walked back over to the conference table, resting his palms against the gleaming teak surface as he leaned forward and looked into his father's astonishingly bright blue eyes. "Tell me something, Dad. How did you know that you were in love with Mother? I mean, *really* in love?"

"*Really* in love? Well now, let me think about that for a minute." Henry sat back in the plush leather chair, cupping his hands behind his neck as a slow, warm smile softened his thin, angular features. He thought for a few moments, his smile growing wider, then said, "It was fairly easy, actually, Nick. Your mother told me."

Shaking his head, Nick laughed out loud. "Mother? Shy, quiet Mother? I can't picture it."

Henry rose and walked over to the window. He stood staring through the glass as his son had done a few minutes earlier, his eyes narrowed as if he were watching a movie unroll in front of him, a private screening of his most cherished memories. "Your mother was quite a woman, Nick, quite a lady. Genteel, well-bred and polite to a fault. But that didn't mean she was weak. Oh no, on the contrary. She was no shrinking violet, and she wasn't afraid to fight to get what she wanted."

"Fight, Dad? Are you sure you're talking about *my* mother?" Nick teased lovingly, as his memories of his mother always centered around visions of the woman sitting at the grand piano in the living room, or arranging homegrown flowers in a cut crystal vase, or presiding at an elegant dinner party. "What did she do, flip you for who got to pop the question?"

Henry turned his head in his son's direction and Nick could clearly see the love the older man still held for the wife who had died ten years earlier. "Your mother and I dated for nearly two years, although I only saw her once a week, on Saturday nights. Your grandfather's business was just getting off the ground, and I was working almost around the clock. Anyway, I think she had begun to believe I was taking her for granted, you know, believing she'd always be there, waiting for me to have the time to see her, and she decided to do something about it."

Nick rubbed a hand across his chin, remembering that, no matter the season, no matter how busy the business was, his father was always home by six o'clock to have dinner with his wife and son and spend his evenings with them. "I take it she found a way to change your life-style."

"That she did, son," Henry replied with a chuckle. "For three straight weeks your mother was 'unavailable,' until I couldn't work, I couldn't eat, I couldn't sleep—all I could do was think of her. When she finally agreed to see me she sat me down and explained that I loved her, and it was time we started talking about getting married. It's a good thing she didn't wait any longer to pop the question, too, even if the war did keep us apart for four years. As it was, it took us more than fifteen years to produce you.''

Nick gave a low whistle of appreciation. ''So Mother actually proposed to you? I can't believe it.''

''Believe it, Nick,'' Henry declared, going over to put his arm around his son's shoulders. ''Your mother and Rosie O'Hanlon—between the two of them, I didn't stand a chance.''

''Who's Rosie O'Hanlon?''

Henry smiled again, conjuring up a mental picture of his wife's next-door neighbor all those years ago. ''Lord, I haven't thought about Rosie in years. Now there was a young lady who knew what she wanted and went after it until she got it. Married at sixteen or some such nonsense, I believe your mother heard later. It wasn't unusual then for girls to leave school and start families at that age. I'll bet the poor fellow never knew what hit him. Anyway, Rosie aided and abetted your mother in the whole scheme, although your mother didn't let me in on that little secret until our tenth anniversary, of course. But, let me tell you, I never regretted being tricked—not for a single moment of all our years together.''

Nick's hazel eyes clouded as he thought about his mother. ''She was a great lady, Dad. I believe I miss her almost as much as you do.''

Henry sighed, gave his son's back a few gentle pats and resumed his seat. ''So, now that we've had that little trip down memory lane, tell me—what's her name?''

Nick's smile was glowing. ''Elizabeth.''

Henry nodded consideringly. ''Elizabeth, huh. Nice. She have a last name?''

''What?'' At the mention of her name, Nick had slipped once more into a pleasant daydream. ''Oh, of course. Sorry, Dad. Her name is Chatham. Elizabeth Chatham. She's our new housewares buyer.''

''Chatham . . . Chatham,'' Henry repeated, mulling the name over in his mind. ''Sounds familiar, but I can't place it right now. So, you want me to tell you if you're in love, is that it? You're nearly thirty-two years old, Nick. I doubt if this could be puppy love. How long have you known this Elizabeth?''

"Two weeks today," Nick admitted, knowing two weeks wasn't a very long time—especially to a man who had dated for over two years and still had to be shocked into proposing. "But we've seen each other nearly every night. I'd like you to meet her, Dad. She's really wonderful.''

Henry looked at his only son, who appeared as earnest as he had as a young boy trying to talk him into buying a puppy, and felt an unfamiliar tightening in his chest. Nick had dated dozens of young women over the years, but he'd never brought any of them home. This Elizabeth Chatham must be some young woman.

"I think Friday evening would be fine, Nick. I'll have Mrs. Gillespie fix something really special. Now why don't you go downstairs and check with Ms. Chatham to see if it's all right with her, while I try to find those Baltimore sales figures. One of us has to keep his mind on the job, you know, and from the look on your face I can see I won't get a lick of work out of you until you've talked to her.''

Nick's face split into a wide grin as he pushed a thick manila file toward his father and quickly headed for the door. "Thanks, Dad. I'll be back in fifteen minutes, twenty minutes, tops—I promise.''

Pulling the folder in front of him, Henry folded his hands on top of it and opened his heart to memories of his wife, his smile wistful, yet happy. "She may be wonderful, this Elizabeth," he whispered aloud in the quiet room, "but she'll have to go some to hold a candle to you, my darling Katherine.''

Elizabeth was lying on her back underneath the frilly white eyelet canopy that, since her earliest memories, had transformed her ordinary bed into a fairy-tale land whenever she wished. A gift from her grandmother, the high, wide four-poster bed had served as a comforting refuge when the world got to be too much for her—her quiet "thinking place." And when she drew the floor-length draperies around the bed, nobody was allowed to disturb her, except for her grandmother, of course, who had always been welcome.

But not tonight. Tonight Elizabeth wanted, needed, to be alone. She had disappeared upstairs as quickly as possible after helping with the dinner dishes, feeling Gammy's too-observant eyes on her all through the meal, so that she had choked down every bit of food on her plate, even the green beans, which she had always hated.

The last thing she needed was for Gammy to give her another third-degree grilling about her poor appetite and Nicholas Lancaster. After two weeks of Elizabeth's seeing him every day at work and nearly every night for dinner, Gammy was already walking around the house humming the "Wedding March." It was embarrassing.

Not only was the situation embarrassing, but it was confusing. Elizabeth's entire life had been disrupted, and she had let it happen. She knew that she had allowed herself to be totally absorbed in Nick, to the exclusion of anything and anybody else. John had complained only that morning that Elizabeth had missed his first freshman basketball game after promising to attend, and Megan had scolded her for failing to take her shopping at Lancaster's for a new pair of jeans.

Elizabeth squirmed uncomfortably on the mattress, feeling guilty. Some sister she was. She had moved back home because she'd missed her family, and yet now she was farther away from them than when she had worked in New York City and traveled home by bus one weekend every month.

Her parents hadn't said anything to her so far, but Elizabeth had seen the concern in her mother's eyes. *They think I'm moving too fast,* Elizabeth decided silently, *and they just might be right. I don't know what's going on, how I feel, even how I should feel. This is all so new, so different, for me to understand it.*

"Hi, Liz." Megan's voice was a plaintive whine. "I can come in, can't I? I mean, you don't have the curtains pulled or anything."

Elizabeth's first reaction was to remind her sister that, even if the bed's draperies were open, the door to her room had been closed, but she stopped herself in time and only said, "Sure, Meg, come on in. I was only resting my legs for a few minutes. The worst thing about retailing is being on your feet all day. There was a one-day sale today and I had to help out on the floor."

"Oh. Gee, that's rough. I'm sorry." Megan stared at the tip of her left sneaker, the one she was digging into the deep rose shag rug.

Elizabeth looked blank for a moment, then sat up and slapped a hand against her forehead as the realization hit her. "Your jeans! Lancaster's is open late tonight because of the sale and you want me to take you over there—oh, Meggie, of course I will. I'm just sorry I didn't think of it myself."

Megan brightened instantly, her freckled face rosy with pleasure. "And that dopey Paulie said you wouldn't take me! Oh, Liz, you're the best sister ever! I'll hunt up Dad's keys and meet you at the car. You'll just love the jeans I want. They're just like my friend Sandy's—all faded and with holes in the knees—really neat!"

Collapsing back down on her pillows, Elizabeth gave a weak laugh. Megan already owned a half-dozen pairs of faded jeans with holes in them. The only thing wrong with them was that those weren't designer holes, they were only old-age holes. As much as Elizabeth hated to admit it, sometimes it seemed true—people would buy anything, as long as it was considered fashionable.

"No wonder I like the housewares department," she mused, searching under the bed for her sneakers. "There's no such thing as a designer potato peeler. Of course," she added consideringly, "there *are* all those fancy food processors that do everything but sit up and—"

"Liz!" Megan's screech swooped up the stairwell and into the bedroom. "I've got Dad's car keys. You coming or what?"

Two hours later, their booth loaded with bright blue-and-white striped plastic shopping bags, Megan and Elizabeth sat in the store restaurant, Elizabeth sipping a cup of coffee while watching her sister devour a double-dutch hot-fudge sundae.

"You sure you don't want a bite, Liz?" Megan asked, licking a dollop of fudge from the back of the spoon. "This is really great."

"Hmm?" Elizabeth had been quietly observing a small group of men sitting at a table in the far corner of the restaurant. His back was turned to her, but she was sure Nick was one of them. He had told her he had an important business meeting tonight. "Uh, no thanks, Meg," she said as her sister repeated her offer, stiffening slightly when the four men rose politely as a beautifully dressed redhead joined them at the table. "I'm not hungry."

Megan peered inquiringly at her sister, then turned around in her chair to see what had put such a sad look on Elizabeth's face. "Wow! Why can't I do that with my hair, Liz? Do you think this stupid red frizz will ever look all warm and coppery like that? Do you think she's a model or something?"

The redhead slid off the forest-green wool coat she had worn into the restaurant and the man Elizabeth had thought was Nick signaled for a waitress to take it. It *was* Nick, and the redhead was sitting down right beside him, her beautiful, perfectly made-up face raised beguilingly as she thanked him for holding her chair.

"Red and green," Elizabeth muttered nastily. "How perfectly ordinary. The woman has no imagination, no imagination at all."

"Gee, Liz," Megan leaned across the table to whisper eagerly, "you sound real angry. Do you know that woman or something?"

Realizing that she was being petty, Elizabeth firmly returned her gaze to the table and her sister. "No, I don't know her, Megan. I was just being catty—and stupid. Please forgive me."

Megan took another spoonful of her sundae. "Oh, darn, Liz, don't go getting all stuffy on me. Come on, you can tell me. Is she one of your Nick Lancaster's old girlfriends? Tell me all the dirt."

Elizabeth propped her elbow on the table and her chin in her hand. Looking once more toward the table in the corner, she grumbled, "I don't know, and I don't care. And he's not *my* Nicholas Lancaster."

Now Megan laughed out loud. "Oh, brother, Gammy was right—you have got it *bad*! When are you going to bring this guy home so we can meet him? You always go out straight from here. Mom's beginning to think you're ashamed of us, but Gammy said if Dad promises to chain John and Paul in the basement she's sure you'll bring him home someday. Liz, you look strange. What's wrong?"

Elizabeth sat up straight and spread her napkin more fully over her lap, trying to hide her old jeans. "You want to meet Nick Lancaster, Megan? Well, don't look now, but he's coming this way. Do I look all right?"

"He's coming this—where? Which one of them is he? Do you look all right? Of course you do. You always do. How do I look? Is he really coming over here? What color is his hair? Is he wearing a—"

"Hello, Elizabeth." Nick's voice was low, intimate, and to Megan's ears obviously extremely sexy. "I thought I saw you sitting over here."

"—suit?" Megan finished on a sigh, looking up at Nick, her mouth opened wide. *"Oh, wow,"* she gushed, too quietly for Nick to hear her over the low hum of conversation in the crowded restaurant.

"Hello, Nicholas," Elizabeth answered, wishing her voice didn't sound so thin, so strained. What was the matter with her? She was reacting even more immaturely than her teenage sister. "I thought I saw you earlier, when we first came in. Is your meeting over?"

Waving his companions on their way and promising to catch up with them in a few minutes, Nick pulled out a chair and sat down beside Elizabeth before introducing himself to Megan. "Elizabeth has told me all about you, Megan," he offered, smiling down at the girl who was staring at him as if he had suddenly grown an extra head. "You're on the school newspaper, aren't you?"

Megan swallowed with obvious difficulty. "Feature—er, I'm the feature editor."

"Oh, really?" Nicholas responded, looking toward Elizabeth. "You know, several years ago Lancaster's worked with many of the local high-school papers, using our Junior World fashions for models chosen by the feature editor for newspaper articles three or four times a year. We supplied our store photographer for the pictures and each feature editor wrote up the copy. We did sport clothes—for both boys and girls—and trendy wear and, in the spring, prom gowns. It was really very successful. Megan, do you think your adviser would like to try the idea again?"

Elizabeth was worried that she might have to reach across the table and physically restrain her sister from grabbing Nick and covering him with kisses.

"Would it?" Megan shrieked, her cornflower-blue eyes wide with excitement. "Oh, wow! Mr. German will really freak! I mean, he'll just jump at the—I mean, I'm sure Mr. German will consider it, Mr. Lancaster. And *I'd* get to pick the models and write the stories? Oh, Liz, I could pick Sandy, and Marcie, and—"

"I know I'm going out on a limb here, Nick, but I think she likes the idea," Elizabeth interrupted dryly before adding, "You don't have to do this, you know."

"The series was very effective, as I recall, Elizabeth, and Megan's school probably won't be the only one I contact," he assured her before rising once more and reaching into his jacket pocket for his business card. "Megan, you have Mr. German phone me and we'll arrange the first session, all right?"

Nick then shook her hand, once more reducing Megan to unintelligible monosyllables, and she could barely choke out a polite thank-you before holding the business card in front of her with both hands and staring at it as if it were printed on purest gold.

"Elizabeth," he went on, looking down at her, "I really have to go now. I have to show Mrs. Halstead around the jewelry department."

Elizabeth ran her tongue around her dry lips. He was talking about the beautiful redhead. "Mrs. Halstead? Is she interested in jewelry?"

Nick smiled and the last of the ice melted from around Elizabeth's heart. "I guess you could say that, sweetheart. She and her husband own one of the largest freshwater pearl outlets in the country. He's home nursing a sprained back and she's been sent to scout us out, to see if Lancaster's is worthy of their product. I think she's pretty impressed so far, but I don't want to leave her alone with the vice presidents too long."

"No, no, of course not!" Elizabeth suddenly felt wonderful, as if she had just taken in a refreshing lungful of sweet spring air. "You'd better not keep her waiting."

"I'll see you for lunch tomorrow as usual?"

Elizabeth's smile faded. They had lunched together almost every day, either by accident or design, but tomorrow was her day off and she had promised she would help her grandmother can the last of this season's tomatoes before going to John's basketball game right after school. "I can't," she said at last, her disappointment obvious.

"Oh," Nick commented hollowly, causing Megan to look at her sister and wink. "Well then, I'll just have to wait until tomorrow night. Dad said to come around seven, if that's all right with you?"

"I'll be ready," she assured him, then watched him as he made his way through the tables and out of the restaurant.

"You'll be ready, all right," Megan said. "God, Liz, why didn't you tell me he was such a hunk?"

Elizabeth's smile was dreamy as she turned back to face her sister. "Yes, he is, isn't he?"

"Oh, Lordy!" Megan derided before downing the last of her cola. "Gammy sure called it right this time. You're crazy about the guy, Liz. And you know what? I think he's crazy about you, too."

"Don't read too much into this, Meg," Elizabeth warned, aware that her heart had skipped a beat at her sister's words. "We've only been seeing each other for a couple of weeks."

"Sure," Megan shot back. "And you wanted to pull that redhead's hair out because you don't like green coats. Cut me a break here, Liz. My sister's gone bonkers for Nicholas Lancaster. Gee, do you think if you marry him he'll let our whole family use the employee discount?"

"Megan, my dearest sister," Elizabeth said woodenly, "shut up and eat your ice cream."

Chapter Three

"Nervous?"

Elizabeth fought her way into the buttercup-yellow silk-and-angora-blend sweater, her head finally poking through the proper opening so that her chestnut curls bounced free to swirl around her face. "Nervous, Gammy?" she repeated on a slight laugh, carefully adjusting the sweater's three-quarter-length sleeves. "Nervous doesn't even begin to cover it. I'm terrified! There, that does it. I bought this outfit last night when I went shopping with Megan. What do you think?"

Rose Chatham sat on the edge of the high mattress, her slim legs lazily swinging back and forth a good ten inches above the floor. "You look like a pretty statue carved out of freshly churned butter, Elizabeth; good enough to eat. That muted shade of yellow has always been a good color for you. But," she offered kindly, "I do think it would look even better if you wore the skirt. Warmer, too."

Elizabeth pulled a face at her grandmother's teasing, snatched the sweater-knit skirt from the bed, and stepped into it. After donning the long matching cardigan and slipping her ivory-stockinged feet into slim bone-colored heels she stepped back to give Rose the full effect of the ensemble.

"All right, now what do you think? This outfit cost me a full week's salary, Gammy, even with my employee discount, so please, be gentle."

Rose hopped down from the bed and walked around her granddaughter, inspecting her from every angle. Elizabeth was a stunningly beautiful young woman, both inside and out, but tonight she positively glowed. *If Hank Lancaster does anything to burst this child's bubble,* Rose decided, *I will personally cut his heart out!*

"Well? Do I pass muster, Gammy?" Elizabeth asked when her grandmother didn't speak.

"You look wonderful, Elizabeth—*almost* as pretty as I did the day I caught your grandfather," Rose assured her, "except for one small thing."

Elizabeth raced over to the free-standing brass mirror and peered into it intently. "What is it? Do I look pale? I still have to put on my lipstick, but I was afraid I'd get some on the sweater."

"A little war paint wouldn't hurt," Rose agreed, "but that wasn't what I meant. You go sit at your vanity table and fix your lips, Elizabeth, and I'll be right back."

Elizabeth watched as her grandmother left the room, then did as she was told, carefully blotting her lips on a tissue just as Rose came up behind her and told her to close her eyes.

Stiffening slightly as she felt Rose's hands lift her hair to fasten something behind her neck, Elizabeth opened her eyes to see her grandmother's treasured single-strand pearl necklace lying against the soft knit of her sweater. "Oh, Gammy," she breathed, overcome with emotion, "these are the pearls Grandpa gave you on your last wedding anniversary before he—I can't wear this! What if the string broke? What if I lost all the pearls?"

"You won't lose them," Rose insisted, handing Elizabeth the matching drop earrings and watching while she put them on. "Besides, if you did, I'd just forgive you like the wonderful woman I am, and then I'd throw this lovely new outfit in the clothes dryer—on High. No, I'm just kidding. Really, dear, I'm not worried a bit.''

Elizabeth put up a hand to settle the necklace more smoothly around her throat and then touched her fingers to her ears. ''They're the most beautiful pearls I've ever seen, such a rich, creamy shade. Grandpa always had excellent taste—in women as well as jewelry.''

Rose dropped a kiss on the top of Elizabeth's head and then quickly turned away, memories of her late husband making her eyes slightly misty. ''I always intended them for you on your wedding day anyway, but I don't want you going to Henry Lancaster's looking anything but your best. Now stop that sniffling before we both make fools of ourselves. Besides, I thought I just heard a car door, and I want to give this Nick of yours the once-over. Just because your parents are out at that bowling banquet doesn't mean this Lancaster fellow is going to think there's no one here who gives two hoots about how late he brings you home.''

Elizabeth blew her nose and gave a small laugh. ''Do you remember my first really 'grown-up' date, Gammy?'' she asked, giving Rose a quick hug, which she knew was all her grandmother would tolerate.

''Tommy Something-or-other, if my memory serves,'' Rose recalled, checking her own appearance in the full-length mirror and deciding that, for an old lady, she didn't look that bad. ''A basketball player, like your brother John, wasn't he? All skinny legs and hip pockets, and a shirt collar three sizes too big for him.''

''Please, Gammy,'' Elizabeth protested, laughing. ''I'll have you know that Tommy Rothenberger was only the biggest catch in the entire junior class. All my girlfriends were green with envy.''

''Which doesn't say much for your junior class,'' Rose sniffed, giving her short curly hair a last pat. ''But I do remember the third degree your father gave that poor boy. I wonder if he ever fully recovered.''

'' 'Do you own a car, son?' he asked,'' Elizabeth recited, mimicking Jack Chatham's deep, gruff voice. ''And when poor Tommy admitted that his car was parked out front,

Dad really went on the attack. 'So, you drive, do you? Do you drive *fast*?' Honestly, by the time Dad was done, all I wanted to do was find a great big hole and hide in it. Tommy had me home by ten and never called again. I thought my life was over. I hated Dad for weeks.''

The doorbell rang and Elizabeth and Rose exchanged quick looks, their calming reminiscences immediately forgotten as Elizabeth nervously bit her lip and her grandmother reminded her granddaughter that she had supposedly outgrown that particular bad habit at the age of twelve.

"Hey, Lizzie," Paul's squeaky, half-grown-up voice bellowed from the narrow foyer, "your date's here. You comin' down or what?"

"So refined, so delicate. So absolutely elegant," Rose commented, her smile wry. "Remind me to have a talk with that boy, Elizabeth; perhaps my were-you-raised-in-a-barn? speech. Now let's go downstairs quickly, before Paul and John decide to try a duet."

Taking up her new bone-colored leather envelope purse and a stylish mohair wool cape she had picked up that past year at Bloomingdale's for a song, Elizabeth walked toward the stairs, Rose close on her heels, only to stop, one hand on the dark mahogany bannister. "You are going to behave, Gammy, aren't you? I mean, I really like Nick, but he's an only child, and I don't think he's used to a madhouse like ours."

Rose looked at her granddaughter, looking so self-assured, so sophisticated—so New York—and saw through to the frightened little girl hiding beneath that sophistication. "And you're politely telling me you don't want me to scare him off. Don't worry, I know how important this young man is to you, honey. After all, he's the first person to ever come between us, isn't he?"

Elizabeth's eyes clouded at the unexpected sadness that had crept into her grandmother's voice. "Oh, Gammy, Nick hasn't come between us! Nobody could! I know I haven't come creeping into your room at midnight to tell you all about our dates like I used to, but that's because there's something different about it this time. I can't explain it, but I guess I'm being selfish with my happiness—and maybe even a little superstitious. I don't think I'm ready to share Nick yet, not even with you. I don't feel right talking about our time together; I don't know why. Please, Gammy, try to understand.''

"I do understand, my darling," Rose answered softly. "I really do, and that's probably why I'm a little sad, even though I'm also very happy for you. Now, go on downstairs and rescue poor Nick before Megan tries to work her wiles on him. She hasn't been able to stop talking about your Nick since she came home last night. If you don't watch it, you'll have all the Chatham women falling in love with him. In fact, just to be safe, I think I'll stay up here.''

Elizabeth kissed her grandmother again, frowning. "Then you aren't coming downstairs after all? I don't understand. You said you were anxious to meet Nick. Gammy, are you sure you aren't angry with me?''

Rose dismissed Elizabeth's question with a wave of her hand. "No, dear, I'm not angry. I've just decided that Nick Lancaster might be better off if he took his Chathams in small doses at first. I'm sure I'll soon get to see him a dozen times a week, if this dinner party at his father's means what I think it does.''

Elizabeth was sidetracked, as her grandmother wanted her to be. "Oh, Gammy, there you go again, dreaming silly dreams. Anyone would think you've already picked out names for your first great-grandchild.''

"John Henry after your grandfather and Nick's father if it's a boy—even if it does make him sound like a railroad engineer—and Katherine Anne, after Nick's mother and your maternal grandmother if it's a girl,'' Rose quipped immediately, winking at Elizabeth before turning around and heading back down the hall to her small combination bedroom and private sitting room.

"How did you know Nick's mother's name?'' Elizabeth called after her, careful to keep her voice low. "Just how well do you know Henry Lancaster?''

Rose stopped, turned around and wagged a finger at her granddaughter. "As I told you when you were eleven and you wanted to know how babies are made—*I* know everything, but that doesn't mean I have to tell *you* any more than you need to know. Have a wonderful time tonight, Elizabeth. You never looked more beautiful."

Putting out one foot to start her descent to the foyer and Nick, Elizabeth warned, "Just don't you dare fall asleep before I get home, Gammy. I want to tell you all about my evening. I *really* do."

Rose closed the door to her small apartment behind her, leaned against it, raised her eyes to the ceiling and spoke to her late husband. "Elizabeth and that young man are getting married, whether they know it yet or not. I can see the same look in that girl's eyes that I saw in yours when you came courting all those years ago. And I'll tell you something else, John; that girl is going to have the wedding you and I missed—the biggest, grandest wedding this town has ever seen. I can promise you that because I'm going to see to it, *personally*!"

It was quiet in the car as Nick turned onto Prospect Avenue and headed north on the narrow, tree-lined street. When they reached the intersection at Eighth Avenue, Elizabeth absently turned her head to look at the rambling, three-story brick-and-stucco Tudor house that had fascinated her since childhood.

"Oh, Nick, I just can't believe it," she was startled into saying. "When could that have happened? They're selling my house!"

Nick slowed the car to make the turn onto Eighth Avenue, then looked to his left to see the realtor's sign in the front yard of the house that sat on the southwest corner. "Your house, Elizabeth? That's funny; I thought we just left your house a minute ago. Or did you just hire those people to pretend to be your family?" he questioned lightly, before seeing her wistful expression.

"That was my family, all right," Elizabeth answered, twisting in her seat to look back at the house, "or at least as many of them that were home. Mom and Dad went to his bowling banquet and my grandmother stayed upstairs, er, resting." She turned forward in her seat once more with a sigh. "That house back there is my dream castle."

They didn't speak again for a while, as Nick could see that Elizabeth was lost in thought, her smooth brow furrowed. He left her alone, happy that she felt comfortable enough with him after the past two weeks to allow an occasional lapse in conversation. "Your dream castle? Sounds interesting," Nick said at last, interrupting her thoughts as they turned onto Macada Drive to enter an area Elizabeth knew to be very exclusive.

"Yes, it is, actually," Elizabeth agreed, willing to talk about the house if it would keep her from worrying about her upcoming meeting with Henry Lancaster, for with the turn into the residential area all her fears for the evening had returned. "Years ago, when the executives of Bethlehem Steel and other companies built their mansions, Prospect Avenue was what this area is now, not that it isn't still grand. But of all the beautiful houses, the Tudor always seemed to draw my attention."

Nick glanced over at Elizabeth and nearly ran the car into a ditch, as his attention was immediately grabbed by the expression on her face, the way her wide brown eyes had gone dark and soft with emotion. *Does she look like that when she thinks of me?* he asked himself silently, praying that she did. "Like a giant-size dollhouse?"

Elizabeth laughed, the sound pleasant to Nick's ears. "Probably. When I was little it absolutely fascinated me, what with its three-story stone turret and all those oddly placed mullion windows. There just has to be a second-floor gallery, if those windows in the middle of the house mean anything.

"Anyway," she continued, "Gammy and I would walk past it all the time when we were out for what she still calls her 'constitutional,' and she'd make up stories about the people who lived there. It's silly, but I almost think the owners should have asked my permission before putting it on the market."

Nick pulled the car into a long, curving driveway and cut the engine in front of his father's house before sliding an arm across the back of Elizabeth's bucket seat. "Do you want to satisfy your fantasy, Elizabeth?"

She turned to him, confused. "How? I doubt they'll open a house like that to the public."

Suddenly Nick felt all-powerful, like a magical genie who wanted nothing more than to grant this beautiful princess her every wish. "No, I don't think the realtor will need to do anything like that, but I can call and get us an appointment for a private showing."

Elizabeth didn't know what to say, how to react. It was one thing to joke about such an idea, but if the two of them were really going to look at houses—well, that sounded serious. Gammy would be delirious, for one thing, and she herself would have a hard time believing that Nick could still be classified as "just a date."

Besides, if she accepted, would she be sending him the wrong message? Would she be tacitly admitting that she loved him and wanted to marry him—or even worse, that she had decided the time was right to get married and he looked like acceptable husband material? Why hadn't they answered this sort of question in any of the how-to articles women's magazines were so fond of printing?

"Well, what do you say?" Nick prompted as Elizabeth remained silent, worried that he was moving too fast and wondering if she were trying to find a polite way of telling him to go peddle his papers somewhere else.

Elizabeth blinked twice, trying to bring Nick's face back into focus. He was so dear, sitting there with such an earnest, appealing expression; so unlike the corporate image he projected at Lancaster's. Her assistant, Judy Holland, wouldn't recognize him. Nicholas Lancaster was a *nice man*, and he was offering to do a nice thing. She was simply reading too much into a very mundane exercise. The house was for sale. They would look at the house. It was simple, very black-and-white. No strings attached.

"It certainly would be different," she said at last, her decision made. "Why not—let's do it!" Her heart skipped a beat as Nick showed his agreement by way of a long, slow, satisfying kiss.

Dinner had been wonderfully uneventful, with Henry Lancaster at home in the role of host, although he would never quite get used to seeing the empty chair facing him at the opposite end of the long dining-room table.

Henry had been openly pleased with Elizabeth, whom he had decided was not only beautiful but extremely intelligent, and their discussion of Lord Byron's *Don Juan* had lasted straight through the dessert course, with Nick surprised to find himself feeling the slightest twinge of jealousy as he had watched Elizabeth walk back into the living room on his father's arm.

Three hours later, after suffering through his father's proud exhibition of his son's baby pictures, Nick and Elizabeth were alone once more, walking hand in hand through the extensive rose garden Nick's mother had planted when he was a child.

"This reminds me of some of the English gardens I saw when I was in London last year on a buying trip. Even now, this late in the season, it's absolutely breathtaking." Elizabeth stopped beside a small statue of a cherub holding a water pitcher on his shoulder. "Oh, what a shame. Look, Nick, its nose is missing."

Nick slipped his arm around her back and Elizabeth instinctively snuggled against him. "I was afraid you might notice that. It's a remnant of my terrible youth, I'm ashamed to say."

"Aw, you did it with your little baseball," Elizabeth teased, looking up into his face in the faint light coming from the patio.

"Nope," Nick responded, flicking the tip of her nose with his finger. "I cannot tell a lie; I did it with my little slingshot. I was deadly within fifty feet."

Elizabeth pulled herself away just enough to turn and face him, her hands now resting on his elbows as his arms lightly encircled her waist. "Your slingshot? You're kidding! Oh, please, don't ever tell John or Paul; I can't bear to think of the consequences.''

Nick promised to keep the slingshot incident secret and they walked on, farther from the patio and deeper into the darkness. Elizabeth, her head resting lightly against his shoulder, took a deep breath of the crisp night air and her pulse leaped as a hint of his spicy cologne teased her nostrils. Involuntarily, she shivered.

"Cold?" Nick tightened his arm around her shoulders, his fingers taking delight in the softness of her sweater as he ran his hand rhythmically up and down her arm, a movement that sent another chill racing through her body. "We should go back to the house."

Trying to hide her disappointment, Elizabeth agreed, saying, "And then I probably should go home. I have to work tomorrow, you know, and my boss is a real stickler for having his employees arrive at work on time."

Nick's voice was low and menacing as he said, "Sounds like a real jerk, lady. Do ya want me ta take care of him for ya?"

Elizabeth laughed, shaking her head. This wasn't the first time they had playacted; both of them seemed to be able to speak their minds more freely if they made a game of it. Playing the game made Elizabeth happy, even while the need for it made her sad. "Oh, no, thank you, mister gangster, sir. You see, I may seem silly to you, but, I sorta like the guy."

"Oh, yeah, lady?" Nick pursued, staying in character. "Well, from what I hear from the boys in the mob, he sorta likes you, too. And that's no line," he ended in his own voice, although it sounded deeper and somewhat husky, even to his own ears.

They had kissed often since their first embrace in the parking lot of the restaurant, but by unspoken agreement they had been careful to limit those kisses to just before saying good-night. Their attraction had been too immediate, too electric, and it had been as if they were both holding back, determined to get to know each other better before allowing this powerful physical attraction to take control and overcome their better judgment.

They weren't teenagers who were falling in love with love. Elizabeth may have worried about that for a while, because she knew she had reached an age where her body was telling her it was time to find a mate, but this was only a vague self-imposed caution. In her heart she knew that this time it was different. This time it was right.

Nick had also been restraining his urge to claim Elizabeth for his own. He had been involved with other women over the years, had even thought he was in love a few times. But meeting Elizabeth had done something to him, had awakened feelings inside him that were foreign to him, and even a little bit frightening. It was as if he wanted to build a high fence around Elizabeth and post a warning against trespassers. He felt an almost overriding need to lay claim to her, to shout to the world that this woman—this wonderful, marvelous, perfect woman—was his, and his alone.

He hadn't needed his father's approval; Nick had been his own man for more than a dozen years. He hadn't taken Elizabeth home to meet his father as if she were some prize he had won or a beautiful art object he wished to have admired. If his father had hated Elizabeth on sight it would have hurt Nick, but it wouldn't have changed his high opinion of her.

He liked Elizabeth. He admired her. He felt comfortable with her. He felt alive with her. He wanted her. "Oh, hell," he said out loud as they stood so close together in his mother's night-dark garden, "I love her!"

Elizabeth, her mind working along much the same lines as his, gasped almost inaudibly and asked, "What—what did you say?"

Nick shut his eyes a moment, realizing he had spoken his last thought aloud. "I think I just said that I love you," he told her, feeling himself drowning in her large, trusting eyes and cheerfully going down for the third time.

Elizabeth bit her bottom lip, then nodded. "That—that's what I thought you said." *So now what, Elizabeth?* she screamed silently. *This is all happening so fast—maybe too fast. What do you do now?*

Nick saw the sudden confusion in Elizabeth's eyes. "I'm way ahead of you, aren't I, darling? I'm sorry."

"No . . . no! That's not it," Elizabeth protested, then fell silent. *Tell him, you idiot!* Her inner voice was screaming at her, while her tongue refused to move. It was like one of her childhood nightmares, the one where she was in danger but couldn't cry out. *You love him; you know you love him. Say something, for goshsakes! If you go home and tell Gammy what a dope you're being she'll have you locked up!*

"Yes, it is," Nick persisted, "and I don't blame you. To tell you the truth, I rather surprised myself. Why don't we just drop it for now, okay?"

Elizabeth nodded vigorously, wondering if she had lost her voice forever, only to find it in time to say something so honest, so revealing, that it immediately made her cheeks hot with embarrassed color. "It's a deal, Nick. Now, how about we kiss on it, just to make it official?"

"Anything you say, Elizabeth," Nick agreed, relief in his voice. "Your wish is my command."

The teasing was back—the harmless game playing—but it didn't last any longer than it took for Nick to take Elizabeth in his arms and cover her mouth with his own. Then the teasing stopped, and the mind-blowing fireworks display that blossomed and burst behind their eyelids sent warm currents of liquid desire coursing through their veins.

Their kiss deepened, as they opened to each other, tasted each other, gloried in each other, their bodies admitting truths their minds still struggled to accept.

Nick's arms tightened around her body as Elizabeth strained closer into his embrace, her fingertips tingling as they reached up to cup his cheeks, to trace the edges of his mouth where it pressed against her own. She was as much his at that moment as she would have been if they had already consummated their love; she lived for him, breathed for him, existed only because of him.

All my life, Nick heard the chant over and over inside his head. *All my life has been lived for this, will be for this.*

Everything I was, everything I am or ever hope to be lies within this woman. I'm the luckiest, the most fortunate man in the world.

They drew apart slowly, then Nick pressed his forehead against hers, his smile slow and satisfied as her eyelids came down to hide her expression, to cover her shyness at the unspoken admission they both knew she had made. "I'll take you home now, working girl," he whispered quietly, kissing both her closed eyes and the tip of her nose. "But only if you promise to have dinner with me tomorrow night."

It was a long ride back to Spring Street, with Nicholas stopping at every corner, to lean across the midseat console to kiss Elizabeth—for Elizabeth to kiss him back.

Gammy's light was still on when they pulled up in front of the house and Elizabeth knew she wouldn't be allowed to go to bed until she had told her grandmother every last detail of her evening with Henry Lancaster, but she didn't mind. As for that strange, wonderful interlude in the garden, well, Elizabeth decided as she watched Nick's taillights disappear down the street, what her romantically minded grandmother didn't know couldn't hurt her.

Chapter Four

"Gammy, this is Nick. Nick, my grandmother—and best friend—Rose Chatham." The introductions over, Elizabeth stood back and held her breath. She never knew what her grandmother would say, and only prayed the adorable, but sometimes trying woman would behave herself.

Taking hold of Elizabeth's hand, Nick acknowledged the introduction. "Mrs. Chatham, it's a pleasure to meet you at last. Elizabeth's been keeping you under wraps for so long, I was beginning to believe you were a figment of her imagination."

"Nicholas Lancaster," Rose responded pertly, looking him over as if he were a floor lamp she might consider purchasing. "Nice. Very nice. Sorry I missed you the other night when you came by to pick up my granddaughter, but it was my pinochle night," she lied easily. "So, Nicholas Lancaster, you like children, or what?"

"Gammy! You promised me you'd behave yourself!" Elizabeth was mortified, embarrassed beyond belief. What she wasn't, was surprised. She had purposely kept Nicholas and her grandmother apart for as long as possible, afraid something like this might happen. Now it was up to Nick, poor man, to find a way to answer her question.

Nick, luckily, had been forewarned, and as he looked down on Rose Chatham from his much greater height he produced his most ingratiating smile. "Only if they're all as beautiful as Elizabeth, Mrs. Chatham," he replied, thinking his answer extremely clever.

"You want pretty boys? Well, to each his own, but I like boys to look like boys. Even John and Paul do, the little brats. And please call me Rose. Mrs. Chatham makes it sound like I'm an old lady, and if there's one thing I keep telling this family, it's that I'm not an old lady."

"Rose it is, then," Nick promised, noticing that Elizabeth's facial features closely resembled her grandmother's.

"So, what are we doing standing out here in the hallway?" Rose motioned for Elizabeth to precede her. "Everybody's around here somewhere, just waiting to get a piece of your young man, Elizabeth. We shouldn't keep them in suspense."

"Don't say I didn't warn you," Elizabeth whispered to Nick as they walked down the hallway toward the dining room, Rose following close behind them. "Now you know why I always tried to meet you at work. Leave it to my loving Gammy to open her mouth and put *my* foot in it."

"I think you were just afraid I'd take one look at your grandmother and leave you in the dirt," Nicholas whispered back. "She's wonderful."

"Hah! I heard that," Rose called after them. "Elizabeth, grab him quick, or I will. He's Henry's son, all right. Lucky for you he takes most of his looks from Katherine."

"You knew my mother?" Nick stopped abruptly at the entrance to the dining room to face Rose. "Rose Chatham, Rose Chatham," he repeated, staring at her, a puzzled expression on his face. "Wait a minute, I've got it now. You must be the Rosie my father told me about. But no, the ages wouldn't fit, would they? I mean—"

"I know what you mean, but you're wrong. I married young, and so did my son, Jack. While your father was busy building an empire, we Chathams got ourselves one generation up on him," Rose explained, enjoying herself.

"Rosie O'Hanlon! This is wonderful. Dad was wondering whatever became of you. Elizabeth, your grandmother was the one who played Cupid for my mother and father. Remember, I told you about it."

"Smart too, isn't he?" Rose quipped, feeling rather full of herself. "Elizabeth, child, what *are* you waiting for? Grab this boy!"

Nick bent down and kissed Rose on the cheek. "Thank you, Mrs. Chatham. I do think you might be the reason I'm here, if my father is to be believed. And thank you for what you just said. I have to tell you, it made my day. I guess I'll just have to keep showing Elizabeth how wonderful I am."

"My grandmother and your parents? I knew there was something, but I just didn't put it all together," Elizabeth exclaimed, looking from one to the other and praying furiously that she could change the subject. "Isn't that a coincidence. I wonder why you never told me, Gammy."

Rose turned to Elizabeth and expressively waggled her eyebrows up and down as she smiled. "No one ever tells someone else *everything*, child. Do they?"

Elizabeth flushed, her grandmother's dart hitting home. She and Nick had been dating for almost six weeks and she had shared only a small portion of what happened on those dates with Rose. "I get your point, Gammy," she admitted wryly, "but now that I've heard what Nick's father remembers, I'd love to hear the story from your side sometime."

"That goes double for me," Nick added just as Paul came around the corner from the kitchen, a stack of homemade chocolate-chip cookies in his hand.

"Hey, Nick!" he shouted familiarly, just as if Nick was a regular visitor, even though this was only his third time in the house. "Liz said you were coming over. You want to watch the Eagles game with us? Dad and John are in the den. It's just about to start."

"Elizabeth?" Nick looked at her beseechingly, just like a little boy asking his mother if it was all right to go out and play, and she laughed as she pushed him toward the den.

"Hello, Mrs. Chatham," he called out as he went past the kitchen and saw Gloria Chatham in the process of pulling a large tray of cookies out of the oven. "It certainly smells good in here."

Gloria, who had told her husband Jack just the previous evening that Nicholas Lancaster was an extremely nice young man, immediately rushed to pile ten warm cookies onto a plate and offer them to him. "Would you like milk with these or coffee, Nick?" she asked as he thanked her.

"Milk, Nick," Paul said helpfully. "They taste great dunked."

"Well, that's that," Gammy concluded once Nick and Paul had disappeared into the den to be loudly greeted with the news that the Eagles had just intercepted the kickoff on the ten-yard line. "We'll be lucky if we see them for a few minutes at halftime. Elizabeth, would you like to try your luck at a little two-handed pinochle?"

Elizabeth leaned back against the doorjamb and closed her eyes, her features glowing blissfully. "Nick fits right in here, doesn't he, Gammy? I don't know why I haven't brought him home more often," she said, sighing. "Dad likes him, Mom likes him, both the boys adore him, and Megan says he's 'boss.' Isn't it wonderful?"

Rose walked past her granddaughter to get some playing cards from the top drawer of the buffet. "Yes, dear, but I have a feeling nobody *likes* him quite as much as you do. As I seem to remember saying before, Christmas is a wonderful time for a wedding."

"Oh, Gammy, stop it," Elizabeth warned nervously. "Nick might hear you."

"So, let him," Rose goaded, sitting down at the dining-room table and beginning to expertly shuffle the cards. "Remember, I've already gotten one Lancaster man down the aisle. But, to tell you the truth, I have more confidence in this one. And from what I can see in his eyes when he looks at you, little lady, Christmas can't come too soon this year."

* * *

Central Park was trying out its brilliant fall wardrobe, the trees sporting leaves that had just begun to decorate themselves in endless colorful hues of the brightest orange and gold. The vast lawns were still lush and deeply green, while the flowers of the season winked in the warm sunlight.

As it was a Thursday, for the most part it was left to the usual horde of tourists to seek out the horse-drawn hansom cabs that were one of the more famous features of the Park. The men who drove the cabs were doing a brisk business— so brisk, in fact, that Nick was beginning to worry.

He had planned everything so carefully, so thoroughly, down to the last detail, but that didn't keep him from being extremely nervous.

He had picked Elizabeth up at her parents' home exactly at eight o'clock that morning, just in time for Jack Chatham, who had been on his way out the front door, to wink at him conspiratorially, for the two of them had had a very private, very personal discussion the night before.

Nick had presented Elizabeth with two perfectly formed long-stemmed red roses as she descended the staircase into the foyer a few minutes later, looking like a lovely wood sprite in her emerald-green wool dress and flowing beige mohair cape, and he was pleased that she had instantly realized that the flowers were meant to mark the second-month anniversary of their first meeting—their first date.

Thankfully Rose Chatham wasn't an early riser, as Jack had warned him that his mother would take one look at him and know that today was the day—the day her oldest granddaughter would become engaged. "Not that I don't think she figured it out the minute she heard you were taking Liz to New York, but I do think it'll be easier if you don't have to try to keep a straight face while she's winking at you and throwing out hints to Liz," Jack had commented as he handed Nick a glass of beer to toast the conclusion of their discussion.

The chauffeur-driven Rolls-Royce he'd hired on a whim had smoothly whisked Nick and Elizabeth out of Bethlehem while they nibbled on flaky croissants, sipped good champagne and giggled like guilty children in the wide midnight-blue velvet back seat. They drove smoothly across the state line out of Pennsylvania and onto the New Jersey Turnpike, then through the Lincoln Tunnel and into New York City.

The mild November weather was cooperating beautifully, just as the morning weatherman had promised three days earlier while Nick lay in bed in his apartment, drinking his second cup of coffee and hatching his plan. It was a beautiful plan, close to a divine inspiration, he had decided modestly, and he'd been on pins and needles ever since, feeling as if Thursday would never come.

Once in the city, Nick had dismissed the driver and then strolled hand in hand with Elizabeth through the Park for an hour before they adjourned to Tavern on the Green to share a leisurely lunch in the restaurant's famous Crystal Room.

Nick knew Elizabeth had enjoyed their lunch thoroughly, for her warm brown eyes had shone with almost childlike delight as she had exclaimed over the multicolored chandeliers and the huge, succulent shrimp while smiling at the small army of waiters that had eagerly anticipated her every wish.

He had gloried in her excitement, pleased that she was pleased, and privately congratulated himself for having been the architect of her pleasure.

"I feel like a queen," she had told him after thanking Bruce, one of their waiters, for refilling her nearly full water goblet for the third time. "You never cease to amaze me, Nicholas Lancaster. Just imagine, driving all the way into New York just to have lunch. And that champagne! I've never had champagne before noon in my entire life. Anyone would think this was some really special occasion."

But it is a special occasion, Nick thought nervously now that they were back out on the sidewalk, leaning his dark head forward to see if one of the cabs was on its way back to the waiting area. *This is probably the second most special occasion in my life, with the first yet to come. Damn it, why didn't I think to reserve a cab? Sloppy, Lancaster, sloppy. It just goes to show what falling in love can do to a man's brain. Who in hell could know everybody and their brother would pick today to take a spin around the Park?*

"We don't have to take a ride, Nick," Elizabeth told him, lightly touching his sleeve to get his attention. "Really, I'd be just as happy if we walked. I've eaten so much it would probably do me good. Bruce said they're filming a movie somewhere around here—some sort of police chase story. Maybe we can watch."

"No!" Nick exclaimed hastily. Too hastily, he realized as Elizabeth looked up at him questioningly. "That is, I really do want to ride in one of those carriages. I never have, you know. Please, darling, indulge me a little. Let's play the tourist all the way."

Elizabeth raised herself onto her toes and kissed his cheek, her joy at being with him making her silly. "Only if you promise to take me to the top of the Empire State Building afterward, Daddy—please, please?"

"Smart aleck," Nick answered, giving the tip of her nose a light flick with his finger.

The cab that eventually pulled up in front of them was one of the newer ones, all red leather and shiny black paint. There was even a huge white horse sporting a hot-pink feather headdress as he stood quietly between the shafts, and a brash young Irishman was perched on the seat, a white cockade tucked in the band of his bowler hat.

The fact that the driver was also wearing faded designer jeans and a blue sweatshirt that said Let's Go Mets couldn't dampen Nick's excitement as he helped Elizabeth up onto the soft leather seat.

"Oh, Nick, this is wonderful." Elizabeth sighed in delight, snuggling into the seat. "I feel like I should bow my head and wave to the passersby, like Princess Di."

Nick smiled at her and shook his head. *It's happening, it's finally happening,* was all he could think, swallowing hard, like a nervous schoolboy about to ask the head cheerleader to the junior prom. "Once around the Park, please, and take your time," Nick commanded tersely, knowing his request sounded like a cliché. He slipped the driver a healthy tip, almost as an apology.

"And what else would you be wantin', I wonder, what with a fine beauty like this dear lady here up beside you?" the young man quipped cheekily, throwing Elizabeth a broad wink.

"Isn't he sweet?" Elizabeth whispered confidentially as Nick gingerly lowered his long, lean frame onto the seat beside her. "I can't understand why anyone thinks New Yorkers are cold. I've always found them to be very friendly, and almost all of them seem to be from somewhere else. It's almost as if New York is several dozen small towns all strung together on the same string, like multicolored beads. While I was living here I met dozens of really lovely people from different areas of Pennsylvania's coal regions."

"You shouldn't talk to strangers, Elizabeth," Nick felt he had to remind her, having learned that, to Elizabeth, strangers were only friends she hadn't yet met. Hadn't she been friendly to him after he had crashed into her that first day? Her openness, her friendliness, was just one of the many things he loved about her.

"Yes, darling," she replied evenly, and he knew she was only agreeing with him to be polite. "You know, Nick, for all the time I lived here, I never went for one of these rides. You're spoiling me, darling, and I love you for it!"

Nick felt his heart do a small flip in his chest as Elizabeth turned her glowing face up to his, her thick, chin-length, sweet-smelling chestnut hair dancing in the slight breeze so that it lightly caressed his cheek as she resettled herself within the circle of his arm. He kissed the tip of her nose as the driver moved the cab away from the curb. *She loves me for that. Please, Lord, let her mean it.*

"It's easy to spoil you, Elizabeth," he assured her, checking his suit pocket for the tenth time in ten minutes, just to be sure the small package was still safely tucked inside. He took a deep breath and tried to relax, looking at Elizabeth out of the corner of his eye.

She was beautiful; small, perfectly formed to fit in his arms, and he felt all-powerful, responsible for her in a way that brought out a tenderness he had never guessed he possessed. *And I'm about to make my possession official!*

She sat beside him, her sun-kissed face animated as she eagerly took in the sights and sounds of the Park, her hands unconsciously twirling the huge yellow-centered daisy he had bought for her from a strolling flower seller, and he leaned his head back to bathe his own face in the warm sunshine, reliving their first explosive meeting.

In his thirty-two years, Nick could not recall another example of the instant compatability he and Elizabeth had shared, or his intense need to see her, touch her, hold her, that had been with him ever since. If he had been right in his first assumption, if he was a victim of love at first sight, he would go happily to his fate.

His feelings for her were physical, he knew—had known from the beginning—intensely so, but they weren't limited to his barely hidden desire to take her to his bed. She appealed to his mind, to his heart, to his recently surfaced desire to make a home, to father a whole brood of chestnut-haired children with huge, laughing brown eyes. Being with Elizabeth had been a mixture of heaven and hell, and even now he wondered why it had taken him so long to ask her to be his wife.

He patted his suit pocket yet again, closed his eyes and reveled in the warm, satisfying feeling that had invaded his chest. This was right, this was so perfectly, so wonderfully right.

Elizabeth closed her eyes and tried to hold back an inane grin. Everything was perfect, completely, absolutely and deliciously perfect. The Park, the weather, the hansom cab—and most especially, the man by her side. *Gammy will go crazy when I tell her about this cab ride!*

She supposed she may have spent happier days in her twenty-six years, but at the moment she couldn't remember a single one. Nothing could compare to the absolute perfection of this day, not even the Christmas when she was eleven and had gotten that fire-engine red two-wheel bike with the white wicker basket and the shiny silver bell on the

handlebar. It was a silly example, she knew, but then she
was feeling silly. Silly and lighthearted—and maybe even a
little light-headed.

Nothing in her experience had prepared Elizabeth for
Nicholas Lancaster, and she still couldn't decide if he was
everything she had ever wanted, or only a dream that was
too good to be true.

The past two months had blended into one long roller-
coaster ride. The times she and Nick had spent together were
the exciting, dizzying climbs to the top of the highest hills,
the hours they were apart the small valleys between, passing by too quickly to allow her to catch her breath, but last-
ing just long enough to build her desire to be catapulted up
the next steep incline and embrace the delicious excitement
of seeing what lay on the other side.

She snuggled more closely against Nick's shoulder as the
cabdriver urged his horse onto the street alongside the Park.
She pretended to be chilly so that his cashmere-tweed-
covered arm would automatically tighten around her.

Elizabeth felt so safe with Nick, so cosseted. Yet she was
always aware of the strong sensual undercurrent that ran
between them, the desire to be one with each other, to belong to each other totally, in every way there was. She knew
Nick wanted her, and loved him even more for not pressing
her to give herself to him—behaving just the way her
grandmother had always told her honorable men did with
the women they really loved.

And their physical attraction had been there since the beginning, she thought now, since the first moment she had
impulsively reached out to comfort him after they had col-
lided in the housewares department. Elizabeth felt herself
blushing as she remembered how she had babbled, saying
anything and everything that had come into her head, trying to cover her nervousness. But Nick had felt it, too; he
must have, because he had asked her out for lunch.

And dinner that night, and the next night, and the next—
and the next. She rubbed her cheek against his jacket as she
remembered her grandmother's prediction that she, Eliza-

beth Anne Chatham, was meant to marry Nicholas Lancaster.

*And that was after our first date! Dear Gammy, she
thinks its wonderful, like something out of those old Hol-
lywood movies. I think she even believes she had something
to do with our coming together. She certainly was acting
strange last night when she made me leave Nick and come
upstairs to help her find her eyeglasses—especially when we
finally found them in the kitchen. I just hate it when she
knows something I don't know.*

"Warm enough, darling?" Nick asked, breaking in on her
thoughts just as she felt a shiver of hopeful anticipation run
down her spine.

*Could Nick have said something to Gammy? Or to Dad,
once the two of them were alone? They weren't acting suspicious, or were they? Could Nick be planning something
for today—something like—oh, no, it's just too ridiculous.
He couldn't be, could he?* Elizabeth looked up at Nick
searchingly, but his eyes were clear and unclouded.

She berated herself for her wild imagination and tried to
tell herself she wasn't disappointed. Did she really think he
was going to propose? It was silly. She'd only known him for
two months. People didn't propose after knowing someone
for only two months. *Did they?*

"Uh, no, I'm fine," she said in a rush as Nick's eyebrows came together in a frown. "I'm just enjoying the
ride."

"Good," Nick answered, and she knew he was wondering what was wrong with her, why she looked and sounded
so frightened.

She snuggled back against his shoulder once more and
surrendered to her daydream, picturing Nick's face as he
asked her to marry him. *Oh, how I love this man. He's so
sweet, so thoughtful—so wonderfully romantic! I believe I
could ride like this forever—into the sunset, my dearest love,
and I . . .*

Nick patted his suit pocket again, cleared his throat, and
called Elizabeth's attention to the large crowd standing near

a barricaded side street. "Look over there, Elizabeth, I think that might be where they're doing the filming your friend the waiter told us about."

"That it 'tis, sir, right enough," the driver piped up informatively, also looking toward the side street. "It's for a television show, you know, the one where that fella with the fancy sports car sticks up for the little guy?"

"Oh, I watch that show all the time!" Elizabeth exclaimed, eagerly leaning toward the left side of the cab to watch until they had moved past the alleyway, and giving Nick the time he needed to slip the small package out of his pocket and conceal it in his fist. "I think Megan's half in love with the hero, although she'd probably strangle me if she knew I told you, Nick. She's going through a phase, I think, and says television is a complete waste. This from a girl who practically grew up in front of the boob tube. Nick? What are you doing?"

"My shoelace has come undone somehow," Nick answered quickly, hiding his smile as he leaned down to retie the lace he had purposely loosened earlier, then placed the package carefully on the floor of the cab near Elizabeth's feet. It wasn't the most original idea he'd ever had, but somehow, considering the way they had met, it seemed to fit the situation.

He sat back on the seat, then fumbled in his pockets. "Damn, I must have dropped it."

"Dropped what?" Elizabeth asked as if on cue, already leaning forward to search the floor of the cab for whatever it was Nick had lost. "I don't see anything—oh heavens, what's this?"

"What's what?"

She sat up slowly, holding the small, square silver-wrapped package gingerly with both hands, eyeing it warily, as if it were alive and might bite her. "This. It's a box. It's got a bow on it," she said, swallowing hard. *Oh, please let this be a ring. Please, let me be right!*

Nick closed his eyes for a moment, knowing he was scared. Not a little nervous, not slightly apprehensive, but downright wet palms, dry mouth scared. What if he had read the signals all wrong? What if Jack Chatham had only been polite? What if Elizabeth didn't want him? What if she lived for her career and had no plans to marry before she was thirty-five? What if she hated him? What if—oh, how had he ever come up with such a stupid idea? He was a grown man, for God's sake, and here he was, shaking like a kid on his first date.

"I—I guess I should open it," Elizabeth stammered, her hands shaking so badly she couldn't loosen the bow. *It's probably a pair of diamond earrings. Men like to give earrings. Oh, please, don't let it be earrings!*

"All right," Nick agreed as casually as he could, swallowing hard and putting his arm around her tentatively. This was it; this was the moment he had been waiting for, working toward, plotting out so meticulously. "If you want to."

Elizabeth made a few more attempts, barely able to see through the tears she was sure he'd notice, until at last she gave up and thrust the box into his lap. "Oh, this is just impossible! Here, you open it for me, Nick! I'm shaking too hard."

Nick shook his head, laughing silently, suddenly not quite as nervous as he had been. Leave it to Elizabeth to turn the simply tied bow into a tangled knot. Her mechanical ineptitude was only one of the many things about her that delighted him. He quickly untied the bow while keeping Elizabeth firmly inside his embrace, then handed her the box, watching as she removed the silver wrapping and lifted the lid.

"Oh, dear," Elizabeth squeaked, tipping the brown velvet case into her hand, Nick's soft breath warming her cheek. He pressed his head close to hers while she slowly pushed up the lid to expose the contents.

It is, it is, it is! Oh, Gammy, you were right, you were so right. He loves me, Nick really does love me! Oh, no, I'm going to cry! Her first tears fell onto the velvet padding surrounding the perfectly formed marquise diamond that twinkled with blue fire between matching rows of baguettes, the whole encased in a thin circle of gold.

"It—it's beautiful," she whispered almost reverently. Her tears were falling freely now, and her full lower lip trembled as she said, "It's the most beautiful thing I've ever seen." *Oh, please, Lord, don't let me be dreaming!*

"And that makes you cry?" *It's all right, darling,* he thought to himself. *I think I feel like crying, too.*

"I'm not crying."

"Yes, darling, you are. Very prettily, but crying just the same." *It's all right, everything's all right. She loves me!*

Elizabeth's hand reached up and touched her wet cheeks. "Oh, dear, I am crying. I'm sorry. This is for me, isn't it? Please tell me it's not just something someone lost in the cab? I think I'd die if—"

Nick relaxed completely, at last. Reaching for the ring and her nervously shaking left hand, he then slipped the diamond onto her finger. It was a perfect fit. Raising her hand to his lips, he stared deeply into her eyes, knowing that no words could possibly add to the perfection of the moment. Then he placed a soft kiss just where the ring encircled her finger.

Elizabeth watched, fascinated, her head tipped to one side, her gaze tender, as Nick's warm lips lingered on her tingling fingers. She felt her body instinctively melting in his direction. "Oh, Nick," she breathed, oblivious to everything except what was happening to them, between them, in the snug cocoon of the New York City hansom cab as the white horse carried them back through the gate into Central Park.

At last Nick, his voice husky with emotion, asked, "You will marry me, Elizabeth, won't you? I love you, darling. I love you very, very much."

Her answer was breathed into his mouth as she gave herself up to his embrace, just as the cab drew up alongside the curb in front of the restaurant.

The driver peeked back over his shoulder, then flicked the reins to set the cab in motion again. "Once more around the Park, Maureen, m'love. And this one's on the house!"

Chapter Five

"So, now the fun starts!"

Elizabeth didn't know quite what she had expected her grandmother to say when she and Nick showed her the engagement ring, perhaps something like "I told you so," but Rose Chatham had surprised her again. "Fun, Gammy? What do you mean?"

Although she was disappointed that no one else was at home when they returned from New York just before dark, Elizabeth was glad that the three of them were going to have some time together to talk about the day. Besides, if this was the response she was going to get from her grandmother, maybe it would be easier on Nick if the Chatham clan voiced their opinions one at a time.

"Yes, dear, you heard me—fun!" Rose repeated, clapping her hands in glee. She went up to Elizabeth and Nick, took them each by the hand and led them to the living room. "Hurry, we don't have much time before everyone comes home from John's basketball game and this place turns into a three-ring circus. Now, come, my children, and you'll hear just what I mean. Nick, my dear, you will indulge me, won't you?"

"Do I have a choice?" As they were dragged along behind the little woman, Nick winked at Elizabeth, clearly enjoying himself. "I hoped your grandmother would be happy about this, but I think I may have underestimated her. She's really thrilled, isn't she?"

Overhearing him, Rose shot back happily, "You bet I'm thrilled! Nicholas, I've been planning for this since the day this child was born. So, no, you don't have any choice, unless you want me to tell your father on you. Now sit down, here, on either side of me and listen. You do want a nice wedding, don't you, Elizabeth?"

The three of them sat on the bright green floral slip-covered couch, Rose still not releasing their hands. Elizabeth lowered her head, avoiding Nick's eyes as she answered her grandmother's question. "Well, to tell you the truth, Gammy, I have thought about the sort of wedding I'd like; every girl does, I imagine. I think I'd like it to be old-fashioned—traditional—oh, you know what I mean. But—"

"But nothing! That's exactly what I want, too, with a nuptial mass, and a long veil, and your cousin Bill singing 'Ave Maria' as you give flowers to the Blessed Mother. I'm going to bawl like a baby through the whole thing, and enjoy every wonderful minute of it. You're going to be the most beautiful bride, Elizabeth. Isn't she, Nick?"

"Absolutely beautiful," he agreed, leaning forward around Rose to smile at his fiancée of six hours. Nick didn't know what else to say. When he had thought about the future it had only included Elizabeth and himself and a home of their own, a place where they could be alone together with their love. Then, a little later, the children would come, to make their family complete.

That's what marriage meant to Nick. A wedding was nothing more than the necessary ceremony that would officially join them together. He couldn't have cared less about anything but getting it over with as quickly and as painlessly as possible. But, obviously, there were certain things about marriage that he hadn't considered, and his confused expression made that very clear.

Rose threw back her head and laughed with delight at Nick's discomfort. "He doesn't have the faintest idea what I'm talking about, Elizabeth! Isn't that just like a man? You would like to get married tomorrow, isn't that right, Nick—or even tonight? Well, I can tell you, it isn't that easy. There are plans to be made, the church to be reserved, flowers to be ordered, a gown to be bought—oh, a million lovely things to do."

Elizabeth suddenly felt uneasy. Rose's plans sounded so exciting, so much like the dreams she'd had herself as a young girl, but she would have to be blind not to see that Nick was looking somewhat harassed. "Really, Gammy, I don't see any real need to go to all this fuss. It's not like we're children, after all. I think we might be past the shoes and rice sort of thing. I'm sure a very small, quiet ceremony would do just as well."

Rose sank back against the couch cushions like a small rag doll whose stuffing had been knocked out, her bottom lip forming a petulant pout. "You're no fun, Elizabeth Anne, no fun at all. And you, Nicholas," she went on, turning her head toward him and impaling him with her steely gaze, "do you really want to marry Elizabeth in some tawdry hole-and-corner affair? What would your father say?"

"I hardly think I'd involve Elizabeth in anything tawdry, Mrs. Chatham," Nick replied, trying hard not to laugh. Elizabeth's grandmother looked about as menacing as a fluffy kitten, but he'd say one thing for her—she certainly knew where to apply her claws.

"Of course you wouldn't, Nick," she agreed, patting his arm. "And please, now that we're going to be family, call me Rose. Now, are you going to let Elizabeth miss the best day of her life just because you're in a hurry? I mean, I can't imagine you'd be just as happy to bop her on the head, throw her over your shoulder and carry her off to your cave, now would you?"

"Oh, Gammy, please don't throw a tantrum," Elizabeth warned, wondering if Nick would ask her to return the ring, believing insanity ran in the family.

But Nick wasn't insulted; he was thinking about his father, about the man's great love of ceremony, about the many times he had heard Henry Lancaster speak of his own wedding day, and the pride he'd felt when his own bride had walked down the aisle to meet him. Would Nick regret it for the rest of his life if he denied himself the same sort of wonderful memory? If he, through his own impatience, denied Elizabeth the day she deserved?

"Rose," he said at last, taking her hands, "my bride is going to be the most beautiful bride that ever walked down an aisle, and her wedding day is going to be perfect, in every way. I don't know where my mind was to even think about a small, quick ceremony. Thank goodness you're here. Please, can we count on your advice?"

"Oh, brother, here we go. Hold on to your hats everybody," Elizabeth grumbled good-naturedly, knowing that yet another man had succumbed to her irrepressible, irascible grandmother and her Irish wiles. Thanks to Nick's well-meaning politeness, they had just relinquished all control over whatever would happen to them between now and their wedding day.

Immediately—after having gotten her own way, as she had been sure all along that she would—Rose was all business. "All right, children! Now you're talking. Elizabeth, Nick, what do you think about a Christmas wedding? Poinsettias on the altar, either white ones or red, I'm not sure yet which it should be—maybe both—and candles, lots of candles. And white bows on the ends of the pews, of course, and, Elizabeth, you should have a cathedral-length train, it's so elegant. We'll have to hurry, of course, as it takes so long for gowns to be ordered. We're going to have to hope you can wear one of the gowns the store has in stock."

"A gown," Elizabeth repeated wondrously, suddenly misty-eyed in spite of her misgivings. "Yes, I think I can see it. Something with a full skirt that rustles when I walk, and a train that bustles up for dancing. We'll go Saturday, Gammy, if it's all right with you and Mother."

"That's my girl! Gloria will cry the whole day long.
Won't it be grand? Now, for the bridesmaids. You'll have
Megan, naturally, and that friend of yours from New York.
What's her name? Beth, isn't it? Yes, of course. Such a
pretty girl, all that lovely blond hair. Wait till you meet her,
Nick, she has the loveliest speaking voice, all soft and
breathy. And for your matron of honor, Jennifer; she's a
redhead, isn't she?"

"I think I'd like to have Lisa as one of the bridesmaids,"
Elizabeth slipped in, remembering the good times she and
her cousin had had together during their teens, when Lisa
had visited during the summer vacations.

"Yes, yes, I was just coming to Lisa. She has black hair,
and your high-school friends, Nora, Lorraine, and Rose-
mary, they all have brown—my goodness, that's quite a mix.
We'll have to be very careful of the colors when we choose
their gowns. Nick, you do have five friends for ushers, don't
you? You'll want John and Paul for the other two; I can
blackmail them into behaving themselves."

"Fourteen attendants?" Nick said, quickly totaling the
number on his fingers. He could feel his control of the situation rapidly slipping away.

"Yes, yes, not counting the ring bearers. Your cousin
Bonnie's boys are just the right age, Elizabeth. Have you
thought of a best man yet, Nick? Oh, dear, let me get a pen
and paper. We'll have to start making lists." She impulsively kissed each of them on the cheek as she clambered to
her feet. "Oh, this is going to be *such fun!*"

Nick stood as Rose scurried out of the room, then sat
down, cupped his chin in his hand, turned his head to the
side to look at Elizabeth and sighed. "I think I'm getting a
headache. You know, darling, it's a good thing I only plan
to go through this once."

Elizabeth smiled and scooted over to slide her arms
around his neck. "I told you Gammy was a handful, and
you, my poor darling, were like putty in her hands. But
honestly, Nick, we don't have to go the whole nine yards if
you don't want to. I'll understand."

Nick took hold of her shoulders and looked down at her face, his heart in his eyes. "Rose is right. Besides, Christmas isn't that far away. You'd be surprised how hardheaded I could have gotten if she had started making noises about a June wedding. You're going to make a beautiful bride, Elizabeth soon-to-be Lancaster. And I wouldn't miss it for the world."

"Oh, Nick," Elizabeth said on a relieved sigh as she sought his mouth with her own. "I do love you. I love you so very, very much!"

"This is wonderful news! Come in, come in, and sit down over here. What do you mean, is it too late? Are you calling me an old man, Nicholas?"

It was almost ten, his father's usual bedtime, but it had taken some time to extract Elizabeth from her family once they had all come home, and even now their congratulations were ringing in his ears. The news could have waited for the morning, Nick knew, but Elizabeth had insisted that it would only be fair to tell both families the same day.

Now he was glad they hadn't waited. Nick couldn't remember the last time he had seen his father this happy. Ever since he had bumped himself up to chairman of the board, Henry had spent less and less time at the store and devoted more of his life to the garden that had been his wife's greatest passion. He was getting older, Henry had complained, and Nick had secretly agreed that his father was beginning to show his years.

Yet as Elizabeth and Nick sat with him in the living room of his home, Henry looked ten years younger. After shaking Nick's hands vigorously and giving Elizabeth kisses on both cheeks, he had immediately gotten down to the business of the wedding, reminding Nick of Rose Chatham's reaction to their news.

Once Mrs. Gillespie had offered her own best wishes and served champagne—a bottle Henry had chosen the night he'd first met Elizabeth, already anticipating this occasion—he announced, "I won't say this is sudden, son, because I could tell when I first met her that Elizabeth here was the woman for you. She's so like your mother, her gentleness shows in her every movement. My dear, have you given any thought to what sort of wedding you'll want?''

Nick leaned over to whisper in Elizabeth's ear. "Here we go again. Why do I get the sinking feeling that when it comes to weddings, the groom is only a convenient warm body to hang the bride on?''

Elizabeth knew Nick was joking, but she also knew he had a point. Everyone was behaving most peculiarly. Her grandmother had barely stopped talking to come up for air all evening, and she even had Elizabeth almost believing that there was nothing else happening in the world that held a candle to the upcoming wedding. Nick, at least to her grandmother's way of thinking, had performed his single function—he had proposed.

When the family had come home, Megan had immediately wanted to know if each bridesmaid would have her own limousine, and put the entire family on notice that she'd rather walk down the aisle bald than be partnered with either of her brothers. Not only that, but she had made known her preference for a green gown—"to match the season, silly''—while Elizabeth knew that her friend Beth never wore green because she thought it made her complexion look sallow.

Paul and John, not known for their tact, had quickly tired of the talk of the wedding and could be overheard in the kitchen conspiring to paint Help me! on the soles of Nick's shoes, a prank that they were sure would have the guests rolling in the aisle the first time the groom knelt at the altar. Nick was the only one who thought that that was funny, she remembered now, looking at him strangely.

Jack Chatham, Elizabeth's father, normally a quiet man who cheerfully left the everyday running of the household to the women of the family, had then announced firmly that he planned to hire his lifelong friend, Jimmy Timenski, leader of a local group called Jimmy Timenski and His Polka Dots, to play at the reception.

"Dad, no!" Megan had groaned, dramatically flinging herself onto the couch. "Not accordions! I'll die, I mean I'll absolutely *perish* from embarrassment."

In Elizabeth's mind, the only sane person left in the family was her mother. After she had dried her tears of happiness, Gloria Chatham had immediately gotten busy formulating a list of all the relatives who would be happy to assist in the baking that would probably go on for weeks preceding the ceremony, so that the reception afterward in the church's all-purpose hall would be overflowing with nut rolls, miniature cakes and apricot kiffle pastries—a particular favorite of the Chatham side of the family.

"Well, actually," Elizabeth admitted now, realizing that Henry Lancaster was waiting for her answer, "my family has surprised me by having quite a few rather definite plans for the wedding."

"Especially her grandmother," Nick put in. "Talk about your 'idea' people—that woman missed her calling. Rose should have been a general. She could probably plan a major campaign, outfit a battle battalion from boots to tanks and have it on its way in ten minutes."

"Rosie O'Hanlon," Henry said, smiling at the mental picture the name drew for him. "She came no higher than my shoulder, as I remember, but she made you feel as if she were ten feet tall. Elizabeth, ever since Nick told me who your grandmother is, I've been anxious to see her again. Indeed, as father of the groom, I believe I remember that it's up to me to have your parents here to dinner as soon as possible. Naturally that invitation will include Rosie. Let me know your phone number, my dear, and I'll give them a call tomorrow morning."

"That's very kind of you. I'm sure Gammy and my parents will be delighted," Elizabeth told him, privately grateful Nick's father hadn't included the other three Chatham children in the invitation. Not that she was ashamed of her siblings, for she wasn't, but things were moving too quickly for her to believe that having Megan, John and Paul in on a discussion of the wedding plans at this stage of the game would do anything but confuse the issue.

"Mrs. Chatham—Rose, that is—would like us to have a Christmas wedding, Dad," Nick said, bringing the discussion back to the ceremony itself. "What do you think?"

"Christmas?" Henry repeated. "I imagine you mean the day after Christmas?"

Elizabeth nodded. "Gammy wanted it to be Christmas Day, but that's really a difficult day. I think the day after Christmas is perfect. Unless it snows," she added quietly, frowning at the thought.

Henry reached into a nearby drawer and pulled out a small calendar, counting off the weeks until the holiday. "That's rather short notice, isn't it? I mean, I'll have to see if the club's available, for one thing. It will probably be closed, but I think I can pull a few strings—cost is no object. And then there's the orchestra to consider. Nick, what was the name of that orchestra they had at the club for the Governor's Ball last spring?"

Nick shifted uncomfortably in his seat, not unaware of Elizabeth's sharp intake of breath. "Richard Burrows and his Orchestra," he said automatically before continuing: "Look, Dad, I think you should know that Mr. and Mrs. Chatham have already begun discussing the reception and the orchestra. You wouldn't want to commit us to anything without first talking it over with them. After all, I really think the bride's family is responsible for such things. Isn't that right, darling?" he ended, looking toward Elizabeth, who could have cheerfully strangled him for putting her in the position of answering such an obviously leading question.

"Well, traditionally, yes, I think so," she replied, unconsciously seeking Nick's hand and squeezing it tightly. "But I was in my friend Jennifer's wedding last year, and I know that the etiquette has changed over the years, so that the financial burden is no longer entirely with the bride's family. As a matter of fact, today more and more couples are paying for their own weddings."

"Nonsense!" Henry exclaimed, rising to his feet. "I never heard of such a thing. Oh, how I wish Katherine was here. She'd know just what to do. Elizabeth, I'm going to call

Rosie tomorrow morning and we'll get this whole thing straightened out. Pay for the wedding yourselves? Not while there's breath in my body you won't.''

Now it was Nick's turn to stand. "Dad, I think you're forgetting something. Elizabeth has a mother and father. I know you and Elizabeth's grandmother go back a long way, but I don't think it would be wise to go over their heads. Besides, both Elizabeth and I have good jobs. I think we should pay for the wedding ourselves. I haven't asked you for money since I was fourteen and got my own paper route.''

Elizabeth looked from one man to the other, seeing as well as sensing that a sudden battle of wills was about to take place in front of her. Rising quickly, she stepped between them to give Henry Lancaster another kiss. "I'll tell Gammy you're going to call her, Mr. Lancaster. I know she'll be delighted. And on my lunch hour tomorrow I'll go to the bookstore and buy an armful of bridal magazines and etiquette manuals. But until then, to be perfectly honest with you, I think I'm just so happy that Nick and I are going to be married that I really can't think of anything else. Everything's happening so fast. Why, we just got engaged this afternoon. Isn't that right, darling?''

"Like I said, son," Henry replied, chuckling, "she reminds me of your mother. A born diplomat. But I have to agree with Elizabeth. Rosie and I will have lunch as soon as possible, just to talk over old times, and she and Elizabeth's parents will come to dinner Saturday night if they're free. We'll put our heads together then. I want to do this thing right.''

"I don't want to say good-night.''

Elizabeth slid her hands down Nick's arms so that they stood facing each other, their hands clasped together at their sides as they stared into each other's eyes. "I don't want to say good-night, either.''

It was past midnight as they stood on the Chatham front porch, reluctant to let this special day end. After leaving Henry Lancaster's house Nick had driven around Bethlehem, the two of them remarking that every year the Christmas decorations were going up earlier on the city streets. They had stopped at a small restaurant for a light snack that neither of them ate, and afterward walked hand in hand down Broad Street, looking at the displays in the shop windows.

But they both had to go to work in the morning and it had been a long day, so that at last Nick had reluctantly driven back to the house on Spring Street. They had been standing together on the porch ever since, still finding it impossible to say good-night and part from each other.

They were engaged now, promised to each other, and it seemed unfair that they should have to go home separately, to lie in their lonely beds and only dream of the day when they would be able to say good-night and never have to part again.

Nick had kissed Elizabeth good-night three times; and three times he had made it only as far as the first step of the porch before coming back to take her in his arms once again. "This is crazy," he said now as he drew her body against his and buried his face in her hair. "I think it would be easier to rip my heart out than to walk away and leave you here. Elizabeth, darling, I don't know if I can go through with this. I want us to be married—now."

Elizabeth felt tears gathering in the corners of her eyes even as she gloried in the slight shuddering of Nick's body as he clasped her tightly to his chest. She knew how he felt because she was feeling the same way. They belonged together, and waiting for Christmas to come this year would be the hardest thing she had ever done.

"I know, darling, I know," she assured him, nuzzling her cheek against the front of his coat. "I just want to run off somewhere private and hold you forever. This is silly; we're mature adults. After all, it's not like we won't be seeing each other tomorrow. Why are we feeling this way?"

Suddenly Nick smiled. "I can think of one reason. *Grrrr,*" he growled, nibbling at the side of her throat. "Like you said, we're all grown-up, aren't we?"

"Nicholas Lancaster, shame on you!" Elizabeth reprimanded, feigning shock. "My mother warned me about boys like you. Lucky for you that your intentions are honorable, or I'd have to scream for my father so that he could toss you down the porch steps on your head."

Moving his lips from her throat to her ear, Nick warned: "Better start yelling, darling, because at the moment my intentions don't have a whole hell of a lot to do with honor. I'm a desperate man, Elizabeth. Now stop talking and give me your mouth."

The porch light flicked on and off three times, stopping Nick just as Elizabeth had turned her face to his, obedient to his playful demand. "Gammy," she acknowledged, sighing. "I think she's trying in her own inimitable way to tell us to stop putting on a show for the neighbors."

"Tell her we'll sell tickets and give her ten percent off the top," Nick said, still intent on getting his own way.

"Nicholas," Elizabeth scolded, giving him one last quick kiss before reluctantly pulling free of his arms, "I'd better go in now, before Gammy decides to come out here on the porch to share her latest brainstorm with us. I wouldn't put it past her, you know."

Nick laughed as he remembered his last sight of Rose as the woman paced up and down the dining room spouting random ideas for the wedding. "Neither would I. All right, darling, I'll go quietly. Just remember—I love you. I love you madly... and passionately... and wildly..." he said, kissing her to punctuate each word "...and eternally... and—dammit!"

The light flicked on and off three more times as Elizabeth collapsed against Nick with a fit of giggles. "Mrs. Williamson across the street must be standing at her window with her binoculars again. Gammy says it's her only pleasure in life, spying on us Chathams."

"That's not funny!" he pointed out, but he looked across the street anyway, just in time to see a lace curtain on the second floor of the corner house sliding back into place. "Like I seem to remember saying before," he said as he backed down the porch steps, "Christmas can't come too soon this year!"

"Good night, darling!" Elizabeth called after him, waving until he started the engine and switched on his headlights, and then finally turning to put her hand on the doorknob. Just as her fingers connected with the doorknob the door flew inward and she was catapulted into the foyer, to see her grandmother standing on the other side of the door.

"Finally! I thought he'd never leave! That old biddy Williamson will be hanging over the back fence all day tomorrow talking about you, young lady. I can't wait to tell her about that rock on your finger. Talk about taking the wind out of somebody's sails. Well, don't just stand there gaping at me, come up to my room. We have so much to talk about."

Elizabeth leaned down and kissed her grandmother's cheek. "We're in love, Gammy," she gushed happily. "Isn't it wonderful?"

Rose looked at her granddaughter, saw the dreamy glow in her eyes and groaned. "Go to bed, Elizabeth. I know when I'm licked. We'll talk in the morning."

Chapter Six

Life, Elizabeth decided while putting a stack of just-completed order sheets into her Out basket, and feeling a giddy thrill go through her as her ring caught the light and became a glittering burst of color, was actually rather wonderful.

She was engaged to be married. That, all by itself, was the fulfillment of a dream. She had always suspected that she wasn't cut out for the dog-eat-dog world of business, and her three years in New York after graduating from Moravian College had taught her that, for her, a career wasn't the be-all and end-all of her existence.

After all, wasn't that exactly why she had come back to Bethlehem in the first place? She had missed her home, had missed her family and she was ready to settle down. Her grandmother's teasing had been right on target; she was ready for marriage.

Using her parents' happy marriage, and her grandmother's stories of her own married life as models, Elizabeth had grown up with a healthy regard for the rightness of the institution, and she had never had any problem seeing herself in the role of traditional wife and mother. She was, she concluded happily, just an old-fashioned sort of female.

But now the reality that she had found with Nick had far surpassed even her wildest dreams. Marriage itself had become secondary; it was the man and the man alone who counted. If Nick had not become the reason for her existence, he certainly had given that existence real meaning. She had known from the moment he'd first touched her hand that he was different, special; but almost overnight he had become the most important person in her life.

Sitting back in her chair, Elizabeth hugged herself tightly to keep from crying out with happiness. Here, in the small office behind the housewares department, she felt as if she would burst into song at any moment. She could dance, she could float on air. Love was the most wonderful, the most lovely emotion in the entire world.

It had nothing to do with curtains on windows or freshly baked brownies cooling on top of the stove. Love, she concluded, had to do with finding that one special person in the entire world who had the power to make you want to have it all, even as you were giving it all away with both hands. The house they would live in, the children they would have, these were all lovely to think about, to discuss, to weave dreams around. But without that one special man, they meant nothing.

She was so lucky, she decided, so very, very lucky. Thousands of people, maybe even millions, lived their entire lives without ever finding that one special person. Why if she had decided to stay in New York, she never would have met Nick at all.

Elizabeth shivered at the thought. Never to have met Nick? Never to have known his love? It was unthinkable. She shook her head, dismissing such an unsettling thought. She *had* met him. They *had* fallen in love. And in just five more weeks, they *would* be man and wife, never to be separated again. Yes, life was wonderful!

"Miss Chatham, the Reading store is on line one," Judy Holland said, poking her head into the office and politely not commenting on the idiotically blissful expression on her boss's face. "Something about a shipment of Christmas tree cookie cutters being lost somewhere in transit. Shall I tell them you'll call back?"

"No, thank you, Judy, I'll take it in here," Elizabeth answered, pushing her hair behind her ear as she picked up the telephone. Halfway through her conversation with the manager of the Reading branch a second light on her telephone lit up and she put the manager on hold while she answered. "Housewares, Miss Chatham speaking."

"Elizabeth, would you believe it, I've found a gown for you—the perfect gown! Do you think you could come home early tonight?"

"Gammy?" Elizabeth questioned blankly, still mentally trying to figure out what the postal service could possibly have done with the cookie cutters. "We've tried every bridal shop in town with no luck. Thank goodness we got that last store to put a rush on the bridesmaids' gowns; at least we have that done. I thought we'd agreed to take the bus into New York City on Friday."

She could hear her grandmother's derisive sniff through the receiver. "There's nothing in New York that could hold a candle to this particular gown," she assured her granddaughter loftily. "Trust me in this, Elizabeth. Have I ever let you down before?"

Out of the corner of her eye Elizabeth could see the light that showed her the Reading manager was still waiting, and now a third light had begun to blink on the console. "Look, Gammy, I really can't talk about gowns now, much as I'd love to. I have to work until closing tonight and again tomorrow, so I won't be home until after nine either night. Can't this wait until Friday? And you do realize that if this gown isn't right, we'll have lost the day in New York."

"Friday at ten o'clock should be just fine," Rose agreed with unusual docility, then added, "and don't waste time arguing with me. Don't you have a job to do or something? I'm hanging up now."

Pulling the receiver away from her ear, Elizabeth looked at it owlishly for a moment before pressing the button that would reconnect her with the Reading manager. Dealing with the problem in short, if not entirely satisfactory, order, she took the waiting call only to hear her sister Megan whine: "*Gammy* said we can't carry roses because cousin Lisa sneezes. Did you ever hear anything so silly? Liz, you know how I *love* roses. Do we have to listen to Gammy? This is *your* wedding, right?"

"I used to think so," Elizabeth quipped, although she doubted her sister understood her sarcasm. "And I thought you stayed home from school today because you had a headache. Shouldn't you be in bed?"

"*Bed!* Really, Lizzie, how can I stay in bed? I'm telling you, Gammy is going to goof up this whole wedding. She's on the phone all the time with Nick's father, planning everything. Dad's really beginning to get mad. Of course I have a headache. How could I help it?"

"Miss Chatham? Excuse me, but do those spaghetti bowls we got in last week come in any other color except red? My customer says her kitchen is orange, and red will clash."

Turning toward the open door of her office, Elizabeth looked at Judy and blinked twice as Megan kept up a running list of complaints in her ear, her tale of woe now having something to do with Paul, who said he was going to drink the champagne toast no matter what their father said about substituting ginger ale in his children's glasses. "What, Judy?" she asked, feeling a headache of her own coming on. She laid the receiver on the desk and looked through a stack of computer pages that lay to one side.

"Oh, yes, here it is. Blue. They also come in blue, but tell her we'll have to special order it for her," she answered before picking up the telephone once more to find that Megan was still talking. "Meg, I have to go now. We'll talk later, okay?" she broke in, and then quickly hung up the receiver before her sister could protest.

No sooner was the receiver back in its cradle than the telephone rang again. "Hello, darling," she heard Nick say, and instantly she felt the tension in her shoulder blades beginning to ease.

"Nick! Oh, you don't know how good it is to hear your voice," she confessed, clutching the receiver with both hands. "We're still on for lunch, aren't we? Please, darling, don't fail me now. I think I'm losing my grip on reality."

"Well, actually, honey, that's why I'm calling," Nick began, and Elizabeth's shoulders tensed again. "Dad just stopped by to talk to me about the wedding, and he wants to join us."

"Oh, no!" Elizabeth groaned. "It's been a madhouse here all morning. I was so looking forward to a few minutes of sanity with you."

"Is that all I can offer you?" Nick teased. "Thanks a lot. You make me sound like a comfortable old shoe, and we've been engaged less than a week."

"Is that all? I feel like we've been going round and round about this wedding forever. And keep your voice down, darling, or your father will hear you, and I wouldn't want to hurt him for the world. What does he want now? He and Dad aren't fighting over the band again, are they? I thought that was all settled."

"Bingo, darling—plus one," Nick answered, letting her know that she was right, he wasn't alone and yes, trouble was brewing once more.

"It *is* the band—and the reception, too, right?" she asked, sagging against the back of the chair. "They seemed to understand each other so well when we went to your father's house for dinner last Saturday. Nick—what do you say we elope? It'd be a lot easier, and then we can be alone. Just think of it!"

"You certainly do pick your times, don't you, darling?" Nick whispered into the telephone, and Elizabeth knew the idea appealed to him, as well. Then, louder, he went on, "So we're all set, right, sweetheart? We'll meet you downstairs in the restaurant at one o'clock. What, Dad? Oh, sure, I'll tell her. Elizabeth, Dad says to bring your appetite with you; it's his treat."

"And if Halloween weren't already past, I'd say it's probably going to be his 'trick,' as well," Elizabeth concluded aloud, smiling as she heard Nick's soft baritone chuckle. "I love you, darling," she said and smiled as he told her that he loved her, too.

After hanging up the telephone for what she hoped was the last time for a while, Elizabeth reconsidered her earlier thought. Life was indeed wonderful. However, with every passing day, it was also getting to be more and more complicated.

Judy Holland poked her head in through the open office door again, calling, "Miss Chatham, the lady says blue will clash with the orange, too. Do you have it in yellow? And, oh, I almost forgot. Your mother is here with some swatches for the bridesmaids' gowns you picked out last week; something about your grandmother saying you'll have to find silk flowers to match the color. Something about somebody sneezing, I think she said. She showed them to me and I think the pink would be pretty, but of course it's your choice. Shall I send her back here or do you want to come out on the floor?"

Elizabeth allowed her forehead to fall into her hands as she released her breath in a long, exasperated sigh, wondering if all brides had to ride this same dizzy carousel of happiness and frustration.

Nick picked Elizabeth up at home at nine o'clock the following morning, knowing she wasn't scheduled to start work until noon. He hadn't told her where they were going, and it pleased him to hear her squeal of surprise and delight when he pulled his car into the driveway behind the Tudor house on Prospect Avenue.

"You remembered! Oh, you darling!" Elizabeth cried, catapulting herself across the console to give him a hug. "Is that the realtor? Is the house empty? I haven't seen lights inside it for the past week. I thought you forgot, not that I would have blamed you. Oh, this is going to be such fun. Gammy will be green with envy when I tell her I finally got to see the inside of the 'castle.'"

"The answers are yes, yes, and, if you tell your grandmother about this I will personally wring your neck," Nick

answered, helping Elizabeth as she excitedly scrambled out
of the car, not willing to waste any time waiting for him to
come around and open her car door. "If we're going to play
house, as you call it, Elizabeth my love, the last thing we
need to do is tell Rose about it, right?"

Instantly Elizabeth was sorry she had mentioned her
grandmother's name. For the moment, she felt that both of
them had had enough of their relatives. After surviving the
trying lunch they'd had with Nick's father the day before,
they had been treated to another scene last night on Spring
Street that had featured both fathers and Elizabeth's
grandmother in the starring roles.

As Megan had said, Rose was now spending time with
Henry Lancaster—nearly every day—and was solidly on
that man's side when it came to having the reception at his
country club; she had no qualms about stating her argu-
ments to her son. For his part, Elizabeth's father, who had
previously agreed to using the country club as long as he
could choose the band, had turned stubborn when Henry
reacted to Jimmy Timenski and His Polka Dots with barely
concealed scorn.

Of course, there was also the very delicate matter of just
who was going to pay for everything. The church hall was
within Jack Chatham's price range; the country club was
not. Rose's offer to share the cost was refused out of hand,
and for a while Elizabeth was afraid there was going to be a
real family battle, but in the end Nick had settled everything brilliantly.

After excusing himself to confer at some length with his
father by telephone, he had announced that the expenses
would be split three ways, with the parents taking a share
each and he and Elizabeth paying for a third themselves.
Furthermore, he had pronounced in his most businesslike
way, the reception would have to be held at the country club,
but only because the church hall could not hold the number of people that were to be invited.

But the best part of all—the part that still had Elizabeth
chuckling every time she thought about it—had been Nick's
solution to "the battle of the bands." The Great Room at

the club, a separate area away from the main dining room that had a floor designed specifically for dancing, was a very large chamber, big enough to accommodate two bandstands. Richard Burrows and his Orchestra would set up their instruments at one end, and Jimmy Timenski and his Polka Dots would be at the other end, accordion and all. When one band was taking a break, the other would play.

"And if you don't like that, you and my father can darn well *hum* the tunes, because that's the best compromise I can work out," Nick had concluded so forcefully that not even the outspoken Rose had dared to object.

"Oh, how I love a masterful man!" Megan had gushed, clasped hands to her breast as she had pretended to swoon onto the couch, breaking the tension and allowing everyone to laugh and shake hands.

Jack and Gloria had quickly admitted their relief to Nick, thanking him for his help as Paul and John went off to watch professional wrestling on television, saying that at least then they could see a *good* fight. Megan had waited until her brothers had left the room to sidle up to Nick and ask his opinion of her new perfume, while Rose had gone back to her endless lists, saying something about adding twenty more people now that she knew the size of the room.

Marrying a successful businessman had its perks, Elizabeth confided to Nick later on the front porch while across the street Mrs. Williamson watched them from behind her lace curtains. "You're fair, but firm. I believe I like that in a man," she teased, kissing his chin. "Mmmn, delicious. You smell almost as good as Megan does. I think she's trying out her feminine wiles on you; but she can't have you. I saw you first. Kiss me, you masterful man."

"Don't push me, lady, I don't have much to lose," Nick had returned, running his fingers lightly across her midriff, knowing she was ticklish, loving Elizabeth's squeals as she struggled within his grasp. Mrs. Williamson's lace curtains had immediately opened wide and Nick and Elizabeth ended up holding on to each other, giggling like guilty children.

With the relief they had felt now that the wedding plans were at last settled—at least some of them, that is—they deserved this "playtime" today, as Nick referred to it before they followed the realtor to the front door.

Once there, Nick deftly removed the key from the realtor's hand and said politely but firmly, "Thank you very much, Mr. Carlson. We'll drop this off at your office when we're done. Come on, darling."

Elizabeth, her hand firmly gripped by Nick's, could only smile politely at the bemused salesman as she was tugged along behind Nick into the house, the door closing in Mr. Carlson's face. "I think that might have been rude, darling," she pointed out pleasantly as she looked around the two-story-high foyer. "He must have rehearsed his sales pitch for hours, poor man."

"Yes, it was, wasn't it?" Nick agreed, unrepentant. "You and Rose were right, Elizabeth. It is a gallery staircase, and the wood carving is beautiful. Where do you want to start, upstairs or down?"

Suddenly Elizabeth missed the realtor. The house was empty, their voices echoing against the high ceiling, and she fought to keep the atmosphere light so that it wouldn't look the way it felt—like she was alone in the house of her dreams with the man of her dreams. After all, they were only playing; only looking. She certainly didn't expect Nick to buy this house for her. It must cost the earth, for one thing, and—oh, who did she think she was kidding? She had only seen the foyer, and already she was falling madly in love with the house.

"Why don't we start down here?" she decided at last, not ready to go upstairs and see the bedrooms.

It was a large house, as big inside as it appeared from the outside, with a number of high, multipaned casement windows and three sets of French doors leading out to the patio that wrapped around two sides of the house. And yet, Elizabeth decided as they stood in the living room and looked through to the library, it was a cozy house. It had lots of corners and hidden nooks and crannies to make it feel homey. She especially liked the wide window seat set in one corner of the dining room, its view looking out over the back garden and a large, droopy willow tree. It was a place made for dreaming.

"What did you think of the kitchen, darling?" Nick asked as they walked back into the foyer. "It certainly seems to have everything in it."

"And then some," Elizabeth agreed, remembering the wide center island that contained the six-burner stove complete with indoor grill. "My mother would love it, as she's the gourmet cook in our household. But don't worry, she taught me well, I promise you. Why, I can even bake my own bread."

"And I can whip up anything that comes in its own disposable tray and fits into a microwave," he replied, dropping a quick kiss on the top of her head. "At least we won't starve." Wrapping an arm around her waist, Nick led the way up the wide, curved staircase, preferring to see the upstairs for the first time this way rather than by using the narrower set of steps they had discovered in the service hallway behind the kitchen.

The wide upper landing wrapped around the front of the house, with three oversize windows admitting a warming stream of early morning sunlight, while a high carved railing kept the center open to the foyer below. There was a large square hallway behind that opening, with doors leading off in every direction.

They discovered five bedrooms and three bathrooms. The smallest bedroom also had a wide window seat, and Elizabeth could easily imagine the room as a nursery, with white organdy tieback curtains on the windows and a large rocking chair in the corner.

But it was the master bedroom that seemed to hold Nick's interest. More than just a room with connecting bath, it was a suite with two dressing rooms and a pair of walk-in closets on either side of one of the large dormer windows. Even his king-size bed would be swallowed up in the massive room.

"So, all done playing, sweetheart?" he asked, leading her from the room and back toward the stairs. "It's getting late,

and we still have to take the key back to the realtor. Are you
ready?''

Still looking over her shoulder, Elizabeth followed meekly
until they were back in the downstairs foyer once more. It
was over. He had said they would look at the house and they
had looked at the house. It was fun, granted, but she knew
that was all it had been. They had already decided that they
would live in Nick's apartment after the wedding, at least
until they had time to catch their breath and make plans to
settle themselves permanently.

After all, she had just begun her job. Although Nick had
offered to let her resign in order to concentrate on the wedding, Elizabeth had decided to stay on, knowing how difficult it would be to replace her on such short notice in the
middle of the busy Christmas season.

But, rational reasoning to one side, Elizabeth had fallen
deeply in love with this house. It had always intrigued her,
sparked her imagination; but now that she had walked
through it, heard the voices of her yet-to-be-born children
laughing in the halls, and seen a misty picture of Nick and
herself readying themselves for bed in their private suite as
the light from the fireplace danced warm and golden across
the pitched stucco ceiling, she knew this was a house she
could never forget.

It was silly. She was being impractical. She was also being greedy. She had Nick; she already had everything she
could ever want. A house was just a house, nothing more.

"I'm ready," she said at last, giving the place one last look.
"Playtime's over, alas, and it's back to the real world. I have
some Christmas tree cookie cutters to locate before the day
is out."

Nick locked the front door and turned toward her questioningly. "You want to run that one by me one more time?
We just got done looking at one terrific house, and all you
can talk about are some cookie cutters? I think you have
some explaining to do."

Elizabeth reached up on tiptoe and kissed his cheek. "No,
I don't. I am about to be a bride. I'm allowed to be vague.
In fact, I'm beginning to think 'vague' is a required course

for brides. That and Harassed 101. But please let me thank you, darling. I just loved seeing the house."

"Did it live up to your expectations?" Nick held open the car door as he waited for her answer.

"Well, the faucets in the bathroom weren't solid gold, but then one can't have everything, now can one?" she tossed back at him, busily arranging her skirt on the leather seat while she averted her eyes. "Silly man! Of course it lived up to my expectations. A person would have to be crazy not to love that place."

Nick closed the door and took his time walking around the car to get in on the driver's side. Sliding in behind the steering wheel, his expression kind, he said, "Maybe in a few years, when we're seriously looking for a place of our own, we'll consider building a Tudor."

Elizabeth commanded her facial muscles to form a smile. "What a wonderful idea, darling. In a few years, when we're ready. This house is lovely, but it's really much too big for two people, isn't it?"

Nick shrugged. "Well, I don't know. We could always set up a bowling alley in the foyer," he said facetiously, earning himself a jab in the ribs from Elizabeth's elbow before he changed the subject to a problem he was having with the new computers in the credit office, and the discussion of the Tudor house on Prospect Avenue was dropped once and for all.

Chapter Seven

"I didn't know there were any bridal shops out this way, Gammy." Elizabeth was beginning to wonder just where her grandmother's directions were taking them. The woman had been behaving strangely ever since she had first mentioned the "dream gown" and now that they were at last on their way to the store, Elizabeth couldn't help thinking that the woman looked ready to burst with excitement. "Are you sure we're going the right way? I could be home addressing invitations."

"Just hush up and turn right at the next corner, Elizabeth." Rose squirmed in the passenger seat of her son's station wagon and patted the large rectangular box perched across her knees. "What do you think I'm doing, kidnapping you?"

"I don't know, do I?" Elizabeth answered, taking her gaze from the road for a moment to look inquisitively at the box. "For all I know, you could have a submachine gun stashed in that thing. Why won't you tell me what you've got in there?"

Rose looked at her granddaughter with an expression that reminded Elizabeth of the Cheshire cat in *Alice's Adven-*

tures in Wonderland and said, "In good time, darling, all in good time. Here's the turn."

Putting on the turn signal automatically, Elizabeth had the station wagon well into the turn before she realized that they were now on Macada Drive. "There's nothing out this way but houses, Gammy. As a matter of fact, Nick's father lives just one more block down this road. But you know that, don't you? Gammy—"

"Pull in Henry's driveway, Elizabeth, and park the car," Rose ordered, adding, "and for pity's sake, close your mouth. Henry's standing at the door, waiting for us."

Rose was right; Henry Lancaster was standing just inside the open door, the smile on his face doing strange things to Elizabeth's insides. "What have you two hatched between you this time, Gammy?" she asked, beginning to worry. "I know the two of you have had your heads together on everything from the menu for the reception to the flowers we're carrying, but don't you think I'm even capable of finding my own wedding gown?"

Sliding out of the passenger seat still balancing the large box, Rose tut-tutted her granddaughter's outburst and practically skipped up the shallow stairs to say hello to her old friend. "I tell you, it was like pulling teeth, Hank, but I got her here. Is everything ready?"

"Of course," Henry informed her with a wink. "Good morning, Elizabeth. You look lovely today. Your mother's here, waiting for you. We've had a nice chat about your school days. You didn't tell me you played the piccolo in the marching band. Would you like Mrs. Gillespie to serve coffee or do you want to see the gown right away?"

Once inside the house Elizabeth saw that her mother was indeed there, holding a cup of coffee as she stood in the entrance to the living room. "Mom? I don't understand. What are you doing here?"

"I came to see you in the gown, of course," Gloria Chatham answered matter-of-factly. "Henry and your grandmother were kind enough to have included me in the surprise. After all, I am the mother of the bride, aren't I? It's lovely, by the way. Henry let me see it."

"I don't believe this; I don't believe any of this." Elizabeth didn't know whether to laugh or cry. Obviously she and her mother had been brought here on a wild-goose chase to play unwilling parts in her grandmother's latest flight of fancy. She loved Gammy, she really did, and she wouldn't want to insult Nick's father, but enough was enough. Nobody—but *nobody*—was going to choose her wedding gown for her!

Opening her mouth to say just that, Elizabeth was astounded to hear herself meekly agreeing to follow Mrs. Gillespie upstairs to try on the gown.

"Here, darling, take this with you," Rose called after her as Elizabeth mounted the first step. "There's a full slip in it and the headpiece you liked at that shop in Allentown last week. Just to help you judge the gown with all the right accessories, of course," she added lamely as Elizabeth looked daggers at her. "Now, shoo! Hank and Gloria and I will wait down here for your entrance."

"Do you believe those two, Mrs. Gillespie?" Elizabeth questioned in exasperation as the housekeeper opened the door to one of the bedrooms. "Gammy even roped my mother in this time. You know, my grandmother picked out my gown for my senior prom, now that I think of it, and even called my date to instruct him on what sort of flowers he was to bring. I love Gammy, honestly I do, but this time I think she's gone too—*oh, look at that!*"

"Beautiful, isn't it?" Mrs. Gillespie walked across the room to where a wedding gown was hanging from an open closet door, its long train tumbled onto the carpet. "It was Mrs. Lancaster's," she explained as she reverently touched the skirt, lightly fluffing it. "They just don't make things like this anymore. Do you know, every single pearl and sequin on this entire gown was sewn on individually? She had it preserved, thank goodness, and Mr. Lancaster had it taken out and pressed for you to see it. I think he's right, it should be almost a perfect fit. You do want to try it on, don't you?"

Elizabeth couldn't speak, but only raised her hands toward the gown a few times as she walked across the room, before stopping in front of it, her bottom lip quivering. Her eyes filled with tears as she stood, transfixed, staring at the most beautiful gown she'd ever seen. "It—it's lovely—gorgeous. Truly. I—"

Mrs. Gillespie, seeing that Elizabeth was on the verge of breaking down, became all business. Going over to the bed and the box that she had laid on the bedspread, she lifted the lid and pulled out the slip, corselette and headpiece she knew she would find there. After draping them across the bed she walked up behind Elizabeth and helped the stunned girl remove her suit jacket. "That's a good girl. Now, what do you say we give them a show?"

Fifteen minutes later Mrs. Gillespie walked down the wide mahogany staircase and summoned Henry, Gloria and Rose into the foyer. They stood on the black-and-white tiles beneath the crystal chandelier and craned their heads upward for their first sight of Elizabeth.

She walked slowly out onto the wide upstairs landing, trying hard to decide if she felt more like Cinderella at the ball or Scarlett O'Hara on her way to a party. She felt beautiful, yet fragile, and more completely feminine than at any other time of her life.

The full ballroom skirt of heavy *peau de soie* billowed over the half-dozen underslips that rustled faintly with her every step, and the pearls and scattering of sequins decorating the floral-design reembroidered alençon lace that accented the bodice and swirled across the skirt sparkled as they caught the light.

The gown had a Basque waist that outlined her slim form perfectly, and her shoulders rose creamily above the off-the-shoulder neckline; the short puffed sleeves standing out to each side just enough to give balance to the full skirt. Age had lent a peachy-beige tone to the gown; the material had a richness and depth to it that Elizabeth had not seen in any of the gowns she'd looked at, and dismissed, in the bridal shops.

The headpiece that Rose had included was the delicate alençon-lace and pearl crown Elizabeth had chosen at one of the shops, with the layer upon layer of tulle attached to the back of the crown adding a heightened pouf while allowing enough veiling for a modest fingertip veil.

She knew how she looked, for Mrs. Gillespie had placed her in front of a full-length mirror before leaving the room, but the expression on her mother's face reinforced her feeling of ethereal beauty.

As she approached the stairway and began her descent, the cathedral-length train swept along behind her. The large flat *peau de soie* bow near the bottom edge of the train matched the bows floating on either side of the skirt below her hips. With her hands lifting the full skirt just slightly above her ankles, her eyelids now lowered to avoid contact with anyone else, she felt herself float down the staircase, a fairy princess, an angel—a bride!

"Just the way my Katherine looked on our wedding day." Henry's voice was choked with emotion, and he reached into his pocket to take out a handkerchief and unashamedly dab at his eyes.

"Oh, Elizabeth!" Gloria gushed, bursting into tears. "You're so lovely!"

Rose was also crying, but she was smiling through her tears, knowing that this moment was so perfect, so healing, so absolutely right. "My granddaughter's quite a girl, isn't she, Hank?"

Elizabeth walked up to Henry and kissed him on the cheek. "I—I don't know how to thank you, Mr. Lancaster. This—well, this is just the most beautiful gown in the world. I'm more than flattered—I'm *honored* that you'd allow me to wear it."

Henry returned her kiss, then said, "You just make my son happy, all right? And give me a few grandchildren before I get much older."

Her face losing its solemn beauty to beam brightly as she smiled, Elizabeth, tears of happiness standing on her eyelashes, threw her arms around the man and hugged him tightly. "That's a promise, Mr. Lancaster!"

"Dad. That's a promise, Dad," he said gruffly, holding her at arm's length in front of him.

"That's a promise, Dad," Elizabeth repeated as Rose and Mrs. Gillespie hugged each other and congratulated themselves on a job well done.

To bring them all back to earth, Rose announced prosaically: "This is all well and good, but I still say we're having green beans with the filet mignon."

Elizabeth laughed and shook her head. "Back to that, are we? Gammy, I talked to Nick, and neither he nor I like green beans. We'd rather serve broccoli."

"Here we go again," Gloria said, sighing resignedly. "Please leave me out of this discussion."

"Thanks, Mom," Elizabeth teased, "I knew I could count on you."

"We're serving green beans," Rose reiterated staunchly, looking to Henry for support. "Everybody else likes them. Besides, you and Nick probably won't remember a thing you eat anyway."

Throwing her arms up in mock surrender, Elizabeth said, "I give up! I'm too happy right now to fight with you. Green beans it is. Mom, Mrs. Gillespie, would you please help me with the gown? I don't want to soil it."

As Elizabeth disappeared back up the stairs with her mother, the housekeeper holding her train for her as she went, Rose nudged Henry in the ribs with her elbow. "See what I mean, Hank? It's all in the timing. We'll get those trumpets in the choir loft yet, I promise. Now, why don't we go over that seating chart again while we're waiting for Gloria and Elizabeth? You did say you wanted the mayor at the same table as the senator?"

"Good Lord, no!" Henry replied, following Rose into the living room. "They can't stand each other. Let me get the chart and we'll go over it again."

Thanksgiving came and Gloria invited Henry and Nick to dinner, which was an enormous meal that always took her days to prepare, just so that her family could wolf it all down during halftime of one of the many football games that kept the men hidden in the den for most of the day.

This year, however, she warned her family that things would be different. After sampling what dinner was like at Henry's house, with Mrs. Gillespie serving course after course in the elegant dining room, Gloria had worked herself into a frenzy, polishing every bit of silver and hand washing her good china and crystal.

Rose did her part by obligingly unearthing a handmade lace tablecloth her own mother had brought over from Ireland a lifetime earlier and Elizabeth and Megan had set the table after Paul and John inserted the extra leaf.

By noon everything was ready and the appetite-inducing smell of roasting turkey filled the house, along with the pleasing but not so traditional aroma of spaghetti sauce and meatballs bubbling on top of the stove. Elizabeth didn't question the spaghetti, as it had been served on every holiday in her memory, right alongside the cranberry sauce and half a dozen assorted vegetables. It was a family favorite, and a family tradition.

It was, however, a revelation to Nick and Henry, but Gloria's excellent cooking overshadowed their surprise and soon they were all seated around the large dining-room table, passing plates and talking about the quarterbacks for the next game, due on at six o'clock.

"I'm telling you, Megan could throw better than that guy," Paul said as he reached in front of Henry for the mashed potatoes, just to have his grandmother deftly smack the back of his hand with a tablespoon. "Ouch! Hey, Gammy, cut that out!"

"Got you that time," John crowed, laughing. "Remember what Mom told us; no boardinghouse reach today."

If Gloria had worried that Henry Lancaster would feel overwhelmed by her noisy, boisterous family she soon relaxed as Henry said, "Paul, I can remember my mother doing the same thing to me that your grandmother just did to you when there was company for dinner. But Nick and I aren't company; we're family. Isn't that right, Jack?"

Jack Chatham, standing at the end of the table as he carved the turkey, replied, "We certainly are, Henry. Would you like white meat or dark? I'm afraid Megan already has dibs on one of the legs."

"Oh, Father, please," Megan complained in a pained voice, eyeing Nick to see if he had noticed her new sweater. "Let the boys have the legs. They're too messy."

"Well, la-di-da," John said singsong. "Would you listen to her? *Father.* Hah!"

Nick reached for and found Elizabeth's hand under the table. "One more month," he whispered, "and we'll be having dinner in our own place."

"Yes," Elizabeth agreed on a sigh. "Alone. Won't it be heaven?"

"Nick!" his father commanded, interrupting his son just as he was leaning toward Elizabeth's mouth. "Stop eating that poor child with your eyes and pass me some more of those meatballs. Gloria, this is delicious. I can't remember the last time I tasted anything this good. You'll have to give Mrs. Gillespie your recipe."

The meal was a success; Gloria's pumpkin pie was its usual triumph, and Nick and Elizabeth were told to go amuse themselves somehow while the women cleaned up the kitchen and the men returned to the den for the football game. They didn't have to be asked twice, quickly taking up their coats and heading for the backyard.

Once outside on the porch in the deepening dusk, Nick quickly pulled Elizabeth into his arms and soundly kissed her. "God, but I needed that!" he breathed against her ear. "Out of town all week opening that branch in Delaware and then seeing you for the first time surrounded by our families. Tell me, when was the last time we were alone? I mean *really* alone?"

Elizabeth moved her head slightly to one side so that he could nuzzle the base of her throat with his lips. "Do those five minutes in your office Monday morning before you left for Delaware mean anything?"

Nick's response was a low growl.

"No, I didn't think so," she answered, running a hand into the hair at the back of his neck. "You want to go to a movie?"

Nick stood slightly away from her and arched his eyebrows at her, replying, "Only if you promise we can neck in the back of the balcony."

"Nicholas Lancaster," Elizabeth declared, pretending to pout, "there are times I believe you only want me for my body."

"Really? And does that bother you?"

Elizabeth grinned. "Nope, seeing that I kinda like your body, too."

"That does it! Let's get out of here," Nick decided, pulling her toward the back door. "We'll tell them we're going to the movies and then—"

"And then—what?" Elizabeth asked, trying not to mention their pact of purposely staying away from closed, intimate places.

Nick, who had visions of his apartment dancing in his head, came back to reality with a depressing bang. Shrugging, he looked around, trying to form an idea. When his gaze locked on the Christmas Star shining on South Mountain he said abruptly: "We're going to take a ride and look at the Christmas lights. Nothing can be any more harmless than that."

Within five minutes they were on their way out the front door, Nick carrying a large plastic container filled with sliced turkey and stuffing that Gloria had insisted he take home with him. After he stashed the container on the floor behind the driver's seat and started the engine, Elizabeth suggested they should start their tour by riding across the Hill to Hill Bridge two blocks away.

"Do you remember how the bridge used to look when they put a tree in the circle in the middle of the intersection?" Elizabeth asked as they drove along. "The traffic jams were horrendous, with people and tour buses coming from all over to see the tree, but it certainly was beautiful. Sometimes progress can be a little sad. When I was a Girl Scout, we'd all hike across the bridge, singing carols as we went."

"You must have made a great Girl Scout," Nick commented, still intent on finding some place to be alone with her. "I would have bought all your cookies."

"Oh, Nick, look," Elizabeth exclaimed, purposely ignoring his remark. "Moravian College has candles in all the windows of the buildings. I love those old stone dormitories. You know, the early Moravians were very big on Christmas. The crèche at the Moravian Church is absolutely beautiful. Let's drive by it, all right?"

Nick knew when he was beaten, and secretly he also knew that Elizabeth was right. They were going to do this thing right. They had already been through their required meeting with the priest, and they were planning a serious ceremony. He was a grown man; he wasn't some hot-blooded young boy who could put his own pleasure ahead of everything else and damn the consequences.

But that didn't mean it was easy; he loved Elizabeth so much, wanted her so much. And she felt the same way, which was the other reason he knew he could wait for their wedding night before making her completely his. Their love was special, and the celebration of that love had to be just as special. Yet it was only Thanksgiving. How would he ever wait until the day after Christmas?

Elizabeth reached across the seat to take hold of Nick's hand, sensing the tension in his body and knowing what he was thinking. "I love you so much," she said softly. "You make me feel so cherished, darling, so special. If we could, I'd love to run away tonight and get married. But I want to come to you the way your mother came to your father, even wearing the gown she wore. It's silly, I guess, and if anyone had asked me a year ago if I would feel this way I would have said they were crazy, but—"

"But love does strange things to people," Nick ended for her. "And it is crazy. Here I am, Nicholas Lancaster, owner of a fair-size department store chain, reduced to driving around town stealing kisses at stop lights. You know, if it had been up to us, we would have been married by now. We aren't children; we don't need all this ceremony. How did we let ourselves get talked into this?"

It was worse than Elizabeth had feared. Nick was really beginning to hate the delay, to hate the whole idea of a big wedding. Unfortunately as each day passed, and certainly ever since trying on Katherine Lancaster's gown, Elizabeth was getting more and more caught up in the idea of a lavish wedding.

Yet, she reasoned silently, when she really came down to thinking about it, becoming Mrs. Nicholas Lancaster was what she really wanted. Maybe the strain was too much for them; if she wasn't careful they would soon be arguing, and all because of a silly wedding.

"You want to go to Maryland for breakfast, Nick?" she asked at last, watching his face as they passed beneath a street lamp glittering with Christmas lights.

Nick darted a questioning look at her as he turned the car onto a side road at the base of South Mountain. "Maryland? Breakfast? Has that wine Dad brought to dinner gone to your head?"

"I think so," Elizabeth answered slowly, "because I'm offering to elope with you—tonight. We can drive down to Maryland, find a justice of the peace and stick around for breakfast before we drive back."

"Just in time to break the news to your family and my father. Are you harboring a death wish you haven't told me about, darling?"

The idea of eloping appealed to Nick, it appealed to him more than he'd ever admit to Elizabeth, but he couldn't ask her to sacrifice her dreams just because he couldn't seem to control his passion to take her to his bed. "Besides, think of Jimmy Timenski and His Polka Dots. Your father tells me they've been practicing every night at the Legion Hall down the street. What could we say to them?"

Elizabeth put a hand over her mouth to stifle a giggle. "And think of all those green beans going to waste," she added, her relief making her feel slightly giddy. "It's almost criminal. Where are we?"

Nick pulled the car off to the side of the narrow gravel road and turned off the key. "All that talk about your exploits as a Girl Scout brought back memories of my Boy

Scout days. Every Christmas we'd climb up here to sing Christmas carols beneath the star. So many different groups did the same thing that it used to get pretty crowded up here every night. See," he said, pointing toward the front windshield, "there's the star, straight ahead."

Nick helped her out of the car and they approached the massive scaffolding that supported the five-pointed star. "It must be forty or fifty feet high," Elizabeth remarked, craning her neck to see to the top of the highest point.

"Fifty-three feet," Nick told her, "if I remember it right, although I can't remember how many lights are on it; hundreds and hundreds. Impressive isn't it?"

"Well, Bethlehem is supposed to be the Christmas City," Elizabeth pointed out, proud of her hometown. "It's only fitting that we have a proper Christmas star. People can see it for miles."

Nick looked at Elizabeth's face, glowing from the reflected light high above them, thinking she had never looked more beautiful. Her cherry-red cape was appropriate for this, the official launching of the Christmas season and for once he was not dreading the hectic days that stretched between now and the close of business Christmas Eve. He only hoped he could be kept so busy that the time would pass swiftly.

"Oh Nick, darling, look," Elizabeth cried excitedly, holding out her hands. "It's beginning to snow. The flakes are huge!"

The snow floated down slowly, catching in Elizabeth's auburn hair and dusting the shoulders of her cape as she spun around in a circle; her arms were outstretched like a small child trying to catch the snow.

Nick knew he was lost. As Elizabeth stopped her whirling, her cheeks flushed from the cold air, a smile lighting her face, he drew her gently into his arms and lowered his face to hers. "I love you, Elizabeth Chatham," he vowed huskily. "I love you so very, very much."

The world faded away as they clung to each other beneath the Christmas star, the snow increasing in intensity so that it swirled around them, dusting the gravel path and clinging to the bare branches of the low trees that crowded the hillside.

His mouth slanted first this way, then that against hers as she opened to him, allowing herself to be drawn more deeply into the kiss. With one hand at the back of her head, he held her against him, tasting her sweetness, as his other hand crept inside the cherry-red cape to caress her small waist. "I love you, Elizabeth," he breathed into her mouth, "I love you, I love you, I love you."

Straining against him, desperate to be closer to him, Elizabeth lost all sense of time and place, of right and wrong, wanting only to please him, to be pleased by him. There was more to love than hearts and flowers, and this deep need to physically belong to each other couldn't be ignored any longer. She was his, she wanted to be his in every way.

"Hey, guys, look at that! There's a couple of people over here—necking!"

Nick pulled back at the sound of a young boy calling to his friends, to see a troop of Boy Scouts coming up the roadway, their scoutmaster huffing and puffing as he brought up the rear. Bringing himself back under control with some difficulty, Nick quipped, "Some traditions die hard in Bethlehem, don't they, darling? It would seem the Boy Scout pilgrimage to the star is one of them."

Hiding her face against his jacket, Elizabeth could only nod her head, not trusting her voice until they had walked past the scout troop and reached the car. "Nick," she said as he helped her into the passenger side of the car, "do you ever get the feeling Gammy has put a hex on us?"

"What do you mean?"

"I mean, we can't seem to be alone even when we're on the side of a mountain. Now tell me, doesn't that seem a little farfetched to be simple coincidence—or even pure bad luck?"

Nick started the engine, then turned the car back down the hill the way they had come. "I refuse to answer on the grounds it may scare the hell out of me. Oh well, darling, I think I can have you back home in time for the second half of the football game. John said he'd save me a seat on the end of the couch."

"Well yippee, and bully for you," Elizabeth groused, sinking down in her seat. "Sure, you can go hide in the den. I bet we won't be back in the house five minutes before they all start on me again because we haven't auditioned a soloist yet for the church. And tomorrow's Black Friday, the busiest shopping day of the year. My life is just one unending stream of fun, fun, fun these days. I don't know how I handle the sheer excitement of it."

"Poor baby," he commiserated with exaggerated concern.

Raising her hands threateningly, Elizabeth warned tightly, "Don't push your luck, buster. These hands are registered with the police."

"But you love me," Nick reminded her happily, amazed at the way they could go from heated passion to silly teasing so quickly, so easily.

"But I love you," she agreed, moving as close as the console allowed to sit with her head resting against his shoulder. "Nick," she asked idly as they drove back across town to Spring Street, "do you think Prince Andrew and his Fergie had all these problems?"

Chapter Eight

"That's funny," Nick remarked as they pulled up in front of the Chatham house, "Dad's car is still here. I would have thought he'd be long gone by now. I think I'd better go inside with you, darling."

Elizabeth looked at him warily, not liking the apprehension she heard in his voice. "You don't think someone's ill, do you?"

Putting a hand under her elbow as they mounted the porch steps, Nick said, "No, darling, not ill. If this prickling at the back of my neck means anything, I have a feeling we're in for another discussion about the wedding. But besides the prickle, I guess I should tell you, I've been hiding something from you, hoping Dad would change his mind."

Elizabeth felt her stomach drop to her toes. "What is it? Don't tell me we're back to the battle of the bands. You seemed to have settled that so well."

"If only it was that easy. No, it's not about the bands." Nick stopped on the porch and drew her to one side. "I have a confession to make to you about my father, darling. Brace yourself—it isn't pretty."

Elizabeth's cheeks paled. "He hates me," she breathed, grabbing Nick's arm. "Oh, I just knew things were going too well. Everyone I talk to says there are all sorts of problems with families before a wedding. My friend Beth told me about a girl who works with her, and she had the most awful time trying to—"

Nick kissed Elizabeth to cut off the flow of words, then said, "Dad doesn't hate you, darling. As a matter of fact, there have been times these past few weeks when I've thought he's merely tolerating me because it's through me that he's discovered you and rediscovered Rose."

Now Elizabeth was angry. What was Nick trying to do— frighten her into cardiac arrest? "Well, then, what is it? I feel like a thief standing out here, casing the joint or something while I can hear voices inside."

Nick took a deep breath, exhaled it slowly and said, "My father is a toy junkie. There, it's out in the open."

"A *toy* junkie?" Elizabeth looked at Nick as if to see if he was completely sober. "Oh, well, that's it then—of course you realize, Nicholas, that the wedding's off. I could never be related to a toy junkie. Nick, *what the devil are you talking about?*"

"*Shhh!* They'll hear us," he warned, pulling Elizabeth farther into the shadows. "And stop laughing, dammit, this isn't funny. Look—Dad has always been crazy about toys. Why do you think Lancaster's has all those wild, oversize mechanical monstrosities perched on every floor during the Christmas Season? The man's crazy for toys. Only now, thanks to modern technology, he's found a whole new outlet for his addiction. *Home computers.*"

Elizabeth was still chuckling, although she was trying hard to get a grip on herself, aware that Nick was being deadly serious. "Computers, huh? I can see your problem, darling, as you hate the things."

"A necessary evil," Nick agreed, nodding his head solemnly.

"All right. You've confessed, and now I know all about your father's failings. But I also *fail* to see the connection; I don't understand what all the fuss is about. What can your father's love of home computers possibly have to do with our wedding?''

Nick arched his eyebrows as he pulled her over to the window that looked in on the living room. Just as he had thought, his father and the entire Chatham family were gathered around the coffee table, looking at a portable computer that sat there, it's green eye glowing malevolently, like an alien space creature. ''Do you see that?'' he asked Elizabeth. ''Dad must have brought it with him, the sneak. Some genius has invented a plan-your-wedding program for home computers.''

''Oh, no,'' Elizabeth wailed, rejecting the idea that something as romantic as her wedding day could be turned into a cut-and-dried computer program. ''What are they looking at now?''

Nick bent down to peer through the glass. ''Unless I miss my guess, they're working out the seating chart for the reception.''

''But that's the thing Beth told me her friend and her fiancé nearly broke up over! Oh, Lordy, Nick, we'd better get in there—fast!''

No sooner had they opened the front door than Rose's voice reached them, saying impatiently, ''That's entirely out of the question, Jack. Why would I want to sit next to Margaret? She's *old*—we have nothing in common. I'm not going to spend the whole reception listening to her telling me about her gallbladder operation again. I wonder if she still carries the stones around with her in that little brown bottle? Daft woman.''

''She squeezes my cheeks, Gammy,'' Megan added, as if to prove her grandmother's point.

''But, Mom,'' her son protested, ''Aunt Margaret is Elizabeth's godmother. She has to sit at the table with us; it says so in the book Gloria found in Elizabeth's room. See— parents may have their own table . . . sitting with *close relatives*—''

''Close relatives *and friends*,'' Rose finished for him firmly, looking over his shoulder. ''I'm going to sit beside Hank.''

"Oh, dear," Gloria asked quietly, "have you forgotten that the groom's family has their own table? Remember, we decided that the families are too large to put them both at the same table."

"Hi, gang," Nick broke in swiftly, realizing that no one had noticed their entrance, "we're back. What's going on? Is Dad teaching the boys how to play football on his computer? I thought the game was still on television."

"Lizzie, you're back!" John exclaimed unnecessarily, scrambling to his feet. "Mom says you're having a bridal table and Megan says that means I can't sit with Eddie and the rest of the guys."

"And we have to be on our best behavior, and Gammy says we have to make sure not to eat like we're at a trough—just like we were pigs or something, for pete's sake—and then we have to dance with our partners," Paul chimed in, joining his older brother in their list of complaints. "You never said this was going to be such a pain. Me and John talked about it a couple of minutes ago, and we decided that we don't want to be in the wedding anymore, Liz. Sorry about that."

"John and I," Gloria corrected, unruffled.

Helping Elizabeth out of her coat, Nick said calmly, "Gee, that's too bad, boys. We'll miss you, but I guess it can't be helped. Right, darling?"

John frowned, looking at Nick. "Hey, not so fast! That's it? We're out of the wedding? But what about Liz's friends, Nora and Lorraine—we're supposed to be their partners, aren't we? You're just gonna let us sit on the sidelines, with nothing to do? Lizzie?"

Taking her cue from Nick, Elizabeth merely shrugged, spreading her hands fatalistically. "What else can we do, boys? I know it's my wedding day, the single most important day of my life, and it will hurt me deeply if my own brothers don't want to be a part of it, but I don't want to force you into anything. If you really want out, you're out. And no hard feelings, honestly. I'm sure Nick will have no trouble replacing you."

"You could use your cousin Steve, Elizabeth," Rose suggested, "and even the boys' friend Eddie, if we're pinched for an extra usher."

Paul glared at his brother angrily. "This is all your fault, you dope. You talked me into this. I *want* to be in the wedding. We told everybody we were going to be wearing tuxes and riding in limousines—and now you've blown the whole thing!"

Nick leaned over and quoted quietly into Elizabeth's ear: "And that's another fine mess you've gotten us into, Stanley." Louder, he said, "Just a minute, Paul—before you get too upset—nothing's written in stone here. If you want back in, just say so. You too, John."

"Only if you agree to play by the rules," Elizabeth added carefully, knowing her brothers much better than Nick did. "And no more plans to wrap Nick's car in plastic wrap so that we can't leave for our honeymoon."

"You overheard us, huh?" John guessed, grimacing. "Eddie said they did it to his cousin's car and it took them over an hour to unwrap it. Okay, we promise to be good, honest."

"Yeah," Paul seconded, then both boys walked over to shake Nick's hand, gratifying their mother who was about to prompt them to do just that from her seat on the ottoman beside the coffee table. "Can we go watch the end of the football game now, Dad?"

"With my blessing," Jack told them, once more examining the seating chart still dully throbbing on the green computer screen. "I don't know why you even came in here in the first place."

Paul was naive enough to answer: "Because we heard you yelling at Megan and wanted to watch the fun," which earned them a speaking look from their mother and had them bounding out of the room on the double.

"Thank heavens they're gone," Megan pronounced from her tucked-up position in a corner of the slip-covered couch. "See, Mother, I told you the plans should be left to the grown-ups."

"Which of course explains your presence," her grandmother quipped, ruffling Megan's curls and receiving a glare from the youngest Chatham daughter.

Elizabeth walked over to the coffee table and sat down on the floor at Henry Lancaster's feet. "Oh, look, Nick. The whole screen's filled with pictures of round tables, just like at the club. And there's the bridal table—my goodness, it's long, isn't it?"

"It has to hold a bridal party of sixteen, my dear," Henry pointed out, moving the cursor along the sixteen small squares that denoted chairs. "I checked with the manager at the club and she says the table will have to go in front of the windows overlooking the terrace. It's the only place it will fit."

Nick leaned over his father's shoulder to see the screen. "I don't like it, Dad. We'll look like the judges' table at an ice-skating competition. I can see it now, Elizabeth—we'll be holding up cards, giving scores on the waitresses for their technical and artistic skill in weaving through the other tables."

"But it's traditional," Rose said, the matter already settled in her own mind.

Elizabeth narrowed her eyes as she looked at the screen. "You're right, Nick. Besides, so many of the attendants will have wives, husbands or dates with them—like Beth's date from New York—and those people won't know anybody else. I thought we'd dispense with the traditional bridal table and scatter the attendants throughout the room."

Gloria seemed to like this idea. "With their pretty plum-colored gowns, the girls would add color to the room, wouldn't they? But, dear, where would you and Nick sit if there isn't going to be a bridal table?"

"With you, of course," Elizabeth answered. "We'll sit with both families, and the priest will also sit at our table. It's quite acceptable, according to the books I've read."

"And that fool, Margaret?" Rose interposed. "Where does she sit?"

Elizabeth looked to Nick for assistance, and he answered, "I've got an uncle who's ninety and nearly stone-deaf. Aunt Margaret can talk all day long and Uncle Fred will just sit there, nodding and smiling. I think they'd be great together."

The laughter that Nick's solution caused broke some of the tension, but only long enough for Henry to clear the computer screen and begin arranging tables the way Elizabeth had suggested. The long bridal table was discarded in favor of a large circular table placed directly in front of the windows in the middle of the room, and Henry began placing smaller round tables around the room, labeling each with a different letter of the alphabet. "There, now we can seat the rest of the crowd. Elizabeth, where do you want to start?"

The first few tables were filled easily and without any problems, the wedding party being seated with guests close to their own ages. Because of Gloria's suggestion, the bridesmaids were scattered evenly throughout the room, like colorful garnishes tastefully arranged on a platter, and the groomsmen were seated near the dance floor, and away from the bar.

Elizabeth gratefully accepted the glass of white wine Nick handed her, winking at him to show that his fears had been for nothing, just as Henry declared: "Jack, you don't seem to understand. I'm not being a snob. We just can't have Senator Billings sitting at the same table with your friend Harvey."

"Why not?" Jack asked. "Billings is always saying he's plain folks, just like his constituents. Well, Harvey Wycheck is one of his constituents."

"Father," Megan pointed out condescendingly, "Mr. Wycheck is a *garbageman*."

"Harvey's a businessman. He owns a fleet of waste-disposal trucks. Besides, where would we all be today, I ask you, young lady, if there were no garbagemen?" her father countered.

Rose was happy to enlighten her youngest granddaughter. "Up to our ears in—"

"Mother, please, don't encourage him!" Gloria interrupted before her mother-in-law could say what was on her mind. "Megan, Mr. Wycheck is a lovely man, and captain of your father's bowling team. I suggest you apologize to your father at once and then go out to the kitchen and unload the dishwasher."

"Yes, Mommy," Megan agreed sullenly, pushing herself slowly to her feet. "But I still say Mr. Lancaster is right. Brother, where are you going to put the Mayor—on the other side of Aunt Margaret?"

It was quiet in the room for a few minutes, Henry busily retitling the dozens of little squares and pushing them first to one table, then another, as the sounds of Megan's heavy-handed treatment of her mother's pots and pans filtered into the room.

Finally Henry sat back, sighed and announced proudly. "There, all done. I put the Senator and Mr. Wycheck at the same table and they can talk to each other or ignore each other; it's all the same to me. I don't know why I thought it was impossible."

"Oh, they'll talk, all right," Rose told him, going over to look at the screen. "Harvey will bend the senator's ear all night long, telling him what a great idea it would be for Bethlehem to have its own professional soccer team. Right, Jack?"

But Jack Chatham wasn't paying attention to his mother; he was looking at the guest list Henry had projected onto the screen. "Hey, this thing's showing that there're over three hundred and fifty people on that list. I thought we'd agreed to keep it to a hundred and fifty on each side. What's going on?"

"Calm down, Jack," his mother commanded. "Hank and I added a few people, that's all."

"Oh really? And who's going to pay for all those extra people?"

Gloria, knowing that she had planned to purchase new slipcovers and drapes for the living room so that the photographs taken before the ceremony would have a pleasing background, found her voice. "Mom, I think you might have thought to consult us before you did this," she suggested mildly, so mildly that Elizabeth knew her mother was close to tears.

"You got that in one, Gloria," her husband said as Nick looked at his prospective father-in-law and noticed that the man's ears looked unusually red. "Well, I'm not paying for them, so you can just push whatever button's on that crazy thing that erases people."

Henry stood up. "There's no need for that, Jack. I'll gladly cover the additional expense."

Knowing Henry had just said exactly the wrong thing, no matter how well meant, Elizabeth felt the urge to duck her head and cover her ears as she waited for the explosion that was sure to come. She didn't have long to wait.

"The hell you will! And it's not the expense; it's the principle of the thing!" Jack exploded, his injured pride overwhelming his normally pleasant disposition. "Gloria, go tell the children to get upstairs to their rooms. Henry, we're going to have this out here and now. That's *my* daughter over there, and I'm the father of the bride. *I* make the plans. You got that?"

Henry, fortunately, "got that," and quickly agreed, knowing that he had allowed himself to be caught up in Rose's schemes without taking the time to think of the consequences. Even if he hadn't realized it, one look at his son's face would have been enough to show him the error of his ways. Nick, he could see, was angry—very angry.

Unfortunately Rose wasn't as easily convinced. She loved her son, she really did, but she had always thought he was just a little too stubborn for his own good—she couldn't imagine who he took after, for *she* was certainly a most flexible person.

"Now see here, Jack," she began, standing in front of her son and poking a finger into his chest, "I told you a dozen times that I want to contribute to this wedding, so climb down off that high horse of yours and let me help. This is a party—we're supposed to be able to look back on Elizabeth's wedding day and know that it was the best darn party anyone ever had!"

"Rose, I think—" Henry began carefully.

"Mom, I said no, and I meant—" Jack broke in.

"Mom? Can't you do anything?" Elizabeth pleaded.

"Oh, wow!" John and Paul said together, standing in the archway.

"I said *no*!" Jack reiterated, and he reached down a hand and pushed several buttons on the computer at random, sending the screen to black.

"Now you've done it!" Henry shouted, rushing to save his latest "baby." "You've erased everything we've done. We'll have to start from scratch!"

"Not with me around, you won't," Nick said through clenched teeth, picking up his coat from the back of a nearby chair and slamming out the front door, forgetting to say goodnight to his fiancée.

"Isn't he masterful!" Megan gushed, standing in the archway, clutching a damp dishcloth to her breasts.

Elizabeth looked at the people who were left in the room, then at the closed front door, her eyes wide, her throat working silently. She spread her hands as if to comment on the bloody carnage that had been left behind by a rampaging army and then, her face crumpling as the tears she had been holding back threatened to fall, wailed, "Look what you've done! You've ruined *everything*!" before running for the stairs, sobbing, a hand to her mouth.

"Well," Gloria observed, hands on hips, clearly taking charge of the shambles, "I hope you're all feeling proud of yourselves. Children, go back where you were, please. Jack, shake hands with Henry and apologize for breaking his little computer. Mother Chatham? What do you have to say for yourself?"

The silence in the living room after Gloria finished speaking was deafening. Rose Chatham dug the toe of her shoe into a corner of the aged oriental rug, averting her eyes from everyone else in the room. "Bridal nerves," she muttered quietly at last, knowing that Elizabeth was normally the most levelheaded person in the world and that most of what had gone wrong tonight could be laid squarely at her, Rose's, door. "That's all it is. Don't make a fuss, Gloria. She'll be fine in the morning."

"Nick, too," Henry put in after nervously clearing his throat. "He never did like scenes."

Jack put his arm around his wife's shoulders, feeling the tenseness in her slight body. "It's not like they're mad at each other, honey."

"No," Gloria agreed in her soft voice, "you're right. They're angry with us. And you know what—I don't blame them. I don't blame either one of them a bit. They aren't children; they're adults, and we're treating them as if they were babies. From now on, this wedding is strictly Elizabeth and Nick's, and we are going to keep *our* noses out of it. Is that understood?"

Gloria Chatham didn't become angry often, but when she did, Jack Chatham—and even Rose—knew it was better to listen to her. Henry Lancaster took his cue from them.

"Agreed," they promised together, not noticing that Rose had crossed her fingers behind her back.

The day after Thanksgiving—called Black Friday in the retailing world—was traditionally the busiest shopping day of the year, and this Black Friday was even worse than usual. Shoppers descended on Lancaster's main downtown store an hour before the doors opened, eager to snatch up the early-bird specials, and Elizabeth had instructed her sales personnel to stand back and let the customers loose in the department for the first few minutes; she was fearful the clerks would be trampled by the stampeding horde.

Two hours after the store opened for business, Elizabeth surrendered the cash register that she had been working to Judy Holland and escaped to her office to catch her breath, knowing that she was going to explode the next time a customer asked her a silly question.

"Why don't you salespeople smile more? I should ask to see your manager," her last customer had complained just moments after the woman had slammed a heavy roasting pan down on the counter in front of three other customers who had been patiently waiting in line, insisting she had been there first.

Slumping into her chair, Elizabeth slipped off her shoes and lifted her feet to rest them on top of her desk, knowing she should never have worn high heels today. "That just goes to show me where my head is," she lamented, rubbing the back of her neck as her aching head continued to throb. "I can't believe I actually cried myself to sleep last night."

Elizabeth closed her eyes, remembering the events of the previous night. What an awful, terrible scene! And what a stupid, childish reaction! She still couldn't believe the way she had dissolved into tears, like a child, like Megan. "No," she corrected aloud, "Megan wouldn't be so silly. Why did Nick have to storm out that way? Talk about a rat deserting a sinking ship."

"I agree," came a voice from the doorway. "Personally, I think he should be flogged."

"Nick!" Elizabeth exclaimed, swiveling her chair around to see him standing half in, half out of her office, a huge bouquet of long-stemmed red roses held out in front of him. "Are those supposed to be a peace-offering?"

Looking down at the flowers, Nick remarked, "Well, I don't think they'd make much of a shield, do you? How are you this morning? I didn't sleep all night."

He looked so vulnerable standing there that Elizabeth's heart, which had never really hardened against him, melted, and she got up and rushed into his arms. "Oh, Nick, what happened? How did it all get so crazy?"

Holding her tightly against his chest, Nick rubbed his cheek against the top of her head. "I'm not sure, darling, but I think it may have to do with something I asked you one day in Central Park."

Elizabeth rested her cheek against his chest. "What a wonderful day that was. It seems a lifetime ago. We should have stayed in New York and found a justice of the peace and avoided all this craziness. What fools we were."

Cupping her face in his hands, Nick tilted her head back so that he could look straight down into her wide brown eyes. "The worst is over, darling. I had it straight from my father's mouth this morning. He was waiting for me when I came to work, all hangdog looking and with profound apologies. Not only that, but he told me your mother made everyone promise to leave us alone."

Smiling, Elizabeth said, "Megan told me as much this morning before I left for work. According to my sister, my mother lined them all up like naughty children and bawled them out. I wish I could have been there."

"But you weren't, were you?" Nick said softly. "Dad told me you ran to your bedroom, crying, right after I left. That's my fault, too, isn't it?"

Elizabeth closed her eyes and shook her head. "No, it was my fault. I've read about the way brides seem to dissolve into tears at the slightest provocation, but I didn't believe it until I found myself facedown on my bed, sobbing my heart out. I figured it was going to happen sooner or later, what with all this rush to have everything done on time."

"Like the seating chart," Nick said, sitting in Elizabeth's chair and drawing her down on his lap. "Do you realize that we haven't even gotten the responses back from the invitations we sent? For all we know Aunt Margaret may be going to the Bahamas for Christmas and Senator Billings might be in Timbuktu. Why were they working on the seating chart now in the first place?"

"Gammy," Elizabeth said, as if that explained everything and, unfortunately, it did. Elizabeth loved her grandmother, loved her dearly, but the woman was going to drive her crazy. "Do you know what I found in my room this morning, Nick? A sixpence! She wants me to put it in my shoe before I go down the aisle."

"I like her," Nick declared firmly. "She's done wonders for my father. I haven't seen him this happy since Mother died. Good Lord, I just thought of something—do you think they'll make a match of it?"

"Don't look so thrilled, darling," Elizabeth warned. "We won't be able to pay them back by planning *their* wedding for them. Gammy already talked to me about your father and herself, and she told me that they're just good friends. Gammy and your father have both loved only one person in their lives, and they're content with their memories."

"That's rather nice."

"Yes," Elizabeth agreed, "it is. Unless you know, as I do, that Gammy says she and your father plan to spend a lot of time together in the future—'raising hell' is the term she used, I think."

Nick threw back his head and laughed, nearly toppling the two of them onto the floor. "Elizabeth, what do you say we move to Arizona after the wedding?"

"Arizona? Lancaster's doesn't have any stores out there."

"I'll *build* one," Nick bargained, pretending desperation. "Single-handedly, brick by brick, if I have to. Elizabeth—marry me and take me away from all this!"

"You idiot!" Elizabeth laughed at his joke until, without warning, the atmosphere in the room changed, becoming supercharged with the knowledge that they were alone together, and in harmony once again. "Nick?" she asked tentatively.

"Hmm?" he answered vaguely, his gaze centered on the hint of cleavage he could see above the front closure of her blouse.

"Let's not ever fight." Elizabeth's voice was low, and deadly earnest. "I hate it. I was so lonely without you, without knowing that everything was still all right between us."

Raising his gaze to her face, Nick saw a hint of tears in her eyes and felt a lump in his own throat. "We'll never fight, darling," he vowed fervently, "and that's a promise."

Their lips met gently, tentatively; the kiss was one of healing, but passion quickly turned it to one of increasing fervor and intimacy. Their bodies shifted, hands moving hungrily over arms, shoulders, backs—striving for a closeness denied them by both the swivel chair and their location just a few feet away from the busy sales floor—until they reluctantly separated.

Elizabeth continued to cling to Nick as he helped her to her feet, protesting, "I don't want you to leave. Can't you just lock the door?"

"As I believe I've said before, lady, you sure know how to pick your times and places," Nick joked, wishing he could lock the door and allow them to give way to their feelings. "Unfortunately we both have work to do. Now unhand me, woman, and let me out of here."

Holding on to his jacket lapels, Elizabeth cajoled, "Only if you promise to take me to lunch."

Nick looked at his watch, seeing that it was almost noon. "I don't have time for the store restaurant today, darling, so it will have to be hot dogs and potato chips at the snack bar. Is that all right?"

"Purest ambrosia," Elizabeth assured him, already putting on her shoes. She grabbed her purse and ran ahead to open the office door, promising, "I'll even let you pick up the check!" So saying, she bowed, flourishing her hand as if to invite him to precede her through the door.

Nick loved her, and all was right in Elizabeth's world once more.

Chapter Nine

Elizabeth sighed contentedly and rested her head against the back of the leather seat, lazily observing the familiar passing scenery as Nick steered the car along the deserted country road.

Sunday afternoons had become her favorite time. It was then that they spent their precious few hours alone together, and the peace and privacy they found inside his car seemed to be the only sanity left in a world gone mad.

Despite all Gloria's good intentions and warnings, life had not become easier for Nick and Elizabeth, even if their families were doing their best to be cooperative. Cooperation couldn't deliver seven bridesmaids' gowns to the bridal shop so that Elizabeth would stop having nightmares about going down the aisle behind attendants dressed in lovely gold-mesh-and-pearl snoods, gold leather high-heeled shoes—and their full-length crinolines.

All the good intentions in the world couldn't locate a single transportation service large enough to fit their needs, and Nick had spent two days calling rental agencies before he had found enough matching limousines for the entire wedding party.

Following a sample checklist in one of the books she had purchased, Elizabeth had already checked with the club manager about the menu, set up an appointment for her formal portrait, conferred with both bands about their selections, personally selected the silk flowers for the entire wedding party, hosted a bridesmaids' luncheon, finalized the seating chart and visited her doctor for a complete physical.

She had done all this while working long pre-Christmas hours at the store and trying, usually in vain, to find a few precious minutes alone with Nick, who was just as busy as she was. Many evenings Nick would come over to her parents' house after waiting for the sales figures from all the Lancaster store branches to be phoned in to his office, just in time to watch the eleven o'clock news with her and her father and then fall asleep on the floor with his head in her lap. She'd sit in the darkened living room with him for a while after her father went up to bed, stroking the hair back along his forehead, then reluctantly shoo him out the door, his sleepy good-night kiss usually landing somewhere to the left of her ear.

For all the romance we've been having lately, Elizabeth thought as she stole a look at Nick sitting behind the steering wheel, *we might as well be an old married couple. I wonder if he's becoming bored with me already?* As if the thought conjured up the words, she asked, "Nick? Wouldn't you want to drive to some secluded place—like maybe your apartment—so we can be alone? After all, we haven't seen each other since Friday."

Nick looked at her quickly out of the corner of his eye, just as if he were on a busy highway and couldn't really afford to take his attention off the road, and said, "We had lunch together yesterday, darling, remember? I'm sorry I couldn't stop by last night, but Dick Saunders and a couple of the guys from marketing insisted I join them for a drink for old times' sake. You know, sort of a good-bye drink. It got kind of late, so I just went home."

Elizabeth folded her arms across her stomach, her chin raised defiantly. "Old times' sake? My goodness, Nick, you're getting married—not going out of their lives forever. Why do you men always act like the groom is a condemned man, getting ready to walk the last mile? Besides, what does that have to do with our going back to your apartment? We've been driving around for almost an hour. I *know* I've seen that cow over there before."

Nick looked at the dashboard clock. "Yes, we have, haven't we? Good. Tell you what, darling, let's go visit Dad. It's Mrs. Gillespie's day off and he might be lonely."

Elizabeth liked Henry Lancaster, she liked him very much, but she wasn't in the mood for a quiet Sunday visit with the man, and she said as much to Nick. "You don't want to be alone with me, do you, Nicholas?" she added, frost edging her voice.

Turning back onto the highway, Nick, his strong jaw set belligerently, countered, "You sound like a wife, Elizabeth. Don't read so much into things, for pete's sake. I want to visit my father—so sue me!"

Elizabeth's right foot began beating a steady tattoo on the floor of the car. "Well I don't! And I don't need a house to fall on me; you don't want to be alone with me. You probably would be happier watching a football game with some of your bachelor friends. Well, far be it from me to disappoint you. Nick, take me home!" *What is the matter with me?* Elizabeth wondered. *I'm acting like a nagging fishwife.*

Pounding a fist against the steering wheel a single time in frustration, Nick exclaimed, "*Women!* I *told* them this wouldn't work. I told them it was a stupid idea. But would they listen to me? No! Of course not! Of course I want to be alone with you, Elizabeth. I want it so bad I hurt! But in the gospel according to your grandmother, grooms are not to reason why, grooms are just to do and die. This whole thing is so damn stupid. I mean, why couldn't they just tell you? After all, it's *your* shower—" Nick slapped the side of his head with the palm of his hand. "Oh, damn! I blew it!"

Elizabeth gasped inaudibly, trying not to believe what she had just heard. She was *so* ashamed! Slinking down on the seat, as if she somehow could shrink into a smaller size—one less liable to be observed by a world that would point its collective finger at her and say, "There she is! That's the one! She blew it!" Elizabeth squeaked, "My *bridal shower*? Oh."

Pushing his hand through his hair in exasperation, Nick shook his head in disbelief at his own stupidity. Then slowly, he began to laugh, at first silently, and then with more abandon. "Yes, that's it, darling—*oh*. I was supposed to keep you away from both our houses until your family could leave for the party and all the guests had arrived safely at my dad's."

"It almost worked," Elizabeth provided soothingly, reaching out to touch his arm. "It would have worked—if I hadn't been such a pigheaded idiot."

"Yes, well," Nick temporized, "it's a good thing nobody ever whispered the secret of the H-bomb in my ear or it would be all over page one of every newspaper in the country by now. I can't believe I told you! Now what do we do? Everyone worked so hard to make the party a surprise."

"I'll just have to pretend that I'm surprised," Elizabeth said, wondering how she'd ever be able to fool her grandmother, who had been able to see straight through her all her life. "Don't worry, darling, I won't let anyone know you gave it all away."

Nick pulled the car into the long curved driveway that fronted on his father's house and turned off the engine. "I thought we were going to share the blame. How did it all get to be my fault?"

"Dick Saunders and his 'farewell' drink," Elizabeth answered with a smile, knowing she was being extremely female, and loving every minute of it. She leaned over to give him a kiss before he got out of the car. "After all, it seems only fair."

Two days later Megan was sitting on Elizabeth's canopy bed, helping her address thank-you notes for the bridal shower guests. "I can't believe you got three blenders, Liz. What are you going to do with them?"

Sitting cross-legged on the floor, Elizabeth sorted through her personal address book looking for an address. "I already returned two of them to the store and exchanged them for a waffle iron. Nick loves waffles and strawberry jam. Can you believe Gammy, Megan—giving me that gorgeous peignoir? The lace on the bodice actually matches my wedding gown. She's so wonderful. I can't imagine where she ever found it."

Megan licked another envelope before replying. "Yeah, it was pretty, but I liked the baby-doll nightgown us bridesmaids gave you. All that black see-through lace—and those red bows—wow! You should have seen yourself, Liz. You got *so* red when we passed it around the room and Aunt Margaret held it up to the light to check the seams and said there was more thread there than in the whole gown."

Megan was silent for a moment, then changed the subject, bringing it around to herself—a subject of unending interest to her. "Liz, may I ask you a question? Now remember, you *have* to tell me the truth. Do you think I'm pretty?"

Elizabeth heard the words and allowed them to repeat themselves inside her head, clearing away the zip code for Manhattan that she had almost remembered without looking it up again in the directory. How should she answer that question?

A year ago, even six months ago, she could have teased, "Fishing for compliments, again, Megan?" and gotten away with it. But not now. Not since Nick. Elizabeth may have been living in her own world most of the time since her engagement, but that didn't mean she hadn't seen the changes taking place in her seventeen-year-old sister. She was sure Megan had a case of hero worship for Nick and while it was rather cute, it was also a very delicate situation, one that needed special handling.

"Pretty, Megan?" she answered her sister at last. "I guess that depends. What kind of pretty are we talking about here?"

Megan pulled a pained face. "Well, I certainly don't mean pretty as in Aunt Margaret pinching my cheeks and gushing, 'Isn't she a pretty little pudding?' I mean, do you think I appeal to men?''

Elizabeth leaned back against the base of her dresser and looked at her sister through narrowed eyes. "Men, Meg? Don't you mean boys?''

Pushing the thank-you cards to one side, Megan hopped to her feet and began pacing back and forth in the bedroom. "*Boys*, Lizzie? Oh, cut me a break! John and Paul are *boys*. I have nothing in common with *boys*." She stopped in the middle of the room and turned to face her sister, dramatically tossing her head. "Did I tell you that I plan to become a writer?''

"A writer? Really? Isn't that wonderful! You're growing up, Megan. I had no idea you'd been seriously thinking about your future. But what does becoming a writer have to do with whether or not you're pretty enough to appeal to boys—I mean, *men*?''

Megan sighed in exasperation, unable to believe her intelligent older sister could be so dense. "Look, Liz," she explained patiently, "how do you expect me to learn anything about the world—about *life*—if I don't get to know some men?''

"When you say men, Meg, do you mean men who have been around a bit—men like Nick?''

"Oh, Liz," Megan gushed, throwing herself back down on the bed so that Elizabeth scrambled to remove the thank-you cards before they were bent, "you *do* understand. Nick is, well, Nick is so *smooth*, you know, so *sexy*. He makes Billy Perkins look like a baby.''

"Billy Perkins. Isn't he the boy who asked you to the Sophomore Sweetheart Dance last year?''

Megan rolled her eyes. "Yes, isn't it dreadful? I mean, really—I'm a writer! I'm going to write for Nick, aren't I? What could I possibly have in common with a *football player*?''

Elizabeth rubbed a weary hand across her eyes. "Oh, brother," she said under her breath, "now what?" Megan was at such a sensitive age, and it appeared that she had chosen Nick for her first grown-up crush. He'd have to be careful.

"Anyway, Liz," Megan went on, oblivious of her sister's fears, holding up her head so that her throat would appear longer, more willowy, like the heroine in the novel she had just finished, "you haven't answered my question. Am I pretty?"

Looking back at her sister, Elizabeth felt her heart melt. "Pretty, Megan? Darling, you're beautiful! Just please, give yourself some time. You have a lot of years ahead of you to break hearts."

"I know," Megan told her happily, picking up a pen and starting to copy another address, "but I have to start *sometime*, don't I?"

"She's got a crush on *who*! Elizabeth, that's crazy. You must have read the situation wrong. For crying out loud, Megan is only seventeen."

Elizabeth was sitting in Nick's office, taking a break from the sales floor to ask his help with her sister. "I think that's *whom*, but I guess that isn't really important now. Look, Nick, I know it must sound ridiculous to you, but believe me, the girl is serious. Oh, I should have seen it coming, but I didn't. I mean, first you help her with that fashion feature for her school paper, and then you treat her like she's all grownup—"

"How the hell am I supposed to treat her?" Nick broke in, still confused. "She's not a pigtailed baby."

"Don't remind me," Elizabeth said, sighing. "Megan has very patiently explained to me that she's grown way beyond mere boys; she's only attracted to *men* now."

Nick sank back into his chair behind the desk. "Hey, you aren't kidding, are you? Great! As if we didn't have enough problems. Now what do we do?"

Elizabeth got up and walked around the desk, to stand behind his chair and slide her arms around his chest. "Well, I guess you could always dump me and run off to Maryland with Megan," she suggested, bending her head to nibble at the side of his neck.

Nick was quiet for a few moments, then said consideringly, "Yes, there's always that, of course. I should have thought of it myself. But you'd probably sue me for breach of contract. I have a feeling you might be nasty that way. Still, Megan is quite pretty."

"Wretch!" Elizabeth exclaimed, nipping his neck with her teeth. "I think I'm marrying a dirty old man. Now, be serious. We have to do something. You know, I had expected Megan to be jealous of you—because you're taking me away from her—but I guess she got over that separation business when I moved to New York. Nick? What is it? You're looking suddenly smug. Have you thought of something?"

Nick answered happily, "Not some*thing*, darling, some*one*. My mother's youngest sister's son, Mike. He's a junior in college and one of the ushers. You and I thought he could be with your cousin Lisa, but we'll have him partner your sister instead. As I remember Mike, he's quite handsome—broad shoulders and all that. He'll get Megan's attention, don't you think? Feel free to kiss me, darling, right after you say thank-you very much."

Elizabeth bit her knuckle as Nick held out his cheek for her kiss. "Not so fast, Nick. Don't you think we'd just be trading one problem for another?"

"Darling, Mike lives in Maine and goes to college in California. Megan can write to him after the wedding, it'll be good practice for her if she wants to make writing her career. And in the meantime, we can show her what a good, solid marriage we have."

Elizabeth congratulated him, leaning forward to kiss him on the end of his nose. "What an absolutely brilliant idea! Tell me, how did I ever get so lucky? I'm marrying a genius. Kiss me, Albert."

"Albert?"

"Albert. As in Einstein. A real genius."

Nick lifted his head and pulled Elizabeth's face down to him. "Yes, I am, aren't I? Come closer, woman. Oh, dammit, now what?" Nick hit the intercom button and growled,

"Marge? I thought I told you I didn't want to be disturbed?"

"Yes, sir," Marge's voice said through the chocolate-brown box, "but it's Ms. Chatham's grandmother on the phone. She says it's urgent."

"I'll take it, Nick," Elizabeth said, already reaching for the telephone. "Gammy, is that you? What's wrong? Is someone ill?"

Nick shook his head and laughed. "Why is it women always think somebody's sick?" he asked the room in general before sobering, as Elizabeth's face had suddenly gone white. "Elizabeth?" he whispered. "What is it?"

"Uh-huh, uh-huh," Elizabeth was saying, shushing Nick with a shooing motion of her hand, "I understand. Well, can he walk? What? Oh—well, that's something, I guess. Okay, Gammy, thanks for calling. I'll be home for supper. Tell John I hope he feels better."

Watching as Elizabeth replaced the receiver, Nick could barely contain his curiosity. "So? What's wrong with John? It is John, isn't it?"

Elizabeth walked around to the front of the desk and collapsed into a chair. "I've got some good news and some bad news, as the joke goes. Which do you want first?"

"Either one. You choose," Nick said, relaxing a bit as he saw that Elizabeth was smiling—even if it wasn't a very big smile.

"The bridesmaids' gowns have finally come in," she told him. "So the girls won't be going down the aisle in their underwear."

Nick grinned at her, waggling his eyebrows. "There goes another fantasy straight to hell—so, what's the good news?"

Trying to look stern, Elizabeth's eyes betrayed her amusement. "The *bad* news is—John broke his foot in gym class this morning. He's in a cast up to his knee. Mom just called Gammy from the hospital to tell her."

Nick was all concern. "You want to go home? I can arrange cover for you."

Elizabeth rubbed the side of her cheek while she mentally pictured John clomping down the aisle on crutches.

"No, that's all right. This is John's third broken bone, if I
remember correctly. Paul's already broken his wrist—and
an ankle, I think. Our family doctor always jokes that the
Chathams have personally paid for his new X-ray machine.
Mom is used to it by now."

The thought that Elizabeth had already considered finally registered with Nick. "Good Lord, how's John supposed to wear a tux? He'll never get the pants over the cast.
Elizabeth, my offer still stands—if we leave now we can be
in Maryland by dinnertime."

It was strange, but seeing the usually unflappable Nick
flustered, Elizabeth suddenly became very calm. She got up
and walked around the desk to stand behind Nick, massag-
ing his shoulders. "Now who's suffering from prewedding
nerves? Gammy says John will be on crutches for a week
and then they'll fit him with a walking cast. I think I've already figured out a way we can keep him in the wedding, so
don't worry, darling. John's cast should be the least of our
worries. Now," she asked, leaning down to kiss his earlobe, "where were we before we were so rudely interrupted?"

Five minutes later the intercom buzzed again, reminding
Nick of a meeting he had planned with his merchandise co-
ordinators, and Elizabeth returned to the housewares department.

Saints Simon and Jude Church wasn't one of the oldest
buildings in Bethlehem but it was one of the most impressive, Nick decided as he parked his car and made his way
across Broad Street in the late afternoon traffic.

A massive building of hand-hewed gray and brown stone,
its twin towers rose high into the sky and the large, intricately traced nave window, carved in limestone in the Gothic
style, rose above statues of the two saints that surmounted
the double front oak doors.

Once inside, Nick stood at the rear of the church, looking down the hundred-foot aisle at the three massive Gothic
wood rear altars that stood against the stone wall. In the
near darkness he could make out the wood trusses on the

three-story-high ceiling and it reminded him of churches he had seen years earlier on a trip to England. He squinted slightly, imagining the brilliant colors that sunlight would produce inside the church as it flowed through the two dozen blue-and-red-mosaic stained-glass windows that pierced the stone walls.

He was early, and no one else had arrived, giving him time to walk down the aisle, conscious of the echo his footsteps made in the cavernous interior. Approaching the main central altar, he admired its black marble front inlaid with deeply carved white marble in the design of vines and grapes, twin carvings of two peacocks balancing the whole.

It was a beautiful church; but now, decorated for the Christmas Season, it was glorious. The three rear altars were adorned with massive red and white poinsettia plants, unadorned Christmas trees lined the stone walls three deep and there were dozens of ornate brass candle holders scattered around the entire altar area.

It was the perfect setting for a Christmas wedding.

A sound at the back of the church brought Nick's attention away from the pleasant daydream he was having: a mental vision of himself standing at the altar rail as Elizabeth, a vision in white lace and satin, her face hidden behind a gossamer veil, floated down the aisle to take his outstretched hand.

"Hi, Nick," Megan said cheerily, coming down the aisle holding a paper plate covered with pink and white and blue bows. "How do you like my flowers? Crazy, huh? Each bridesmaid—and Liz, of course—is going to carry pretend bouquets we made out of the bows that came on her shower presents. Gammy says it's traditional, but I think she made it up, just to keep me busy during the party and away from the onion dip."

Nick nodded in reply, but he wasn't really paying attention. Looking over Megan's shoulder he asked anxiously, "Where's your sister? I called her office but her assistant said she'd already left. I want to get this rehearsal over with."

Megan laughed. "Nervous, Nick? Relax, it's only pretend. The real thing doesn't happen for three whole days. Did I tell you that your father brought your cousin Mike over to meet me? We're going to the movies together tomorrow afternoon. Oh—here she comes. Darn it, Gammy's with her. She promised to stay home out of the way. Father Chuck doesn't stand a chance; Gammy will be giving orders right and left, just you wait and see. She would have made a great mother superior."

Elizabeth was walking toward him now, wearing the flowing mohair cape that she had worn that day in Central Park. She held a mass of white bows and streamers in her hands. Her face was bright, yet somehow solemn, and he imagined that her mind was now working along the same lines as his had been a few minutes earlier. He didn't know why, but it made him feel better. "Hello, darling," he said as she joined him, kissing her lightly on the cheek. "Are you ready for our rehearsal?"

Elizabeth only nodded, unable to speak. She'd been attending Saints Simon and Jude since she was a child...so why hadn't she ever realized before just how *long* the aisle was? How was she ever going to get down that aisle without tripping, or stepping on her gown, or dissolving into tears like a baby? This big wedding business was insane—how had she ever allowed herself to be talked into it?

Nick took her hand, noticing that it was ice-cold. "Elizabeth? Darling? Are you all right? I think everyone else is here now, in the rear of the church, but if you want to sit down for a moment, I don't think anyone would mind."

"I—I—"

"All right, boys and girls! Father Chuck, everyone is here now, so let's get this show on the road." Rose Chatham walked briskly down the aisle, clapping her hands to gain everybody's attention. "Elizabeth, get to the back of the church to make your entrance. Jack, go with her, you're the father of the bride, you know. Nick, good to see you. Now go away. You don't belong out here until the music starts. Now, if you please, Father? Anytime you're ready."

The priest raised his eyes to the vaulted roof and—at least Nick thought so—sent up a silent prayer before addressing the bridesmaids and ushers about their duties in the processional, concluding his instructions by saying, "If that's all right with you, Mrs. Chatham?"

Luckily it was, and the rest of the rehearsal went off smoothly, a fact that worried Rose, who had always heard that a good rehearsal meant a bad opening night. When Elizabeth reminded her that this was a wedding, not a Broadway show, Rose only sniffed, then went off with Henry Lancaster to make sure everything was in place for the rehearsal dinner at a nearby restaurant.

Just before the meal was served, Rick Jamieson, Nick's college roommate and best man, stood to make the traditional toast to the prospective bride and groom. Holding his glass high, Rick turned to the guests of honor and said, "Elizabeth and Nick, as you stand on the brink of committing matrimony, let me quote to you the words of the illustrious Benjamin Franklin: 'Keep your eyes wide open before marriage, half shut afterwards.'"

"What's that supposed to mean, Rick?" Nick asked, laughing.

Rick pulled a face, winking at Elizabeth. "Darned if I know, old man, but it sounded good, didn't it?"

"I have a better one," Rose said from her place halfway down the table, and the entire party rose for another toast. "To my darling Elizabeth and her Nick. 'A new commandment I give unto you, That ye *love* one another,' the Gospel according to John."

"Amen," Henry whispered, draining his glass.

Chapter Ten

Elizabeth leaned over and looked at the alarm clock. Eight in the morning. The wedding wasn't until three o'clock. What was she supposed to do with herself in the meantime? Oh, why couldn't she sleep!

She had a hairdresser's appointment at noon, but she certainly didn't have to get up at eight o'clock. Besides, her stomach hurt; it felt tight, like someone had tied her insides up in knots.

The weather! She had forgotten about the weather. She'd watched every major television station's weather report last night and two of them had forecast snow. How was she to keep the hem of her gown dry if it was snowing? What if it snowed so much that half the guests didn't make it to the ceremony? Whoever heard of getting married in the middle of winter in Pennsylvania! Why did she think June weddings were so popular?

Throwing back the covers, Elizabeth dived through the draperies she had pulled around the four-poster bed and ran, barefoot, to the window. Pushing aside the curtain, she looked out, then leaned her forehead against the bitter cold pane. It was all right. The sun was shining. How could she have been so worried? Everyone knew television weather-men didn't know what they were talking about!

"Elizabeth? I thought I heard you moving around up here. May I come in?"

"Mom!" Elizabeth exclaimed, turning to see her mother standing in the door, a lap tray in her hands. "Oh, you brought me breakfast. How wonderful. But I couldn't eat a thing, honestly."

"Nonsense," Gloria scoffed, clicking out the tray's collapsible legs and motioning for Elizabeth to climb back under the covers. "I've only brought you some tea and toast. You have to keep up your strength. Nervous, darling?"

Pressing her lips together tightly, Elizabeth nodded. Suddenly without warning, she felt close to tears. This was the last morning she and her mother would have alone together in this room. Everything was so final now, everything was the last thing, being done for the last time. "I—I guess it's another case of bridal nerves. Silly, isn't it?"

After positioning the tray across her daughter's lap, Gloria sat down on the edge of the high bed. "Oh, I don't know, Elizabeth. I think I can remember feeling a bit nervous myself, all those years ago. There's something so final about getting married, isn't there?"

Now Elizabeth nodded vigorously, happy her mother understood. "I love Nick, honestly I do, but—"

"But marriage is a big step and you can't help but have some last-minute doubts," Gloria finished for her. "That's perfectly natural. You two only met a few months ago. But you've got a level head, Elizabeth, and I know you've thought this all out carefully."

Talking around a bite of toast, Elizabeth countered, "But have I, Mom? I mean, maybe I just fell in love with love. I mean, I'm twenty-six years old, and God knows Gammy thought I was on my way to becoming an old maid—so what if I just convinced myself that I was in love because I was afraid I'd never meet the right man?"

"Oh, my," Gloria responded, looking closely at her daughter, "you do have yourself in quite a tizzy, don't you? So you were getting desperate, and Nick is just the male body who happened along at the right moment? Do you really think that's what happened, Elizabeth?''

Elizabeth's chin fell against her chest. "It sounds pretty silly when you say it like that, doesn't it?''

Gloria reached out a hand to gently stroke her daughter's hair. "Nick Lancaster is a wonderful man, darling, and he loves you very much. We can see it in his eyes every time he looks at you, just as we see the love in your eyes when you look at him. Do you really think your father and I would allow you to marry Nick if we didn't think the marriage was right, in every way?''

Biting her lip to keep back her tears, Elizabeth shook her head. "Gammy would laugh at me.''

"Your grandmother had me up half the night, giving me helpful hints on how to handle you this morning. She saw this coming, darling—you know your Gammy. Now she also gave me a detailed list of instructions for you. I have it here somewhere.''

Elizabeth laughed shakily, brushing away her tears with the back of her hands. "That also sounds very much like Gammy. What does she say?''

Gloria reached into her apron pocket and pulled out a small piece of paper. "Let's see, oh, yes—here we go. 'Elizabeth—get up at eight.' Well, she had that right, didn't she? 'Finish crying on mother's shoulder at eight-thirty; eat breakfast.' Honestly, that woman!''

"What next? I hope I don't have to do push-ups or anything.''

"No, the list gets pretty basic from here: the bridesmaids will arrive at one, already in their makeup, to get dressed, and there's a complete schedule for the bathroom this morning, so that all of us may take a shower without running out of hot water. You're first, darling, and you're supposed to take a long bubble bath.''

"That sounds delicious," Elizabeth remarked, brightening. "Being first in the bathroom—ahead of John and Paul—is like a gift from heaven. I guess I'd better get to it, huh?''

Gloria folded the paper and returned it to her apron pocket. "Are you sure you don't want me to drive you to the hairdresser? I'd still have plenty of time to dress when we got back."

Elizabeth shook her head. "No, I think I may need the time alone, if it's all right with you. Mom?" she said as her mother moved to get off the bed.

"Yes, honey?"

"I love you, Mommy," Elizabeth whispered, her voice husky, reaching out her arms.

Gloria cradled her oldest daughter close, fighting back a few tears of her own. "I love you, too, baby. I always will. Be happy."

He was numb. Completely numb. It was eleven o'clock in the morning and he was still sitting in the kitchen of his apartment, nursing his third cup of coffee and hoping that it would eventually make some impact on his brain.

It was ridiculous! Here he was, a man who was cool under fire, the victor in countless business confrontations—the man who had just three weeks earlier concluded a deal that would more than double the size of Lancaster, Inc. by annexing a large southern department-store chain—and he was having trouble remembering his best man's name!

Rick Jamieson sat across the table from his college friend, lazily waving his hand back and forth as if trying to see if Nick responded to stimuli. "Yo! Nick! You in there anywhere? Come out, come out, wherever you are."

Nick blinked twice, and swallowed the cold dregs lying in the bottom of his cup before pouring himself another cup from the decanter that sat on the table. "Yuk! Oh—Rick. What's the matter? Were you saying something?"

Rick, a psychologist, pulled at his earlobe, an unconscious habit he'd acquired while listening to his patients tell their life stories. "Yes, I was, as a matter of fact. I was asking you if Beth is romantically involved with anyone at the moment."

"Beth?" Nick didn't know what his friend was talking about. "Who the hell is Beth?"

"Blond. Beautiful. Bridesmaid. Beth. Word association, Nick, word association. She's Elizabeth's maid of honor. Ring any bells now?"

Nick nodded. "Beth's the one from New York, right? No, she's not involved with anyone—but she's a nice woman, Rick. She's not your usual love 'em and leave 'em type; she could get hurt. So watch it, okay?"

Rick stood up and carried his coffee cup over to the counter. "Got it, old friend. I'll be good." He sat down again and looked across the table, wearing his professional, interested face. "So—you want to talk about it?"

Sitting up straight, Nick looked at his friend warily. "Talk about it? Talk about what? I don't know what you mean."

Once again Rick tugged at his earlobe. "You sure about that? I don't mean to pry, but you look like you just lost your last friend. I thought bridegrooms were supposed to be happy—or hungover—the morning of their wedding. I'd hate to think I gave up Christmas skiing in St. Moritz just to watch you jilt that pretty girl. *Are* you having second thoughts?"

"Second thoughts?" Rick had Nick's full attention now. "No. Why the hell would you think something like that? I love Elizabeth."

"Okay. Then maybe you can tell me this," his friend persisted, "since when do you put seven teaspoons of sugar in your coffee?"

Nick took a sip of coffee from his cup and shivered as the sickeningly sweet liquid assaulted his taste buds. "Good Lord! What's wrong with me? My mind's turned to mush!"

Rick leaned back in the kitchen chair, balancing it on its two back legs. "Well, normally I'd tell you to call my office for an appointment, but in your case I think I'll make an exception. You're scared, old friend. Scared right out of your socks."

"Of what? Elizabeth and I love each other. It's not like I'm afraid we're making a mistake. This marriage is right— for both of us."

"I'm not talking about that kind of scared," Rick corrected. "Tell me—when do you and I walk out of that side room and approach the altar?"

Nick's eyes shifted, avoiding his friend's interested gaze. "When the music starts—no, I didn't mean that. After Gloria is seated, right? But the ushers have to roll down the white runner first, don't they?" Nick buried his head in his hands. "I don't remember! Why don't I remember?"

Rick dug in his pocket and pulled out a folded sheet of paper. "I bow to a wisdom greater than mine," he said, unfolding the paper and shoving it across the table to Nick. "Mrs. Chatham handed me this last night. It's a complete list of everything you have to do today, up to leaving for the reception after the ceremony. If you look at it, you'll see that you're supposed to be shaving in—let's see here—fifteen minutes. Better get going, buddy."

Nick took one hand away from his eyes to pick up the paper, reading down the list slowly, and marveling at its completeness. "Rose," he said, shaking his head. "It's all here, every move I have to make. That woman never ceases to amaze me."

"Yeah," Rick agreed, helping his friend to his feet and guiding him toward the bathroom. "I've been thinking about her. You know, if everybody had a grandmother like that, it might just put me out of business. Or make me a millionaire," he added consideringly.

"Hey, Gammy!" John shouted loudly from the hallway. "The cake is here already."

"Hurray for the cake," Rose responded abstractedly from the dining room. "Now get back in here so I can figure out what to do with you—*the cake is where?* Grab that delivery man, John, and don't let him leave!"

"What's going on, Mom?" Jack called down the steps as he saw his mother advancing down the hall with all the delicacy of a charging bull. "It sounds like there's a war on."

"I don't believe it," Rose was muttering under her breath. "I just don't believe it! If I told those people once, I told them a dozen times—*we* live on Spring Street, the *cake* goes to the country club! I tell you, it's true what they say, you just can't get good help these days— *You!* Hold it right there, young man, and come back here this instant," she called to the deliveryman, who was already halfway down the porch steps.

"You'll have to pick one, Mom," Jack pointed out from behind her. "I don't think he can hold it there and still come back here. And stop yelling at him, you're scaring the guy. It's really getting to you, isn't it, that everything isn't perfect after all your plans? You know what they say about the best laid plans, Mom."

"Hey, that's some cake, isn't it?" Paul said, joining the rest of them in the now crowded hallway. "Look at all those flowers glopped all over it. They're sugar, aren't they? Where's the little bride and groom dolls?"

Rose closed her eyes and began slowly counting to ten. "One—I'll thank you, Jack, to stop grinning. Two—I'm not upset. Three—I never get upset. Four—John, go back into the dining room and try one more time to get those pants over that cast. Five—young man, this cake does not belong here. Please check your delivery slip. Six—Paul Chatham, if you lay so much as one finger on that icing I will personally break both your— *Now what?*"

Gloria hastened out of the living room to pick up the phone extension just inside the dining room. A few moments later she held her hand over the receiver and called out frantically: "It's the church housekeeper on the phone. Father Chuck is in the Emergency Room. They think he may have had a heart attack. Poor man, and he's so young! Now what do we do?"

Elizabeth, who was just returning from the hairdresser's, held open the front door as the delivery man staggered out under the weight of the cake. "What?" she asked as she closed the door behind her and leaned on it, her heart dropping to her toes. "Oh, no. Nick and I liked him so much. Now what are we supposed to do? Gammy?"

Seeing the panic in Elizabeth's eyes, the panic in all her family's eyes, Rose took a deep breath—and then took charge. Removing the phone from Gloria's nerveless fingers, she asked the person on the other end which emergency room the priest had been taken to, hung up, and then pulled out the telephone directory.

"What are you going to do, Mom?" Jack asked, leaning against the dining room archway. "Have the poor man paged in intensive care?"

Making a face at her son, Rose dialed the emergency room pretending to be Father Chuck's sister, and within five minutes had all the information she needed. "It was just a muscle spasm he got playing basketball this morning in the church hall. He's fine, and is already on his way back to the rectory," she was able to tell everyone as she hung up. "Honestly, you people get upset so easily. I tell you, it's a good thing you've got me around. Now, John, how do those pants fit?"

"I still can't get them over my cast, Gammy," he told her, balancing on one foot as he tried to pull the material over his plaster-encased lower leg. "You're going to have to split the seam some more, I guess."

The doorbell rang and, as John hopped into the kitchen on one foot so nobody could see him with his pants down around his knees, the front door opened, admitting four of the bridesmaids. "Elizabeth!" Jennifer exclaimed in delight. "Your hair looks wonderful! Gosh, I'm nervous! Hey, does Beth still own a little red compact with a bumper sticker on it that says 'I'd rather be skiing'? We passed a car like that on the thruway near Easton. It was pulled off on the shoulder with the hood up."

Jack was already picking up his car keys. "Gloria, do you want to go for a little ride? I think we could use a few minutes of peace and quiet. Mom? How does this fit into your little schedule?"

Rose stood in the dining room, slowly shaking her head. She couldn't understand it. She had planned everything, down to the last detail. How could it all be falling apart like a house of cards at the last minute? Then she remembered that it had bothered her that the rehearsal had gone so well, and she smiled at her son. "Actually, Jack, I feel better now that we've hit a few snags. Now I know the ceremony will go off without a hitch. Well, don't just stand there gaping at me—get moving before that crazy Beth finds herself a good-looking man to fix her car for her. There's no room for another guest on the seating chart."

The priest spread his arms, saying, "And now, for the first time in public, let me present to you Mr. and Mrs. Nicholas Lancaster!"

Elizabeth felt Nick's warm hand squeezing hers tightly as they turned to face their guests, who were all on their feet in the pews, applauding. She could see her mother and father in the pew directly behind the bridesmaids, her mother leaning her head against her father's shoulder as he cradled her waist.

Gammy, she noticed, had been true to her word, and was sitting with Henry Lancaster, the two of them unashamedly wiping away happy tears in between their enthusiastic clapping.

She wasn't surprised to see that nearly everyone in the church was looking a bit misty-eyed. It had been a beautiful ceremony, from beginning to end. Elizabeth was now amazed that she had been nervous before; that she had stood at the rear of the church holding on to her father as if he could lend her some of his rocklike strength.

But the moment Jennifer, her matron of honor, had stepped onto the white cloth runner that led down the aisle and Elizabeth had caught her first glimpse of Nick waiting for her at the altar, all her fears had disappeared.

She had only been vaguely aware of the guests that stood on either side of her as she moved down the aisle, her entire world centering on the man who waited for her, his heart and his pride shining in his eyes. When her father had lifted her veil to give her a kiss she had smiled and said, "Goodbye, Daddy," bidding farewell to the life she had known, before taking another step forward and saying, "Hello, Nick," willingly embracing their future together.

And now it was over, the ceremony that had bound them together, tying silken chains around them that they were more than willing to bear. They stood together, looking out over their guests, their heads reeling with joy. Nick leaned toward her slightly and whispered facetiously, "We done good, wife, now let's get out of here!"

Still holding hands, they walked back down the aisle, never stopping until they reached the street and Nick helped Elizabeth into the waiting limousine. A chilled bottle of champagne awaited them there, and they lingered only until the rest of the bridal party were in their limousines before pulling away from the church and heading for the reception.

"I don't know why your grandmother insists on this, Liz," her father protested as he led Elizabeth onto the dance floor. "We already did all of this earlier. I danced with you, you danced with Henry, Nick danced with your mother—all God's children danced with everybody else. What are the two of us doing out here alone?"

Elizabeth was enjoying her father's discomfort. Never one to seek the limelight, he was uncomfortable enough in his tuxedo, without Gammy pulling one of her little stunts. "I don't know, Dad. She says it's one of her little 'extras.' You know, sometimes that woman absolutely scares me."

Just then the musicians—from both bands—struck up the music, and the strains of "Daddy's Little Girl" filled the room. "Oh, Dad," Elizabeth marveled, "it's the song you used to sing for me when I sat on your lap and you played the piano. I think I'm going to cry again."

Jack Chatham's eyes were none too dry, either, as he clasped his oldest daughter to him, his feet barely moving to the music as he rubbed his big hand clumsily, affectionately, up and down her back. Out of the corner of his eye, he could see his mother standing at one side of the dance floor, a broad smile on her face as she watched her son make a spectacle of himself by falling apart like a sentimental fool. "I love you, honey," he said gruffly just as he felt Nick tap him on the shoulder, rescuing him from the moment like a good son-in-law should. "Take good care of her, son," he warned gruffly before searching the crowd with his eyes, longing for the comfort of his wife's understanding arms.

"Come on, Lizzie—wind up and wing it!" John yelled from the sidelines. Brothers were so encouraging. Elizabeth waved to him, still marveling at how good he looked, dressed in his tuxedo jacket and a pair of black sweatpants that sported a hand-sewn strip of black satin down each side. Only the foot of the white cast poking out from the hem of the pants gave him away.

Elizabeth looked over her shoulder at the bridesmaids and guests who were waiting for her to throw her bouquet and gasped, "Gammy! What are you doing there?"

"I'm single, aren't I?" her grandmother quipped, and a few moments later, when Elizabeth turned around to see who had caught the specially made nosegay, the woman held it up triumphantly, saying, "Not so bad for an old lady, huh?"

When Nick threw the garter, Rick Jamieson caught it by leaping three feet into the air and snagging it with one finger. After he had slipped it on Rose's leg, to the accompaniment of cheerful hoots and suggestions, Elizabeth had slipped out of the room and made her way upstairs to change.

Gloria and Megan went with her, the rest of the bridesmaids graciously giving them a few minutes alone together as Elizabeth changed into her baby-pink wool suit and recombed her hair. "Everyone's enjoying themselves," she said, looking in the mirror to check her makeup. "I think it's a good time to slip away, don't you?"

Gloria was standing at the other side of the room, taking great pains to hang the wedding gown just so, doing her best to keep busy. "Unless you want to listen to your grandmother's instructions on how to handle the honeymoon—yes, I think this is the perfect time. Megan, hand me that plastic bag. I want to cover the gown before something happens to it. You were a beautiful bride, Liz. Your father and I were so proud of you."

"Did you get a chance to talk to Mike, Liz? You know—Nick's cousin. Isn't he terrific! He says he's going to invite me to Maine this summer to visit his family."

Elizabeth turned from the mirror to smile at her sister. Nick's plan had worked. "Megan," she began, thinking that she had never seen her looking quite so grown-up. "I'm really going to miss those little talks we used to have in my room. Will you do me a favor?"

"Sure, Liz," Megan answered, taking her sister's hand. She didn't want to admit it, but she was going to miss those late-night talks herself. "Anything."

"Will you keep an eye on Gammy for me? She likes late-night talks, too, you know, and she's a great listener when you've got boy problems."

"Gammy?" Megan made a face. "She always says I'm still wet behind the ears. She'll laugh at me."

"No she won't," Elizabeth assured her. "She loves you very much—she loves all of us. In fact, now that she's got me settled, I wouldn't be the least surprised if she made you her next project."

"Really? Gee, I wish I could believe—"

"Megan!" Rose called loudly, entering the room. "What are you doing up here wasting time? Mike's downstairs, wandering around like a lost sheep. Go dance with him."

Megan looked at her sister and grinned. "Yes, Gammy," she said, giving her grandmother a kiss as she sped out of the room.

"And I expect you to come to my room tonight to tell me all about it," Rose called after her. "I'm an old lady; I have to get my thrills somehow. She's going to break a dozen hearts before she's through," she declared happily, looking at Gloria and Elizabeth. "Now, what do you two think you're doing—setting up a sewing circle? Nick's already waiting downstairs, champing at the bit and ready to leave. You'd better find him and get moving before Aunt Margaret spies him and you never get out of here."

"What's this?" Elizabeth asked, reaching down to pick up a small packet of brochures that were held together with a rubber band and that Nick had tossed onto the seat.

Nick turned the car onto the main highway, leaving the Country Club and all their wedding guests behind. "Oh,

Rose handed that to me on our way out the door. It's a bunch of folders listing things to do in New York City. I think she's got every minute of our honeymoon planned, right down to which restaurants we should go to for dinner. Quite a woman, your grandmother."

Elizabeth laid her head on his shoulder and sighed. "I'm surprised you didn't strangle her on the spot. After all, I think we're capable of planning our own honeymoon."

"I am, at any rate," Nick told her, loosening his tie. "Darling, what would you say if I told you we aren't going to New York?"

Lifting her head to look at him in the darkness inside the car, she said slowly, "I think I'd say it was fine with me. But where are we going? I packed winter clothes, so I hope you aren't planning on someplace with a beach."

"Nope."

"Not going to tell me, are you?" Elizabeth asked, snuggling against him once more. "Does Gammy know about this?"

"Ah, that's the beauty of it, darling. *Nobody* knows about it. We're married now, and from now on, we'll make our own plans."

"Sounds heavenly," Elizabeth said. "So—where are we going?"

Nick grinned at her, obviously quite pleased with himself. "That, my dearest wife, is for me to know and you to find out!"

"Yes, the food was wonderful, Rose, thank you for recommending the restaurant. What? Oh, that's nice. We can use another silver platter. Who sent it? My Uncle William? It's a shame he couldn't come to the wedding; you would have liked him." Nick sat up slightly in the bed and adjusted the pillows at his back.

"I thought you were going to tell her we went to see the Statue of Liberty," Elizabeth whispered, her fingers slowly marching up his bare chest.

"*Shh!* What? Oh, that was Elizabeth, Rose. She was just asking me if I wanted another cup of coffee. Do you want

to talk to her again? No? Well, then I guess I'll say goodbye now. You'll call my father and tell him we're fine? We'll
call him tomorrow morning. How long are we staying in
New York? To tell you the truth, I don't know. But we'll call
every morning, I promise. Say goodbye to Gloria and Jack
and everyone for us, will you? Goodbye, Rose."

Nick leaned over and replaced the telephone receiver, then
rolled onto his back and dragged Elizabeth down across his
chest. "Come here, wife. I haven't kissed you in at least ten
minutes. I think I'm suffering from withdrawal symp-
toms."

Elizabeth obediently kissed him, then quipped, "I think
you might be suffering from guilt, darling. How can you lie
so easily? We had take-out pizza for dinner last night, for
heaven's sake!"

"Well, you were the one who told your mother we were
window-shopping at Tiffany's yesterday," Nick temporized, nibbling on her ear. "Personally, I think we're pretty
clever. Nobody suspects a thing."

Elizabeth pushed herself over onto her side and looked
around the room. Her canopy bed fit perfectly between two
of the dormer windows in the large bedroom, and Nick had
already started a fire in the fireplace, which lent a warm
golden glow to the rest of the room. She didn't know how
he had done it, but somehow Nick had gotten stock boys
from Lancaster's to take down her four-poster bed and
move it to the house on Prospect Avenue after everyone had
left for the wedding. Then those same stock boys had
transferred all of Nick's furniture there as well.

Their house on Prospect Avenue. Elizabeth felt a tinge of
pleasure run through her as she remembered how she had
felt five days earlier after leaving the wedding reception,
when Nick had first driven the car into the driveway and
parked behind the house. He had called it his wedding
present to her, and she had cried on his shoulder as he had
carried her across the threshold into the house.

For the last five days they had honeymooned in the house,
learning about it and each other, alone together in the world
they had made. After all the hustle and bustle of preparing

for their wedding, the house was like an island of peace, and Elizabeth was reluctant to ever let the world in again.

Every morning Nick had telephoned either his father or the house on Spring Street, reporting in dutifully and telling whopping fibs about the fun they were having in New York. It was wonderful, a bit silly and just what they needed after months of listening to everyone else tell them what to do.

"How long do you think we can stay here before we have to face everybody?" she asked him now, her bones turning to water as he began nibbling at the side of her throat.

Nick turned her more fully into his arms, his lips a scant inch from hers. "I'm aiming for June, myself."

Elizabeth felt her heart leap. "I love you, Mr. Lancaster," she told him earnestly, raising her hands to encircle his head.

"I think I can live with that, Mrs. Lancaster," Nick admitted happily, just before their private world grew even smaller, with room in it for no one but each other.

* * * * *